"Birdie." Temple's voice was hoarse with wanting. "I cannot stand this. Step away now or give up the right to cry nay later."

Birdie understood he was giving her the chance to retreat from the fire that threatened to burst into flame inside both of them. Love for him surged through her veins and she felt no desire to move away from him. Ever.

"Temple, do you still think I am a child?"

"I would not feel this way about a child," he rasped. He caressed the sweet curve of her cheek. From somewhere came the unfamiliar desire to protect her, even from himself, if need be. "I will understand if you ask me to leave. You are still so young. And this marriage was not of your own mind."

"I may be young, Temple, but I do not think I was ever a child," she whispered. "And I did want this marriage…."

Dear Reader,

Taylor Ryan's first book, *Love's Wild Wager*, was part of our popular March Madness promotion featuring talented new authors. With her second book, this month's *Birdie*, she returns to Regency England and Ireland to tell the touching story of a woman of noble blood who is raised on the streets, married off to a titled lord, captured by Irish bandits and, finally, must banish her husband's suspicions and prove that she loves him. Quite a past to overcome, but Ms. Ryan's heroine, Birdie, is up to the challenge.

Romantic Times had great things to say about this month's delightful new Medieval from award-winning author Margaret Moore. *The Norman's Heart* is "A story brimming with vibrant color and three-dimensional characters. There is emotion and power on every page."

Our two other titles for the month include *Man of the Mist* from Elizabeth Mayne, the sweeping tale of a Scottish officer who finally returns to claim his young bride, now a grown woman. And from longtime Harlequin Historical author Lynda Trent, *The Fire Within*, a haunting story of lovers who must choose between the past and the future.

Whatever your taste in reading, we hope Harlequin Historicals will keep you coming back for more. Please keep a lookout for all four titles, available wherever books are sold.

Sincerely,

Tracy Farrell
Senior Editor

Please address questions and book requests to:
Harlequin Reader Service
U.S.: 3010 Walden Ave., P.O. Box 1325, Buffalo, NY 14269
Canadian: P.O. Box 609, Fort Erie, Ont. L2A 5X3

TAYLOR RYAN

Birdie

Harlequin Books

TORONTO • NEW YORK • LONDON
AMSTERDAM • PARIS • SYDNEY • HAMBURG
STOCKHOLM • ATHENS • TOKYO • MILAN
MADRID • WARSAW • BUDAPEST • AUCKLAND

ISBN 0-373-28912-X

BIRDIE

This edition published by arrangement with Harlequin Books S.A.

® and TM are trademarks of the publisher. Trademarks indicated with
® are registered in the United States Patent and Trademark Office, the
Canadian Trade Marks Office and in other countries.

Printed in U.S.A.

TAYLOR RYAN

A passion for solitary mountain trails, a love of restless cloudy skies and a propensity for daydreams on rainy afternoons led her to trade a penthouse condo and hectic corporate life for romance in the rugged Pacific Northwest. All of which she shares with Lou and Joe, who give purrs and approval...no matter what.

To Doris June Haney...
a remarkable woman of humor, wit and incredible
strength of understanding...and someone I'd want as
a friend even if God hadn't generously given her to
me as my mother.

This one's for you, Mama!

Chapter One

Eleven-year-old Birdie ran light-footedly through the rapidly emptying marketplace toward the King's Guard Tavern. Her bare feet fairly flew in anticipation of a hot meal and a stolen moment away from the whining demands and painful slaps of old Maude Abbott. The January thaw that ushered in the germs and hopes of 1829 London had melted December's great snowdrifts into a stew of mud, but the girl nimbly leapt across the flooded sewer ditches without noticing the putrid smell and raced down Haymarket Street.

The King's Guard Tavern welcomed gents and their gaudy ladies of the evening inside from the cold of the gathering night. Its dimly lit and overheated depths promised watered spirits, hot food and a reasonably clean bed for an hour or more dalliance. Easing the alley door open just the tiniest bit, Birdie pressed her eye to the crack to scan the room for the heavyset bar master.

It was a well-known fact among the unfortunate children of Haymarket slums that Old Hardin was not fond of giving away food to nonpaying street waifs. He had chased her out the door more than once with loud curses and well-aimed blows. Only when the little girl was positive he was nowhere to be seen did she slip her thin body through the crack and into the warmth of the room. Pressing her back to the wall, she attempted to remain small and invisible, waiting for her only friend in the whole world to take note of her.

Flo Bender was standing behind a tall counter washing pewter mugs. Pretty and plump, with soft brown hair caught up in a white muslin cap, she was laughing and calling out ribald remarks to the departing gents as the taproom rapidly cleared. When a lamp flickered in the slight breeze from the alley door, she glanced around to search the shadows for Birdie, as if anticipating her arrival. With a wide smile of delight, she quickly waved the little girl further into the room, flapping her towel at her and calling out.

"Come on in, Birdie. He's gone for now. I got a spot of hot supper saved for ye. Just knew ye'd be by, seeing as how it's market day and all."

Greatly encouraged, Birdie cautiously slipped behind the table closest to the alley door, keeping a ready escape if required by Hardin's untimely return.

Plopping a bowl of steaming rabbit stew in front of her, Flo planted fists on ample hips and studied her little friend in open disgust. "I swear, yer nothing but a wasted little kitten. Worse every time I see ye. Bones just poke through yer clothes. Nothing better to wear than dirty rags!"

Birdie raised sad, sunken eyes to her friend and shrugged. A bruise on her cheek was beginning to turn brilliant with reds, blues and purples. The tender flesh beneath her eyes was dark from lack of rest.

"Maude gave ye that blue mark, I suppose," the barmaid stated, already knowing the answer. She slid the bowl of steaming food closer. "Eat up, now. I'll fetch ye a bit of mulled wine. Strengthen yer blood, it will."

Without waiting for a second invitation, Birdie tore into the stew with both hands, wolfing it down as if she were afraid someone would snatch it from beneath her nose at any moment. She did not lift her head until every last scrap had disappeared. Then, wiping her hands on her shirt, she pushed the bowl away and accepted the wine from Flo with gratitude. She winced and placed a hand against her cheek for a moment.

"Does it pain ye much, Birdie?" Flo asked, pulling her hand down to take a closer look.

Birdie shrugged away Flo's hands, as if the matter meant little to her. "Maybelle's at Maude night and day again," she muttered. "And I think she's listening to her this time."

"Birdie, if yer gonna . . ."

The little girl's head snapped up and she narrowed her brown eyes into a hard stare. "Don't be starting on me, too, Flo. We been all through this last time. Ye do what ye have to and ye'll never hear no blame from me. But I'll make out some other way than servicing the toffs off the streets."

Flo waved aside the crude remark and flopped down onto the bench. She flipped her apron and sniffed in defense of herself. "Laying on me back for a couple of gents of me own choosing is better than what Maude Abbott has in store for ye. Better than what ye'll get at Maybelle's place."

"Aye..." Birdie nodded, for she couldn't deny Flo's words. Maude Abbott meant to hand her over to Maybelle's house of gentlemen's pleasure just as soon as the price was high enough, and no other fact was truer.

"Just look at ye!" Flo exclaimed in exasperation. "Near starved! Filthy and ragged. Ye know that Maybelle will have ye before yer thirteen."

Birdie rubbed her mouth with the back of her hand. "I know it, Flo, but what am I to do? I ain't got nothing else."

"Ye got something, Birdie. Ye got youth. And ye got bosoms the size of melons. Them two things will earn yer keep and more, if ye'll just make use of 'em," encouraged Flo. "Yer a pretty little thing if ye was cleaned up. And ye can see with yer own eyes, 'tis not so bad here."

Birdie would only stubbornly shake her head. "Coming here is just the same as going to Maybelle's, Flo. What would ye do if ye got caught with a babe? Lose yer work and be out on yer bum in the street, that's what. And Maude would have another throwaway baby on her doorstep. No! That's not for me, I tell ye! I'm a lady! My mam told me so..."

"A lady! Birdie, don't I know what ye have in yer head? Didn't I help ye nurse yer mam when ye was just a babe yerself?" Flo asked in earnest. She leaned forward and tried to raise the stubborn little girl's head, but Birdie, knowing what was coming, refused to look at her. "Ye may have been born of good blood. True enough, yer mam was as refined as the likes of us will ever see. But ye can't be no lady and live in the Haymarket slums. And ye don't have no way out. Ye got to look at things straight, Birdie, not through some fancy dreamworld."

"If I've told ye once, I've told ye a hundred times, Flo. I ain't going to end up on the streets," Birdie declared, pushing her lower lip out in defiance and stiffening her chin. Her sherry brown eyes snapped in the dim light of the taproom, warning that it would do no good to push her.

"Aye, ye've told me. But ye got to see reason. Ye've lived under Maude's thumb for five years now. Ever since yer mam died. I don't want to hear one more time about ye being a lady. Your mam died coughing up blood, right here in this slum, for all her fancy talk. Yer da done run off. If you ever had one. I can't remember ever seeing one," Flo yelled, her voice gaining volume as her frustration rose. "Ye ain't no lady! Hell, Birdie! Ye ain't even got a damn last name!"

Birdie would only push her bottom lip out farther and shake her head. She knew what she knew. And she knew she was a lady. Her mam had told her so more than once. A call for ale, coming from the other end of the tavern, ended the argument. Flo pushed herself away from the table with an exasperated look and a sad shake of her head.

"I swear, Birdie," she said through gritted teeth, "ye'd think ye had the queen's jewels between yer legs! The way ye protect it!"

Flo rushed across the room to tend the gent. One could never tell, he might be tempted to part with a bit of coin for a warm bed partner this night. While she might wish her life was different, she was not the fool to think it would ever be so. And somehow she must talk some sense into her little friend before she disappeared into the hell that was Maybelle's and was lost forever. The only place worse than Maybelle's was the street, for there, girls were robbed, beaten and murdered.

Birdie downed her wine in a dark mood. No matter what the question, the answer always seemed the same. Laying her body down for strangers. Reaching inside her shirt, she pulled forth a greasy black bag, tied tightly and hung about her neck with a twisted piece of cord. With dirty, broken nails, she tugged at the knotted cord and finally pulled out a small brooch. It was a hand-painted miniature of a beautiful woman on an ivory oval edged with gold filigree and of obvious value. She lived in terror that Maude would discover her one and only treasure, for there was no doubt it would bring a handsome price at the hockers'. Turning the miniature to catch the light, Birdie fought tears, just as she did each time she looked at the sweet face. The elegance of the beautiful woman with masses of titian hair was revealed in every line of her lovely face. Amaryllis, her mother.

"Oh, Mam," she whispered. "Why did ye have to die and leave me here? At least ye could have told me who I am. Given me my da's name."

"Here, Flo! Step lively now and fetch a pint for your boss."

In a flash, Birdie ducked beneath the table. Her heart thumped deafeningly in her ears with panic. Old man Hardin had slipped up on her in her reverie. With eyes watchful, she began inching her way along the floor to the alley door. The last time he had snatched her, he had dealt such a ringing clout on the side of her head that she'd seen stars for days. She'd sworn then that he'd never catch her again! Rising quickly, she flew out the door, slamming it back on its hinges. Without a glance over her shoulder to see if he was giving chase, she ran and ran, ducking around corners and into alleyways until finally her bursting lungs forced her to a halt.

She crouched against a slimy brick wall, her chest heaving and her throat burning as she gulped icy air in great mouthfuls. Cupping her hands over her nose and mouth, she tried to warm the air a bit before she breathed it, until gradually her heartbeat slowed and the stitch in her side allowed her to stand upright. Opening her palm, she looked again at the miniature of her mother. And as if by magic, a soft, loving voice whispered in her ear.

"Always remember, my precious. A girl's maidenhead is like a bubble. Once it's broken, it can never be repaired. It should be saved for the man you love more than your own life."

"I know, Mam. I'm trying," the little girl murmured, oddly comforted by the sweet voice in her head. She swiped the matted hair from her face with a fist. "I'll be strong. I'll run away from this place! And—" she giggled at the thought "—with my queen's jewels!"

Carefully, she restored the miniature to its bag around her neck, tugging the cord tight. Satisfied of its safety, she glanced around to gauge her whereabouts. It was rapidly approaching dark. Maude would have a healthy share of her hide for being out this late, and for not being home to put out supper for the other unfortunate orphans who made up the rest of their little family. The clanging of rigging and the salty smell of fish meant the wharf. Not the best place for a young girl to be as light failed. Slipping down the dark side of the alley, she cautiously peered out.

The tinny sound of music came from a tavern, accompanying the drunken roar of laughter that rose and fell in cadence. The street was heavily veiled by the damp, salty fog that wafted ominously in the semidarkness, obscuring her vision. Best to put distance between herself and this place before some drunken sailor appeared to cause her grief. Shoving off the wall, she darted out of the alley and slammed into the barrel chest of a brawny giant of a man who materialized out of nowhere.

"Humph! Whaaa—" came a startled grunt as hard hands roughly grasped her skinny shoulders.

"What's ye got there, Sid?" a second voice came from behind the bulk of her captor. Birdie struggled to free herself but the beefy grasp was like iron. "Why, 'tis a blinking lad! And a wild one at that."

The giant rumbled a laugh. Birdie, with her hands against the mountain's chest, could feel his voice more than hear it. So near was he, the odor from his unwashed body burned her nose. Desperately she struggled to break his hold.

"Lemme go!" she yelled with false bravado.

"Here! Leave off with all that, boy," he roared, shaking her like a rag doll.

"Let's see what ye got," the second voice slurred, heavy with drink. The man stepped to the side of her captor and leaned close to peer in the darkness, trying to see her face. Birdie's heart pounded in her chest and panic tugged at her mind. Weaving slightly, still gripping her shoulder in a bruising hold, the giant pulled a bottle from his pocket.

"Give over with the fighting, lad," he advised. Tipping his head far back, he swilled long and deep from the bottle. Thin rivulets escaping from the corners of his sucking lips slid down his chin and into the open neck of his shirt. Wiping his mouth along his forearm, he handed the bottle down to Birdie. "Have a swig of this. 'Twill put some hair on ye chest and make a man of ye."

"Now, Sid, he don't need to be a man if ye've a mind to use him for a girl, now does he?" the second man wheedled, pushing the bottle gently away from her with a nasty little snicker. "Saves us the price of a lady. That's what it does!"

Planting a foot against the giant's belly, Birdie gave a mighty shove and twist, succeeding in breaking the man's hold. Falling hard on her shoulder and striking her head sharply on the ground, she rolled away and leapt to her feet to make a swift exit as if her life depended upon it, as well it might with these two. The drunken Sid dropped his bottle to shatter on the wet cobblestones and made a desperate grab for her, catching the collar of her striped shirt. Her momentum, combined with his jerk, easily ripped the rotted shirt from her back. Birdie, choked for a second by the collar, gasped for air as spots danced before her eyes. The one called Sid, holding her torn shirt, stared at her in disbelief.

"Cor! Just look at that, would ye? Lad's a scrawny little wench!"

"Watch out, ye fool! Don't let her get around ye!"

"Stay back, the both of you!" she shouted, attempting as much bravado into her thin child's voice as possible. Her mind reeled. She had to get around these two. No time to plan! Her shoulder ached and her ears buzzed as if bees were inside her brain. She shook her head to clear her vision.

Sid, intent on snatching her, ran a beefy tongue over his thick lips. Birdie shivered in disgust. A rumbling in her head clouded her thinking. The rumbling grew louder and Birdie panicked. She could not hold them off all night. They were edging closer and closer. She must do something. She must get away from here! Deciding the slow-witted Sid to be the lesser of the two evils, she chose to attack him. Moving quickly, before her mind had a chance to reject the plan as faulty, she jumped the distance to the giant man.

Using her head as a battering ram, she struck him a brutal blow between the legs.

"Ow..." he bawled in pain. His bellow battled with the loud rumbling in her head as he doubled over to grasp his wounded crotch with both hands. Not waiting to assess the damage she had done, or to clear the ringing in her ears, Birdie sprinted straight ahead into the road. The rumbling overwhelmed her. A high-pitched scream came from nowhere and went on and on and on... until blackness mercifully overtook her.

The coachman stood on the brakes and sawed at the mouths of the four blooded horses, sickened by the bump he felt as the front coach wheels bounced over the small body in the road. The young postilion jumped to the ground, just as a gray head poked through the side window. The two toughs, seeing the noble crest embellishing the door of the magnificently appointed traveling coach, melted into the dark alley.

"Ben, is there a problem?" the marquis quizzed.

"We've hit someone, m' lord. Darted out into the road as quick as a cat." Bending to peer beneath the coach, the softhearted boy gave a moan. "Aw, 'tis a child, m' lord. And dead, I think..."

"Oh, I hope not. Libby, get down and help them see to him. If he's not dead, bring him up," the marquis ordered, waving his hand at the woman across from him. Turning to peer out the window again, the marquis missed the look of disgruntled dismay from the tall, heavyset woman in black.

"Bleeding heart!" she muttered as she stiffly climbed down, clutching her dark cloak around her tightly corseted bulk. Ben was gently pulling the ragged little girl from beneath the wheels. The woman bent over the still form, sniffing in disgust. "It is a slum child, a girl, and damn ripe, if you ask me!"

"But she's alive!" Ben looked up at the woman expectantly. "Those men were going to, I mean... Mrs. Fitzwaters, you can't just leave her in the street!"

"His lordship says to bring her up, so bring her up," ordered the woman.

The unconscious child was carefully laid on the soft leather squabs of the elegant coach. Ben wrapped his pilot coat tightly around her body. It would make for a cold ride atop without it, but the poor mite was welcome to it, he generously thought. The marquis leaned over to peer into the dirty face.

"A girl, you say, Ben? And alive?"

"Aye, she's just a wee thing, m' lord. Being attacked by two rabble in the alley. Ain't nothing but a rack of bones. Poor thing needs some fresh air and plenty of good food. Make her right as rain, 'twould,'' said Ben. He watched the old man's face closely for pity and was gratified at what he saw.

"Well, there's plenty of both at Blanballyhaven. I suppose we can share a bit of it with one small girl,'' the marquis decided. Clapping a hand on the young man's shoulder, he ordered, "Move on, Ben. We'll commend her to the care of the ship's surgeon.''

"Yes, sir!'' the boy exclaimed. With a beaming grin, he leapt to the ground and closed the door. Within a thrice the coach lurched forward and the elderly marquis steadied the covered form with one hand.

"Excuse me, Lord Daine-Charlton. But do you feel that is wise?'' the woman asked. Having served as the marquis's housekeeper for thirty years, she was granted some license for familiarity. "It could be a well-planned hoax. Probably set street rabble and thieves upon us for all your kindness.''

"Really, Libby,'' admonished the marquis with a wry smile. "She's just a child. And I seriously doubt any plot she could think up would have included throwing herself beneath the wheels of a fast-moving coach.'' He watched the woman's face for any sign of compassion. When he saw none, his voice became stern. "If the ship's surgeon can save her, she will sail with us to Blanballyhaven. She will sleep in your cabin and you will nurse her diligently. Then, once she has fully recovered, you will see that she is trained for some position of service. Do I have your complete understanding on this, Mrs. Fitzwaters?''

"Of course, my lord,'' Mrs. Fitzwaters murmured. She lowered her head in mock agreement, and to hide her obvious opposition from the marquis. A slum child! The man should have been a man of the black cloth, for all his misplaced saintly charity. He was truly becoming senile. First of all, adamantly refusing to travel with his valet, which had embarrassed Mr. Travers beyond repair below stairs. Then, when pressed upon the matter, reversing his decision to extremes, insisting upon transporting half the servants of Daine Hall to Ireland. She sighed in resignation and set her mouth firmly. Yes, senile as a box of rocks. But when she looked up again, the veil of respectful servitude was firmly in place once more.

Chapter Two

Birdie was floating in a soft, warm cloud. Her dear mother gently held her, rocking her ever so carefully against her warm breast, crooning a monotonous lullaby. She didn't want to wake, for when she did, the dream would be gone and reality would be hunger and cold, with only a dirty straw pallet against the draft that sneaked through the rough plank floor.

"No..." she moaned as awareness insistently returned and the light behind her eyelids brightened. Slowly her eyes opened a crack. A tense throbbing pulsed at her temples and the light greatly intensified the ache. Overhead, a copper sea lamp rode easily from side to side, giving a tiny squeak at each arch. Birdie's eyes flew open wide at the strange sight, only to clamp tight again as blinding pain knifed through the center of her forehead. Covering her face with her hands, she held her breath, praying for the pain to go away. Gradually, it lessened and she was able to slit her eyes open the tiniest bit.

"Cor!" she muttered. It all came back to her, twisting her heart in place. Had Sid caught her? Was she dead? She rotated her eyes, slowly lest the awful pain return. Through a small round window she could see a rail. Beyond that a vast body of water, which rose and fell, causing her stomach to rise and fall with it. From overhead, she could hear a strong wind. A distant, muffled creaking and groaning persistently sounded, as if someone were in great agony. Outside a bell clanged, four double rings.

"Well, child. About time you were awake," a gentle voice called. "I was beginning to think you were going to sleep the whole of the voyage."

Birdie's eyes flew wide, and she started to spring upright to defend herself if need be. The abrupt motion brought the pain ripping through her head. "Aaaow! My head!" she cried. Grabbing her forehead with both hands, she nearly dislodged the white bandage there.

"Best lie still a bit, child. You've been sick and your head's not going to take kindly to your leaping about." Gentle hands pushed her back to the bed.

"Where am I?" she asked, staring around the room through slitted eyes once more. More wood panels greeted her, and across the ceiling ran wooden beams with metal instruments of torture hanging in neat rows. She struggled weakly with the man. He smiled gently, showing twin rows of white teeth in a sun-browned face.

"It's all right. I'm ship's surgeon. No harm will come to you here, I promise," he soothed. "You were hit by the marquis's coach. Do you remember?"

Birdie grew still, blinking rapidly into the smiling face above her. The corners of the blue eyes crinkled as his mouth widened into a friendly smile again, but she still did not trust him.

"Where am I? Why is the room moving?" she demanded.

"You're on board the *Bonnie Blue,* bound for Ireland."

"A ship? I'm on a ship?" Startled, again she tried to sit up. Her head throbbed and stars danced before her eyes. "Aaaow! My head hurts fierce."

"Here, child. Let me help you. Easy now. Don't jump around so." The surgeon eased Birdie into a sitting position and plumped the pillows behind her back. "Better? Are you hungry? You've been asleep for a very long time."

"A long time?" she whispered. First, a part of her life gone with no memory of it, and now to find herself in this strange place with a kind man offering food? 'Twas more than her mind could take in! Still suspicious, she studied the man dipping soup from a small iron pot on the washstand. Of medium height and average looks, he had nothing to make him special until he smiled and his blue eyes twinkled with merry kindness. The smell of rich beef broth reached her nose, causing her stomach to rumble and cramp. Eagerly she reached out to grasp the two-handled mug as he came back to her.

"Careful now, it's hot, and your tummy's been empty for a spell," he cautioned. "Go slow. No one's going to take it from you. There's a whole pot. You can have as much as your heart desires."

Trying to slow her gulps, Birdie raised her eyes to him. All she wanted? Why, there was even real meat floating in it. Though she'd resolved to drink the entire pot, half a portion filled her and made her drowsy. When it seemed she would drift into a healthy sleep, the memory of the two toughs in the alley shot through her mind. Raising the covers, she peered down the length of her naked body. Gathering the blankets about her, she darted an accusing look at the surgeon.

"Where's my clothes?" she demanded, narrowing her eyes into as mean a look as she could manage.

"Thrown into the sea. Rags they were and not fit to be on a body. We'll find you something else when you're ready to regain your feet," he stated. With another grin, he correctly guessed her worries. "Have no fear. You've everything you came on board with, except filthy rags and a bloody head." His grin turned to a laugh as she continued to glare at him in suspicion. "Would you like to hear about your accident and where you are? Or would you rather close those sleepy eyes and drift off?"

Birdie pondered a moment. Considering the rapid changes in her life, she thought it best to hear the worst, so that plans could be made if need be. "I best be knowing," she whispered.

"Fine. Snuggle down then and I'll not be offended if you drop off to sleep in the middle of the telling," he quipped, tucking the covers neatly around her. "'Twas a dark night," he commenced, as if telling a fairy tale, "and the grand Marquis of Stannisburn was speeding along the wharf in preparation for departure aboard the mighty ship the *Bonnie Blue,* when, from out of nowhere, the merest slip of a lass ran right in front of his coach. Even when she should have by rights been killed outright, the good Lord saw fit to save her for better things. She escaped with a broken head—" he tapped her lightly on the head "—and that's mending nicely. Although I was a little worried when she did not wake up and show me her merry brown eyes." Birdie smiled sleepily at the gentle teasing. "Now, the marquis, being a true gentleman with a kind nature, would not hear of leaving her in the middle of the street and ordered her carried to me. And that's how you came to be on board the *Bonnie Blue,* bound for Ireland."

"What's Ireland?" Birdie asked, desiring his kind, soft voice to go on.

"Ireland is another country," he explained, then went on to describe further when he saw her confusion and the frown knit her pale brow. "It's an island not far from England. We'll be sailing into the Lough Swilly before you can blink an eye."

"What's an island?" Her brow furrowed further.

"An island is a piece of land completely surrounded by water." With a grin at her questions, he leaned over her to tap her on the nose.

"Aaaow..." wailed Birdie. Sitting up abruptly, she practically bumped heads with the surgeon. "'Tis sitting on water? 'Twill sink if we step on it?"

"No, child," he said with a laugh, pushing her down. "It's quite safe. Why, you've been living on an island the whole of your life and it didn't sink, now, did it?"

The frown didn't disappear from her face. Such great ideas boggled her mind. Never had she thought past Maude's and Haymarket Street, her own miserable little world. Now, juggled by fate, here she was sailing to another country, an island named Ireland. "Haymarket's an island?" she asked.

"Actually, I meant England, but I think it's safe to say the slums of Haymarket are an island of sorts...for the likes of you. Now, settle down or your head will begin to hurt again," advised the surgeon. He was saddened at the little girl's ignorance and his inept attempts to enlighten her.

"What am I to do on this Ireland? I have no coin to pay for my ride, nor for yer care of me," she said, fearful of her fate at the hands of strangers, be they ever so kind. She felt all weepy and her head hurt ever so fierce.

"There now, don't you worry. Just concentrate on getting your strength back. His lordship is a kind man. I'm sure he'll find a position of sorts for you at Blanballyhaven," he reassured her. "Now, let sleep take over and heal that head of yours. I'll be here when you wake again."

"Blanballyhaven? 'Tis a magical name. I'll be a lady there. A lady at Blanballyhaven in Ireland..." she murmured as sleep overtook her. Then a sudden thought roused her again. "What's yer name, Doc?"

"George Hughett, but you just keep calling me Doc. Now sleep."

Rain came during the night, a savage downpour that scourged the ship, rattling with a strange metallic sound against the bulging lower sails and thumping the deck in a hypnotic pattern. Birdie woke in the early morn to the sounds and peered out the porthole at the bleak water heaving restlessly, its surface pebbled with raindrops. The room moved in ceaseless motion. She slept a healing sleep most of the day.

The next time she opened her eyes, the pain was gone and hunger growled at her belly. Eager to be up and about in this new world, she eased out of the high bunk and wound the blanket tightly into a toga just as the door jerked open. Startled, she looked up into a pair of cold black eyes.

"Well, I see our little stowaway is on her feet." The housekeeper's voice grated, and she was pleased to see respect on the girl's pale face, just as it should be. "How's the head? Are we mending?"

"Yes, mum," Birdie murmured, watching this awesome lady with trepidation.

"You'll be well enough to work once we get to Blanballyhaven." Folding her hands in front of her and drawing herself up to an impressive height, the woman reeked authority. "I am Mrs. Fitzwaters, housekeeper to the marquis. I will be assigning you a position in the house, and if you work hard at your labors and show proper respect for God, you will do well enough."

"Y-yes, mum," Birdie stammered. After living with Maude Abbott's abuse, she supposed she could put up with this one just as well.

"Now, what's your name, girl?"

"Birdie..."

"Birdie? Birdie what?"

"Just...B-Birdie." She dropped her eyes to the floor in shame at having no more names to give to the housekeeper.

"Just as I thought. A bastard with no name. Should not wonder, considering the slums where you were whelped! Well, it's of no matter."

"Mrs. Fitzwaters!" The sharp voice brought Birdie's eyes up from the floor to face the door and a stern Dr. Hughett. "You will have ample time to browbeat this child once she is well. For now, I refuse to have you upsetting her. If you will please excuse us..."

"I was unaware I was browbeating anyone, Dr. Hughett. But I shall yield to your wishes as I have no desire to impede the child's recovery," the housekeeper huffed. With a haughty look down a very long nose, she swept from the cabin in a flurry of starched black skirts in a regal manner.

"Don't be frightened, child," George said, drawing Birdie gently to the bed. "Mrs. Fitzwaters is not a bad person, just very set in her ways."

"'Twill be no worse than Maude," she answered with a bright smile. "As my mam always—" Suddenly wide-eyed, she grabbed for her throat. Her treasure! It was gone! "Aaaow...my locket!" she cried in a wail of anguish.

"Here now. It's safe. I laid it here. See? No one's touched it."

Snatching the grimy pouch from his hand, Birdie clutched it tightly to her breast and sobbed in relief. If she had lost it, her heart would have been broken. For then, she truly would have felt alone. Slightly mollified, she tugged the blanket tighter about her, sniffling.

"Better now?" George quizzed. Then to distract her and stop her tears, he waved toward the door. "Good, because I have a surprise for you—" Throwing open the door, he called, "Bring it in!"

The young cook's help edged around the door toting a monstrous hip tub easily twice as big as himself, followed by two brawny sailors with buckets of steaming water. These were unceremoniously dumped into the tub, filling it to the rim. Great clouds of steam rose from the tub to fog the windows and heat the cabin. Birdie watched with ever-widening eyes. Did they mean to cook her? She backed away as far as the cabin bunk would allow. Seeing her hesitation, George crouched down before her.

"It's the marquis's hip tub... for a bath. Haven't you ever had a bath before?"

"A b-bath? You mean an all-over washing?" Birdie clutched the blanket tighter and cringed back against the bed. She swiveled frightened eyes from the tub to Doc, then back again.

"Evidently not," murmured George. With a sigh of resignation at such a simple thing as a bath being denied any child, he smiled reassuringly. "It's the marquis's own tub. And look!" With a flourish, he produced a small cake of delicate pink soap. Holding it aloft, he watched her expression flicker rapidly from fright to suspicion to curiosity. "Smell!" he said, thrusting the soap beneath her nose. "Never known a woman yet who could resist the smell of verbena."

Birdie jerked back but not so quickly as to miss the cloying sweet smell of flowers. "Oh! 'Tis sweet!" Snatching the soap from his outstretched hand, she held it beneath her nose and inhaled deeply. "'Tis wonderful!"

George laughed at her amazement, greatly relieved to see that she had at least one female weakness. "Now listen. This is how it is. I will leave the cabin and you are to climb into this tub... without the blanket. Scrub every inch of your body with that soap. Every inch now, you understand?"

Birdie looked at the tub full of steaming water with trepidation, then at the soap wistfully. She nodded; she did so want to smell as nice as the soap.

"Now the hair. It must be washed, too. I sadly fear there are things creeping about in that great mass of hair you've got. I can call Mrs. Fitzwaters to help you wash it but she'll probably snatch you bald-headed in the process, or..."

"Not the witch! Please!" Birdie begged. She could not bear to have the kindness spoiled just yet. Again she sniffed the soap.

George's voice was tender as he reassured her. "Child, I promise I can be trusted. If you will allow me to wash your hair, then I will take you on a stroll about the deck when it's dry." Satisfied with the eager nod he received, he noisily latched the door behind him to assure the little girl of her privacy.

Much later, wearing the oversize striped shirt and the canvas pants of the cook's help, and wafting the scent of verbena, Birdie hesitantly ventured up the stairs on bare pink toes. As he had been watching for her, George waved her toward him. Self-consciously, she gathered the loose pants about her waist and ran lightly across the deck. Soft, clean hair blew back from her small face, pink from vigorous scrubbing. As she reached his side, George's smile disappeared and his eyes grew wide at the sight of her.

"What's wrong? Have I done something wrong?" she asked fearfully.

When he saw her shrink away as if wanting to disappear from his anticipated anger, George's eyes instantly softened and his smile returned. "No, child, I was just amazed at the breathtaking beauty all that dirt was hiding," he teased. To her obvious delight, he offered her his arm as a gentleman would a lady. Her face lit in a smile that broke his heart. So young and so beautiful to have been so ill treated, he thought. "See, we are just entering the mouth of Lough Swilly," he explained to distract her. "We will sail to the end and dock at Buncrana. We are in the far northern tip of Ireland, in County Donegal."

"County Donegal," Birdie parroted, loving the sound of the musical names. Eagerly she ran to the rail and gazed at the craggy rocks rising into towering cliffs amid swooping, screaming terns. A warm afternoon sun shone brightly but did not burn off the mist hanging heavily on the mountaintops. George smiled at the picture she made in her boy's clothes, straining on tiptoe to see over the rail. Her hair, freed of dirt and grease, curled in a riotous mass seemingly too heavy for her small head. And the color! It was the color that had struck him dumb. It was a startling deep russet red, bursting with golden highlights, and so curly it bounced in tight ringlets, now set ablaze as the sun touched it.

The Marquis of Stannisburn, leaning heavily on his cane, walked slowly up to the surgeon and laid a hand on his shoulder in a gesture of warm familiarity. "I say, George, who have we here?" He pointed his cane to the young person hanging over the edge of the ship.

"It's the child involved in the carriage accident, my lord. On the wharf? Apparently her name is Birdie."

"Well, then I have amends to make. Pray, introduce me to the young lady, George," instructed the marquis.

"Certainly, my lord. Birdie, please, come here," he called.

Birdie spun toward them with a smile on her face. The marquis was startled speechless. For such a young child her beauty was stunning! The face was pale and much too thin, but the wind had whipped roses into the cheeks. The generous mouth curved in a smile over pearly teeth. Her eyes were bright brown with golden lights beneath dark, surprisingly delicate eyebrows. Her russet red ringlets danced wildly about her face in the sun and wind. She was a child of the golden sun, the rich earth and the pink roses of summer.

"I say," murmured the marquis. He cleared his throat gruffly, discomfited at his immediate reaction to the child's looks.

George ducked his head to hide his amusement. Holding out his hand, he drew Birdie forward. "Child. May I present Charles Daine-Charlton, the Marquis of Stannisburn... your benefactor?"

Birdie stared up at the old man in awe. Never had she seen one so noble. He was a burly, straight-backed man with a walking stick and a magnificent waxed mustache. His mop of hair was white and blew about his hatless head, revealing pink scalp beneath.

"Cor, Doc! 'Tis truly grand, ain' he?" she whispered.

George nodded his encouragement at her uncertainty. "Yes, he is. But kind, too. You may address him as your lordship," he prompted gently. "And thank him for rescuing you when you were injured."

As the old man's eyes were kind, Birdie hesitantly returned his smile with one of her own. "Thank ye, yer lordship, for saving my life," she said, bobbing a small curtsy taught to her by her mother practically before she could walk.

"You are most welcome, I'm sure. But do not forget that I am also the cause of your injuries," he teased, then held up a hand when she would protest. "George, my friend, you do not mind if I steal away your young lady for a stroll?"

"Of course, I mind greatly, but I do have duties that are pressing. Such as salvaging my flooded surgery after a certain young lady's bath." With a tender laugh and a small bow, he took his leave of them.

The marquis held out his hand. Birdie shyly slid her tiny fingers into his much larger palm. Taking a turn around the deck, the marquis suddenly pointed with his cane, high over their heads. "There she is!" he exclaimed excitedly. "Blanballyhaven!"

Looking up and up and up the cliff, high over her head to the very top, she caught a glimpse of a fortress . . . no, a stone-walled castle. " 'Tis where I'm going to live?" she asked in wonder.

"And would you like to live in a castle?"

"I don't know, yer lordship. I've never been to one before," she answered candidly. She craned her neck far back to stare at the stone walls and towers.

The elderly marquis laughed at her childish honesty and gazed up at his Blanballyhaven. " 'The castle I was born in stands over the sea,' " he quoted.

Birdie shifted her gaze to his face at the tearful tone of his quivery old voice. "Ye was born there?"

"Yes, and now I come home to die."

"Aaaow! No, yer lordship," she cried. Birdie tugged at his hand and longed to throw herself into his arms. Distress registered plainly on her small face, much to the old man's surprise. It had been a very, very long time since anyone had cried over him.

"Oh, but not for a long, long time yet. Can't kill off an old man like me easily, you know," he quickly modified, patting her head. "Don't cry, please. Come . . . Look at the water. This, the great Lough Swilly, you know, and the longest sea inlet in Donegal." Birdie obediently leaned over the side of the ship and stared down at the fast-moving water, dashing tears from her eyes. Blue it was, with flashes of green where algae rose near the surface. White froth foamed as the ship, moving briskly in the wind, cleanly cut the swells. "It was named for a sea monster with sixteen heads and hundreds of eyes that lived in its depths in the sixth century," the marquis gently teased her with history and myth.

With a gasp and a widening of her eyes, Birdie stumbled back from the edge with terror in her voice. "A—A monster, you say?"

Having limited experience with children, especially ignorant children, Lord Daine-Charlton sighed at his mistake. Sorry for frightening her with his story, he took her hand to lead her to a bench so that he might ease his aching legs. "Now, listen to me, Birdie." Pulling her arm toward him, he set about rolling the sleeve of the striped shirt up to reveal her hand. "They say the Lough Swilly lived there in the sixth century. This is the nineteenth century we are living in at present. Do you think it possible that he could live that long?"

After a moment of thought, Birdie narrowed her eyes at him as if calculating. "How long is a century?"

Pleased at her quickness, he replied, "A century is one hundred years. That would be thirteen hundred years. He'd have to be very, very old by now."

"Aye, but maybe he had babes, and they is much younger," she reasoned. Her eyes grew wide at the thought of many, many monsters of the type he described.

Lord Daine-Charlton tipped his head back and laughed at her sally. "I swear to you, child, I have never heard of a Lady Lough Swilly, so I doubt there ever were young ones. You must take my word for your safety."

Birdie regarded the elegant lord with all her childish wisdom for a long moment, then asked in earnest, "Yer lordship, do ye know everything?"

"Everything about what, child?"

"Just everything about... Why, everything."

"No, child. Not everything," he answered, attempting to keep his face as serious as hers. "Though I have lived seventy-odd years and one does overhear a bit in that length of time. What is it you would have me tell you?"

"Why—" she glanced at him in surprise "—all of it!"

"All of it?" He chuckled, then touched her head gently. "Poor little mite, so hungry for knowledge. Well, Miss Birdie, there's nothing an old man likes better than the sound of his own voice. I suppose I can be sharing some of it." Very much excited, the child threw her arms around his neck and hugged him with all her strength. Gratified at her show of affection, the marquis smiled at her through eyes suddenly misty. Settling his gnarled hands on the gold head of his intricately carved walking stick, much as an orator who is embarking upon a lengthy speech would do, he pondered her for a moment. "Now where shall we begin?"

Birdie seated herself on the bench at his side, and leaning onto his knee, she lifted her face. "With Ireland and Blanballyhaven!"

The Marquis drew in a deep sigh as he gazed down into her face, drinking his fill of it. Her warm brown eyes were bright and her cherry mouth parted slightly in her eagerness. The sun touched the creaminess of her skin, kissing it with a golden hue. The russet red ringlets blew across his face, wafting a caress of delicate verbena scent.

"How old are you, Birdie?" he asked, gently cupping her chin in his large hand and tracing a thumb over the satin skin of her cheek.

"I don't know," answered Birdie. She was puzzled by his searching look but eager to get on with the lesson.

"Ten or possibly eleven?" he guessed, a smile creasing his face. "My dear, you are going to be a force to reckon with in a few years—" He paused to shake her face with a teasing hand. "And I may be an old man, a very old man, but I pray I live long enough to see you in all your glory. Then, my dear, may God have mercy on me *and* the entire male population!"

"My lord," George interrupted. "I'm sorry to say it, but I feel I must take your companion away. This has been a busy day for one so recently out of her sickbed. I heartily feel a nap before supper would be in order."

"Yes, yes, of course," agreed the marquis, clearing his throat. "Run along, child, and we'll have other times to talk."

Thoroughly disappointed, Birdie found herself more tired than she had thought as she snuggled down into the blankets again. George looked down at her with a speculative and sad expression.

"Tell me, child. Was your life so terrible that you had to be afraid of everything and everyone?"

"Not so afraid as . . . ready, I guess. But 'tis going to be better now."

Looking up at him with a smile, she melted his heart. Such a strange mixture of innocent child and wise woman, as if a very old soul lived inside her. He wished for nothing more than to take her in his arms and swear to protect her for the rest of her life. But being a ship's surgeon, constantly at sea, and having no female relative to take her in, he could not offer much. Besides, the age and looks of this child somehow made the whole idea highly improper. Best she go with the marquis, he thought with a sigh. Her future lay in that direction.

"Are you excited to be going to a new home?"

"Aye . . . b-but—" She shivered despite the warmth of the blankets, causing George to lay a concerned hand on her cool brow. " 'Tis so strange, and . . ."

"Scary?" he finished for her. "Just remember, the marquis is a good man and you can always turn to him. If you work hard in your new position, you can learn a skill. Then return to England if you want, and seek employment in one of the great houses. There are positions aplenty from which to choose. Maybe you'd like to be a nursery maid and tend the master's babes? There's kitchen maids to upstairs maids... Or maybe you'd like to take care of the silks and satins of her ladyship. Be a lady's personal maid?"

"Nay, none of them! I would be the lady what has the lady's maid."

Her quiet, sincere confidence startled him. Then with a grin, he patted her shoulder. "I shall miss you greatly, little one. You shall be a wonderful woman in a few years, even if you will travel a long, rough road if you maintain that attitude. A lady, indeed!" He shook his head in humor, but Birdie held her tongue for she had heard it all before. "Now, drift off to sleep. I'll wake you with supper."

Left alone, Birdie allowed a sigh to escape. Unsure of how many days had passed, she could only imagine how worried Flo was. While she did not wish to give up her dubious good fortune, she would have gladly given a lion's share to her friend. Flo would think her stolen or murdered in some dark, dank alley. She would have searched the slums for her, but with only the two toughs knowing what had happened to her, the tale would never be told. Her mood sank lower.

" 'Tis 'alf-witted, I am," she whispered to herself as a tear slid into the pillow. Then, as always when a feeling of helplessness came over her, the sweet, loving voice of her mam whispered in her ear.

"Watch your *h*'s, my darling. Remember, you are a lady..."

Chapter Three

Birdie tucked a stray russet curl inside her large, Gypsy bonnet. Twitching the cotton ties under her chin, she sneaked a furtive peek from beneath the straw rim to confirm she was unobserved. Although anyone who knew her would not have been surprised at her actions, she had no wish to be censured. The disinterested piebald sheep dotting the hillside formed her only audience, thus settling her quandary. Undoing her string garters, she kicked off the heavy, suitable boots and yanked the cotton stockings from her feet. Divested of such encumbrances, she dug her toes into the cool grass and giggled to herself.

"A pox on your head, Libby Fitzwaters!" she spouted in glee.

She was fully aware her behavior was outrageous for a proper scullery maid, and she should be busy in the kitchen as the stack of dirty dishes seemed never ending, but oh, how she hated the time spent in the dark cubbyhole, sticky from heat and overpowered by the strong, acid stench of lye soap. It surely must be the most disgusting position in all of the house, but Mrs. Fitzwaters had declared it her intent to begin Birdie's service at the bottom and advance her through the ranks as talent revealed itself. And although Mattie O'Donnell, who ruled the kitchen, had protested that she was just a wee little thing, into the scullery she had been flung.

Raising her face to the sun, Birdie soaked up the glorious warmth and pretended she wasn't running away. She pretended she was a lady of leisure with the whole afternoon to do as she pleased. Holding her arms out, she let herself fall backward into the grass. It was as soft as a bed of goose down and smelled as sweet as spring. Stretching her arms over her head and arching her back, she allowed the straw bonnet to crush under her head. Silly old thing, anyway! Hadn't she told Mattie that having red hair didn't auto-

matically mean freckles would follow? Hadn't she presented her
flawless, creamy nose and cheeks for inspection over and over
again? So many rules, and most made with no thought to common sense at all, or so it would seem to a young girl raised in the
slums of London.

Take the rule about stockings! Bloody things must be washed
and darned every week, and were hot as Hades much of the time.
But Mrs. Fitzwaters cared a great deal about her rules. Sitting up,
Birdie carefully rolled the hated stockings into the toes of her shoes.
The white apron was flung on top, followed by the bonnet. With a
vigilant glance around, Birdie turned and fled, ducking and dodging through the tall grass sprinkled with spring flowers, until she
was out of sight of the castle and quite out of breath. Stopping, she
flung her arms out and began to spin. Free! A whole afternoon
free! Not that there weren't plenty of free afternoons to roam the
hills, for Mattie had never restricted her to the kitchen unless she
had to. And what Libby Fitzwaters didn't know didn't trouble
Birdie. The last two years had greatly lessened any terror she had
of the demon housekeeper.

Walking with a healthy stride, arms swinging, Birdie set off over
the hills. The years of plentiful food and abundant love from the
motherly Irish people had caused the thin, half-starved orphan to
blossom into a beautiful budding young woman. Her arms were
round and soft, belying the actual strength there. Her legs stretched
long and supple, tightly muscled from the hills of Ireland, as all her
stolen free time was spent out-of-doors. Rounding a high, stone
wall, she paused to gaze expectantly over a valley with a score of
different shades of green, deepening here and there from the
shadows. Putting two fingers to her mouth, she whistled a high,
shrill note that echoed down the valley. Laughing at her own silli-
ness, she spun away, thrilling in the pure joy of being young and
healthy and free on such a wonderful afternoon. Lifting her skirts
above her knees, she ran along the wall, letting the momentum
lengthen her stride until, bare feet racing, her body flew pell-mell
down the hill.

"Look out!"

As if coming from nowhere, a horse loomed over the wall, eyes
rolling white in its high-flung head, nostrils flaring wide and its
chest streaked with foamy lather as their paths intersected. Caught
in the middle of her whirlwind race down the hill, Birdie could do
no more than twist sideways and throw herself from beneath the
savage hooves as they struck dangerously close to her head.

"Ye gods!" she yelped as she tumbled head over heels down the
hill, coming to rest in a boggy dent of black mud. Lying on her

belly in the sticky mess, she fought to catch her breath and slow her spinning head.

"Are you injured?" An incredibly deep voice came from above her, sounding annoyed as blue blazes. "You there! Answer me! Are you injured? Oh, hell's teeth! Take the leathers, Mike. I'd best see to her." Tossing the reins to his groom, the young man dismounted and stalked down to bend over her. Exasperated at having his gallop cut short, and wondering at the girl who would lie on the muddy ground rather than regain her feet, he scowled disagreeably. "I say, may I help you to your feet?"

Biting her lip and shaking her head to clear it, Birdie glanced up, only to stare straight at muscular legs molded by tight-fitting buff pantaloons and gleaming black Hessians with absurd, tiny red tassels. She stifled an exclamation as her eyes traveled upward to a black riding coat with no less than sixteen capelets spanning broad shoulders. One elegant hand held a beaver topper while the other was extended toward her. By the time she had reached his face, her head was tipped back as far as it would go, and her mouth could only gape at the sheer magnificence of this sight. He was more than handsome. Outrageously beautiful leapt to her mind. Yes, that seemed a more apt description. But to mar his beauty, every muscle, every feature seemed bursting with foul temper, from the indentation in his chin to the neatly trimmed mustache and the scowl on his forehead. Two heavy black brows accented pigeon gray eyes, while the lowered lids did little to conceal the dangerous glint of irritation there.

But for the proper cut of his clothes, he could have been a buccaneer home from the sea, brandishing a sword, long and bloodied from lopping the many heads from sea dragons. A sigh escaped Birdie. When he reached his hand farther down to her, she placed her own within as if mesmerized, not noting the black mud until he grasped her hand to roughly haul her to her feet. Pulling a snowy handkerchief from his pocket, he swiped at the mud on her face, then, giving that up as hopeless, he rubbed at his own muddied hand in disgust.

"Damned balmy thing to do, girl! Spooking a man's horse like that, coming off a blind jump. Could have broken his leg, not to mention my neck!"

Bracing her fists on her hips, Birdie glared up into his face. Beautiful he might be, but the lad displayed no manners. "Y-yon horse, ye be saying? And what of me own neck? 'Tis thinking, I am, that ye should not be so careless with where ye be jumping the bloody beast! And no hint of apology coming from ye, neither!" she spouted, lapsing into a musical, lilting brogue.

Jerking his head up in surprise, the young man looked at her aggressive stance with raised eyebrows. Impossible to tell much about her with black mud caking the length of her, but she showed a deal of spunk and displayed a set of beautiful eyes, he thought. Worth a dalliance if one had time to spare, which unfortunately he did not.

"Oh! So you would take me to task for placing you in danger, would you? Very well, I shall play your villain," he conceded, sweeping her a low bow and flourishing his topper in shameless prank. "And may I know the name of the fair damsel I have so carelessly endangered?"

Taken aback by the sudden change from anger to amusement in the gray eyes, Birdie could only blink at his courtly actions, then glance down at her gown, hopelessly mud-stained. Mattie was going to be furious with her for this day's work. "'Tis B-Birdie..." she stammered. As always when asked her name, she prayed he wouldn't ask for more, as the shame of being nameless had never left her.

"Ah, the Lady Birdie is most beautiful, " he exclaimed. Snatching her dirty hand, he carried it to his lips. Turning it as if looking for a clean spot, he finally brushed his mustache softly against the inside of her wrist. Sweeping a flower from the ground, he presented it to her with another gallant flourish.

Birdie blushed and accepted the flower carefully. He was the most beautiful man she had ever seen. Truly bigger than life. Tall as a giant, brown as a foreigner, his hair jet black. He smelled of Nun's soap, and his pantaloons, of buff, fit his skin as if he were naked. A prince from a magical land. Exactly as she'd always known a prince would be. Reminded by his grin and tilted eyebrow that she was caught staring, she swept a low, graceful curtsy, spreading her skirts over bare feet. "'Tis most welcome ye be, I am sure, my lord."

"And you are most welcome, also, for the pretty thank-you and for this, as well," he mocked, stepping quickly to her.

"Oh..." Birdie gasped as she was suddenly grabbed by strong hands and crushed against a powerful chest. She glimpsed a devilish grin before her lips were captured beneath his. Never having been kissed before, she could only squirm against the strange feel of another person's mouth upon her own. The pressure lasted barely a second, then he whispered against her mouth, his breath soft and sweet, the mustache tickling her lips.

"Ah, my little tempting Irish colleen, would that I had the time..." Sighing regretfully, he set her away from him. One more dazzling smile at her stunned, muddy face and he marched back to his fractious mount. Taking the reins from his laughing groom, he swung easily into the saddle. "Hurry and grow up, Lady Birdie! Your sweet prince awaits." With a wave, he spun the prancing animal and galloped back up the hill in the wake of his groom.

Birdie stood for a moment with her hand pressed to her mouth, stunned to her very toes. His words ran over and over in her head, tumbling and playing havoc with her heartbeat. 'Hurry and grow up. Hurry and grow up.' Her first kiss! And from an English gentleman at that! Her overactive imagination wound up. Her prince! That's who he was! And exactly as she'd dreamed of him. Her hand pressed again to her mouth, only this time her fingers scratched at her upper lip where his mustache had tickled.

Mattie O'Donnell surprised everyone now and then by her free and easy use of strong language. This was one of those times. Having been dunked in a tub of water and washed from stem to stern, Birdie now sat in front of the fire brushing her hair dry. Mattie stood at the scullery sink scrubbing mightily at the mud-stained blue serge dress.

"Damn ye for yer carelessness! 'Tis a new dress, Birdie. Besides being gone so long as to make me think the wee people had stolen yet another child. For ye be a child still, even for those splendid bosoms ye sport. To tempt them by roaming these damned hills... Sheesh! 'Tis too much, I tell you!"

"Makes no sense to be fashin' yerself over the wee people running off with the likes of me, Mattie," Birdie countered. "If they even tried, me fine prince would come riding to me rescue, he would. He'd fight them off with his sword and claim me hand to wed as his just reward."

"There ye go again. Talking about this fine prince. And don't ye be mocking me with yer use of the brogue, me sassy lass. Ye be making fun of the wee people and they'll be laying a charm about yer head," Mattie scolded sternly. She scrubbed hard at the dress, taking her irritation out on the stains. "I've seen them with me own eyes, I have."

Birdie's mouth softened with a smile. She'd heard this tale, invented by tired mothers as a nighttime tale meant to scare little children into staying in bed the whole of the night, many times. "And just where would that have been? Tell me where?"

"In Glencolumbkille, that's where. I seen them riding down the mountain on their horses," Mattie said, spreading the offending dress before the fire. "Here's yer dress. 'Tis the best I can do with it."

Birdie laughed, determined not to let the cook stray from the tale and back into her scolding. "I do not believe in such things as wee people."

"Ah, well," Mattie muttered, taking the poker to stir up the fire, a thing she always did when people downfaced her. "Maybe there's none any longer. There's many a wonder gone out of this world since meself was a wee lass."

"Where's Glencolumbkille, Mattie?" Birdie asked, partly to mollify the dear woman and partly out of endless curiosity. Not once had she been away from Blanballyhaven since that fateful day the marquis's giant coachman, Condor O'Donnell, had deposited her tired and hungry little body at his mother's kitchen table to feed and clothe and love.

"'Tis a fair piece into the mountains," Mattie said, taking the brush from Birdie's hand. She stroked through the ringlets, curling the drying hair around her fingers. "I was raised there. Terrible poor place, 'tis now. Good only for tending goats and starving. 'Twas the only place left to the people when the English stole the farms away from the O'Donnells."

Birdie nodded her head. This was another familiar and much loved tale. "So cruel! To take the people's land."

"Aye, 'twas that," Mattie agreed. "'Twas after the big revolution. The English came to fight, and when they won, they gave all the land to their own. The Irish walked the land, hungry and homeless. Blanballyhaven was O'Donnell homeland forever, then one day they say, 'Go away. 'Tis yers no more.'"

Birdie's heart wept for the kind people who had befriended her so generously, for wasn't she English? And they should hate the English, shouldn't they? "Mattie, why are you so very kind to me, when I'm English?"

"'Twas a terrible long time ago," Mattie said, with laughter in her voice. "And besides, ye be just a little bit of nothing, that's what ye be."

Birdie leaned her head back against the woman who was like a mother to her. "'Tis a terrible thing to have no home. But so much hate betwixt the Irish and the English..."

"Aye. There be bands of angry Irishmen living in the hills, just waiting for the time to strike back." Mattie stroked the brush through the girl's hair. "Not everyone has forgiven, nor forgotten, the fight for freedom. But then some have! What of the looks I see coming from young Enus? That's not hate!"

"'Tis nothing," Birdie said, blushing furiously. "Besides, I'll not be settling for the likes of Enus O'Malley. I have a prince waiting for me. One day I'll be a real lady..."

"None of that, lassie—" Mattie bopped the girl on the head with the hairbrush. "'Tis but a dream, and 'twill never be coming true. What's true is that stack of dishes awaiting ye. And ye had best get at them."

Birdie pressed her lips together. She had grown used to keeping her own counsel about her dreams and about the things only she believed to be true. She was a lady! And there was a prince for her! Never before could she imagine a face for him. Until today. Now she knew him. He was tall, dark and handsome. His shoulders were broad . . . broad enough to carry the world, she thought romantically. His voice carried authority, his gaze was commanding and his sword lethal. He was capable of taking care of her in every way, and she would always be first with him. Not first in his arms perhaps, as some other woman would long ago have had that honor, but she would be first in his heart. He was going to wait for her to grow up, and then he would be there forever!

Chapter Four

The library was dark. Thick, sooty, smoky dark. The silence so profound it rang loudly in her ears. Standing motionless for a moment, Birdie let her eyes adjust to the night. Ever so slowly, threatening outlines began to take on familiar shapes. The hump of an ogre turned into a winged back chair. An eerie lump became the curved back of a divan. Easing the door closed behind her, she held her breath when the sound of the latch clicking into place seemed to reverberate throughout the room. Standing as still as a statue, she waited for the cry of alarm to be sounded from the footman on night watch. When none seemed to be forthcoming, she let her breath whisper past her parted lips. Sweeping her eyes over the library, she took stock without moving her head. The scent of newly snuffed beeswax candles lingered on the air and mingled with that of dampened fireplace ash.

Deliberately taking a deep breath to hearten herself, she felt her way along a table's edge to the desk. Sliding her hand over the plane of the leather padded surface, she bumped the cold weight of a sterling candle holder. Fishing a stolen lucifer from her skirt pocket, she touched off the branded wick. The bright light caused her dilated eyes pain. Throwing a hand over her eyes, she flopped down in the leather chair.

"Damn!" she muttered. Even her whisper seemed to echo from corner to corner of the cavernous room. Again she held her breath and waited. Nothing. Slowly she exhaled. She knew punishment would be severe if she was caught in the library. It was not an allowed area for the scullery maid to be found, particularly past midnight. And well she knew, old Libby Fitzwaters would like nothing better than to punish her for breaking her bloody rules.

Easing from the chair, she stepped to the tall bookshelves. Reverently she ran hands over the books lined there like forgotten soldiers standing at eternal attention. So many, all leather-bound and gilt-edged. Pulling one slender volume down, she flipped the stiff pages. The smell of musty old paper and dust met her nose. Quickly she stifled a sneeze in the folds of her skirt before randomly selecting two or three books to carry back to the desk. Under the circle of candlelight, she opened them one by one. Peering closely at the pages, she ran her finger under line after line. The finger moved slower and slower and finally came to a stop. The tense shoulders slumped and tears traced down the porcelain cheeks. Pushing the books away from her, she laid her head on her arms and allowed the sobs to overtake her. So deep was her misery that she did not hear the door open, or see the hunched figure shuffle into the room.

Lord Daine-Charlton moved with faltering steps. His frail and slightly stooped body was aided in its progress by a stout cane in his right hand and whatever chair or table came under his left. The past years had not been kind to the ailing marquis. The waxen features of his lined face clearly showed his illness. But his clear blue eyes were still lively and sharp as they looked at the sobbing girl at his desk. He understood deep grief when he saw it. He would have retreated unobserved but for his infirm, unwieldy body, which seemed to bump into furniture of its own accord.

Suddenly aware of another person in the room, Birdie jerked her head up and stared with tear-flooded eyes at the marquis, a rather frightening sight hunched beyond the arc of light. With an audible gasp, she jumped to her feet and puffed out the candle, plunging the room into darkness. A dim glow from the entry hall traced through the open door, casting shadows to run the length of the floor. Birdie edged around the desk, looking for a path to escape.

"No need to take flight, girl. I am a very old man and could do you no harm even if I had that purpose in mind," said the marquis. His gentle voice reached Birdie and halted her. He shuffled to the desk, pulled the candle toward him and attempted to strike a lucifer with his trembling hands. Then with a snort of disgust, he motioned for her to approach him. "Damnation! Come light this infernal thing!"

Stepping hesitantly to the desk, Birdie quickly restored the meager light. "I m-meant no harm, my lord."

"I have my doubts that you could harm anyone," he announced gruffly. "What's your name, girl?"

" 'Tis Birdie, my lord. Don't you remember me?" She came closer to him. "You brought me from London with you when you came."

"Of course. The little girl who wants to know everything." He chuckled, easing his stiff body into the chair with a sigh. "And have you learned a great deal during your stay here?"

"Aye, my lord," she confessed to him with a giggle. "If the counting of china passing through my dishwater could be passing for learning, then I'm learning a great deal."

"Any knowledge that enters the brain and wasn't in residence before is considered learning. But why would you be wandering the library in the dead of night?" He craned his head back to look up at her, then, irritated, stabbed a bony finger toward a chair opposite. "Sit, girl, sit!"

Perching on the edge of the chair brought the marquis into the candlelight. For the first time she noticed his greatly reduced state and it saddened her. Fresh tears came to her eyes. Ducking her head, she concealed her distress from him. "I—I'm sorry . . ."

"Enough apologizing. Now tell me. What were you doing in the library at this time of night?" he persisted.

Without raising her head, she sniffled. "I must better myself," she muttered. While she knew it was not her fault that she was ignorant, it still shamed her to say it out loud.

"Speak up, girl. I can't understand you," he admonished gruffly. Leaning forward, he cupped her chin with a hand knotted with age, lifting her face to study her. His dry flesh rasped against her soft skin. "Come now. No more weeping, you understand?"

Swallowing hard, Birdie tried to control her tears. Clearing her throat, she answered louder, "I must better myself, my lord."

"Well, I cannot fault a person for wanting to better themselves." Reaching for one of the books, he turned it to read the title. "German poetry—" he tilted an eyebrow at her in doubt "—in German? Do you read German, my dear?"

"Nay, m-my lord."

"Well, then that would seem an odd choice, wouldn't it?" Sitting back and resting hands upon the curved head of his cane, he studied her closely, waiting for her to confide in him, as he was sure she would do.

Holding the silence as long as she could, Birdie finally began to stammer a great muddle of nonsense to the marquis, involving ladies and returning princes. When she threatened to burst into tears again, he held up his hand.

"I do not know of what you speak. Just tell me what you want, child."

Birdie raised sherry brown eyes to the marquis's watery blue ones. Thinking to see disgust at her ignorance, she was startled to see only kindness and interest. Could she trust this man with her secret? Remembering Doc's words on board the *Bonnie Blue,* she decided to take a chance that he would help her. Or at least listen in sympathy.

"I want to read!" she gasped in desperation. "I cannot better myself if I cannot read."

"I see." He pondered the situation a moment. "And you thought you could perhaps teach yourself if you could see the books?"

"Aye, but I've never seen a book before. I didn't think they would look so...so..." With a shrug, she sought the right way to explain. "The words. I couldn't do it! I cannot make them out!"

"Why is it so important for you to read? To better yourself...er, tell me your name again, girl?"

"'Tis Birdie, my lord... Just Birdie. And I would be a lady, your lordship," she stated simply, as if that explained it all.

"A lady?" The marquis was stunned, then amused, then saddened. Poor little thing thought she could learn to be a lady from books. "But, Birdie, a true lady is born a lady. A girl born in the slum can't learn to be a lady, not from books especially." He tried to explain it gently lest she burst into tears again. He had no wish to break her heart, but surely she must see that while she could improve her mind, she could never alter her station in life.

"But I thought being a lady was in the blood," she persisted. "If a lady 'twas living in the slums and she had a babe while there, can't that babe be a lady, even if 'twas born in the slum?"

"Yes, I suppose so," he said, nodding his head. She was seeing reason so fast. Such sharp wit for a child of her background, he mused. Leaning back in the chair, he clasped both hands on his cane again, satisfied he was handling this situation beautifully.

"So there!" Birdie stated, glaring at him in defiance.

Puzzled, he waited, but she did not continue. A frown knit his bushy white eyebrows together. "So there? So there... *what?*"

"I am a lady born, but I must learn to talk and act like a lady," she reasoned. Sensing his doubts, she drew her mouth into a straight line. So, he would require proof, she thought. Quickly tugging the top buttons of her blue serge gown loose, she pulled a small flowered pouch from her bodice, where it hung on a ribbon provided by Mattie.

Lord Daine-Charlton, glimpsing the whiteness of her throat and firm rise of her young breasts, cleared his throat and stammered in discomfort at her actions. "Ahem... Really, my dear. I mean to say..."

Ignoring him, Birdie worked the knot loose with great difficulty and opened the pouch. It had been opened rarely the past years. Cheerful Mattie, with her ample lap and motherly scolding, had filled many holes in Birdie's lonely young life. Carefully lifting the miniature from its protective pouch, she smoothed a finger over its surface. A soft smile laid claim to her face as she looked at her beautiful mother. Handing the priceless object with two hands to the marquis, she said in a proud tone, " 'Tis me own mam. Lady Amaryllis."

With a trembling hand, Lord Daine-Charlton leaned toward the light and studied the miniature. It was obviously a very expensive piece, near solid gold and heavy. The portrait had been painted by a master, each tiny stroke perfect. "She is beautiful, Birdie. And very obviously a lady of quality."

"Thank you, my lord."

Cradling the miniature in his hand, he studied Birdie seriously again. Could this girl have stolen the brooch and then from loneliness created a mother for herself? No, he rejected that idea, for there was something very similar in the eyes. The dark eyebrows were shaped the same, also, though the hair color differed. Birdie's hair was a darker, burnished red, where the miniature showed a light reddish blond. There was no doubt in his mind that Birdie would surpass the beauty of the woman in the portrait when she was grown. Even with her lapses of speech, there was the carriage of the aristocrat about the girl, and none of the coarseness of features found in the lower classes. Handing the brooch back to her, he smiled at her pride in her mother.

"Tell me about her, Birdie."

" 'Twas only a babe when she died. But I remember the softness of her hands on my brow, and her sweet voice, 'twas refined…n-not like mine." Turning to him, she became very serious. "Something terrible happened to her, my lord, for her to end up alone and lost in the slums."

"Do you remember anything she might have told you about your father… or his people?" The marquis was greatly intrigued with this beautiful young girl as well as with her sad story.

"Nay, only that he was bad, and that I should never seek him out. She couldn't stop weeping at times like that." Pausing, she wondered whether to mention her mother's voice in the night, then thought it better not to. "She died of the bloody flux, coughing up blood. 'Twas no one for me, so they sent me to Maude's. They all took her beautiful clothes and what furniture there was left, what she hadn't sold. But I hid this—" She nodded to the miniature. Her head was tipped down with the red ringlets falling in charming disarray from beneath the white mop cap.

Lord Daine-Charlton's eyes narrowed in thought. The girl provoked a strange tenderness in his chest. "Birdie, if you were a lady, what would you do?" he asked softly, watching her expressive face.

"Since naught would change the fact of my poverty, I would seek to work like any other impoverished lady. Mayhap a governess? I have a way with children, just not the proper learning to school them."

Her head came up with determination. The stern set of her little chin and the tightness of her luscious mouth left him with no doubt she would succeed at anything she attempted. But he also doubted any woman would be stupid enough to have a girl with such exceptional beauty in her home, or around her husband or sons. No, domestic service was not the answer for this girl.

"It would be a great deal of hard work, you know, to make up for the lost years," he cautioned, watching the play of emotions on her face.

"Aye, 'twould be for sure," she admitted, restoring the miniature carefully to its pouch. She sat back with a sigh, comfortable in their silence. She expected nothing from him. His kindness of just listening, and not scoffing, seemed comfort enough for her.

Lord Daine-Charlton pursed his lips and stared into the fire, lost in faraway thoughts. His voice was low when he spoke, as if he spoke for his own ears only. "I am a very old man. I have lived a great time already. Survived nearly all my family, had two wives. Not that I really loved either of them, merely convenience, you understand. Arranged, actually. Or expected, anyway," he mused absently. Birdie leaned forward to catch his soft words. "I have lived a life fueled by ambition and notoriety, though great wealth and status came from it. I have known the great sorrow of hatred, but never the exquisite joy of a grand passion. At the time I must have thought the wealth and status would warm me in my old age." The white head lifted and he studied the fresh face in front of him. "I would trade all that I have amassed for grandbabies to climb upon my knee."

"Aye, family..." Birdie sympathized with the loss of family. "'Twould be nice to belong to someone."

When the emotion seemed close to the surface for both of them, the old man visibly shook himself. Drawing a large printed handkerchief from the pocket of his robe, he noisily blew his nose.

"'Tis late, girl. You had best see yourself off to bed. I wager the morning starts early beneath Mrs. Fitzwaters's hand." He dismissed her gruffly, with an abrupt, almost embarrassed wave of his hand.

"Aye, that it does," she agreed. Rising, she reluctantly moved toward the door. "Good night to you, my lord."

"Birdie," he called. "If you had asked, I would have allowed you free use of the library. You need not have slipped in after dark."

Pausing with her back to him, she answered in a low voice. "Nay, my lord. For the likes of me, sneaking 'tis the only way. You forget the freedoms you enjoy be denied to others. 'Tis forbidden to be in the house except for quarters. And 'tis forbidden for the likes of me to speak to the likes of you."

"The hell you say!" he bellowed. "Who has forbidden you to speak to me?"

For a moment, Birdie quailed before his anger. Then, as if gathering herself, she lifted her head and squared her shoulders. "'Tis no matter, my lord. 'Twouldn't change the ways of the world to carry tales, now would it?"

He reckoned by the set of her shoulders that it would do no good to press her, and chuckled. Besides, he did not have to think long to lay claim to a name. "Girl, come here. Seat yourself again," he demanded, slapping the vacant chair with his cane.

Birdie did as he demanded, quaking inside. Was he to rail at her head, then? Perhaps dismiss her? She had nowhere to go but out into the hills.

"Birdie, I do not know if I do the right thing. Perhaps I am wrong to give you false hope in bettering your life. I see something in you, a strength and a breeding that I cannot in all good conscience send back to the kitchens to waste its vitality in the scullery." He slammed a fist into an open palm and stared hard at her. Then, as if coming to a hard decision, he reached for her small hand.

Birdie stared back at him with wide eyes, startled and not understanding the things he said. She allowed him to take her hand and leaned toward him, wondering if she should call someone, for he did look feverish. There was a flush to his sallow skin and his eyes did burn brightly.

"I have but a little time left to me in this life. I should be allowed to spend it as I wish. I can think of no person, save a great-nephew I see rarely, who will mourn my passing. I can think of no person that I can say I truly helped in this life. Birdie—" Again he stopped to stare at her. Abruptly, he dropped her hand and waved her away. "Get yourself to bed, girl! It is late!"

Birdie fled, totally confused and strangely saddened, as if she had come very close to something precious, only to have it slip away unrecognized. Easing quietly into her bed, she took care not to wake the two kitchen maids sharing the room with her. Good girls they both were, but she wanted no questions just now. She shivered, and a sob gathered in her throat and tears slipped unheeded into the coarse cotton of the pillow covering.

"Hush, little bird. Don't you cry," a soft, loving voice whispered into her ear. "Mama's here and the sun will shine on the morrow."

Birdie's hand slipped around the little flowered bag containing the miniature of her beloved mother, and she gave in to sleep, oddly comforted.

Chapter Five

Braced before her work board, Mattie hummed tunelessly beneath her breath as she kneaded the rising bread dough. "One more time up with ye, then into the oven ye go, me beauty," she said to the bread, patting it affectionately.

Birdie stood with her arms buried to the elbows in hot, sudsy water. Her apron was sodden and the front of her gown was wet through to her skin. Steam rose around her in a steady mist. The stench of strong soap hung heavily in the stuffy air of the scullery, effectively blocking any of the enticing aromas drifting about the kitchen. To her right were stacked clean dishes, and on her left, those still to be scrubbed. Perspiration ran down her flushed face and stuck her gown to her back between her shoulder blades. The stone floor was hard under her shoes and hours of standing there caused her lower back to ache. The light was provided by a single lamp placed well away from the washtub, hardly extending its arc to any advantage. A measure of dim light came in from the arched doorway, which had been left open with the scant hope for a breath of cool air. When that light dimmed, Birdie glanced up to see Mrs. Fitzwaters's considerable bulk blocking the doorway.

With one look at the housekeeper's face, it was apparent she was livid with rage. The normally straight body was rigid with fury and the face set so tight it wanted to crack. "Birdie! Come with me!" she barked.

Birdie's heart sank. The dragon had somehow learned of her transgression and meant to punish her. Hurriedly drying her hands and arms on a rag, she made ready to follow the woman to her doom. Passing through the kitchen in the housekeeper's wake, she shrugged her shoulders at Mattie's raised eyebrows. The cook's eyes narrowed and her mouth pursed but she said nothing. Birdie knew there could be no rescue from that quarter.

Following Mrs. Fitzwaters through the servants' hidden doorway, Birdie could only gape at the marvelous sights of the castle. She had never been through the door during the light of day, and her senses swam at the luxury. Passing through the entry hall, they paraded up the curved staircase and along the wainscoted hallways, where family portraits stared down at the interloper. As she trailed the housekeeper into a bedchamber, the bulbous eyes of the ancestors, all of whom seemingly suffered from goiter, appeared to judge Birdie. All goggling and damning this miserable product of the slum class, she was sure.

"These will be your chambers from this day forward. I am having your...er, things moved. Such as they are," Mrs. Fitzwaters said with a stern look at the wide-eyed girl. "Birdie, Lord Daine-Charlton has seen fit to do something totally against my better judgment, but as it is not our place to question our betters, I shall endure. His lordship has requested that you be instructed in social refinements, such as the daughter of the house would expect. While I do feel he is giving you airs that are ill-advised, you must work hard to show appreciation and prove his interests in your future are not wasted. Do you understand?"

"Y-yes, Mrs. Fitzwaters. I—I shall . . ."

"See that you do. Now, you are to be dressed and ready to dine with his lordship in one hour. I took the liberty of laying out a suitable dress for you there, and have assigned Franny to see to your needs." With this and one more austere, appraising look, she swept out of the room, shutting the six-paneled door rather more sternly than necessary.

Birdie's courage fell before the grandeur of it all. Nothing could have prepared her for this. The opulent silk-and-satin-draped room was beyond anything her imagination could have conjured. What could it all mean? When the door behind her opened to admit an upstairs maid, she jumped with a squeak of alarm. She could only gape at the plump girl in her black starched uniform and nervously pluck at her wet apron, trying to gather enough sense to claim herself not an idiot. The cheery little maid bobbed her a curtsy and gave her a broad smile and a cheery wink. Birdie returned the bob, worrying her bottom lip with her teeth. She had seen her in the servants' hall, but as their stations had been vastly different, she had no ready acquaintance with her.

"Me name is Franny, miss. And I shall be attending yer needs, if it pleases ye."

"Franny? 'Tis me . . . Birdie," she hissed, pointing to herself as if to clarify the obvious fact.

"Aye, I know that, but Mrs. Fitzwaters says from now on I am to call ye miss and treat ye as such," Franny whispered with a tense look over her shoulder, as if she feared the housekeeper would burst through the door to reprimand her at any moment. She swept the door wider to admit two gaping footmen with buckets of steaming water. "I thought ye'd be wanting a bath before lunch, miss. Washing the stench of the scullery off ye before ye dress, ye see."

Birdie glanced down at her pink hands, wrinkled from their long submersion in the dishwater. Surely further washing could not make them any cleaner. "Franny, did she tell you why all this is happening?"

"Not a word, just that I'm to make ye presentable in an hour," she admitted, then cocked her head to one side at the worried look on Birdie's face. "Don't fash yerself, Birdie. Whatever 'tis all about, 'tis only the fairies' good work, and ye should not be questioning the fairies too closely, now should ye?"

As Franny arranged the bath in the dressing room and added scents to the water, Birdie prowled the bedchamber. Such a vast difference between master and servant! While the servant quarters were quite comfortable and serviceable, they were bare of ornamentation and luxury. These apartments were sumptuous, with tapestry-hung walls to shut out the drafts and thick carpets to cover the stone floor so that one seemed to be walking on pillows. The chamber was dominated by a four-poster bed so tall it required a ladder of three steps to reach the feather mattress. Ornate shelves and rosewood tabletops displayed tiny clocks, all ticking in unison. Birdie could only shake her head in wonder.

"Bath's ready, miss."

Birdie hesitantly entered the small dressing room to find a sizable tub set behind an oriental screen and thick toweling warming before an inviting fire. "Am I to keep the dust from all this, Franny?" she asked, waving a hand back into the bedchamber. "'Tis so much! Have you ever seen such?"

"Seen lots of it! All in Dublin. Come now, into the tub with ye while the water's hot. And rest yer mind, somebody else will have the dusting of all them clocks, they will," Franny said, pushing Birdie's fumbling fingers away from the bodice ties of the blue serge gown.

"Here, what are you doing?" Birdie demanded in surprise. Grasping the bodice of her wet gown, she backed away from the forward girl.

"Fa, Birdie...I mean, miss." Franny laughed. Placing her hands on ample hips, she clucked at the slight girl who was now her charge. "A lady never dresses or undresses herself. And for all that matter, ye haven't got a thing I haven't seen before. Just more of it!"

"I—I'm sorry, Franny." Birdie stepped forward and dropped her hands compliantly, though her face flamed scarlet to be standing in front of the older woman without her clothes. She wanted to do whatever would make her a lady. Slipping into the tub, she allowed her russet ringlets to be lathered, remembering George Hughett. Dear Doc, the first person to ever be kind to her. He had promised to visit and it was nigh two years with no sight of his smiling face. Probably one of those promises grown-ups made to children but had no intention of keeping.

The dress provided by Mrs. Fitzwaters proved to be too small and way too tight in the bust, much to Birdie's disappointment. She stood with her arms out from her sides, not daring to breathe for fear of ripping the seams.

"Aw, 'tis a shame. Such a pretty thing, but even letting out the seams wouldn't do," said Franny. Ceasing her tugging and pulling, she stood back to ponder the problem. She tapped her pursed lips with a forefinger, as her mind sifted through the possibilities. Suddenly her face brightened, and she flew from the room in a flurry of black skirts.

Birdie regretfully drew the pink gown over her head and spread it carefully on the bed. Looking down at the white lawn small-clothes, she blushed at their thinness. Alone in the vast room, she moved on slippered feet to the tall pier glass to study her reflection. Displeased at what she saw, she pulled her face into a distorted mask at the image in the mirror.

"Too short by far. Just a skinny old thing, and these great bosoms on me chest! No prince will ever look at me with a glint in his eye."

"Ye be talking to yourself like one touched in the head," Mattie replied from the doorway, shaking her head at one who would converse with herself. "Besides, young Enus has a blinking fit every time ye come in range of his eyeballs!"

"Mattie!" Birdie yelped, covering herself with her hands. Then abandoning the fruitless effort, she ran to draw her surrogate mother into the room with a furtive attitude about her. "Do you know what all this is about? Mrs. Fitzwaters brought me here and says I'm to stay. And then she just left! Didn't rail at me or nothing!"

"Damned if I know," Mattie admitted, then gave a shake of her head. "If the marquis was not so aged, I'd have me suspicions. All I know is Franny called for help to ply a needle over some gown she's found. 'Twas a-standing on her head in a trunk muttering about your bosoms, she was."

"Here 'tis!" Franny burst into the room, all out of breath. "I remembered where I'd seen it and there it was," she crowed. Her cheeks were flushed and the tidy brown bun at the nape of her neck was no longer tidy. But she was holding a gown over both arms with a decidedly triumphant expression. "'Tis a bit much for daytime, but would ye just look at these seams? A full measure! 'Twas just made for alterations. Besides, time's running out. So 'twill have to do."

"Oh, Franny! 'Tis grand, but—" Birdie fingered the fragile amber silk in awe. "You didn't filch it, did you?"

"No!" Franny protested in mock outrage. "'Twas stored away upstairs, along with things that belong to nobody anymore. Now slip it on so Mattie can make it fit ye. 'Tis late and I still have to do yer hair."

In praise of Franny's efforts, Birdie stood a scant time later, ready to descend the staircase. The old silk gown glowed a mellow gold in the candlelight, accenting the russet ringlets hurriedly tamed into simple order. Seams had been altered to accommodate her splendid breasts, which still threatened to burst over the low *décolletage* at the first deep breath, then nipped in again to display her tiny waist to perfection.

"I can't even see my feet for this skirt!" Birdie wailed. "I'll not make it down the stairs without tumbling head over heels and breaking my neck."

"Nonsense, lassie!" Mattie admonished her, tucking her needles and threads safely into their basket. "Those slippers be paper thin. Keep yer hand on the banister and feel with yer toes. Remember the look of your mam in that picture you wear around yer neck. Make her proud of ye."

Doing just that, Birdie safely arrived at the arch of the dining hall with her dignity in one piece, and at the same time as Lord Daine-Charlton. Demurely clasping her hands in front of her, she paused and nervously waited for him to notice her presence.

When he did, the plunging neckline immediately drew his eyes. "Good Lord!" he exclaimed.

Birdie paled at his exclamation and tugged at the neckline self-consciously. "The dress Mrs. Fitzwaters sent me...'twas too small and couldn't be altered. Franny said not enough seams to c-cover... Uh, I m-mean..." Her words stumbled to a halt with a blush creeping upward to her face.

"Ahem. No, I imagine not," the marquis murmured in humor. His mouth spread in a grin of delighted appreciation of her problem. The girl was exquisite. Her skin was delicate bone china with crushed berries for lips, brandy wine for eyes and morning sunrise for hair.

"Did I do wrong? Was it all right for Franny to make this one over?" she asked, fearful that he would be displeased and send her back to the scullery.

"It is a gown more suited to a ball, but yes, I think you and...uh, Franny...did well. Very well, indeed. Come, my dear," he reassured her. Taking her hand to escort her into the dining room, the marquis tucked it into the crook of his arm to Birdie's great delight.

Seated, the marquis faced Birdie down the enormous length of the dining table laden with sterling and crystal. They were attended by the butler, the underbutler and four footmen. For most of the ten removes, Birdie kept her eyes on her food, raising them occasionally to dart nervous glances at the old man. The underbutler stood at her elbow, ready to correct her table manners and usage of the heavy sterling. She had never imagined there could be such a thing as tangible amusement, but there was. While the staff behaved correctly for the most part, they displayed their understanding of the marquis's intent for Birdie in tiny ways. A raised eyebrow, a slight twitch of the lips, a smirk here and a sneer there. Every one caught by Birdie inflamed her temper until she could stand the strain no longer. Sitting up straight, she slapped the startled underbutler's hand when he would replace an incorrect fork in her hand.

"Cor, man!" she admonished him. Turning to Lord Daine-Charlton, she complained angrily, "'Tis as if they expect me to shove my food into my mouth with the knife, your lordship!"

The marquis laughed his rumbling laugh. "A lady ignores her servants for the most part, Birdie. Pretend they are not there. I am sure they mean no disrespect to you...nor to me. Do they, Hudson?" He stared hard at the English butler, a rigidly correct man who squirmed a bit beneath the stare as the others were in his charge and therefore his responsibility.

"Of course not, my lord!"

"There, you see, my dear. Hudson says no, so just ignore them."

Birdie jumped quickly to her feet as her chair was being pulled from beneath her by the underbutler in a not too subtle indication that it was time to leave the table. "'Tis hard to ignore a man who would take the tools from my hand as I try to put food in my mouth!" she muttered.

Lord Daine-Charlton levered himself stiffly from the table, then moved to offer his arm to her gallantly. "Come along, Miss Birdie. We shall not stand on ceremony tonight. Hudson, please serve my port in the drawing room. I shall join the young lady there with her tea.''

Birdie allowed him to hand her down the hallway with her nose in the air, duly ignoring the servants as they stared after them. Rounding the doorway into the drawing room, she gazed in awe at the opulent room. A sea of blue carpet stretched far past the circle of candlelight and hinted at islands of chairs and tables beyond. Various dour ancestors stared down at them in the gloom from their gilded frames.

"Your lordship? Are all these sour people in the pictures your family?'' she asked, sinking into the offered seat before the fire.

Hudson fought to restrain a laugh as he served Lord Daine-Charlton his port. Birdie frowned at him in irritation, but then accepted the tea as if it had appeared out of thin air.

The marquis grinned and waved the butler from the room. ''No, Birdie. Those are O'Donnells, to the last one of them,'' he explained.

"O'Donnells? Why not Charltons when 'tis your house?'' she asked, puzzled.

"The Charltons reign over Daine Hall in England. As is their rightful place, since it is the place of their heritage. Blanballyhaven has been the O'Donnell stronghold since the sixteenth century. It's only right they should hang here and glower down upon us, for we are the interlopers here.''

"I don't understand,'' she said soulfully. How ignorant she must seem to him. ''You use so many big and strange-sounding words.''

"Well, I shall try to explain in simpler terms then, my dear. You see, in the fourteenth century, County Donegal, all these lands as far as the eye can see, were given to the O'Donnell clan. It was they who built Blanballyhaven and raised their families here. They battled with other clans and protected it with their lives. According to the journals my father discovered, this castle was built as a signal tower for guarding against attack in Lough Swilly.''

Birdie eagerly leaned forward. This was what she wanted. To learn, to understand the history and the land. ''I would be interested to know more...''

Lord Daine-Charlton smiled, and with a shake of his head he cleared his throat. ''Birdie, while it is true that I am a very old man, you must not think the sight of your splendid...ahem, charms spilling out of that bodice does not affect me. Pray sit upright or I shall not be able to continue with the tale.''

Birdie quickly straightened in her chair to tug at the offending neckline, her face a flaming pink. ''I'm sorry,'' she said, flustered with embarrassment. '' 'Tis just the way I'm put together.''

"Pray, do not apologize." He chuckled. "You will give your husband heaven on earth someday. But first, before the history lesson, let us speak of my plan. I am greatly taken with you, Birdie. I see something in you that your... ahem, unfortunate circumstances belie. A breeding that even the slums could not obliterate. I wish to aid you in your search for knowledge."

"Oh, do you truly mean it?" she exclaimed. "God bless you, my lord."

"Do not thank me in such haste. It will require a great deal of work on your part. Are you agreeable to hard work?"

"Oh, yes!" She beamed in delight at him. "I will not let you down."

"Good! From this day forward—" he toasted her with his port, then drank deeply "—I shall treat you as the daughter of the house and instruct all others to do the same. I shall take charge of training your mind personally as I readily admit it is to my pleasure and benefit to do so. And as for a governess..."

"Governess? Am I to start all over as a babe, then?"

"Of course not! That, my dear, would not be possible," he said with a pointed look at her chest, charmed with her innocent blush. "But someone must teach you to walk, to talk and act every inch a lady. Instruct you in dress, needlework, directing servants and... er, well, all the other things a lady does." He studied her delighted expression and sparkling eyes. She was a fragile, exquisite bud that had struggled for existence in a bed of weeds. And he so looked forward to watching her bloom. "It will be hard work, Birdie. Do you think you are equal to the task?"

"Aye, my lord," she assured him with a determined set to her mouth that convinced him she was capable of most anything her heart desired. "I shall work night and day, if it takes that. I will make you, and my mam, proud."

"I do believe you will, my dear. I do believe you will."

"God bless you, my lord," she said with a sigh. Then, unable to contain her tears of joy, she quickly dropped to her knees and laid her cheek against his dry, knotted hand in thankfulness. The other hand gently stroked her hair. The very tenderness in the gesture released the tears and she wept. Wise in years and experience, the marquis let her sob out her happiness.

Chapter Six

The marquis was seated in the mahogany-paneled library behind the enormous desk, its entire leather surface littered with estate ledgers. His valet, Frederick Travers, was solicitously attending his fractious master, but turned when Birdie hesitantly poked her head around the door. Mystified as to how such a vision of loveliness had materialized in the gloom of Blanballyhaven without his taking note, the little man was rendered quite speechless. His mouth dropped open to hang there. Irritated at his inattention, the marquis glanced up to scowl at the man's besotted expression and followed his gaze to Birdie. An immediate smile of delight and welcome burst over his face.

"Birdie! At last! Travers, ring for tea if you please. Travers? *Travers!*" he barked. It required a rather sharp poke in the ribs by Lord Daine-Charlton's bony finger to gain the valet's attention. "Tea, blast you!"

"Ouch! Yes, my lord. Of course, my lord! Tea, of course," sputtered Travers, bowing himself across the room in hurried little steps.

"My dear, please seat yourself. I must say you are looking exceptionally radiant. A welcome sight for these old eyes. I had begun to despair at ever seeing you again. It has been a sennight since I've had the pleasure of your company," he called, shoving papers aside.

"'Twas the same thought I had, your lordship. I was afraid Franny wouldn't let me leave my room again in this life. And the things she's been doing to me! Mud baths! And salt rubs to take the skin from my body, I swear." She laughed, pleased that he so obviously approved of her efforts. "Your lordship..."

"I think we should do something about that 'your lordship.'" The marquis flung up his hand to interrupt. "Perhaps you could call me . . . Charles?"

"Oh, your lordship . . . I couldn't do that!" Birdie exclaimed.

"Hmm . . . Let's see then. 'Your lordship' is just, well, too deuced formal for the kind of friends that we shall be." The old man pondered, tapping his pursed mouth with a forefinger.

"I could mayhap call you . . . Sir Charles? 'Tis still respectful," she offered tentatively.

"Not exactly correct by British standards, but it shall be as you wish!" he exclaimed. Rising stiffly from the chair, he leaned heavily on the desk until he had his feet securely under him. Shuffling around the desk, he held out his hand to her. Birdie slid hers into his with a rush of affection. Squeezing her hand lightly, he guided her toward the two chairs positioned cozily in front of the fireplace. "Sir Charles it shall be then. And what shall I call you? Let's see now. Perhaps . . . beautiful and exquisite and charming? For, my dear, you are all that and more—" he bowed stiffly over her hand "—and if I were a much younger man, there's all manner of things I should enjoy teaching you."

"Your lordship . . . I mean, Sir Charles, 'tis a randy old goat ye be. I should not think to be safe in yer presence," she teased in her thick brogue. Nevertheless, she flushed a bright pink at his outrageous compliments.

"No, my dear. You are ever safe with me. I am too old for love, but in my younger days—" Flipping his coattails out of the way in an eloquent manner, he seated himself across from her. "Ah, yes, in my younger days I was a force to be reckoned with!"

Tea arrived with Hudson supervising two footmen carrying a large sterling service. All three stared openly at Birdie with astonished expressions. Other than pinking prettily about the cheeks, she did not appear to notice they were in the room. When they would seem to stumble over themselves in confusion, the marquis snorted in exasperation.

"Out! All of you!" he finally commanded, thumping his cane mightily on the carpet. The men scattered like guilty spaniels. When the room was cleared again, Sir Charles scrutinized the heavy tea service with aversion. "Damn! I fear I shall now have to call one of them back to pour the bloody stuff!" Holding a trembling hand out toward Birdie, he made a disgusted sound at the infirmity and weakness advanced old age had dealt him.

"I can pour it," Birdie offered, totally awed by the extravagance of the tea service, "if you will but tell me how." The teapot, ornately encrusted, looked to weigh a stone at least. The cups sitting on tiny saucers were paper thin and dwarfed by the sterling creamer and sugar bowl.

"I have watched it done with a grace that would astound a mere mortal, but to tell you how it is accomplished escapes me. Mrs. Fitzwaters will be able to teach you that, for sure...among a medley of other things, as our Mrs. Fitzwaters has proven herself a wealth of information...knowledge even I never suspected she possessed. But for now..."

"What say you to muddling through as best as we can?" suggested Birdie. She approached the service with a confidence that she did not feel. "If there's nobody about to see us do it wrong, then how terrible can it be?"

"Wonderful idea!" Sir Charles exclaimed, settling back to enjoy the mere sight of her movement. "I shall hate to see your honesty and frank manner destroyed, my dear. It's so refreshing in a female, but alas, not the thing in society. You must learn to dissimulate."

Birdie tipped the teapot awkwardly, pouring tea into a delicate bone china cup held gingerly in her hand. Placing several toasted pastries on a saucer, she carefully carried them to the old man. Repeating the process for herself, she slipped into her seat to watch the marquis closely, to observe how one went about this business of having tea.

"Sir Charles, Franny says she came to Blanballyhaven as wife, for 'twas nigh impossible to keep an O'Donnell from Donegal. 'Twas like asking the mist to leave Ireland, she said. What was her meaning?"

The marquis smiled at her. A treasure of a girl for a man who loved history. "You remember me telling you this land was O'Donnell land? The Irish feel powerfully drawn to their land and fought many bloody battles in the attempt to retain it. The clashes of the clans have gone on for years. Even now that England rules in Ireland, the pull of the land remains in their hearts. And it's because of this that England will never truly conquer Ireland."

"If Ireland be such a powerful fighting island, how did the English take it from them? This...Donegal...be a far and distant place, but even here England rules." Birdie again leaned forward in eagerness to learn.

"There was a great rebellion in the late 1600s. English armies, led by a man named Cromwell, came into Ireland and defeated the Irish armies. The men were killed or deported into slavery...no quarter given. Women and children were reduced to wandering the land, homeless and hungry. Thousands died for famines raged the country."

"But why wouldn't they win? 'Twas their own country and must have been so many of them. A great fighting nation, on their own land, willing to die for it . . . 'twould seem to me they would have might on their side. And knowing the land like the back of their hand, why didn't they win?" she demanded.

Sir Charles smiled behind his teacup at her passion. The winter would prove to be most entertaining with this young mind soaking up knowledge like a dry sea sponge.

"Eat your pastry, child. And I shall try to explain the mystery of the Irish people to you." When she dutifully bit into the sweet tart, her eyes eagerly watching his face, he cleared his throat and placed both hands on the head of his cane. "The Irish have always been separated into clans of great strength. Each clan existed as absolute monarch over their own lands, thus dividing Ireland into small countrylike sections. No one man, no one Irishman, has ever proved influential enough to unite all the clans. The heads of the clans could never be together in one room long enough, nor at peace with each other long enough, to elect a leader. Thus divided, they were easily conquered. The only thing they have ever agreed upon is their hatred of the English."

"Mattie says 'tis still alive . . . the hate. That bands of men gather in the mountains and talk rebellion." Birdie again crossed to the tea service, lifting the pot this time with more confidence. "More tea, Sir Charles?"

"Nay, Birdie. Please ring for whiskey?" Turning, he noted with humor her confusion. "There . . . the bellpull just by the door. A tug upon it will ring a bell in the kitchen. Someone will come. Do you see it?"

Tugging the rope gingerly, Birdie smiled. "Aye, Sir Charles. I've heard the bell but never knew where 'twas coming from."

"Birdie, you will easily learn to run a house as large as this for knowing the kitchens as you do. A lady has a housekeeper only to relay her orders. She never relinquishes total control to another woman in her own house. She is like a general and her housekeeper is her first officer."

The door opened quietly and the underbutler slipped into the room, attempting to keep his eyes from straying to Birdie.

"My lord?"

"Whiskey, James."

The man bowed and retired to a sideboard to pour the amber liquid into a crystal glass. Birdie paid careful attention to the bottle he used and the amount he placed in the glass. She wished to refill it for the marquis, should he require it. As the underbutler left, she resumed her questions.

"Mattie says they had no freedom. Freedom to run their own country and freedom to own their own land. And that they will someday fight again for that."

"When Ireland lost the war, they forfeited their land and their power to govern their own country. And while they may gather in knots in the hills and talk, they have no true power to act. Talk has always been the downfall of the Irish. It has long been said, if you put an Irishman in a tavern by himself, he will toast his God. If you put two Irishmen together, they will toast each other. But if you put three Irishmen together, they'll start an argument that will end in bloodshed."

Gripping his cane, the marquis started to struggle to his feet with his empty glass. Birdie quickly slipped from her chair and gently took his glass. Walking to the sideboard, she took the glass stopper from the crystal decanter she had seen the underbutler use. Not knowing whether to reuse the same glass or fill a clean one, she chose the latter.

The marquis beamed at her as she moved across the room to hand him the glass. He listened to the pleasant rustling the heavy fabric of her skirt made as it swayed. A pleasure only a man who loved women the whole of his life would notice and rejoice over. A pleasure he had forgone for too many years, since his last mistress had departed, certainly. It was not a good thing for a man to be without a woman. Even for a man as old and useless as himself, he mused.

"You are a joy for a man's old age, my dear. I would never have believed it possible, but when a man becomes too old to feast with the body, it is just as pleasurable to feast with the eyes," Sir Charles said, enjoying the blush that flushed her delicate cheeks. "I shall miss you when you are gone."

"G-gone, your lordship?" Sudden fear struck her heart. Was she to be sent away, then? Was the dream to end so soon?

"Aye, my dear. You are far too beautiful for an old man like me to keep hidden. Even in this forgotten place the young swells will ferret you out. Can't be helped. But your absence will leave a great hole in my heart," he teased with an appreciative glint in his eye.

Greatly relieved, she teased him in return. "Aye, a handsome young prince a-sporting a bonnie black mustache and astride a great white charger will come to carry me away." But in her mind's eye, she saw the beautiful young gentleman in the glen calling for her to hurry and grow up as he waited for her.

"I think, actually, you are too beautiful to waste on the Irish lads," Sir Charles stated somewhat solemnly. In his mind, there began to form an idea, an idea of launching Birdie into London society. What a fuss they would make over her beauty.

"Do you *truly* think I am beautiful?" Birdie asked, earnestly leaning forward. "I mean, as beautiful as me mam?"

Sir Charles thought to tease her about fishing for compliments as any debutante of the ton would have done, but studying her serious face, he realized she was asking for an honest answer, for there was no coy flirting about her.

"Aye, Birdie. Fully blossomed, you will be even more beautiful," he answered just as seriously. "In society, there seems to be an eternal image of the perfect woman. This image changes sometimes year to year. One year it may be dark hair and limpid eyes, though most usually it is blond and insipid. But among the beauties, there is always those women who stand apart. They may not be the most beautiful, may not conform to the trend of the season, but for some obscure reason, possibly their wit or style, some women just have a flair that makes them devastating. You are going to be one of those women, Birdie. With your determination, your frankness, your keen mind, your charm and, for the not at all obscure reason, your perfection of face and form. Aye, you are more than beautiful. Birdie, you quite take a man's breath away."

Birdie sat very still with her hands limp in her lap. The sherry brown eyes were wide and blinking slowly as if she were greatly stunned. Slowly the tip of her tongue appeared to moisten her dry lips. With awe plain in her voice, she said, "Cor, your lordship! What a blinking ball of blarney!"

Throwing his head back, the marquis roared with laughter. He laughed until tears streaked down his face, and Birdie, unable to help herself, laughed with him. Even the news that Mrs. Elizabeth Fitzwaters had been assigned the instruction in refinements to Birdie's lacking education could not destroy the pleasure the two found in each other's company. But, three days afterward, when the house was in an uproar and it would seem war had been declared, Sir Charles retreated to his library and firmly closed the door for most of the daylight hours.

An enormous woman, towering over everyone in the household and carrying a bulk of weight corseted as solid as a stone wall, Mrs. Elizabeth Fitzwaters was a formidable opponent. Traveling with the marquis, she ruled his residences with an iron will. She stalked the hallways of Blanballyhaven with her head in the air and a stare down her long nose at everyone and everything, instantly appraising and finding most seriously lacking.

The absurdity as well as the very inappropriateness of the idea of turning a slum child into a lady set Mrs. Fitzwaters's teeth on edge, but she had agreed upon a task and she was a woman of her word. Teach the chit she would, but make it pleasant, she would not. She was determined, along with the required subjects, that the child would learn to be God-fearing, to realize her station in this life and return to it! Not one week into the task at hand and she was confronting the staff on their manner of relating to Miss Birdie. Striding into Mattie's domain, she demanded, in no uncertain terms, that the motherly cook cease serving her unruly charge meals in the kitchen, as it was unseemly to her newly elevated station.

"Is that so?" Mattie exclaimed in a hoarse, angry voice. She planted her hands on ample hips and gave an indignant, disbelieving glance toward Travers, with whom she was sharing a pot of tea and sweet rolls fresh from the oven. "And just what harm do you think I be doing the lassie?"

"It makes no difference and I do not deem to explain myself. You have only yourself to monitor. And I must say, you should have more sense, a woman of your years, than to sit there simpering like some moonstruck girl with his lordship's valet. You would be better advised to see to your duties in a God-fearing way."

"Oh, I would, would I?"

Undaunted, Mrs. Fitzwaters swept her scornful gaze over the shocked Travers, who, teacup halfway up to his mouth, stared dumbfounded at her. As if catching himself staring, and becoming aware of the comical picture he must present, he carefully eased the cup to the table, gulping mightily at the sight of this paragon in full, haughty glory.

"And you, Mr. Travers, having been in the employ of his lordship for a goodly number of years, know better than most how his lordship would view this sort of amoral behavior among staff members? Disgraceful!"

Mattie, her face red and sullen, began to bang pots. "All right," she muttered, to turn the anger away from the innocent valet. "I'll see what I can do about the lassie. But I'm not above thinking I was doing her no harm. She's just a dear wee thing and been as close to me as my own daughter for these last years."

"Thank you, Mrs. O'Donnell." Mrs. Fitzwaters acknowledged the capitulation. "I trust you will carry out your word." And with that, she elevated an eyebrow at Travers with significant warning and marched from the kitchen.

"Of all the bloody hell . . ." Mattie sputtered, plopping down at the table across from Travers. "The high-handed and mighty . . ."

Travers still sat staring at the doorway after the housekeeper. "Yes, isn't she just magnificent? Totally correct in everything she says and does."

Mattie could only gape at the man, then shake her head in disbelief and mutter into her apron, "Ye gods and little fishes!"

Chapter Seven

A strong wind blew lustily across the hills, coming straight down from the mountains. It carried the very bitterness of winter on its breath as it rattled the windowpanes and caused the tapestries to stir against the stone walls. A fire burned brightly in the hearth, wavering a bit now and then when the wind found its way down the chimney.

Lord Henry Templeton Daine paced the vast and chilly drawing room. His highly polished Hessians rang out sharply against the smooth stone floor each time his lengthy stride crossed the space between the two carpets. It was advancing toward noon and he was restless at the delay. His great-uncle, having sent for him on a matter of dire urgency, now seemed to be taking his own time quitting his bedchamber. Even though he and Viscount Sayers, who had thought it a lark to accompany the ill-tempered Daine on this command appearance, had arrived chilled to the bone in the dead of the night, Lord Daine's keen sense of family duty had prodded him to rise early to be prepared for the interview. But all that had gained him was a solitary breakfast and a long, tedious wait.

A snort of frustration escaped him as he paced to the window overlooking the east lawn. His greatest desire was to settle this matter, whatever it was, and return to London posthaste. The little season would be under way shortly and he did not wish to leave Sophia alone in London, especially with others viewing his absence as license to ardently press their own suits. He would not have chosen to visit Ireland just at present, but a summons, after all, was a summons.

The entire journey had been a misery. The crossing had been rough, as must be expected at this time of year, and the long road from Buncrana, never an easy trek at best, had proved nearly impassable. He sincerely hoped it had all been extremely necessary. He felt sorely pressed to dispense with whatever duty awaited him and be out of Ireland before the fierce winter took hold of Donegal. For once that happened, he was truly trapped at Blanballyhaven. And this castle, never one of his favorite haunts, was enormous and drafty as hell's teeth. In fact, if his opinion was to be sought, the estate was only perfect for autumn shooting and should be duly avoided the rest of the year.

He had attempted to explain the possibility of entrapment and the limits of Blanballyhaven's creature comforts to Lord Sayers, but regardless, it apparently seemed just the thing for the fair-haired man to pack his bag and follow along behind as if it were no more than a sight-seeing jaunt through the park. Although the miserable trek last night had seen even that usually quiet, amicable gent in a foul temper and in a hurry to seek the warmth of his bed. It was not a surprise to Lord Daine that he had yet to see hide or hair of him this morning. Lord Sayers was not a particularly close friend, although they did frequent the same clubs and seek the same amusements. But as one usually did not have the choice of brothers-in-law when one selected a wife, he supposed the inoffensive Oliver would be as good as any, and no worse than most.

Turning from the window, he paced the length of the room once more, again cursing the delay. His great-uncle Charles might be an ancient and eccentric old man, but he had always been a favorite relation. The suspicion that his lordship was at last about to join his ancestors could not but occur to him. Not that he hoped in any way the marquis was ailing, but after all, he was into his eighties by now. While Lord Daine had little desire to step into the man's shoes, they would bring him a great number of advantages he could ill do without. He mentally counted back the years since his last visit. It had been close to three . . . no, four years at least.

Raking his hand through his unruly hair, he attempted to maintain a light mood. Wouldn't do to be in a blue devil in front of the old boy. A chilly blast of wind moaned down the chimney and sprayed ashes onto the rug. Lord Daine shivered and vividly recalled warm London hearths, cheerier company and soft, inviting arms.

This for sure, he would not live at Blanballyhaven when he succeeded. Not only was it too far from London and his interests, but it was a dashed unpleasant place, full of dark corners, secret passages and too much history. Even Sophia's pale silver beauty would be hard-pressed to lighten this gloom. Although the thought of a secluded honeymoon here with that beauty quite put a different light on the place, he mused. A slight smile replaced the forbid-

ding frown on his face and his stance somewhat eased. They could
ride the hills, fish the lakes, tumble in the heather.... No, Sophia
was more suited to Paris and opulent ballrooms than the wilds of
Ireland. In fact, a manager of top rank would be in order for
Blanballyhaven and one visit a year required of him. No more, no
less.

Placing both hands on the mantel, he stared into the fire. The
flames glinting on his uncovered head gave to his thickly curled hair
the blue black sheen of a raven's wing. His dominant features, with
a slight hawkish cast, were set to advantage by warm, sun-browned
skin, as though he spent much of his time in the sun, when in fact
the opposite was truer. His eyes were large, a sober shade of gray,
and held a searching look, surprisingly unmarked by any lines of
dissipation despite his notorious habits. At present a guilty scowl
disfigured his fine forehead at the thought of succeeding, for in
truth, he did not wish ill health upon his great-uncle.

Temple was, in fact, a wild young man and had at one time been
an object of concern for his father. That gentleman, however, had
been deceased a long decade. The sudden independence at such a
young age, two and twenty, probably accounted for the wasting of
time in the delights of unshackled living. The marquis, being his
legal guardian, had done his duty and seen the boy through Oxford, then washed his hands of him, although Temple had never
created an all-out scandal. Lord Daine-Charlton was always anxious and delighted to see his great-nephew, and the visits were a joy
to both, quite probably, as they both suspected, because the visits
were seldom close enough together to be counted in the same year.
The door opened and he spun to see Travers bowing to him.

"Travers! You old dog!" Temple greeted the valet affectionately. "Has life been treating you fair?"

"No, my lord," the valet said in a muffled tone. Affecting a
woeful face, the thin man mutely shook his head in a negative
fashion. "It is simply that I am a victim of unrequited love."

Quite taken aback at this blunt offering in answer to a reasonable and civilized question, Temple drew the man into the room
and closed the door behind him. Observing the downtrodden look
on the narrow face, he fought back amusement. Somehow, one did
not readily equate love with Travers.

"Well, it has happened," he announced in a voice he strove to
keep steady, "to the best of us. It has been said that even the
strongest man cannot hope to stand against the pull of their charms
forever."

Travers's weak, almost colorless eyes took on an eager light.
"My lord, you too? My very best to you! Although I—I hope your

quest is met with more favor than mine has thus far. But there is ever hope..."

"A truer word, Travers...a truer word." Temple bit his quivering lip and continued in a credibly even tone. "From your long face, am I to take it the lady is, er..."

Anxious to state his case to any sympathetic ear, Travers spoke in a breathless rush. "Oh, my lord, I have reason to believe she will not always be adverse, but thus far I have lacked encouragement." Glancing around as if to catch eavesdroppers on their very private conversation, he lowered his voice. "Does the marquis have knowledge of your lordship's own fallen state?"

"Not as yet. I plan to inform him this trip."

"Splendid, my lord! He will be quite taken aback, I am sure. It has been his greatest wish for ever so long to see your lordship settled and establishing a nursery." Again came the careful sweep of the room with his eyes, and a lowering of his voice still more. "And with the greatest of luck there shall be nuptials below stairs in the near future, as well. With the greatest of luck."

"You've bent the knee to the lady, then?"

"Y-yes—" His voice broke, but Temple was unsure if with indignation or suppressed sobs. "And then she refused! Called me a libertine, she did. A snake in the grass! A viper! *Me!*"

"See here, Travers—" Temple sought to relieve some of the stricken man's emotion with a touch of levity "—I begged you to stay in London with me. My neckcloths have been the shame of the ton. But you insisted on coming to the wilds of Ireland, and just look where it has landed you. I have heard the women are truly heathens here. A real danger to a town bloke."

"But, my lord—" Travers lifted his sad face to peer into the young man's eyes "—my Libby, Mrs. Fitzwaters, is a London jewel."

"Mrs. Fitzwaters! The marquis's housekeeper? Good Lord, man!"

"Yes, exactly. A true paragon, isn't she? I have carried this torch for the longest time, you know."

Seeing the man did not truly wish to be relieved of his misery, Temple merely patted his shoulder comfortingly. The valet was a small, sparse man with thinning hair and pale, near colorless eyes. His being in the old marquis's service was much talked about among the ton, for his very flighty gestures and exacting manners irritated the marquis to absolute rudeness much of the time. But for all his affectations, Travers was a top-of-the-trees valet and much sought after by the Tulips of the ton.

"I do not intend my visit here to be of any great length, Travers. I would deem it an honor if you wished to accompany me back to London and civilization," Temple offered with a smile, for it was common knowledge, and a great joke between him and his great-uncle, that he had been attempting the theft of the valet for the same number of years he had been in long pants. But now it had been made clear why Travers had declined to leave Lord Daine-Charlton's employ. The skirts always seemed to rule a man's life, even a man as self-contained as Travers.

"Thank you, my lord, for your kindness." As if coming to himself, the valet straightened and resumed his formal air of service. "Lord Daine-Charlton will see you in his private sitting room now."

Following the valet up the stairs and down dark passages, Temple felt more than a little apprehensive, and with a rueful smile remembered earlier occasions when he had been summoned to attend the formidable marquis in his London house, almost always for a reprimand of some severity. The thought made him grin and consequently brightened his face so that he looked in the best of humor when he walked into the musty bedchamber.

The marquis's lined face creased into a smile but his tone belied the pleased look. "Humph!" He coughed, rapping the floor sharply with his cane. "So you're here. Took long enough about it, didn't you?"

Temple, unaffected by his great-uncle's gruff manner, merely grinned anew. "I came, my lord, as soon as your letter reached me."

"Humph!" the marquis grunted again, waving the young man to the chair opposite. The light from the window fell full on his great-nephew's face and the older man studied him carefully. The boy was entirely too handsome for his own good, he thought. As he regarded him closely, his eyes softened. Perhaps it was not fair to blame Temple wholly for his life-style, not when he considered how favorably most women responded to his austerely handsome face and his aloof manner. Startled, Sir Charles took himself sternly to task. He must not, even in his own mind, defend Temple. It would never do for the boy to guess that he was not always angry and shocked at his exploits. It would weaken his position if that truth were known. And, with his plot in motion, strength of strategy was everything. Aloud, he said, "I see by your face that excessive living is taking its toll on your health."

The tone was severe but Temple merely smiled again. "Couldn't possibly be that hell's midnight trip up this godforsaken mountain on the worst roads in Ireland that you are reading on my face?''

"Why ever did you not make the trip in the light of day as any sane person would have? Damned dangerous, what with the rebels, you know, unless—'' Sir Charles raised his eyebrows as the thought struck him ''—you were thinking to find me upon my deathbed?'' The young man grinned and merely inclined his head ever so slightly. "Then you are a fool, boy!'' he remarked frankly. "This family is cursed with long life. My father died at seventy-seven. Your father would have lived a long and fruitful life, too, if he'd had the sense God gave a goose and stayed away from strong drink and wild horses.''

Leaning back in his chair, Temple loosened his black coat of superfine and crossed his buff-clad legs to contemplate the tassel on his boot. He knew that his great-uncle would take his own time bringing the subject around to his summons. But he had news himself. A bit premature, perhaps, but the chance Sophia Sayers would refuse his offer was minute. And the opportunity to inform his uncle of his pending nuptials in the flesh was to be relished.

Sir Charles scowled again and regarded his heir keenly from beneath his bushy white eyebrows. "Well, so you obey a summons, do you? Some pretty things I've been hearing about you. So it's married women now, is it? That's too close to scandal, by damn!''

"The liaison was over and done with before the tale reached your ears,'' Temple admitted, unperturbed as he did not trouble himself that he could ever be disinherited by this man. They dealt too well together. Although his great-uncle's sources were unfailing, whoever they were. Little of the ton's business did not reach his ears, regardless of his residence.

"Nonetheless, it is time you were settled and forgetting other men's wives. You need one of your own to worry about,'' barked the marquis, moving the discussion toward his purpose.

"I agree wholeheartedly,'' Temple interrupted, catching the old man unawares.

"What's this? You agree? Damned change of tone from the last time I spoke to you on this same matter.''

"A man matures. He sees where his responsibilities lie, and he shoulders them,'' Temple said with a slight shrug. "I am not unaware of your age, and while thankful you continue in good health, I realize I am your only heir. I am conscious of the need to produce an heir for my own succession.''

"Amazing good sense. Can't say why it makes me dashed uneasy to hear you speak like that. Makes me think I'm talking to an imposter, indeed.''

Sir Charles glanced at Temple's elegant figure with a warm pride that he could never quite suppress, no matter how outrageous the tales from London. Despite his miserable midnight journey, there was not a wrinkle in the finely cut morning coat, not any tired slump of those wide shoulders. Oh, to be that young and that grand again. He hated to cast a cloud over this amicable sitting but it must be done. Freshly exasperated with himself, he gave a deep sigh. A pretty pass he had come to if he feared a snubbing from his own heir. With a great effort, he raised himself on unreliable legs and, with the aid of his heavy cane, hobbled to the window. Below him, on the garden path, was his love, his joy, just as he had expected her to be. For he knew only the very worst of weather could confine Birdie indoors.

"Come, Temple," he called. "I will show you the true sunshine in a man's life." With a hand on the boy's shoulder, he drew Temple beside him and pointed through the window to the garden below.

Temple pressed his face against the cold windowpane to see a girl of some tender years dashing toward the castle. Heedless of the weather and the wind, she ran, her russet hair flying about her uncovered head. Leaping a low hedge with grace and agility, she unexpectedly displayed a length of shapely leg. He heard her cry of triumph as she swooped down and gathered something into her hands, evidently discovering something she had lost.

"Who is she? A servant's child?" Temple quizzed with a chuckle at her antics. Sir Charles smiled to see his amusement, a satisfied gleam in his eye.

"Assist an old man back to his chair, would you? And ring for Hudson, if you please."

Mrs. Fitzwaters answered the bell, stepping quietly into the room. "Excuse me, my lord. Hudson is elsewhere at the moment. May I assist you until his return?"

Temple eyed the woman with the newly acquired knowledge of a love interest and was forced to drop his eyes in amusement.

"Oh, Libby," the marquis said. "Would you please ask Miss Birdie to join us for tea?"

Without a word and always correct, Mrs. Fitzwaters bowed slightly and backed from the room. "Miss Birdie, indeed!" she fumed, stalking through the halls to dispatch a footman, much younger than herself, to climb the stairs with the summons. "Senile old fool!"

"Miss Birdie?" Temple tipped his eyebrow toward his curls. "What new development is this?"

Sir Charles hesitated, disliking to break the congenial mood of the moment. "There is a matter on which I would speak to you. One that is very dear to my heart."

"You may speak to me on any matter you choose—" Temple agreed so amicably that his uncle eyed his heir warily "—always provided it is not a further tirade against my numerous deplorable habits."

"Of course not, Temple. I wanted to speak to you on the subject of marriage."

"Ah, not the last theme then, but a well-worn old one nevertheless." His eyebrows drew together in a formidable frown. "Uncle, why do this? You have made your point perfectly clear and I, in my turn, have told you just this morning that . . ."

"Temple, I insist you wed," Sir Charles interrupted bluntly, then cleared his throat in readiness of the coming confrontation.

Temple hesitated. Studying the serious expression on his great-uncle's face, he pondered that this was, perhaps, not the same old harangue. A small worry teased at the back of his mind. Could it be possible that his great-uncle's health was not as it seemed and his desire to see his heir wed his one last wish?

"Uncle, as I have said, I intend to wed this year . . ." he commenced, then leaned forward to eagerly share his secret, only to be abruptly interrupted by the marquis thumping his cane on the floor and raising his voice.

"Temple, I wish you to wed Birdie. Here and now, within the week."

Silence fell heavily in the room. The wind moaned at the window casements and billowed the drapes. The marquis studied the face of the young man, watching the range of emotions play over his countenance before he gained control. Astonishment and disbelief, then anger and finally back to his characteristic calm.

"Surely you jest, my lord," declared Temple. The tone was deadly, and the face was set in a stormy cloud.

"Believe me when I assure you that I do not jest," stressed Sir Charles adamantly. "I realize I am asking a great deal, but I have my reasons."

Rising, Temple paced to stand before the fireplace, his very stance disapproving and withdrawn. "Am I permitted to inquire into those reasons?"

Clearing his throat, the marquis stodgily told Birdie's extraordinary tale, relating the accident, the rescue, her upbringing and great desire to overcome the slums. Telling of her strengths and her quick mind, he left little out of his story except her great beauty and the sensual young woman she had grown to be. Though, try as he might, he felt it was an impossible task to convince Temple just how special and loving a young woman Birdie had grown to be.

Temple remained quiet as he listened to the unbelievable fairy tale of the lady found in Haymarket slums. He feared for his great-uncle's mind, for surely this was all a fabrication. A figment of his aging imagination. A man as family conscious, as scandal aware as Lord Daine-Charlton to even hint that his heir, heir to the vast holdings of the Daines and the Charltons, would marry a slum child suggested a disturbed mind. Even if she was smart enough to fool an old man into thinking she could be lost royalty, the idea was preposterous.

As if he were capable of reading his nephew's mind, the marquis attempted to reassure him. "I know you are thinking I have taken leave of my senses, Temple. But I assure you, I would have recognized a hoax. The child has given me love and devotion in my old age. I love her as I would a daughter of my own loins. I am prepared to take whatever steps necessary to protect her after my death."

"Then marry her to Travers. Or to Hudson. Not to your heir!" Temple emphasized, anger flaring in his voice. He turned hard eyes upon his great-uncle, silently demanding to be told that this was all a joke of the rudest nature.

Sir Charles found his great-nephew's habit of riveting the twin coals of his gray eyes on one disconcerting, to say the least. Even as a small boy, he had the ability to send a chill of foreboding up one's spine with that direct stare. There was no doubt that Temple's eyes were his most arresting feature. They could flash with anger one moment and sparkle with gaiety the next. At times he could be haughty and insolent, then appear graceful and charming, drawing all those around him. He was a multifaceted gentleman, and Sir Charles desired to trust him with the happiness and safety of Birdie, who was the most loving, caring person he'd ever met. His blue eyes hardened. He would not be intimidated or diverted from his plan.

"She is not a servant, nor shall she be wife to a servant," Sir Charles rasped, then laid down his ultimatum. "Temple, this is my decision. I cannot stop you from succeeding, and I cannot stop Daine Hall from becoming yours one day. They are yours by right of entailment, as is the title. And that is as it should be. However, there is Stannisburn and Blanballyhaven, which are mine solely, to do with as I see fit. It pains me to say this, boy, but if you do not take Birdie to wife within the week, I shall wed her myself. There could be no hope of an heir, of course, so nothing shall jeopardize your succession. But Birdie shall have the protection of my name and the bulk of the Daine-Charlton wealth.

"Daine Hall cannot stand on its own. You need the other two to support your life-style. You'll soon find yourself without funds, and consequently Daine Hall impossible to maintain. I have no wish to cut you out, Temple. You are my blood and I am fond of you. Marry Birdie, settle down, and I'll make you a present of Blanballyhaven on your wedding day. It will serve you well and provide a giant income. May I have your word on this?"

Temple turned his back on his great-uncle's question. In angry confusion he walked to the window. His sight turned inward, he saw nothing of the sweep of lawn below him or the ocean beyond. He was rather pale but, although greatly disturbed, gave no other sign of inner turmoil. As much as the ultimatum angered him, he could not deny his great-uncle the right to dispose of his property as he wished. But a slum child! Thoughts of the beautiful, sultry Sophia, every inch a lady, flitted through his mind. A mental groan escaped him.

Without turning, he asked, "Am I allowed to even meet the girl beforehand?" His tone was sarcastic and displeasing to his great-uncle's ear.

"Your approval of the girl's appearance or manner would not in any way alter my decisions concerning her," snapped Sir Charles.

The marquis's voice was gravelly as he fought to keep emotion out of it. Nothing must deter him from his determination to carry out his threat. He watched Temple's expressionless back. He had a certain reluctant respect for his great-nephew and was pleased that the young man had not succumbed to the violent rage he had expected. What was more, he himself had been wild in his own youth and knew well that by imposing such an ultimatum he was exposing himself to the young man's hatred. The thought that Temple might mistreat Birdie had entered his mind but had been quickly dismissed, for no one who knew Birdie could abuse such goodness. Confident that his decisions were right and would work to advantage in the long run, Sir Charles held his silence. The boy would understandably need time to sort his thoughts and become used to the idea.

Unaware of his great-uncle's consideration, Temple furrowed his brow and ran a restless hand through his hair. Incredible, he thought, the old gent had fallen in love with the chit, and now he must marry her as part of his inheritance. Incredible, indeed! Quickly his mind ran over the possibilities, anger clouding his thoughts before reason and calmness took over. His great-uncle's demands were unforgivable. He should accept the absurd challenge and remove himself from Blanballyhaven posthaste. But in all honesty, he did not relish life without funds.

Again the perfect picture of Sophia Sayers came to him. While it was true he was fascinated with the lovely Sophia, and he did believe her to be the perfect Lady Daine-Charlton, he knew his life would not waste away if he were denied her hand. Just as he knew with a certainty that lady would never consent to wed him if she believed his fortune in jeopardy. She may well profess undying love, but money and social position meant everything to Sophia Sayers. Taking a deep breath, he sighed. Deliberation really was not required. Without his fortune, he could not have Sophia. But with the fortune came the demands of his great-uncle. It would seem Sophia was not destined to be his.

"You would actually marry her yourself?" Temple asked, still without turning to face his great-uncle.

"Yes, I would. I will take any step to protect her after my death. But, Temple," he cajoled in earnest, "she is so alive, so seeking, so eager to learn. I am too advanced in years to inspire passion in a young girl. She needs a husband worthy of her."

"Worthy of *her!*" Temple muttered in anger and disbelief, turning from the window to approach his great-uncle. He was pale but calm as he made a stiff bow to the marquis. "Very well, my lord. I yield to your demands. I agree to wed . . . er, Birdie, within the week. And as the week will be done in two days, I suppose that means immediately."

Sir Charles regarded the young man with great affection. His eyes sparkled with his relief and good humor. "I am grateful. You will not be sorry once you have taken the time to win the girl's affections. Temple, she will truly change your life in more ways than you could ever expect. Sit! Sit! No! Ring for Hudson! We must have a toast."

Chapter Eight

A sharp rap at her bedchamber door startled Birdie. Before she could utter words to grant entry, the formidable Mrs. Fitzwaters whisked into the room. Her starched black skirts rustled in her indignant haste.

"Do come in, Libby," said Birdie, her voice laden with sarcasm, which, as expected, was totally wasted upon the housekeeper.

"I was sent by his lordship to see what was taking you so long. He has requested your presence for tea and, short of combing the hills, you have the house in an uproar searching for you. And—" she clicked her tongue at her charge's untidy appearance "—you are nowhere near presentable! And that flighty maid of yours nowhere to be found, I suppose. Come! I see I shall have to help you myself." The heavy woman paused behind Birdie and planted her hands on well-corseted hips. Her double chin quivered with outraged sensibilities. "Imagine, guests in the house and you sitting before your mirror. Sitting and mooning over your reflection. Vanity, pure and simple! One of the most deadly sins, as I have repeatedly told you."

"Guests?" Birdie's interest was immediately sparked. Company at Blanballyhaven was rare indeed. "Who, Libby? Who?"

"Do not ask me for another word until you are properly groomed. Quickly now. Out of that soiled gown." Roughly, she twirled Birdie around, tugging at the buttons on the back of the gown. "I've far more important matters to attend without playing lady's maid for you, miss. There's no time to wash your hair. I will just have to do my best with it. Now into the tub. Quickly now."

Birdie suppressed a retort and, having little choice, submitted to the rushed grooming. She steadfastly refused to allow the repri-

mands to distract her from the excitement of new faces at Blanballyhaven. "Guests! How exciting. What shall I wear?"

Ignoring her question, Mrs. Fitzwaters held up the soiled gown
for inspection. "For shame! I doubt even Franny can get these
grass stains out! Whenever are you going to stop behaving as a
runaway child?" Holding the damp gown away from her as if it
were a drowned rat, Mrs. Fitzwaters moved toward the mahogany
wardrobe to select a fresh gown.

Birdie quickly washed the day's romp from her body and submitted to rough toweling before holding her arms aloft for a green
sprigged muslin gown to be dropped over her head. Adjusting the
rather plain gown, the housekeeper nodded once in satisfaction at
her choice.

"There! That will do nicely. It's a respectable gown that a God-
fearing young miss should wear," she declared, indicating the
dressing table stool. "Hurry now. You have kept your betters
waiting overly long as it is."

"This gown is so old, Libby," complained Birdie, flipping the
skirt about her. "I would much prefer to wear the new yellow silk."

"I daresay you would. Which only goes to show that you have
very poor judgment and ought to listen to someone older and wiser.
That gown shows entirely too much of your bosom for decency,"
stated Mrs. Fitzwaters. Pushing Birdie onto the stool, she ruthlessly attacked the mass of snarls in the russet curls. "Hold still
now, or I shall never have you presentable in time."

"Who is the company, Libby? That stuffy old Lord Murray?
Stinking up the library with his foul cigars. Pinching my cheeks
when Sir Charles is watching and my bottom when he's not?"

"Do not be disrespectful of his lordship's friends. It is Lord
Daine, his lordship's heir and great-nephew, arrived last night from
England. And his friend, Lord Sayers," Mrs. Fitzwaters an-
nounced.

Birdie twisted her head around, wincing as Mrs. Fitzwaters
stretched one of her curls out to the roots. "Arrived last night?
Libby! Why is it you never tell me these things?"

"I was under the impression that I just did. Sit!" The woman
clamped one large hand on Birdie's shoulder as she attempted to
rise. "Unless you want to rush into the library looking as woolly
as a newly washed sheep, you will not go until I have finished. Do
you want to embarrass Lord Daine-Charlton with your ill-
mannered ways?"

Birdie bit her lip in excitement but did as Mrs. Fitzwaters commanded. Two lords from London! How exciting! Sir Charles's
nephew? Then the thought of facing one of the family, a member

of the ton, struck her with trepidation. Would he see a lady when he looked at her, as Sir Charles said he did? Or a slum child, ignorant and stepping out of her place? Birdie squirmed on her stool, her head snapping back as Mrs. Fitzwaters worked more vigorously against the knots.

"Whatever tempted you to be out in that gale anyhow? Any self-respecting miss would have been working on her needlework. You're a hoyden and that's a fact!" the housekeeper proclaimed, tossing the comb to the dressing table. "There! That is the best I can do with you twisting this way and that."

"Do I look all right?" Birdie took one last anxious peek in the mirror, unnecessarily pinching color into her rosy cheeks and flipping the ringlets framing her face. Without waiting for a compliment, which probably wouldn't come anyway, she jumped to her feet and dashed to the door. Then, as an afterthought, she rushed back to Mrs. Fitzwaters and swept her into an exuberant hug. "Oh, thank you, Libby!"

She was out in the hall and halfway down the steps before Mrs. Fitzwaters recovered enough to make any retort. With a small shake of her gray head and a click of her tongue, the woman turned back to straighten the room. Had she taken time to glance into the mirror, she probably would have been horrified to see the hint of a smile upon her normally stern face.

Pausing to take three deep, calming breaths, Birdie eased open the library door a crack to cautiously peer inside. Her range of vision was limited to half the fireplace and the backs of the two winged back chairs placed there. Sir Charles's veined hand waved back and forth from one chair as he spoke to someone out of her line of sight.

"Excuse me, miss."

Spinning with guilt written over her face, Birdie faced Hudson and the two footmen bearing the heavy tea service. "Oh, I'm sorry, Hudson," she murmured.

Quickly stepping aside, she stood behind the opened door until they had positioned the sterling service on the gilt table before the camelback sofa. Her heart beat so loudly, she feared they would hear it within and think the natives were rising in revolt. Bowing himself from the room, staid Hudson gave her a broad wink as he passed. Birdie grinned at the butler with thanks for the heartening gesture. With a deep breath and pretended confidence, she sailed into the library with chin held high. After all, how terrible could it be?

Three steps into the room, her unbelieving eyes met those of Lord Temple Daine. Her prince! The thought flashed through her

mind that he had used the three years to great advantage. Lounging in front of the fireplace mantel in the posture of studied nonchalance, he appeared so much taller, so much broader, so much
more formidable...and so much more beautiful. His hair seemed
darker, very black, and there was a certain supercilious curl to his
lips that she did not remember. She hungrily devoured him with her
eyes. Nothing could have been more perfect than the set of the
black morning coat across shoulders that would never require
padding, and the pale pantaloons positively clung to a pair of finely
molded legs. He took her breath. A single fob dangled at his waist
and a fine diamond pin in the folds of his cravat were the only
jewelry he affected, but the result was elegant. He raised his head
and, with a hard expression that almost caused her bouncy step to
falter, watched her progress across the room.

Oliver turned at her entrance. Having just sauntered down the
stairs to seek out the company, he was not privy to Birdie's amazing tale, or the harsh demands of the marquis upon his heir. Interest sparked as he duly took note of the fresh young woman rushing
through the door, not so much for her startling beauty but for the
interesting thunderstorm that darkened Lord Daine's face at the
very sight of her. Something was amiss here, and it just might prove
to be the making of the trip. He pursed his lips and resolved to
watch this drama unfold with the utmost attention.

Following his great-nephew's stare, Sir Charles turned to see her.
"Ah, my dear, at last." The marquis made an attempt to rise, but
Birdie quickly stilled the motion with a touch of her hand on his
shoulder. "I was afraid the lure of the hills had claimed you for all
time. I fretted you would be unable to join us before dinner when
you could not be found. My dear, may I present my great-nephew,
Lord Henry Templeton Daine. And his friend, Viscount Oliver
Sayers. Lord Sayers, Temple, this is my ward, Miss Birdie."

"Lord Sayers. Lord Daine," Birdie said in a voice pitched low
with nervousness. She dipped into a small curtsy and dropped her
eyes. Her prince! Would he recognize her? Would he see that she
was indeed grown-up now and sweep her off her feet and truly
make a lady of her?

"Miss...ah, *Birdie*." Temple cruelly emphasized the missing last
name.

The dark head bowed over her hand. The manner was polite but
the words hinted at...what? Anger? No, more ridicule. Birdie felt
her face drain of color. Why? What had she done but walk into the
room?

"Birdie, would you please pour for us?" Sir Charles beamed at
her in pride. "I have been telling Temple our interesting tale. And

I am anxious for him to see how graceful you are. Lord Sayers, please be seated.''

Oliver carefully arranged himself on the sofa, taking care to place himself in the best possible position to watch the three faces before him in much the same manner one selected an appropriate seat for a theater performance.

So, Birdie thought with a tightening of her lips, I am to be exhibited before the lords of the ton. See how well the slum scum pretends to be a lady. Seating herself behind the tea service, she executed the duty with a flawless grace and manner. Noting the Lord Daine's set face and stilted acknowledgment when accepting the cup, she greatly wished to fling it at his head. But she loved the old marquis far too much to disgrace him or to prove the nephew's obvious thoughts correct. That she was indeed a no-name product of the slum.

Oliver accepted the teacup, admiring her grace and style. Her performance was flawless and would have played well in any drawing room in London. The girl was more than beautiful, he thought, almost mesmerizing in that one could become quite lost discovering, in minute detail, the different perfections of her face. He glanced again at Temple and pondered that one's black expression. Everything about him bespoke anger and violence. Very interesting, indeed.

Although Oliver knew of Temple's interest in his sister, and in fact expected him to bend his knee before her upon his return to London, he also knew of his reputation with the ladies. And while he could well understand the *tendre* Temple had begun to exhibit for his lovely Sophia, he did not think him so besotted as to ignore the charming possibilities presented him in this far-flung part of Ireland. This choice little dumpling could make this cold and miserable pile of stones much more inviting during their stay in this heathen country, but apparently the possibility was lost on Temple, or the interview with the marquis had not gone well. Not well indeed, by the look on Temple's face. What Oliver could not understand was Temple's obvious antagonism toward the girl. What part did she play in this scene?

"Birdie has been studying very hard. I'm sure you will find her most knowledgeable in history, for which she seems to have developed a certain passion," Sir Charles commented, opening the floor for polite conversation.

Temple merely nodded and remained aloof. He was not prepared to engage the chit in polite conversation, and at that particular moment was not overly interested in what she knew or did not know. He greatly wished to be anywhere but the stuffy sitting room and drinking something a vast deal stronger than tepid tea.

Sir Charles cleared his throat uncomfortably. "Isn't that right, my dear?"

Birdie could only answer the marquis's question with monotone syllables and concentrated on keeping her hands still in her lap, for they did so want to twist and turn upon themselves. She dared not trust a teacup to them, as they were most untrustworthy, and heaven knows, she'd broken enough of the china in the dishpan to avow to their fragility. She greatly desired to be off in the hills, striding this nervousness away, instead of listening to the marquis embarrassingly praise her fine points to the disinterested young man as if striving to justify the high price he intended to set upon her head to a prospective buyer. Whenever she did chance to raise her eyes to him, he was never looking at her but at some distant place over her head.

"History? That seems vastly amusing to me, as most in our range of acquaintance deem to avoid any subject more strenuous than what one's to wear to the next entertainment," Oliver remarked, greatly enjoying the tension-charged atmosphere in the library. He flipped the lace back from his wrist and smoothed the buff over his thigh with an elegant hand.

Startled, Birdie leaned away from the blond man. She had been so engrossed in Lord Daine, that she had given no thought to the other guest. Now studying him from beneath the fringe of her lashes, she wondered if indeed he was a man, or could he be a boy? To guess his age was difficult, so smooth were his cheeks. He was finely boned and quite slender... as if his maker couldn't quite make up his mind, girl or boy, and had left the decision until the final moment, only to find it was too late for a definite one.

"I do beg your pardon, Lord Sayers," she apologized.

"I was merely trying to rescue you from center stage in what seems to be a very stressful position," confided Oliver. He waved a nonchalant hand over the small, strained company.

Birdie stared at him for a moment at this direct assessment of the situation. His smile was open and seemed harmless. Eager to have attention redirected as he stated, she relaxed somewhat and returned his smile. "I must say, I welcome the diversion, although I would not want it said that I provoked arguments and strife in polite company."

"Oh, but, my dear Miss Birdie, didn't you know that strife lends the highest level of entertainment to one's life. Especially other people's strife." Oliver laughed with such obvious good humor that Birdie giggled with him.

Sir Charles frowned, partly in disgust at the young man who could only be readily classified as a parlor fop, and partly to see Birdie's interest move in a direction contrary to his wishes. He glanced at Temple, but the thundercloud he saw there did not seem to be lessening, nor was there any arousal in his eyes. He sighed in exasperation. Had the boy gone dead inside? Did he not see how charming she was? How sweet and fresh? How lovely?

Temple watched the sweet curve of Birdie's throat as she laughed. So the minx was an experienced flirt, even in the wilds of this place. Breeding will tell, he supposed, for she would readily fall into Oliver's prank. He carefully set his teacup on the tea tray, when he actually wished to hurl it forcefully into the fire. Birdie turned to him with a raised eyebrow and reached for the tea service. He declined a second cup of tea with an abrupt wave of his hand, without meeting her eyes or speaking a word to her. Birdie paled at the open insult and lowered her eyes in embarrassment.

The hour passed with the thickness of molasses left on the stoop on a chilly day and was a visible strain on Sir Charles as he attempted to instigate some contact between the angry, distant man and the confused, nervous young girl. Vastly amused, Oliver sat back and watched the intrigue without attempting to detract from it. It was a relief to at least three of the company when, as soon as politely possible, Birdie excused herself and fled the room. Temple hastily took leave of his great-uncle with the excuse of freshening for dinner. In short order, and in the face of Sir Charles's gruff dismissal, Oliver followed suit and sauntered away, although he considered himself suitably attired for a country dinner and saw no reason to retire above stairs again.

Gratefully Sir Charles allowed Travers to settle him before the fire with a stiff drink. Exhausted by the whole interview as if he had climbed the highest mountain, he was suddenly afraid he had made a terrible mistake, one his little Birdie would be made to pay for with her happiness.

Chapter Nine

The wind had died, and though the air was still crisp, the sun struggled to warm the late afternoon. Unconsciously tramping to her favorite spot not ten minutes' strenuous climb above the castle, Birdie plopped herself down in the grass. Tipping her porcelain face to the fading sun, she let it dry the tear trails on her cheeks. Out in the sun again without a hat, Birdie thought. Mattie would be scandalized. In a fit of childish anger and ill humor, she yanked her skirts up to her thighs and undid the ribbon garters. Jerking off her boots and stockings, she dug her toes into the icy grass in childish defiance. Her only concession to propriety was to tuck her green sprigged gown down to hide the sight of her bare feet.

Hugging her knees to her chest, Birdie tried to will her mind blank. To stifle the painful thoughts as her dream lay dashed in shards at her feet. Of course, she had always known he wasn't truly a prince, and he most certainly hadn't been waiting for her to grow up. In all honesty, he probably did not even remember kissing her so ardently that day in the glen. She dashed a buzzing gnat away from her face in irritation. That was all fine and good, but what did she replace the dream with now?

The thought sobered her. She must make realistic plans concerning her future, for after all, she was a woman grown and educated now. And Sir Charles was not a young man. He would not be around forever to protect her in her little pretend world. And it was apparent any plea of hers for sanctuary would fall on deaf ears with the new marquis, should Sir Charles pass away. But what could she do? Too young and too pretty, Franny says, for a governess. And she could not, *would not*, go back to the kitchens. Bowing her head, she moaned aloud into the cloth-covered knees.

She had no place in this world. No name and no place. And now no dream. Who was she to be, then?

Raising her head, she was startled to see Lord Daine treading in her direction. His arms swung easily at his sides, one holding a beaver topper; his stride was long and forceful. Such grace in so large a man surprised her. If she sat very still, perhaps he would pass by without seeing her, she thought. But the fairies were full of devilishness today, for he looked straight at her and veered in her direction. Birdie did not rise when he approached to tower over her, but craned her neck way back, shading her eyes against the dying sun with her hand.

"I do not wish to disturb you, Miss Birdie. Mrs. Fitzwaters gave me your direction and I thought to speak a moment with you," Temple said. Without waiting for an answer, or perhaps not caring one way or the other, he swung off his short capelet to spread it carefully next to her and arranged his long body gracefully beside her, placing the topper out of harm's way.

"Now, Miss..." He paused, raking his hand through his blue-black hair. "Deuced inconvenient, that... Not having a last name, I mean."

Birdie tilted an eyebrow and regarded him with sarcasm. "I assure you, my lord," she countered, "I have always found that unfortunate fact more of an encumbrance than you ever shall."

He had not known what to expect from the shy, nervous girl he had observed over the last disastrous hour, and her spirited remark took him slightly aback. "Please forgive my manners. I did not mean—" He halted his apology to stare into her face, his experienced eye taking in the flawlessness with pleasure. "I will give you one thing, you are a pretty thing!"

She affected a haughty look that would have made Mrs. Fitzwaters proud and turned her head to snub him, drawing the creamy shawl closer about her shoulders. "I do wish you would stop evaluating me as if I were on the auction block. I assure you, Lord Daine, your opinion means nothing to me."

"Miss...*Damn!*" he exploded, then forcibly collected himself. "I know this will seem most odd, but I wished a word with you in private."

Birdie did not look at him. So, he would follow her into the hills to tell her she was a scheming wretch and to warn her against taking advantage of a dying man's sympathies, for it would not further her cause one bit. Well...let him! He would not make her cry!

"Miss...Birdie," he said, raking his hand through his unruly hair again. "You must think this strange," he began again, "but it would do me great honor if you would consent to become my wife?''

Birdie's eyes grew very large and she snapped around to stare at him. She wondered if he were drunk, then quickly dismissed the idea for she had poured the tea herself, though his cheeks were certainly flushed and his hair could only be called disarranged. On the other hand, it was a chilly climb to the steep slope, and he would keep running his hand through his curls in that distracted manner. She repressed a desire to laugh...and cry. Clearly she was unsure which fit the circumstances more.

"Pray, Lord Daine, are you feeling quite well?" she asked, far more calmly than she felt.

Rising upright, Temple stared at her for a moment. Then, as he considered how distracted he must appear, a chuckle escaped him. Infinitely easier, he drew a bit closer to her. "I said you would think it odd, and I am not at all surprised to find you think me a trifle disguised, as you so clearly do."

Birdie gazed at him appraisingly. Whatever would he do if she flung herself into his arms and cried yes! Yes, yes...a thousand times yes! What would he do if she disclosed that she had lived with love for him burning brightly in her tender heart since she was thirteen? Probably leap to his feet and bolt down the hill. Perhaps even tripping over himself, to tumble head over heels to the bottom, breaking his neck in the process. Then she would be left with the unpleasant task of telling Sir Charles that she had murdered, inadvertently of course, his great-nephew. No, best to keep that bit of information to herself. Instead she merely inclined her head slightly and continued in Mrs. Fitzwaters's parlor tone.

"Indeed? If that is so, you will not be offended if I say that I am completely taken aback by your offer for my hand?"

Her easy manner apparently helped him relax, and he grinned at her in a way that brought all air to a halt before it could reach her lungs.

"No offense taken," he said appreciatively. "But now that this is clear, perhaps I ought to explain why I have made you this offer."

Her sherry brown eyes twinkled. "Perhaps you should. But I do hope you are not going to say you have formed an attachment for me, for I shall know immediately that you lie through your bloody teeth."

He met her inquiring eyes beneath lifted eyebrows, not at all sure what to make of her. One moment she was all propriety, and the next, a minx with an unruly tongue. "I would not insult your intelligence in that manner. It's just that Uncle Charles wishes us to wed. He cares very deeply for you and wants to see you protected after his death. In fact, to be brutally honest with you, Miss, er, Birdie, if I do not, he threatens to tamper with his will."

Birdie felt her heart stop. She went numb all over, but then how could she be numb and hurt so savagely at the same time? So he would be blackmailed into marrying his uncle's... What was she anyway? She raised her eyebrows inquiringly, successfully hiding the pain that threatened to overtake her. She glanced at him, then looked down the slope to distant greens and blues.

"What an awkward situation. And you think I would make you a proper wife? Yes, how stupid of me. Of course you do, otherwise you would not be here, would you, my lord?" she mocked.

Temple chose to disregard her sarcastic question as it did not seem to require an answer, at least not an answer he would politely give. "We are to wed before this week is past, and as this is midweek already—" He paused, but could not help the bitterness that crept into his tone. "I do understand, having heard your tale, that your situation is not altogether a happy one. A trifle insecure at present, but surely something of this sort is what you intended all along."

An icy chill flashed up her spine and for a moment she was silent. Pain as she had never known filled her chest and she found it difficult to breathe. The cruelty of the man! The out-and-out cruelty!

Temple, watching her, began to wonder if he had gone too far, for her face was quite pale. This proposing was no easy business when one wished greatly not to be doing it at all. And doing it while nearly blind with rage made it all that much more difficult.

Birdie sighed prettily and looked at him with a positively wicked glint in her eye. "All 'tis arranged? But didn't ye think that I would not accept yer bloody offer? Which I shall not be doin', ye know?" she snapped, her brogue thick and lilting.

"Wh-what...?" Temple stammered. "I did not understand..."

Leaping to her feet, Birdie planted both hands on her hips and swished her skirts in a fair imitation of Flo Bender. "Your offer is being thrown in your face, and you can go straight to bloody hell, for all I care!" Moving quickly, Birdie snatched up her boots and flounced down the slope without a backward glance.

Stunned for a moment, Temple stared after her slight figure stalking away. Then a smile played at the corners of his sensuous mouth and he lazily gained his feet. Why, the saucy little wench, he mused. She certainly was a surprising contradiction. The thought of taming her pleased his bachelor instincts and he set off after her.

She had gotten only as far as the brook when she realized he was following her. Rounding on him, she snapped, "Go yer own way, ye hear! Or I'll be forced to call on some brawn to topple ye over."

"I do beg your pardon, but I believe you are forgetting these." He grinned, carelessly holding her stockings aloft with his fingertips, taunting her with his amusement as heat colored her cheeks. Taking a reluctant step toward him, she snatched the stockings as if he would have kept them from her.

"Blighter!" she snapped. Angrily, she stuffed the stockings into the boots, once more turning her back on him to storm away.

"You are most welcome," he called after her. "Aren't you going to put them on? I'll wager the water will be deuced cold on bare little toes."

Birdie froze, fighting the unladylike urge to throw one of Mattie's strong words into his smug face. "You—you are no gentleman!"

"What? You would defame me when I so gallantly rescued your stockings? For shame, Miss Birdie."

Birdie steeled herself to wade across the brook. The water would be no more than ankle-deep, but being fed by mountain snow, it would be icy. Besides, when she hiked her skirts, she would give him a clear view of her ankles, which was doubtless what he was waiting for. The cad! But to turn and go back was equally unthinkable, for she would not give him the satisfaction of besting her. While she hesitated, worrying over her most dignified action, he reached her in a few quick strides.

"I cannot allow such a slur upon my character to go unanswered. I am a gentleman and quite capable of gentlemanly behavior," Temple declared. Without waiting for a retort, he swung her into his arms as easily as if she were a child, which in fact she was. Holding her tightly to his muscled chest, he stepped into the icy water of the brook.

"Put me down!" Birdie swung one of her boots, landing a blow soundly to the side of his head and knocking the topper into the water. "Put me down, you mean-streaked blighter!"

"Damn!" Nearly losing his balance, he growled. "As you wish!" He abruptly dropped her into the water.

Gasping as she landed on her bottom with a teeth-rattling jolt, Birdie felt the water soak into her muslin gown. "You . . . you . . ." she squealed, totally at a loss for words strong enough to blister his ears. She struggled to her feet, thoroughly weighted down by heavy sodden skirts and petticoats. He was already standing on the opposite bank, scowling at an oversize dent in the side of an obviously ruined beaver topper. Birdie doubled up her fists, her eyes snapping with outrage. Floundering out of the water, she swung wildly at him. He sidestepped all her blows easily, a slow smile crossing his face.

"Stand still and fight like a man," she challenged. "I'll damn ye to the fairies, I will!"

"Dear me," he drawled. "If I'm to be damned to the fairies for a little wetting, I might as well go with a smile on my lips."

With that he pulled her abruptly to his chest, pinning her wrists behind her with one strong hand. Twining the other in her hair to tilt her head back, he rendered her helpless. Whereupon he leisurely plundered her mouth. Birdie's mind reeled with shock at the touch of his warm lips. She shivered violently, but not from the chill of her clinging, wet gown, or from the gathering chilly dusk. An astonishingly consuming heat spiraled through her veins and robbed her of all strength in her legs. She yielded to him, sagging against his chest.

Loosening his grip on her hands, Temple pulled her slight body tighter to his. Birdie slipped her arms around his neck, allowing his insistent tongue to invade her mouth. She had just begun to return the embrace with inexperienced fervor when he caught himself and set her abruptly from his grasp. Breathing hard with raging arousal, he released her as if the touch of her scalded him. Shocked at the violence of his reaction to her, he took in her flushed face and half-closed eyes speculatively. This raw, barbarous desire was not something he wanted to feel for an unwanted slum-child bride.

"Breeding will tell every time," he drawled.

Birdie blinked her eyes several times. His words slowly reached her fogged mind. Tears of fury and pain welled in her eyes at his unfairness. She had not asked to be kissed by him. Nor had she asked Sir Charles to make him marry her. All she had wanted was for someone to love her and desire to be with her forever. Pressing the back of her hand to her trembling lips, she fled on down the hill in tears, forgetting her boots and stockings lying in the water.

In wonder, Temple watched her until she was out of sight, then rubbed a finger across his lips, speculating on the sweetness of his stolen kiss. It had been soft, sweet and unbelievably innocent. A wonder he had not expected. The lush feel of her ripe body was still freshly imprinted against his and his body cried out for release. He supposed he had been too long in the company of sophisticated ladies, for his manner with children most definitely wanted correcting. Damn her for being so desirable. For, after all, she was just a child. An untutored child. He did not want to feel sorry for hurting her, but he did. Still, her temper! What a joy she would be to instruct in the art of lovemaking. There was no mistaking her response to his kiss. Childish, yet willing, he thought.

Temple waded into the brook to retrieve the boots and stockings. She would make some man an admirable mistress. His amusement turned to a grimace. That was the rub. Mistress! But not a wife! His face settled into a grim expression. Most definitely not *his* wife! But then that was not to be avoided, was it? The decision was made, and it was irrevocable. To make the best of the situation, he might as well enjoy what was to be. Once he tired of her, and there was no doubt that he would, as untutored schoolgirls were never to his liking, he would ship her down to the country. She would deal nicely at Stannisburn, while he resumed his life as he wished in London.

Chapter Ten

Birdie spent an extremely restless night. She had secluded herself in her room after returning soaked to the skin, her emotions out of bounds. Franny had been agape at her appearance. Not one but two gowns ruined in one day! Being too confused to speak of the incident to anyone, Birdie had taken refuge in Mrs. Fitzwaters's haughty manner. It had been the only way she could avoid tears. Pleading a chill, she had crawled into bed and pulled the covers over her head.

Now as dawn broke through the crack in the draperies, streaking a pale shaft of light across the patterned rug, Birdie stretched like a contented cat beneath the satin comforter, before curling into a small ball on her side and tucking her feet into the tail of her cotton night rail. Her mind ran over yesterday. The argument, the wetting, none of that mattered overly much. What did matter was that Lord Templeton Daine had offered for her hand, even though he had been coerced into the act by Sir Charles. But his disgust for her, and the situation in which his great-uncle had placed him, was extremely obvious. It brought home all too sharply her precarious position. If, heaven forbid, Sir Charles succumbed to age, she would be alone and, again, homeless. But to wed under the threat of blackmail was a terrible thing. Their life together could never be happy, for he had made it very clear he thought her a nameless upstart from the slums. She rolled over and threw an arm over her eyes with a groan.

The memory of Temple clasping her body to his, the pressure of his warm, full mouth covering hers flooded her senses. Warmth coursed through her veins, centering in the pit of her stomach, and built quickly into an indescribable ache that she had not the experience to recognize as desire. How wonderful to have him love her and want to hold her that close all the time. But then the thought of her reaction to his kiss, and his scalding setdown regarding that reaction, was humiliating. She clenched her teeth and sat up.

"What to do?" she fretted. She must speak to Sir Charles! That's what she must do. He must be made to see that there had to be another way. A much saner way! How could she live day after day with such humiliation, especially feeling the way she felt every time she looked into that beautiful face. She would be forever wanting him, and would be forever miserable for that wanting was not to be satisfied.

Ringing twice for Franny, Birdie began impatiently dressing herself. Selecting a golden merino gown that clung warmly to her body and set off the golden highlights in her hair, she caught the russet ringlets loosely behind her head with a tortoiseshell comb. A hasty, yet flattering style, that framed the creamy cheeks with caressing russet tentacles. Running lightly down the hall on cloth-slippered feet, Birdie sped past a breathless Franny puffing hurriedly up the stairs.

"Never mind, Franny."

"Ye gods and little fishes! Such goings-on!" Franny exclaimed in the manner of Mattie, whipping around to stare after her charge's scurrying figure.

Birdie tapped briskly on Sir Charles's door, then entered before Travers had time to cross the floor. Her eyes quickly adjusted to the room's somber interior of linenfold oak paneling as she breathed the familiar scents of leather and musty age, scents she would always associate with this old man she loved so dearly. Sir Charles looked up with a beaming smile.

"My dear, this is a wonderful surprise. We haven't shared breakfast like this in months. Come, sit close to me. My eyes aren't what they used to be and I do not want to miss one bit of your beauty. Travers, fetch a breakfast tray for Miss Birdie."

Clicking her tongue much as Libby was known for doing, Birdie crossed the darkened room in a brisk manner. "Your eyes are the same as they have always been, but it seems you insist on sitting in the dark," she fussed. "Why ever won't you allow Travers to open your draperies?" Walking to the towering windows, she threw back the heavy, musty drapes to flood the room with weak morning light. Sneezing lustily three times, she performed the same task with the second window. "I swear, 'tis dusty in here. Have you been chasing the maids around the bed again, so that they cannot find time to clean this room, Sir Charles?" she scolded, fanning the dust motes. "We must see about new drapes for this room come spring, and perhaps a new rug."

The marquis laughed at her wrinkled nose. Patting the bed beside him, he indicated she was to sit close to him. Doing so, Birdie studied him. He had lost weight this past year, and his once good looks had finally succumbed to Father Time. His jowls hung in wrinkles and folds, and the blue eyes watered weakly. He had the air of a man who was indeed in ill health. To hide the sudden tears that sprang into her eyes at the sight of his failing, she smoothed the silver wings of thinning hair over his ears and fussed with the frayed collar of his ruby, brocade dressing gown.

"Really, Sir Charles, you should allow Travers to trim your hair," she scolded him tenderly. "And...and get some new clothes. I declare, this morning gown looks like something your great-grandpapa might have worn. You see? You spend all your fortune on me, trying to make a pig into a peacock, and neglect yourself shamefully."

"Nay, my dear," he said, touching the back of one trembling blue veined hand to her smooth cheek. "I merely add gilt framing to a work of art, a masterpiece worthy of much more. If I were a younger man, I'd make you into a blushing bride myself. Blan-ballyhaven needs a mistress such as you."

"Fah, yer lordship." She dismissed him with a graceful wiggle of her fingers. "If you were a younger man you'd be chasing after every skirt in London town, and never cast an eye over the likes of me, you randy old goat!"

An expression of genuine amusement crossed his face. "You speak an interesting combination of the King's English, Haymarket slang and Irish brogue, my dear. One could never venture an idea of your origins."

"I quite think there are those who would take great pleasure in reminding me of my humble origins. It drives Mrs. Fitzwaters to vapors. Very possibly the reason I do it," Birdie admitted with a devilish twinkle in her eye.

"So that war goes on, I see."

"Yes, I fear I try her patience mightily. Only one of my deplorable habits, as Mrs. Fitzwaters informs me daily. And I must say, she is quite correct. You must confess you agree, I truly am disgraceful."

"I think we will survive your disgraces. Though what passes here in the hills of Ireland will not do in a London drawing room. But you are a child, after all, and should be expected to act like one on occasion."

"London!" she snorted faintly, letting the remark on her age pass unnoticed. "I greatly fear the haut ton would see through my little charade very quickly. From what I read, breeding and bloodlines are everything to them. They pair the children of the great houses and fortunes as one would pair the best of the stables.''

"I think you harbor no small resentment toward something you have yet to experience, Birdie. Perhaps a small amount of charity would be in order. At least until you can form your own opinion of the race. Although I would grant you some license, in that you have been harshly treated through some unfortunate incident that befell your mother,'' Sir Charles gently admonished.

She caught his hand to press a kiss to the back. "I'm sorry, Sir Charles,'' she whispered, resting her eyes on his hand held tightly in both of hers. "I spoke with Lord Daine, I mean, he sought me out yesterday...''

"Did he ask for your hand in marriage?''

Birdie glanced up in distress. "Yes, yes, he did. But surely you must see that I cannot marry him.'' She rested imploring eyes on his face. "He does not care for the idea, nor me, in the least. Surely there must be some other way.''

"Birdie, my dear, I have thought of nothing else for years. I cannot see you alone once I am—''

"No!'' she cried out, leaning toward him. "Do not say it! You will not be gone for a long, long time yet.''

"Do not treat me as if old age has addled my wits! I am old, Birdie, and not in sound health,'' he admonished her again, when she would hide from the truth. "You are very young, and very, very beautiful. Both of which render you extremely vulnerable. I had thought at first to settle enough money upon you to make your independence assured, but you would still be alone and unprotected. Do you remember those two men who were intent on attacking you when I first saw you?'' Birdie nodded her head, unable to answer for the tears in her throat. Sir Charles acknowledged her answer and continued. "There are those kind of men in all walks of life. Money would make you doubly attractive to them. Only these so-called gentlemen would attack you with sweet words and honeyed lies. You could not protect yourself from them, for you have not the experience to recognize them.''

"Could I not just stay here? I would be safe enough with Mattie and Franny and...and Condor. Libby! Libby would guard me.''

"Birdie, we have never lied to one another, and we won't start now. The only way for you to be safe, and truly free, is to marry. A woman has no voice in this century. She is only as strong as the man who takes her to wife,'' Sir Charles gently told her.

Birdie stiffened, for she knew he spoke the truth. "But he hates me so," she whispered. "I truly would not mind just living here . . . alone."

"He does not hate you. He merely hates being told what to do. He does not even know you. He will love you once he allows himself to know you as I know you." He cupped her chin and raised her head so their eyes met. "Somehow I must make you understand!" Lines of worry were deeply etched around his mouth as he tried to explain. "Yes, I could extract his promise for you to live here the rest of your life, but if something happened to him, there would be a new heir. What of him? Besides, Birdie, your beauty is too great to waste hidden in the backcountry of Ireland. Do you not want to return to England? And with your rightful place restored to you, the chances of discovering your history, and your family name, could come within easy grasp. Isn't that what you've always wanted?"

Birdie could only nod her head, tears streaming down her face. The old marquis took both her hands and pulled her, sobbing bitterly, down to his chest, where he cradled her tightly. "I do not wish to leave you, Sir Charles. I love you as my father," Birdie cried, clutching the faded lapels of his dressing gown.

"I do not want you to go, either, my dear, but we must be sensible. I doubt Temple would consent to stay here so that I might dandle your children upon my knee." He attempted to jest with her. "Come now, sit up and dry your beautiful eyes. You're soaking my robe and will have Travers accusing me of something babyish." Pushing the girl up, he swiped a thumb across her wet cheeks. She smiled a watery smile and swiped at her face with the backs of her hands in a childish manner, sniffling loudly. "Birdie, look at me." When he had her full attention, he demanded harshly, "Please, will you do this for me? Will you trust me to know what is right for you one more time? Your word, Birdie . . . for me."

Owing him so much, and having his request presented to her in such a manner, she had no alternative but to give him her solemn promise. "Yes, Sir Charles. I will do as you ask."

"Good! Now run bathe your face and seek out Temple. Tell him you will accept his offer and the wedding will take place in the chapel day after tomorrow." With a stern but loving look, he sent her out the door just as a confused Travers appeared with her breakfast tray.

"Miss Birdie? Miss Birdie?" he called. Turning toward Sir Charles, he glanced helplessly from the tray to her retreating back. "I say, such strange . . ."

"Just set it down, man!" Sir Charles ordered. "Took your own sweet time getting here. She lost her appetite!"

The confused little man set the tray on the table beside the door, ruefully thinking that it must now be carried the distance back to the kitchen. He shook his head in resignation. "I must say! My dove will have to be told of Miss Birdie's behavior this morning. Her charge, after all."

"Humph!" With a grunt, Sir Charles chose to ignore the fussing valet and returned his attention to his own breakfast tray.

"I must say, I do hate to see my dove upset."

"Good God, Travers!" Sir Charles thundered, slamming down his fork. "How can you insist on calling that great moose of a woman your dove? From what I've observed in all of twenty years, she has never even noticed you."

"My treasure is a very sensitive woman," Travers hurriedly explained. "I assure you, her heart warms toward me on a daily basis. It will not be long before she capitulates and swoons lovingly into my arms." Clasping both hands over his heart, a mooning Travers anticipated such an event to the marquis's dismay.

"I certainly hope, my good man, that you have some assistance lined up in anticipation of that happening, for I do not doubt that more strength than you possess will be required or she will smash you to the tiles with her bulk." Sir Charles exploded, throwing his napkin on his tray in irritation. Would that were Temple declaring devotion to his little Birdie with such fervor, he thought wearily.

Temple retired to the library after deliberately partaking of breakfast at cock's crow to avoid subjecting his foul mood upon undeserving company. Having found sleep elusive, he had ridden the hills at dawn in an effort to ease his racing mind. He had ridden until the mists had turned to rain and finally driven him to seek shelter. He had thought that taking strenuous exercise would relieve his depression and his anger, but that had not been the case. His black mood was not directed at anyone in particular but life's joke in general. He could still hope for a miracle to save him from this marriage not of his choosing, but not being an overly devout man, he had inwardly resigned himself to the fact that in two days' time, he would have a wife.

At that moment the library door swung open. Oliver sauntered in with a decided frown on his face, until he saw Temple. "Ah, there you are. I was beginning to think I'd been abandoned in this cavernous place. Although, from the scowl on your face, I'd wager the weather is no less inclement inside than it is outside."

"Sorry, Oliver," apologized Temple. He waved the slight man into the room. "Come in. Come in. Hasn't been much of a holiday for you, has it?"

"I shall not pretend that I was promised anything different," Oliver remarked. He seated himself before the desk and scanned the ledgers and pages strewn about. "You warned me that this could be a bandberry chase, and it was at my own insistence that I tagged along. So there, I've admitted to having no one but myself to blame for my discomfort. I take it from your foul temper that the interview has not been to your liking? Your great-uncle, I mean . . . although he does appear in good health . . ." He paused to allow opportunity for confidences. While he would never have pegged Lord Daine as one for lamenting his woes into any available ear, it did seem that anyone with as heavy a burden as he appeared to have upon his shoulders would lose balance sooner or later and spill the tale about the room. Human nature, after all, was only human nature.

"Yes, his health is adequate for his age. He is just as set in his ways as ever," Temple muttered. He tapped his fingers upon the desk in an unconscious gesture of unleashed irritation.

"Reminds me of my father," Oliver mused. "Determined to retain the reins to the family at all costs. Waited until the horses were nearly out of control and ruin was breathing down our necks before he admitted to age and ill health."

Oliver watched the expression darken on Temple's face. The thing Oliver wanted to hear above all else, and the main reason Sophia had been so insistent that he accompany Daine on this miserable journey, was that the old boy was at death's door and Daine to succeed within the year. Sophia did have her heart set on becoming a marquise.

Temple's mind wandered, and when he did speak, it would seem that he said the words more for himself than for an audience. "No, it's more than just wanting to rule the roost that has this old bantam rooster crowing from his henhouse. He's determined to place all his hens and chicks under someone else's wing before he goes feet up."

Oliver lifted an eyebrow and contemplated the troubled man behind the desk. Without actually prompting, he answered in an urging manner. "Never having been a country squire, I'm not at all familiar with poultry or what a rooster might or might not attempt should demise be imminent."

Temple looked up, startled that he had spoken aloud. Oliver was watching him with such a concerned expression that he smiled a wry smile. "I might as well spill the beans. I mean, it's not as if it'll be a secret for much longer, and after all, you did leave the warmth and comfort of several London boudoirs to follow me on this adventure, now didn't you?''

"Yes, I did at that. And I feel I'm over my head, what with poultry and all. So heave over with the details, Temple,'' Oliver demanded. He laughed gaily as if it were all a great game they were playing.

"It would seem that I am to be wed...day after tomorrow,'' Temple stated simply.

"Wed!'' barked Oliver, sitting up straight in shock. "To whom?''

"The lovely little Birdie, of course.''

"But...'' Oliver calmed himself with an effort before he could blurt out the obvious and destroy the camaraderie between the two of them. Sophia would never forgive him if he did not come home with the complete story. Of course, Sophia might never forgive him anyway, not if Lord Templeton Daine came home wed to another. This news was not welcome news. Less so for the unfortunate bridegroom as for Sophia...and of course himself, as well.

Temple leaned forward on the desk and placed his hands over his face. "I know...Sophia...'' he groaned, rubbing vigorously at his face. "But, in all honesty, Oliver, I have been given no choice in the matter. It's wed the girl or forfeit the bulk of the inheritance. And to be straight with you, I can't see Sophia living on a tight allowance, now, can you?''

Oliver chose not to enter into the discussion of Sophia and her love of the noble life. A title to Sophia meant the funds to support the life-style, as well. For her, as well as for him, Daine without a fortune was useless. He bit down hard on the soft flesh of his cheek to stop the outcry of indignation he felt. Two deep breaths and he was sufficiently calm to continue his semblance of sympathetic friend. He shook his head now in mock sorrow.

"Life is not always content to move in the direction we, as mere pawns, wish it to go. I suppose the old gent has his reasons for wishing the fair lady upon you. And while I will agree that sister Sophia is not going to be pleased, as I do know her heart is deeply engaged, I do hope you are not too devastated. A wife is a wife, after all, isn't she?''

"A fine sentiment, Oliver. I do not relish the task of telling Sophia. I have no wish to cause her unhappiness. That was never my intention.'' Pushing back from the desk, he idly thumbed through the ledgers.

"One can always refuse, can't one?'' Oliver asked hopefully. He asked the question, but he could tell by Temple's expression that if it were a viable option, he would have chosen it. He watched him closely. He liked to observe emotions; they were like signposts set along the dark unknown of another's personality, marking vulnerable points.

"I have been apprised of the dire circumstances should I point-blank refuse the girl. And I have the utmost respect for the strength of Uncle Charles's threats. No, he has stated he will merely marry the chit himself." Scanning the gross profit figures on the page, he frowned at the amount just from wool sales. So much, and so dearly needed to maintain Daine Hall. "No, there is no way out! Even if the girl herself balked . . . but no question of that, now, is there? She has too much to gain. A title, a fortune and a position in London society. Hell, a last name!" Leaning back in the chair, he raked his hand through his hair.

"A last name?" coaxed Oliver. "I do not comprehend . . . a title, yes. But a last name?"

"Ah, yes," drawled Temple. His tone turned sarcastic. "You haven't heard the best part of the story. It would seem that my little bride-to-be is an orphan. An orphan who was raised in a baby mill in Haymarket."

"Extraordinary!" exclaimed Oliver.

"Oh, it's more than that!" he taunted. "The girl confesses to having noble blood. Her titled mother, through some act of an uncharitable God, ended up in Haymarket, then passed on without giving the girl a name. Now, what was the mother's name? It was a flower, if I remember right. Rose? Lily? No, something unusual, more exotic."

Oliver became very still. His throat convulsed several times as if he were very, very dry. Carefully, like one who's suffered a great shock or been very ill for a long time, he placed his hands on the arms of the chair and gained his feet. Moving as if in slow motion, he advanced to the sideboard and splashed a stiff shot of whiskey into a glass, then down his throat.

Temple, lost in his own unhappiness, took note of nothing more than the whiskey. "Yes, exactly. Share a drop of that with me. It's enough to turn your stomach, isn't it? Notwithstanding the girl's charm, to carry her as wife back to London in Sophia's place, fairly unsettles the stomach."

Oliver splashed another generous share in his own glass before doing as Temple bid. He drew a deep breath before turning back to the desk and Temple. "But as you say, the girl is not without her own charm and beauty. And who knows, there might be something to her tale after all."

"That I have serious doubts about," scoffed Temple. "But all this is mere speculation, and in the overall picture of marriage against disinheritance carries no weight. I shall wed the chit and that is that."

"So, I've come all this way to be part of a reluctant wedding party, have I?" Oliver teased with a show of good humor he did not feel. "So, enlighten me? This short, duty-bound trip we undertook? Will it now stretch into a prolonged honeymoon? You are aware of the tight schedule. The ship's captain was more than explicit when he said one week and no more."

"Yes, I am aware that he sails in one week . . . five days now. Nothing has changed on that note. I plan to be on that ship when it departs Lough Swilly. I was more than explicit on that fact myself," Temple swore. His expression was such that Oliver did not comment further.

The heavy library door eased open once again. Temple looked up impatiently, for he had no wish to be further disturbed. Birdie stood there hesitantly. Obligingly both gentlemen rose to their feet. She stepped inside and dropped a silly little curtsy.

"I . . . I . . . am sorry to interrupt, but may I please speak with you, Lord Daine?"

"Of course," he replied. Obviously he was not to be allowed a day of solitude and peace in which to feel sorry for himself.

"And I shall excuse myself. Miss Birdie, a good-morning to you. Temple, we shall continue this at another time," Oliver said with a significant look at Temple. Bowing deeply to Birdie, he slipped out the door. Temple motioned Birdie farther into the room. Neither noticed the door closing to within an inch of the doorjamb, halted from latching by a slim white hand.

Birdie sat down on a straight-back chair before the desk. One that Temple speculated was reserved for interviews with the farm manager or servants. He did not correct her, or suggest they move to more comfortable seating, but seated himself behind the desk again. There was a silence, as if she sought words to express her thoughts. Because he realized she might be operating out of her depth, Temple spoke first.

"Perhaps I should apologize to you for the wetting incident of yesterday . . ."

"No, no, it was my fault." With a wave of her hand, she dismissed his apologetic words. "I acted badly and . . ." Again there was a pause as she collected herself. "I spoke with Sir Charles this morning. He has gained my oath that I will wed you before the week is past. He is not well, and he asked me to do it for him." She raised stricken eyes to him. "How could I say no? I would do anything for him. You must realize he is very dear to me."

Temple dropped his head and tented his face with his hands, pondering. He had not expected anything different and had no right to feel disappointed.

Birdie interpreted his gesture as distress and her heart sank even deeper. He simply did not want her. "I understand how you must feel . . ." she began tentatively.

"How could you possibly?" Temple muttered behind his hands.

"My lord, you seem to forget that I am being forced into this marriage, as well! Haven't I been up all night trying to form a means of escape, also?" Birdie allowed the pain of rejection to be overshadowed by anger. "No sense playing the melodramatic. I have come up with a solution, and one solution only . . . if you will but listen."

"Of course, I will listen," Temple answered, lifting his head in surprise. He knew he was not a totally unreasonable man, but the thought that she might resent the marriage as much as he had not occurred to him. "But I think there is no alternative except to do what my great-uncle wishes." He could not help his voice sounding sarcastic. As he saw Birdie's eyes flicker, he thought perhaps he had been cruel to the child. He could tell by the slight reddening of her eyes that she had been weeping, and she did in fact look no better rested than he felt.

"What I was . . . going to suggest," Birdie said, the words coming a little jerkily from between her lips, as if she hated to beg for favors. "If you will . . . give me a little money . . . not much, but enough to . . . just disappear."

The young man stared at her as if he could hardly believe what he had heard. She would give up everything she stood to gain? "I presume you have somebody in mind to accompany you?" Perhaps she had a lover among the footmen, he thought.

"No," Birdie said, tilting her chin upward. "I would just go away, regardless of what I've promised Sir Charles."

"And where would you go?"

"I expect . . . I truly do not know. If I could accompany you back to England, then . . . I imagine . . . perhaps a small cottage in a small village somewhere," she ventured, blushing at her ignorance. She lifted her chin defiantly and glared at him. So he would push her to admit it, would he? "I've never been anywhere but Haymarket Street . . . and here. I honestly don't know what else there is!"

"What could you do there . . . in a village? Do you have any skills?"

"I—I could teach. Franny says I am too... b-beautiful to be a governess. But maybe I could teach the poor children... there. I would not need much to live on each year."

"You surprise me no end. Could you be happy living like that?" Temple asked, truly puzzled by this young girl.

"Happy?" She shrugged as if happy were not the issue. "I only require food to eat, clothes for warmth and someone to feel... love for me." She said these last words almost under her breath as she clenched her hands in her lap.

"What of your plan to become a lady?" Again he sounded sarcastic.

Her head snapped up in defiance and she leapt to her feet. Rising to her full height, she dared to look down her small nose at the heir of Daine-Charlton. "I *am* a lady! I was *born* a lady! I had only to learn to *act* a lady... for my upbringing was at fault, not my *blood*," she grated between her teeth. "I did wish to right the wrong done to my mother, whatever it could have been. But I fear that might never be possible, for I do not even know where, or even how, to commence such a search."

Temple tilted an eyebrow at her. He sensed a strong emotion, other than defense of her blood, about the girl. It felt as if it might be fear. It might be easy to be a lady and vow revenge while safely tucked away at Blanballyhaven. But to return with him, a virtual stranger, to London and join society must seem a daunting future. Suddenly she seemed very young and very vulnerable to him. When he was away from her, it was easy to imagine her a schemer, but in her presence she became nothing more than a child, an innocent, untutored child in need of a protector. With a sigh of acquiescence, he thought to himself, Forgive me, Sophia, but I have no choice.

Rising, he walked around the desk to perch one hip on the edge and leaned toward Birdie. She sat down abruptly to put distance between them. "While your plan may have seemed reasonable in the dark of night, I fear the light of day often brings sanity with it. I cannot do as you ask. I will not go against my great-uncle's wishes." He leaned closer still. With a deep sigh that stirred the hair on her forehead, he continued. "His concern is that you not be left unprotected. You would not be safe by yourself, even in a small village. Not looking as you do."

She did not understand for a moment, then, when his insinuation filtered through her, she blushed prettily. "Oh, you mean... men... who would make things difficult. Yes, I seem to have problems with that."

Allowing his gaze to roam over her face and then down to her bosom straining the gold merino, he grinned wickedly. "I very much imagine you would."

Blushing even more furiously at his implication, Birdie made a little gesture with her hand. "If you truly want me to disappear, that need not be any of your concern."

"I did not say I wished you to disappear. *That* was your idea," he reminded her. Letting his eyes drift over the sweet curves of her face, he decided she was truly, fantastically beautiful. His loins stirred at the thought of her face contorted in newly awakening passion. He cleared his throat but did not move from her. Seemingly uncomfortable under his searching gaze, she looked away. He realized there was something different about her profile that he had not noticed in any other woman. An intriguing mixture of infant and adult. "You do not think that being a marquise would compensate for being married to me?" He bent forward, leaning closer to her when she would not answer. He would have sworn she was trembling at his nearness. Was she frightened of him? "Does the idea of being my wife really disgust you so much?"

"No...*No!* It is not that!" Birdie said quickly, turning her large eyes to his. "I think you are ... magnificent!" She caught herself and looked away again. "But I feel you must be in love with someone else and I should hate it that you should wish every day of your life that you had not married me."

Temple was astonished. There wasn't time for servants' gossip to ferret out the fact of Sophia, unless Travers had been uncharacteristically indiscreet. "What leads you to think that I am in love with someone else?"

Birdie's eyes flickered, but she would only shrug. How could she tell him that he was the most perfect man she had ever seen and there just had to be hundreds of beautiful ladies who were in love with him ... and it only stood to reason that he must love one of them back.

After a lengthy pause, he said, "I think, Birdie, if you and I are to wed, and it looks very certain that we will, that it would be a gross injustice to both of us for there to be any secrets between us. We should make a pact, here and now, that we will always tell each other the truth."

Birdie drew in her breath. Her eyes searched his face for evidence of the truth of which he spoke before she declared in a strong voice, "I will never speak anything to you but the truth. I promise!"

"And I promise you the same," he replied. Taking her small hand in his much larger one, he stroked the back of it with his thumb. "And therefore, so that there need be no more misunderstandings between us, I will confirm that there is another lady. I was going to offer for her hand once I returned to London, but I will swear to you, upon my word, Birdie, when we marry I shall put her out of my heart and my life. I will work to make our union one of trust and, in time, affection."

Birdie released the breath she had been holding since he had admitted he loved another. He was promising her a chance of making their marriage one of commitment and . . . yes, perhaps even love. Her heart brimmed with feelings.

As he finished speaking, Temple looked at Birdie, realizing there was a different expression now in her eyes. Without moving, without saying anything, she seemed suddenly to have come alive. She glowed, there was no other word for it. She had a radiance that made her already breathtaking beauty even more paralyzing.

The door behind them eased shut on well-oiled hinges. Not one minute later, a resounding rap on that door interrupted the mood. Birdie looked down without realizing her love for this man had shown so brightly in her eyes as Hudson stepped around the door.

"His lordship has expressed a wish to see you in his chambers when it is convenient, my lord," the butler announced with wide eyes, taking in the nearness of the two and the becoming blush on Birdie's cheeks.

Rising quickly and dipping a curtsy to Temple, Birdie slipped past the butler and ran lightly up the stairs. Frantically searching through the little leaded glass box Sir Charles had given her to keep the treasured portrait of her mother safe, Birdie drew forth the likeness. Clutching it tightly in her hand, she flung herself down upon the satin counterpane.

"Mam, I am to wed," she whispered. "Speak to me, Mam. I so wish to be close to you now. Everything you could have wished for me is to come true." Only silence came to surround her. Her mother's sweet voice did not come to whisper into her ear. "Do you hear me, Mam? Pray God that somehow you can see my good fortune. I am to be wed, and to a man I adore more than my own life. Remember, Mam?"

Chapter Eleven

The morning of Birdie's wedding dawned bright with the promise of sunshine. No early mist dared hang over the castle on such a special day, though the distant mountain tips glistened with newly fallen snow. The sweet, snappy smell of greens filled the air and no one could deny winter was peeping around the corner, even with the brilliance of the sunshine. As the sounds of nightingales gave way to the cuckoo and the dawn lit the tart greens, purples and reds of Blanballyhaven's gardens, the castle came alive.

The ceremony would take place in the small chapel at Birdie's request, with only Mattie, Libby, Hudson and Travers attending. A simple supper to follow was laid close to the library fire for Sir Charles's comfort, rather than the cavernous dining room, though the table was set with fine linen napery and decorated from one end to the other with hothouse flowers. All in all, a simple affair to commemorate the union of the heir of Daine-Charlton to the young girl with no name, who would be the next Marquise of Stannisburn.

Lord Sayers had departed at first light with a complement of outriders, hard bound for Buncrana. So great was his desire to be away from Blanballyhaven before first snow, he had forgone witnessing the wedding to carry notice of three passengers for the return voyage to London to the ship's captain. His absence was readily excused. His reluctance to participate in the nuptial celebration was placed at the door of his relationship to the jilted Sophia, even though she had no knowledge of that fact yet.

Taking the chance to escape the excited bickering of Mattie and Franny, and the reprimands of Libby, Birdie spent a long morning roaming the hills deep in thought, for she knew her time at Blanballyhaven was coming to a close. And though they might return for autumn shooting, it would never be the same. The realization that she might never see Sir Charles again in this life, or Mattie, for she was not a young woman, either, was painful. No, she was closing the door on the book of her childhood and she was torn between eager anticipation and tearful reluctance. Finally, finding no peace, she ended her last foray as an unmarried miss and returned to the castle.

Passing quickly through the halls toward her own bedchamber, Birdie was startled to hear a muted sob from the apartments used by Lord Daine. What? Was the man reduced to tears at the thought of marrying her? Noting the door ajar, and hearing renewed sobbing, she peeped in. Travers, midway in the laying out of his lordship's formal attire, was seated before the dressing room door with his hands covering his face.

"Travers?" she asked softly, so not to startle the man, who seemed to be in the throes of despair. Travers raised his head, and Birdie saw that a red mark violently discolored his cheekbone. "Oh, Travers! Did Lord Daine do that?"

Travers had given over to bitter laughter. " 'Tis the work of Elizabeth Fitzwaters!" He was silent for a moment, then he heaved a deep sigh. " 'Twas this morning, I was preparing his lordship's breakfast tray, when she came to me. Said she had decided to join her life with mine. Says to me, 'Mr. Travers, I will marry you just after the Christmas fuss is done.' "

"But that's wonderful, Travers."

Travers gave another bitter laugh. "You'd think so, miss. Indeed you would. And doesn't it seem that a man is surely entitled to embrace his fiancée?"

"A very natural thing, Travers."

"Natural, indeed, but not to my Libby." Rising from the bench, the small valet paced the room in agitation. "Overcome with joy, I jumped to my feet and folded her exquisite form...begging your pardon, miss...into my arms. Well, miss, no sooner had I done so than she ups with her fist and lands me a cruel blow in the face. 'Lecher!' she called me." Travers shook his head and sank to the bench once more. "I say, miss, a man of strong passions maybe, but lecher?"

The image of thin, effeminate Travers embracing the bulk of Libby Fitzwaters was almost the undoing of Birdie. Fighting for control over her laughter, she managed to squeak, "I am so sorry, Travers."

Dropping his hands, Travers regarded her earnestly with tear-reddened eyes. "You would ask how a man can live without tenderness of feelings from the woman he loves above all else, is that what you would ask?"

"Yes. Yes, indeed," Birdie said, comparing her own situation. "How does one live with a love that burns so brightly in the face of another's lack of it?"

"With a great deal of hope, miss. Never you fear, little by little I shall strip Libby's virtuous petals until I have revealed the tender heart within."

While Birdie had begun to suspect there was a lighter, softer side to the housekeeper, she very much doubted there existed a tender heart. For the most part the woman was judgmental and condemning. She did not envy Travers his marriage and was by no means sure that he could achieve a happy conclusion to his dream . . . any more than she could her own. "I wish you the best, Travers."

"That's kind of you, miss." Then, with greatly diminished gloom, Travers rose to his feet with dignity resumed. "We shall be quite a family, miss. Taking London by storm, we will."

Stunned for a moment, Birdie could only stare at the man. "I am not sure I understand your meaning, Travers."

"Why, Miss Birdie!" he exclaimed. "'Tis the reason my dove agreed to be mine. We are to accompany you to London when Lord Daine makes his departure. Such an ideal situation, don't you think? Newlyweds caring for newlyweds?" He fairly beamed. "And now I must see to my lord's dress. And you must dress, also! Time is short! Shoo! Shoo!"

Thoroughly dismissed, Birdie escaped into the hall. Closing the door gently behind her, she leaned on it, speechless. A gale of laughter threatened to burst forth, and fearing the earnest little man might overhear her, she hurriedly clamped a hand over her mouth.

Temple, advancing down the hall, was witness to her actions. He sauntered to her side. This was most unusual to find a bride exiting her intended's apartments on the morning of her wedding.

"Birdie?"

Glancing up into his puzzled face, Birdie removed her hand to speak but laughter bubbled forth. Clamping her hand over her mouth once more, she grasped his arm and drew him into the sitting room across the hall. Falling helplessly onto a ruby sofa, she was overcome with hoots of laughter. Tears streamed down her face, and hiccups erupted as she tried to explain herself.

"They are to . . . married . . . hit him in the face . . . going with us . . . oh!"

Temple's sun-browned face split into a wide smile at her helpless humor. Despite her disjointed words and pointing toward the door, he could not understand the cause of her merriment, and therefore he reclined on the sofa beside her in an unperturbed pose and waited for her to recover. When she did subside into merely hiccups, he pulled a crisp handkerchief from his breast pocket to gently dab at her tear-streaked cheeks.

"And, now, do you think you can tell me what has you so far into the rafters?" he teased. Gently cupping her chin, he turned her face to dab at the tears on the opposite cheek.

Birdie gazed at his full mouth and the startling white teeth as he smiled. "The very first time I saw you, you had a luscious black mustache, and when you kissed me it tickled." Her voice came softly as she allowed him the liberty of her cheeks. His very closeness made it difficult for her to breathe.

Leaning nearer still, he inhaled the floral scent she used, mixed with a tinge of outdoor freshness. Her eyes were huge and her breath, through slightly parted lips, was whispery against his face. She was a delectable child and easy to be tender with. Turning a bit, he lightly touched his lips to hers.

"If you fancy tickling, I shall grow it again, just for you."

Carefully edging away from him, Birdie eased from the sofa. "I must go. Franny must be waiting as it's late. Besides, the bride-groom isn't supposed to see the bride on the wedding day."

Standing with her, he lightly ran a finger across her satin cheek. "There's a number of things a bridegroom should not do before the wedding, so you had best fly away, little wren."

Staring up into his beloved face, Birdie ran the tip of her tongue over dry lips as if tasting the feel of his kiss. Her cheeks flushed a delightful pink with pleasure. Then her eyes grew large and she drew in her breath. Tonight was her wedding night. "Ye gods and little fishes!" she whispered, then fled to her bedchamber in high spirits to prepare for her wedding.

Temple laughed at her disappearing figure. She was easy to tease. Easy to be kind to. She was a tender, young thing that he was about to pledge to protect for the whole of her life. It was a sobering thought. What he wanted most was to take her into his arms and see just how much of her was woman and how much still a child. He wanted to crush those rosy lips beneath his own, fill his hands with those unruly, fiery ringlets and make her whimper. He wanted to hear her whisper his name and answer with his own whisper. But the very act of whispering her name brought back with sudden clarity the fact that she did not have one. And that bothered him no end.

It bruised his ego and tampered with his opinion of himself that he could not help but ponder the rumors that were sure to run riot through the ton when they made the discovery. Nor could he help but weigh the very rightness of Sophia's sophistication and background against the wild enthusiasm for life he sensed barely controlled beneath the satin skin of Birdie.

Birdie looked like a goddess as she walked down the bridal carpet unrolled the length of the chapel, hands clutching the small Bible Mattie had handed her. The scavenged gown of heavy white satin had mellowed to clotted cream with age and the color enhanced her pale skin. A heavy train of priceless Valenciennes lace was anchored to her head, covering the thick russet hair that Franny had swept up and back from her forehead to fall in ringlets of red fire past her waist, framing her strong yet delicate features and her luminous eyes. She would have so liked to have Sir Charles walk beside her down the aisle, but the elderly man was unable to stand without assistance and waited for her now beside Lord Daine, at the altar. As she passed the tall candelabra, the candles cast light and shadows over her face, giving it a radiance that bespoke of her happiness. Her delicate beauty brought a gasp to Temple's lips. Sir Charles heard him and smiled.

Birdie's gaze fell upon her husband to be. He was tall and so beautiful in his black formal wear. The sight of him brought a slight flush to her cheeks and a pounding of her heart for what would follow this night. How I love thee, Temple, she thought. And how fortunate I am. No woman could be more fortunate, for all my dreams are coming true at this very moment. She was marrying a man she adored and, given time, she would make him love her just as much in return.

As Birdie took her place between Sir Charles and Temple, a plaintive, traditional Irish melody filtered through the still air. Softly, the pledge was intoned in solemn yet joyous Latin words that made the two of them one for life. At last, she belonged to someone. She could hear the soft tears of Mattie and Travers behind her. Temple barely had time to lift Birdie's veil and brush his lips lightly over hers before the servants crowding the doorway began to shout "Slainte! Slainte!" and they were drawn out to be escorted to the library amid shouts of well-wishers.

"Health, long life to ye!"

"Land without rent!"

"A babe in arms each and every year!"

Temple stole a sidelong glance at his bride's radiant beauty. Her face was as animated as an excited child on Christmas morn. Allowing that the well-wishing and toasting might never end, Temple made a short, abrupt speech and shut the door firmly on the servants. Feasting and dancing for the staff would go on below stairs until the wee hours of the morning. Sir Charles greeted them from his chair before the fireplace.

"Escaped them, I see," he called with a laugh. Birdie wearily moved to drop a kiss on his dry forehead.

"I am so tired. Their enthusiasm exhausts me. I noticed you did not tarry, but fled like a coward," she teased, arranging her heavy draperies to seat herself amid the froth on the sofa, as no chair could have contained the voluminous skirts and petticoats. She lapsed into a teasing brogue. "I didn't fash meself when ye turned up missing, for I knew ye'd be under the stairs with a buxom lass filling each of yer arms, ye old lecher!"

"Nay, Lady Daine," Sir Charles answered with an exaggerated leer. "You know I lust for married women only, so you had best be locking your bedchamber door from this night forward."

Having never heard Birdie and his great-uncle carry on their tease, Temple elevated his eyebrow in wonder. Was it possible there had been something physical between these two? Was he the victim of a conspiracy to legalize his great-uncle's mistress? Shaking his head, Temple scoffed at his own suspicion. Impossible, he told himself. The man was just too old. And the child too young, too innocent.

Slipping one small gloved hand beneath her heavy hair, Birdie rubbed the ache in her neck. Temple, seeing the move, vowed to send her off to bed soon after supper. The child was weary, and he still harbored plans to depart for Buncrana at first light. Walking to the back of the sofa, he released the pins holding the heavy lace veil on her head. Lifting it away from her, he draped it over the back of the sofa. Instantly, the frown furrowing her brow, eased.

"Oh, thank you, my lord. I thought my neck would surely break from the weight of the thing."

"Perhaps we should drop the 'my lord,' and you could call me simply by my name, Temple," he said, moving to lean casually against the mantel. "As we are now related quite closely, are we not?"

Birdie blushed and smiled at him shyly. "If that is your wish . . . *Temple*."

Hudson and the underbutler had forgone the revelry below stairs to wait upon the family. Together, they served a quiet, elegant dinner with twelve separate removes, each with Mattie's personal, loving touch upon it. Birdie could not help but dawdle somewhat. She was ever so conscious that this marked her last night as a child. By morning, she would be a woman in every way. Lady Birdie Daine, wife of Lord Templeton Daine. Her eyes darted reflectively to her husband's dark profile again and again. He was so handsome, and her heart seemed to ache with the love it sought to contain. While she welcomed the night and the act that would truly bind them together as one, she also feared leaving the library and the safety of her beloved Sir Charles's presence. If she cried and begged, would he allow her to stay with him? To remain a child? Casting another glance at Temple, she thought, No, I do not wish to remain a child. I want to build my life with this man.

Temple noticed her frequent glances and her hesitation but did not press her. He was unsure if it was fear of him and his love-making that made her dawdle over her supper, or mere tiredness. He had thought to set her mind at ease earlier with the fact that he would not intrude on her privacy this night. It was not in his nature to bed infants barely out of schoolrooms. Wife or not!

Mattie, Franny and a group of maids, all tipsy by the look of them and the sound of their giggles, appeared at the library door, requesting Lady Daine's presence. Puzzled, Birdie innocently went to the door. Grabbed by eager hands, the girl was dragged squealing up the stairs to her bedchamber. A similar fate would have awaited Lord Daine had there been any brave enough to lay hands upon him. As it was, he was left to have a final brandy with his great-uncle before retiring to the bridal chambers.

Sir Charles cleared his throat and tentatively approached a touchy subject with his great-nephew. "I hope in time, Temple, you will find it within yourself to forgive me for meddling in your life this way." Temple merely smiled a tight smile that did nothing to relieve Sir Charles's concern and inclined his head slightly. Not to be put off, the marquis bravely forged ahead. "I do not have to tell you, the girl is young and inexperienced. She is not well-known to you, so you can not know how tender her heart is. I would caution you to go slowly and carefully, with solicitous thought before each action."

Temple abruptly left his position in front of the fire to pace the length of the library. "I will make the best of what I can only refer to as an unsavory situation, Uncle. Truthfully, in reference to your meddling, I cannot say that there is anything to forgive. You have your responsibility as head of the family to do as you feel best." Pacing back the length of the room, he paused by the door to turn a stony face to the marquis. "As to the other, she is my wife now. I think you should leave her well-being in my hands. Good night, Uncle."

Sir Charles sat still for a moment, gazing at the closed door, then rubbed a trembling hand over tired, watery eyes. He could not bear the thought of his Birdie frightened. Or worse, treated roughly.

"Dear Birdie. My dear little Birdie. What have I done to you?"
Lifting his head with resolution, he refused the mental pictures.
No! Temple might be angry but he would not abuse a young girl
as revenge. He would not believe his great-nephew would be other
than gentle for his bride's first time. Drawing a shaky breath, he
cursed fate for bringing love into his life amid the foulness of old
age.

Birdie's bedchamber was crowded, and the shrill voices of the
women rose and fell as in a cadence. As they giggled and made
snide remarks concerning the health of his lordship's member, no
one except Franny noticed the weary droop to the bride's eyes.
Birdie gave a deep sigh of relief as Franny impatiently shooed everyone out the door, except for Mattie, who defiantly refused to
budge.

Insisting Birdie slip into a warm bath, delicately scented with
attar of roses, Franny proceeded to rub every inch of the tired back
with a sweet-scented lotion, soothing away the knots of tension.
Mattie sat beside her, weeping softly.

"Mattie, for heaven's sake," cried Franny. "Ye'll be for having
her scared out of her wits! 'Tis a wonderful thing to be discovering love with the man ye love."

"Aye, 'tis just that she's all grown up. And a lady, just like she
always said she'd be," sniffed Mattie, dabbing at her eyes absently with the hem of her best Sunday gown, as her customary
apron tail was missing.

A sharp tap on the door drew gasps from the two women and a
high squeak from Birdie. Three pairs of eyes were riveted on the
door. Oh, God! Birdie thought in sudden panic. Was it Temple
already? "Franny! Get rid of him!"

Mrs. Fitzwaters stepped into the room. If she was startled in any
way at the frozen stares of all three women, the only evidence of it
was the elevation of one forbidding eyebrow. "Franny? Mattie?
That will be all now," she barked. Mattie bristled for a fight at the
woman's tone, but Birdie gathered first one then the other of the
women into a tight hug.

"Off with you now. Would you have me keep my husband
cooling his heels in the hallway most of the night?" she quipped as
she waved them reluctantly out the door.

As if sensing the overwhelming emotions the young girl must be
feeling, Mrs. Fitzwaters drew her gently toward the dressing table.
"Come, let us get you dressed, my lady." Raising her arms, Birdie
allowed the towel to fall to the floor as the nightdress Mrs. Fitzwaters carried slid over her body. "I wish this nightdress and robe

to be my gift to you on this day of your wedding," Mrs. Fitzwaters said, flipping the hem down straight.

Birdie looked at herself in the pier glass. The sleeveless nightdress was of satin, cut without fullness to cling suggestively to the curves of her body, and the same color as the blush that touched her cheeks.

"Oh, Libby, it is truly beautiful. Thank you so very much. I shall always treasure it," she said in an awed voice.

"No need to go into raptures, a simple thank-you will suffice." Drawing the delicate scalloped edges together, the housekeeper laced the rose ribbons, closing the front opening of the nightdress from navel to throat with love knots, which Birdie would never have imagined she knew how to effect. The robe, worn open and flowing, was filmy lawn, as fragile as a spider's web with every inch of the front panel, from shoulder to hem, embroidered with pink satin thread into intricate flowers and vines and songbirds. Pushing her down upon the stool in front of the dressing table, Mrs. Fitzwaters picked up the silver-backed brush to dress Birdie's hair.

"But you must have spent hours over this embroidery," Birdie exclaimed, fingering the delicate lawn robe.

Mrs. Fitzwaters sniffed. "It was my time to waste, I suppose."

"Oh, Libby, I didn't mean . . ."

Mrs. Fitzwaters cut her short. "It is quite all right, my lady. I know exactly what you meant. I thank you, but as you know, I am not one for giving or receiving flowery speeches."

Ducking her head to hide a smile, Birdie said, "Yes, Libby."

"See that you remember it," demanded Mrs. Fitzwaters. The housekeeper's stern eyes lingered for a brief moment on the girl, then her hand smoothed the shoulder of the robe. "As you are well aware, my lady," she continued in her most forbidding voice, "I do not hold with frivolity. Never have and never will. However, you are a young thing, and after all, it is your wedding day. I daresay, like most young things with your head stuffed full of nonsense, you prefer pretty to plain." Removing the pins and clasps from Birdie's hair, she allowed it to tumble down her back in a gleaming russet waterfall.

Trying to control her tears at the woman's gruff tenderness, and maintain a light, teasing voice, she said with a slight smile, "Yes, Libby. I prefer pretty to plain." Tipping her head back, she relaxed as Mrs. Fitzwaters drew the brush through the ringlets one hundred times, until they hung in luxuriant waves like a mantle down her back. With a surprisingly adept twist of the brush, Mrs. Fitzwaters pulled the heavy hair to the top of Birdie's head and secured it there with a few pins. Surveying her work in the mirror, she further astonished Birdie by pulling several frivolous tentacles loose to caress the cheeks.

"Well, Libby," Birdie teased, turning her head this way and that. "Do you think I will compare with his lordship's other flights of fancy?"

Mrs. Fitzwaters pursed her lips. "A vulgar expression, my lady. And one I dislike to hear on your lips. Flights of fancy, indeed!"

Birdie's smile faded, and she raised fearful eyes to meet Libby's in the mirror. Her tenseness was returning. "Thank you, Libby, for everything," she said in a low voice.

With one of her rare smiles, Mrs. Fitzwaters said, almost gently, "Have no fear. He will not be able to resist you."

"Do you think so, Libby?" Birdie's trepidation was reflected in her tone. "I don't fear…what he will do, but rather that I will not please him."

"Believe me when I say, Have no doubt that you will please him." Mrs. Fitzwaters marched over to the door, her heavy tread causing the china clocks to shudder and rattle. "I'll leave you now. Mind you don't rumple yourself." She paused to give the girl one last look. "Do not let this turn your head, but I will allow that you look very fetching and that is all that is expected of you this night." With that and a brief nod of satisfaction, she closed the door firmly behind her.

Birdie stared at her reflection in the mirror. Her eyes were huge, sherry brown pools in her pale face. "All that is expected of me?" she murmured to the reflection. "I very much doubt that! But it cannot be too bad or there wouldn't be so many babies born—" she gave a quiet little laugh "—and Flo would have complained a great deal more about having to do it so much!"

Chapter Twelve

Finally left alone to await her husband's pleasure, Birdie paced the length of the room. Her eyes swept the ivory, blue and rose chamber, trying to see it through Temple's eyes. Would he think it as pretty as she did? Nervously she paused beside the high bed, taking in the neatly turned-down counterpane showing creamy, inviting linens...her bridal bed. Drawing a tremulous breath, she clasped her hands in front of her.

"Sheesh! It's as light as day in here," she whispered to herself. Quickly, she doused most of the wall sconces and all but one of the candles on the dressing table. Standing beside the door, she pretended to be Temple, just entering the room. A frown furrowed her brow and her small teeth worried the pouty bottom lip. "Now 'tis too dark, fool! You would not have the man fumbling about to find you, now would you?"

Shielding a taper with her hand, she lit the four thick beeswax candles set into tall holders mounted at each corner of the bed. With that done, the room glowed warmly and, as was her want, dimly. In her quest for less brightness, she had unwittingly created a very sensuous atmosphere. The wavering candlelight struck the sheen of the satin nightdress, accentuating the movement of her body beneath.

Studying the room once more, she moved the bottle of wine and two stemmed glasses to the table next to the bed. Then when that seemed too obvious, she moved them back to the dressing table once more. Drawing a deep breath and exhaling slowly to calm herself, she stood at the foot of the bed and waited, and waited...until she could stand the strain no longer.

"Damn! Will he never come?"

Restlessly moving to the terrace doors, she unlatched the lattice and threw them open. At once, a brisk wind ruffled the sheer draperies and billowed the robe around her. From the other side of the castle, she could hear the ocean pounding the base of the cliff below the walls of Blanballyhaven. Her heart pained at the thought of leaving Blanballyhaven. How she loved it here . . . her only true home in all her sixteen years. She breathed deeply of the cold night air, the scent of winter heavy but sweetened by mists and the promise of rain. It smelled clean and the dampness caused the tentacles framing her face to curl up tightly into ringlets.

For Birdie, this night held trepidation and exhilaration. She felt blessed that she was able to give her innocence to one she loved, for how many times had it seemed destined to be taken from her by force, bartered or stolen by others, against her will. Suddenly, as a whisper in her ear, her mother's soft voice, so silent the past few years, came to her.

"Always remember, my precious. A girl's maidenhead is like a bubble. Once it's broken, it can never be repaired. It should be saved for the man you love more than your own life."

More than my own life? Would I give my life for Temple? she thought. Did she truly know the man she had pledged her life and body to? Or was she in love with a fantasy of a man who carried the face of Lord Templeton Daine?

Hearing Temple's voice in the hall dismissing Travers, Birdie latched the window and quickly moved to her dressing table, rushing to seat herself before the mirror. By the time the voices tapered off and the footsteps moved on past her door, she was smoothing her hair as if it had been her only occupation for these past two hours. Listening closely over the pounding of her heart, Birdie paled. The footsteps did not return. Leaping to her feet, she ran lightly to press her ear to the wood panel of the door. Absolute silence. Taking a deep breath, she eased the door open just enough to view the hallway. No one moved in the dim light of the wall sconces. To step into the hall, she knew, was to draw the attention of the footman on night duty sitting at the end of the lengthy corridor. She would die before she would let anyone know she was searching for a husband of barely four hours, already absent from his bride's bed. Gently she closed the door, gritting her teeth at the loudness of the latch clicking into place.

Walking back across the beautiful room, Birdie stood before the pier glass to stare at her reflection. The beautiful, desirable woman that stared back at her did not match the childish feelings of rage and abandonment she was experiencing. Gripping the delicate lawn robe in both fists, she thought to rip it from her body. But the care that Libby had taken to make it stilled her hands. Slipping the robe off, she tossed it to the dressing table. Pouring herself a hefty glass

of wine in one of the crystal stemmed glasses, she toasted her reflection.

"May you be blessed with a babe in arms every year, lass," she
muttered with a sad smile. "If you are woman enough to do the
deed by yourself." As she tossed the wine to the back of her throat,
tears filled her eyes, and she addressed the forgotten woman in the
mirror. "You knew he didn't want you from the first. You have no
right to be whining now, my lady!"

Wetting her finger and thumb, she pinched the flame from the
candle sitting atop the dressing table. With a sigh, she mounted the
three steps to the bed, and kicking off her slippers, she slid beneath the cold sheets. Shivering in the thin nightdress, she curled
into a tight ball on her side. The sadness and disappointment lay
heavy on her heart, then rose to fill her throat with unshed tears.
Though her eyes filled, and one by one the tears slipped down to
wet the pillowcase, she was unable to truly cry. Her throat ached
and she wished to beat her fists into the mattress and wail, but
something stopped her. Perhaps she was growing up. Or perhaps
she knew that nothing would help ease the pain of Temple's rejection. A yawn took control of her face. The day had been long and
she was exhausted, physically and emotionally. With the tear trails
drying on her face, she slept.

Temple opened the door of Birdie's room, then softly closed it
behind him. The slight breeze flitted through the room, wavering
the candle flames at the corners of the bed. The small figure under the covers did not stir. Stepping quietly to the dressing table,
he lightly fingered the filmy robe thrown there and glanced at the
two wineglasses. A smile curved his full lips. So she had expected
him after all. Moving to the bed, he stepped up the wooden steps
to stare pensively down at the sleeping child. For a child she did
seem, curled on her side with one hand tucked beneath her cheek.

Unable to resist the impulse, he slowly lifted the sheet to gaze
down at her body. As the cool air touched her, she protested with
a small whimper and curled tighter. Temple let the coverlet drop
back on her sleeping form. Turning, he carefully sat on the side of
the bed. He had thought not to come at all, but he could not hu-
miliate her by his absence. He was too familiar with the workings
of large houses to expect that something like sleeping in his own
bed would not create gossip in the kitchen by morning. So here he
was, sitting on the edge of a bed with a belly filled with guilt for
desiring a child with a woman's body. No doubt about it, his life
was going to be different as a wedded man, he chided himself.

Standing abruptly, he strolled to the dressing table and tossed
down a glass of wine. Throwing his black velvet dressing gown over

Birdie's, he savagely kicked off his slippers, noting ironically how close to hers they landed. Dousing all but one of the candles, he slipped beneath the covers to lie beside his sleeping bride. The soft feather mattress gave under his weight, and with a deep sigh, he settled himself on his back, arms behind his head, hoping that sleep would show kindness and overtake him.

Giving in to the pull of his greater weight beside her, Birdie rolled toward his warmth without waking. Snuggling against his side, she laid one hand upon his bare chest and threw a satin-covered leg over his groin. She tucked her cold foot between his crossed calves with a sigh. Easing his arm down, he pulled her closer to ease the ache in his shoulder and closed his eyes. Sleep still eluded him as the warmth of her body soaked into his side.

Try as he might, Temple could not ignore the softness of the full breast pressed into his rib cage. Gritting his teeth, he fought to clear his mind and accept sleep, but it seemed impossible for him this night. Turning his head, he tried to see Birdie's face, but with it tucked into his neck, his vision was limited to a tangle of curls spread over his chest. Unable to withstand the weight on his groin, he eased her onto her back, gently moving the thigh and arm.

Turning on his side to face her, he studied her in the dim light. He wished now he had left the other candles burning. Her face, in slumber, was so tender and young, the lashes long and curved over the softest of cheeks, and the mouth pouty, slightly open, as if inviting the tip of his tongue to enter and tease. The steady rise and fall of her chest drew his eyes downward. With one hand, he easily flipped the love knots free, one after another, until the gown lay unfastened from her smooth throat to her navel. Without moving the fabric aside, he slipped his hand into the opening and gently cupped the breast there. The firmness delighted him, the soft mound overflowing his hand. Even in her sleep, the girl was responding to him, he noted as the nipple hardened beneath his palm. Drawing the fabric back, he feasted his eyes on her bared breasts, full, creamy mounds topped with pink, crinkled nipples. Again he groaned.

Feeling the worst kind of cad, Temple rolled from the bed and strolled across the room, raking his hand through his midnight hair. He must remind himself again that although she was his wife and his for the taking, she was still a child. Barely sixteen was a child, no matter how magnificent her body or how beautiful her face! If he took advantage of her innocence tonight, as his driving need was urging him to, he would hate himself in the light of day. His desire for her was only a product of the abstinence of the past three weeks. Nothing more!

Striding to the long terrace doors, he threw them open and stepped out onto the terrace. Gulping cold air into his lungs, he flexed strong arms over his head. The icy cold of the stones stung his feet, and the mists Birdie had so enjoyed earlier had thickened into rain that beat against his bare chest and shoulders. The snappy cold reminded him that winter was closing fast on Blanballyhaven and he must be off if he wished to escape being snowbound. Temple raised his face to the heavens and fought the urge to expel some of his pent-up sexual energy with a great shout.

"Are you daft, man?" called a voice behind him.

Temple wheeled to stare at the slight figure standing in the open doorway. Wind and rain whipped the thin nightdress against the curves of her body, causing the thickness to gather in his groin again.

"Damn!" he muttered. Quelling the urge to rail at her for something not necessarily of her doing, he reentered the room. Slamming the doors and latching the shutters, he turned to Birdie. "I'm sorry. I didn't mean to wake you."

Taking note of the drenched trousers, bare chest and feet, Birdie cocked an eyebrow at him. "You would want to make me a widow before you have even made me a wife? You're soaked through! Your hair is even dripping!"

"We seem to be a pair, for you are soaked to the skin, as well, dear wife," responded Temple. With a laugh, he waved a hand at her nightdress.

Glancing down at herself, Birdie wailed, "Oh, my new nightdress!" Rushing to the dressing table, she struck a lucifer to the candlestick, then stepped in front of the pier glass. She looked a mess! Her hair was half in and half out of its pins, wet and tangled into a riot of ringlets, and her nightdress was wet and clinging to her body. " 'Tis ruined! And Libby worked so hard on the fancy stitching."

"Mrs. Fitzwaters gave you that garment?" exclaimed Temple in dismay. He came to stand behind her, peering over her shoulder. "She belts poor Travers a black eye over a simple embrace, then gives a child a nightdress like that? The woman is a mass of contradiction, indeed!"

"I am not a child! Besides, it was an appropriate gift—" looking at him in the mirror, Birdie narrowed her eyes "—for tonight was supposed to be my wedding night for want of a bridegroom."

"You *are* a child," he insisted. "And I had thought not to come at all, but deemed it best to refuse to fuel the fire of servants' gossip."

Reaching up a hand, he pulled the remaining pins from her hair, allowing it to cascade down her back. For a moment, he buried both hands in the rich, silken flame of it as if to warm himself. His touch on her scalp sent gooseflesh creeping along her bare arms. Shifting his body with a slight moan, he abruptly lifted a neatly folded towel from the dressing table bar.

"Your hair is wet through. You're going to catch a chill, at which time our Mrs. Fitzwaters will have my head on a platter!"

Try as he might to treat her as a child, he could not keep his eyes from her candlelit reflection. Beneath the wet nightdress, her breasts swayed enticingly as he rubbed vigorously at her head with the towel. Her nipples were puckered and stiff with cold. Although the nightdress was open to her belly, the satin was too wet to loosen from her skin. Even so, Temple could see the deep cleavage and curved inner sides of both breasts. The satin molded itself to her flat belly and muscular thighs with a slight rise between, hinting at a furred paradise. How he longed to splay his fingers over that taut belly and pull her soft buttocks back against him.

"Damn!" he exploded, striding forcefully across the room. "Find something to cover yourself ! Get out of that wet... Damn!"

Pulling the towel from her head, Birdie turned to stare at him in astonishment that quickly flared into anger. "And what of your own wet self?" she yelled, flinging the towel at his rigidly held back.

Lighting the second taper, she carried it through the door into the dressing room. Flinging the doors open to her massive wardrobes, she pulled out the first robe her hand touched. Dragging the wet nightdress over her head, she wrapped the robe around her. Tears threatened to spill down her face. Pressing the heels of both hands tightly into her eyes, she breathed deeply to calm herself. She would not cry! She would not! Bending, she retrieved the satin nightdress from the floor. How beautiful she had felt in it, and now it was ruined. Carefully, she spread it over a chair, hoping it would dry unstained.

Walking back to the dressing table, Birdie picked up a comb to untangle her hair, hopelessly knotted by Temple's rough toweling. Temple turned when she reentered the room. The towel he had been drying his chest with stilled in his hands. Birdie, standing between him and the candlelight, was silhouetted clearly through the thin silk robe. He watched as she raised her arms to drag the comb through her hair, causing the robe to pull tight over her bottom.

"Hell's teeth! Didn't you hear what I said?" he erupted in frustration. Striding to her, he gripped her arm to pull her into the dressing room, where he frantically pawed through the wardrobe himself.

"Don't you be laying your hands on me!" Birdie yelled, stamping a small foot furiously. "I've had just about enough of your high-handed . . ."

"Here! Don this damn thing, for God's sake! And mine!" he brusquely interrupted, drawing forth a heavy flannel coverall of tartan plaid. He faced her angry stance and held out the nightdress. If he had not been in such pain from his dictatorial body, the situation would have been hilarious. Imagine Lord Henry Templeton Daine frantic to cover the temptation of a delicious female form with a hideous flannel coverall.

"I do not understand you," Birdie railed, her chest heaving in angry humiliation. "But do not fash yourself. If 'tis so damned important to you that I put the blasted thing on, then I'll put the blasted thing on!" Furious, hurt, humiliated, she jerked the sash closing the robe and flung it savagely on the floor. "But then I would be seeing the back of you through the door and—and—" she stammered, shrugging the robe from her shoulders and flinging it after the sash, "and never darken it again!" Gripping a handful of the flannel coverall he was holding out to her, she jerked on it but Temple did not let go.

As she stood fully naked in the candlelight, Birdie's creamy skin glowed warm and inviting. Temple's eyes eagerly roamed over her body. Her breasts were high and amazingly firm, rising and falling rapidly in her agitation. Her waist was small, hardly more than the span of a man's hands, then flaring into slim, pleasing hips. Her legs were longer than he had thought, and well muscled for a woman. Bringing his eyes back up to the little nest of auburn nether curls, he exhaled a long sigh.

"My, God, you are beautiful."

Birdie stood still under his scrutiny. A hot blush tinted her breasts and crept up her throat to her cheeks. But even hotter was the sinking, burning feeling in her belly. His near naked body displayed heavy muscles beneath his hairy chest, the candlelight creating interesting shadows. Dropping her eyes in confused embarrassment, she gently tugged at the robe they both held. Clearing his throat, Temple quickly let go and shoved both hands deep into his trouser pockets.

Slipping into the flannel robe, Birdie walked to her dressing table and sank to the bench on weak legs. Again she dragged the comb through the curls. The snarls brought tears to her eyes, but she did not stop. Somehow she welcomed the pain as a diversion. Anything to ease the strange hollow feeling inside. Temple came to lean a shoulder against the doorway, watching her. Clearing his throat again, he sought to repair some of the damage he felt he had done with this hellish night.

"Are you very tired? The celebration, I mean . . ."

"N-no, not very," she stammered. "I think just getting away from the crowding . . . they all wanted to stay . . . then I slept . . ." She did not finish the thought, for it brought to mind her disappointment when he had not appeared.

"I agree. The servants are quite overwhelming in their well-wishing and merrymaking," he murmured. Straightening, he moved to stand behind her once more. His hand slowed in its combing, her eyes meeting his dark stare in the mirror. Warm brown eyes with thick lashes, filled with what? Wonder? Trepidation? She truly was just a child and totally unaware of her power over him. The thought amazed him, as he had no experience with untutored maidens.

"You are so beautiful that it is almost unreal."

Birdie's breath caught in her throat. Her heart pounded so loudly she feared he could hear it. No, it was he that was so beautiful. Massive, dark and . . . and irrepressibly drawing. "No, I—I think you must have a touch of fever . . ." she said, her voice low and tremulous. Holding her breath and resisting the temptation to drop her eyes from his searching ones, she prayed that he did truly find her beautiful. More beautiful than the lady in London.

Gently sinking his hands into her hair, he nodded toward the mirror. "Your mirror does not lie. Can you not see it?" Moving his hands in her hair, he fingered the silky stuff. " 'Ringletted wench of my love,' " he quoted in a teasing voice, a tender smile on his lips, " 'your kiss is an awaking dew.' " He tilted her head to one side, and his lips brushed her ear lightly.

" 'No shrinking virgin here but a girl aching and tender for the sweet comforts of thy love,' " she said, finishing the phrase he had begun.

Temple stared at her for a moment then grinned his wicked grin. "You are full of surprises, Birdie. I bet Mrs. Fitzwaters never knew you read that one!"

Impulsively, Birdie spun on the stool and flung herself against him. Wrapping both arms around his waist, she clung to him in a childish embrace. Her cheek burrowed against his flat belly.

"Oh, God, Birdie," Temple moaned. Then, as if a decision had been made, he gripped her arms forcefully and dragged her up his body. His hungry mouth came down on her soft one so hard it hurt. Birdie whimpered. His kiss immediately gentled, the painful pressure altering into a sweet, tender searching.

Relaxing her body, Birdie leaned into him, surrendering to him. His hands loosened their grip on her arms and slid around her in a different way... a caressing way. His head bent deeper, his mouth playing on hers, nibbling, sucking her pouty bottom lip. Birdie whimpered deep in her throat as she awakened to the pleasure of it all, responding with womanly instincts as old as time to every touch, every stroke of his tongue. Her hand crept up his back to the nape of his neck, tangling in the crisp hair there. Gently, so gently, he curved her body to his, his warm hand sliding down her spine to rest against the rise of her buttocks, to draw her tightly against him. Her breasts crushed against his chest, her hips fitted snugly into his, so closely that she could feel the length and strength of his arousal. A trembling started in her legs, threatening to rob her of her ability to stand.

Sighing, Birdie gave in to the weakness and sagged against him, allowing her head to fall limply away, rolling onto his shoulder. His mouth nibbled and sucked the delicate skin of her neck and along her collarbone. The trembling advanced up her thighs and across her belly, bringing with it a burning, yearning need that built rapidly. His scent filled her nostrils and her body cried out for him, willing him to do whatever he would with her.

His mouth returned to slant across her slack one. Slipping a searching tongue inside, he devoured her sweetness. His chest rose and fell with an unsteady sigh, and he eased his hold on her, dropping his hands to his sides, where he clenched them as fists.

"Birdie." His voice was hoarse with wanting. "I cannot stand this. Step away. Step away now or give up the right to cry nay later."

Birdie understood he was giving her the chance to stay a child in his eyes, to retreat from the fire that threatened to burst into flame inside both of them. Looking up into his beloved face with eyes half-closed, she saw the tightly clenched lips, recognized the fight to control himself, to give her this one last chance that she neither wanted nor welcomed. Love for him surged through her veins and she felt no desire to move away from him. Ever. Yes, she loved this man. More than her own life.

"Temple, do you still think I am a child?"

"No, though I wish to hell I did."

"But why?"

"Because I would not feel this way about a child," Temple rasped. He reached out and caressed the sweet curve of her cheek. The lines of his mouth softened as he looked at her. She was so young, so vulnerable. From somewhere came the unfamiliar desire to protect her, even from himself, if need be. "I will understand, Birdie, if you ask me to leave. You are still so young. And this marriage was not of your own mind.''

''I may be young, Temple, but I do not think I was ever a child,'' she whispered, drawing a hand through the dark hair over his chest, amazed at the heat of his skin. ''And I did want this marriage . . .''

''Step away from me, little wren . . .'' he whispered.

''I cannot,'' she whispered, swaying toward him with eyes fluttering shut. ''Do you not understand? I have worked so hard to grow up for you.''

Offering no second chance, Temple swiftly stripped the flannel from her body and lifted her slight frame effortlessly. Hooking her arms around his neck, Birdie was clasped against his warm chest, feeling the strength and limitless power there, and felt safe at last.

Carrying her to the bed, he then lowered her into the feather mattress. Straightening, he unbuttoned the black lounging trousers and let them fall to his feet. Birdie, suddenly timid, closed her eyes quickly. The mattress gave beneath his weight as he joined her, his warm flesh searing her beneath the linens.

''Open your eyes, Birdie,'' he whispered against her neck. ''Don't hide from me inside your head.''

Obeying him, she stared into his smiling gray eyes. A rosy blush tinted her cheeks, and embarrassed by his frank pleasure and the feel of his naked body against hers, she squirmed and ducked her head to his neck, to draw the smell of him deep into her nostrils. She would never have guessed the very smell of him could be so exciting. Raised on his elbow, he deliberately ran his hand the length of her, from her throat to her tightly clenched thighs, lightly brushing the auburn curls. The edgy nerves in her body reacted and the trembling began in her legs again.

''You are so perfect,'' he whispered. ''I want to know you, every satin inch of you.'' Easing his body partially onto hers, he ran his tongue across her nipple. It immediately tightened and rose to invite more of the same. Sucking it deeply into his mouth, he slid his hand over her hip to draw her tightly against his groin. The very basis of his maleness pulsed and jerked. A moan of almost agony escaped him.

Sparks flashed from Birdie's nipple to her belly. She could feel his heated ardor, seemingly enormous against her thigh. When Mattie had told her that a man's friend grew larger in excitement, she had never imagined her to mean, well, huge! Such a wondrous thing to have! She longed to touch it, to explore it with her fingertips, but feared he would be displeased. All the shyness and strangeness Birdie had expected to feel disappeared in primitive sensations. Arching her back to push the nipple deeper into his mouth, she murmured low in her throat. Why had no one ever told her how good this would feel?

"This is what it's like," he whispered huskily, moving his hips against her side, "to have a man desire you."

Birdie was drowning in sensations. So many new sensations, and she wanted to enjoy and remember each one separately, but her mind would fog beyond all reason. "Wait . . ."

"Mmm, I can't—" his mouth took hers in a searing kiss, and she thought her heart would burst "—Birdie . . . little wren."

Her hands slipped across his back, holding him closer as he whispered against her bruised mouth. His hand covered her breast again, massaging gently. Her toes curled, her body grew tauter with molten feeling in the pit of her belly. Moving his mouth to her other nipple, he drew the sensitive peak to attention, relentlessly demanding she respond to him. His hand smoothed over the silky skin of her rib cage as she arched toward him. The muscles of her belly jerked under his hand and she clenched her thighs again and again against the itchy fire inside her.

The movement of her flexing thigh on his inflamed manhood was unbearable. Sliding his hand across her belly, he dipped a finger into the auburn curls, bringing a sharp cry from her. Finding her mouth again with his, he stroked the insides with his tongue, thinking of other moist places he would taste later.

"There's nothing to fear. Open for me, little wren," he murmured into her mouth, caressing her lower lip with the tip of his tongue.

Helplessly Birdie let his hand spread her legs. His knee slid over hers, drawing her leg between his, baring her to his stroking fingers. She was so consumed with flames that she was quaking. Sucking her tongue into his mouth, he filled her maiden tightness with a finger, stroking, drawing moisture from the inside to the outside, opening her, readying her.

Twining her fingers in his crisp hair, she pulled his mouth tighter to hers. She was going to die, she thought, squirming beneath his relentless fingers. She felt herself expand toward him in her nakedness as he moved over her, to grind his body into hers, mixing his scent with hers, marking her, claiming her as his and his alone. Her tortured nipples ached as they ground into the coarse hair on his chest. A groan of helplessness escaped her lips as he murmured into her mouth, low and muffled with unrestrained desire.

"I have been overly long without, Birdie, but I shall try not to cause you more pain than I must."

"Temple...Temple..." she moaned over and over, begging but not sure why. Just please don't let him stop!

And then he was pushing against her...there! Parting her, his body slowly becoming one with hers. As his arms encircled her tightly, he pushed down into her, spreading her, searing her...making her his for all time. For a second, her body stiffened with resistance. She whimpered and tried to move away from him. Hooking her knee with his hand, he pulled it to his waist, whispering gentle encouragement to her. Responding to his words, she opened more to him, and he slipped deeper, filling her, tearing her apart with the size of him. She felt an instant of fear that he was piercing her to her very soul and she would never again be as she was before. She pushed against his weight, but then he was kissing her again and everything was right.

Holding still, Temple gave her time to soften around his size. Muscles stood out taut in his jowl as he fought for control against her tight, moist heat. Her body tensed and pulsed against the invasion. Slowly her lips and body responded to his kisses and patience. Rotating his thrusts, shallow at first, then ever deeper until she was truly his, he reassured her in urgent whispers.

"You are so sweet, Birdie. You are mine forever now. Put your arms about me, Birdie. Ah, little wren!"

Thrusting with a gentle cadence, he slid his hands beneath her bottom to help her find the rhythm, stripping away her shyness and asking with his hands and mouth for her to tell him what gave her pleasure.

Holding him close and stroking his flesh with her hands, Birdie reveled in the closeness she had never shared with another human. Truly she belonged to someone now. Confused by her strong emotions, she turned her face into his neck and felt tears prick her eyes. Darting a tongue out, she tasted the flesh of his shoulder and neck.

Temple drove deep and held her to him with a shudder and an extended groan. Burying his face into her neck, he nipped the tender skin there with his teeth. Slowly the tenseness left his body and he eased from between her legs to lie at her side. She felt weak and drained. Tears of happiness filled her eyes and slid down her face.

"Are you all right?" he whispered, gathering her close. Nuzzling her ear, he felt the wetness and looked up in surprise. "Here, no tears. I promise you it will never be painful like that again. It's just that you are so small and I am...well..."

Smiling at his worry, she turned to snuggle her bottom into the spoon of his body, drawing his hand to place between her heavy breasts. " 'Tis nothing. 'Tis nothing at all," she whispered, luxuriating in the security his arms gave her. She belonged to him now. Now and always.

Burying his face into the sweet-smelling hair, he gently caressed her breasts until her eyelids fluttered and she fell into an exhausted sleep. Without waking her, he pulled her body in close to his, entwining it in the cocoon of his arms and legs. Propping himself on one elbow, he stared down at the sleeping girl. She looked exactly as she had before he had taken her. Peaceful and innocent still. She amazed him. She enthralled him. She was so young to be filled with such passion. In all his experience, he had never known a woman so openly aroused when making love. Truly, innocently aroused, experiencing and responding to the sensations as they occurred, with no performance for effect on her part. Not that he dabbled much with sixteen-year-old maidens, mind you. He smiled at the thought. Perhaps he should have if this one was indicative. He knew she had not peaked, but with each time, he knew her body would learn and soon flower as a woman's. He looked so forward to teaching her.

Easily, so not to wake her, he slid his hand between her breasts. His body flamed with need for her again, expanding to slip between her thighs and nudge the heat there, slick with his essence. He longed to wake her and take her immediately but restrained himself, knowing she would be tender.

Birdie stirred in his arms, and her bottom moved slightly, capturing him, sliding him across tender, sensitive flesh. "Again?" she murmured sleepily, then raised her thigh to grant him full entry. "Oh, yes . . . again."

Chapter Thirteen

"But, Temple, why must you leave today? Surely you could tarry for at least a fortnight." Sir Charles scowled in vexation at his pacing great-nephew. The boy's agitation was contagious. His great-uncle seemed to have caught it not fifteen minutes after the announcement came to ready the traveling coach.

"No! As I have already explained, I have pressing matters to attend in London," Temple said with strained patience, yet again. "We will depart as soon as the bags can be prepared."

"You know you should not leave until I can provide you with outriders. They will be back from Buncrana in a matter of days. What can that possibly cost you?" Sir Charles demanded, rapping his cane on the floor in anger.

"It will cost me the ship!" Temple stated rather loudly. "I have told you of the captain's schedule for departure from Buncrana. The breath of winter is in the air this very moment and you know what that means. It's this ship or none!" Returning to stand on widespread legs before the fire, he glared in irritation at all this fuss. "You are aware as I am, Uncle, that once the snow and ice strike this godforsaken place, there will be no traveling until the spring thaw. Is that your wish? To see us bound? I would be eating my pistol in that fortnight you just mentioned!"

Sir Charles threw up his hands in despair. "Bah! There was never any talking sense to you, Templeton! Just as bullheaded as your father..."

Again pacing the length of the room, Temple raked his hand through his black hair. Enough of this! He wished to be back in London as soon as possible. Not only was there Sophia to contend with over this hasty marriage, but he wished to place his child bride in a more familiar setting, to view his situation with a sane mind. For it would seem his mind and his body were strangers to him. With a wry sneer, he mused, Whoever would have thought something so manageable and well thought out as his life could have turned on him with such a vengeance in just twelve short hours? But then, whoever would have expected Birdie to be so sweet, so beautiful and so passionate that in the course of one wedding night she had quite touched his heart. He was thoroughly confused about the entire affair. He declined to call it love!

Sir Charles refused to be denied what he considered a rational answer to this idiotic idea of rushing off to Buncrana this very minute. Rapping on the floor again with the polished ironwood cane and straining his weak voice with some semblance of the authoritative tone it used to carry, he stormed down the length of the room.

"What would be so wrong, I ask you, with staying here at Blanballyhaven for one month, two months... or, for that matter, the entire winter? In my opinion, it might do you a world of good to avoid that way of life permanently." The old man's voice cracked as it rose in pitch to an almost hysterical level. "That's my opinion, you hear?"

Pressed beyond endurance by the marquis's harping, Temple replied with a touch of sarcasm, "With all due respect, Uncle, in matters concerning myself and Lady Daine, I fear my opinion must carry the bulk of weight." Turning his back on his great-uncle, as well as the discussion, Temple placed a hand on the windowframe and stared moodily out to the ocean, though in truth, it was almost impossible to distinguish gray mist from gray water.

His thoughts immediately returned to this morning and his bride. Her shy, hesitant smile and pretty blush when she had first awakened to find herself cradled in his arms had been expected. The perfect response for a new bride. Then to confound him ever so much, she had leapt from the bed and padded to the dressing room, wonderfully naked and totally unconcerned by his delighted stare, to retrieve a breakfast tray placed there by her maid. Such a wonderful contradiction! The very thought of her small body with its rounded curves brought a groan and a quickening of his body. He could charge up the stairs right now to take her back to the bed, knowing full well she would welcome him with a laugh and open arms. Never had he been so aroused by a woman, and he truly doubted he would ever tire of her. Her every movement, every thought, were a marvel to him.

Swinging from the window, he again raked his hand through his hair and paced the room. Lord, what was wrong with him? He was acting like a lovesick knife boy! And over a mere slip of a girl. A slum child, no less! It should be no different than bedding a willing upstairs maid. Temple gritted his teeth together. Damn! Why should these sudden and devastating feelings for a wench overtake him now? He refused to admit he might be in love with this captivating little chit. There wasn't a woman alive that could snare his heart on a permanent basis. He had boasted of that at any time.

And if there just possibly was such a woman, she certainly wouldn't be this small figure of an unsophisticated girl with red ringlets and merry brown eyes. A girl with a decided propensity toward trouble . . . a romp, a hoyden, a guileless chit with an unruly mouth, without the faintest notion of how to go on in the circles he inhabited. Also, he suspected ruefully, the devil's own temper reigned in that luscious little head of hers, and it was more than likely that she would keep him in hot water for the rest of his life. But that did not matter. At present, nothing mattered except that she consent to spend the rest of his life with him.

That unbidden thought surprised him. What hold had she on him that he would mentally concoct a thought like that! Obviously he was only reacting to the deprivation of interesting female company for longer than he was used to, then swept along by Birdie's sweetness. Once he was at Daine Hall in Grosvenor Square, his thoughts would return to normal. If the pleasure of his little bride began to pall, he would fall back upon the plan to have her live quietly at Stannisburn while he maintained his London residence.

In the meantime, he was truly looking forward to her introduction into society. How her beauty would sparkle. He wished to drape her in sumptuous satins and glittering diamonds. He wished to take her to the opera, the theater, the symphony. There was an entirely different side of London to show her. A side of silks and satins, music and dancing. Blast! What was wrong with him? One moment he was damning her for unsophistication and thinking what a disgrace she'd be in society, and the next he could not wait to put her there! Hell's teeth! He was truly bewitched!

Immediately his mind's eye flashed back to last night. Having left the bed to fetch the wine bottle and light the other three candles, he had returned to find her sneaking glances at his body before casting down her eyes demurely and pulling the linens to her chin. Standing beside the bed, he had teased her.

"Come, Birdie. Aren't you even a little bit curious? Look at me." She had flipped the cover over her head and turned her back to him, he remembered with a tender smile now. Easing under the covers with her, he had turned her toward him and cradled her in his arms. "No secrets between us, Lady Daine. Especially not here!" Drawing her tightly against him, he had tried to explain.

"There are things, so many wonderful things we are going to discover together. Things that will bring a blush to your pretty little cheeks, but only until you lose yourself in the pleasure of them. Nothing is terrible or ugly between a husband and wife. Nothing is forbidden." Throwing the counterpane back, he had bared her soft curves to the candlelight and his eyes.

"The candles!"

"In our bed, Birdie, nothing that brings pleasure is forbidden." Stroking his hand down the smooth length of her body, he dipped into every crease and curve on the tour. "Touching you gives me great pleasure. I want the same for you." Taking her hand, he pressed the palm to his lips, then placed it on his chest. "Touch me, little wren."

With her eyes wide in wonder, she had caressed the ridges of muscle in his fur-covered chest. Tentatively stroking his brown nipple, she had laughed when it crinkled the same as hers. She felt the strength of his back, and her small hand had even caressed the rise of his hip and buttocks, but had slipped away when he had rolled onto his back.

"Don't stop there," he had admonished her. She had colored so prettily, her cheeks flushing pink.

"I cannot, Temple," she had whispered. "I do not know how you want to be touched."

"Then I shall show you."

Taking her hand, he had kissed her fingers one by one, then smoothed them over his chest, guiding her hand over his belly, past the black mat there to encircle him gently. God, the feel of her hand holding him, stroking his heat. Clearing his throat, he jammed his hands into the pockets of his pantaloons.

"Dwell on something else, man!" he cautioned himself. "Or the departure will have to be postponed for a more pleasurable trip back to bed!" Narrowing his eyes in serious thought, he resumed his distracted pacing.

Sir Charles watched his pacing, muttering great-nephew with a sinking heart. Something was terribly wrong. The night must not have gone well or he wouldn't be so eager to quit the place. To drag Birdie into the morning mist in such a hurry to return to London was not only unseemly but too dangerous. Much, much too dangerous. Somehow he must make the boy see logic.

"Temple . . ."

"All 'tis ready, my lord," Hudson announced from the door, closely followed by Birdie, drawing her gloves from her reticule. Moving quickly to drop upon her knees beside Sir Charles, she buried her face in the woolly robe wrapped around his legs.

"Here, here! What's this?" He placed a hand on the fur toque that sat snug over her russet curls in the awkward manner of most men when confronted with a show of womanly emotion. "It's not the end of the world, my dear. I shall see you before the season is gone, for I must return to witness your triumph in society, now mustn't I?"

Raising a tear-streaked face to him, she studied his dear old face as if to memorize it for all time. "I shall miss you so, Sir Charles. I owe you my life."

Sir Charles searched her face for signs of mistreatment, for any sign that told him he should demand Temple leave the girl with him. But the only signs he read were her misery at their parting.

"Come, Birdie, we should be off," Temple announced. He lifted her to her feet with a stern hand beneath her elbow.

Sir Charles had so wanted to see the two of them together day after day, to be sure Birdie was happy. To have them leave so soon, and Birdie in tears, was too much for the old man. Tears gathered in his weak eyes and eased down his cheeks. Was he never to know if he had made the best decision for her? He tried once more to dissuade his great-nephew from this rash and reckless act.

"Temple, too much of the journey will be in darkness. You are being reckless. At least, let Birdie come with me in the spring, if you must be so damned foolish to risk your own neck—"

"Nay, Sir Charles," Birdie interrupted him. With a tender smile at Temple, she dropped a kiss on the old man's cheek and whispered in his ear, "Mayhap there will be a babe begun when you come home in the spring."

The look of happiness on her lovely face heartened the old man and he knew he could protest no more. She belonged to his great-nephew now and it was his own doing. No, he could protest no more. She was another man's wife.

Travers arrived to help the old marquis to his feet. Mrs. Fitz-waters stood near the foot of the stairs to direct the footmen carrying case after case from her ladyship's bedchamber. Though it had never been mentioned, Birdie hoped Sir Charles would move his entire household back to Daine Hall in the spring. She was terrified to think of him alone at Blanballyhaven. Terrified that his ill health was more serious than he allowed, and he would not endure the harsh winter. Drying her tears, she turned sad eyes from the sight of his struggle to rise. Moving to stand beside Mrs. Fitz-waters, she set about drawing on her gloves.

"Have Travers make him come with you in the spring, Libby?"

Mrs. Fitzwaters snorted, then gave her a stern look from the great height of her straight nose. "Mr. Travers will have enough to do to organize himself. I shall see to his lordship personally."

"Do what you think best, Libby."

"I always do what I think is for the best, my lady. As you know, I am not one to leave things to the last minute . . . as with the wedding."

Watching Temple's tall figure darken the doorway as he directed workmen, Birdie felt her heart give a lurch. He was her husband. Her husband! She thought to pinch herself. "Wedding, Libby?" she asked absently.

"I am to wed Mr. Travers, sinful lecher though he is, on the day after Christmas, my lady."

Birdie spun with a wide smile for the housekeeper. "Oh, Libby! Why didn't you tell me a date had been set?"

Mrs. Fitzwaters fixed Birdie with a meaningful look. "I was under the impression that I just did."

"I do so wish you the greatest happiness, Libby. And Travers, too."

"Humph! That remains to be seen. Mr. Travers, as I have repeatedly told him, is a wicked man, too inclined to look upon the wine bottle as his friend. But if my influence can save him from the fires of damnation, then I've no doubt we will be tolerably happy."

Feeling a pang of pity for the unfortunate Travers, Birdie thought over her own happiness and unwisely offered a bit of advice. "Be kind to him, Libby. Poor Travers loves you so."

Mrs. Fitzwaters's lips pursed disapprovingly. "Poor Travers, indeed! Rest easy, my lady. If the man merits kindness, you may be sure he will receive it."

Birdie looked at her wonderingly. "I never know what to make of you, Libby. You seem so cold and hard, but . . . you do love Travers, don't you?"

"That is for me to know, my lady." Mrs. Fitzwaters directed a severe look at Birdie. "I am not for wearing my heart on my sleeve, unlike someone I could mention."

Birdie dropped her eyes and flushed pink in confusion. Were her feelings truly so evident? She glanced again at Temple's elegant, commanding figure in the doorway. Yes, she supposed they were, for even now she could feel herself soften and turn to mush inside. Yes, she supposed her eyes were like mirrors to the love that filled her heart. But was that such a bad thing?

"Lib, my dove?" Travers hurried to them. "Her lordship says they are ready for her ladyship and her personal's case." Gazing up at his light of love, Travers waited patiently for her answer.

"Well, Mr. Travers, her ladyship is right in front of you. Here is her case," admonished Mrs. Fitzwaters. "And do not call me Lib."

With a grim shake of her head, Birdie was thankful that the rapid departure had, at least, saved her the unpleasantness of traveling in close quarters with this volatile pair.

The chaise stood in the yard with a restive team of four bright chestnuts. The air smelled of damp horseflesh and fresh morning mists from the mountains. She breathed deeply and closed her eyes with a smile. Dear Blanballyhaven, how she would miss it. With the last of the baggage being lashed to the boot, she gave hurried kisses and hugs to Mattie, Mrs. Fitzwaters and Franny.

"Franny, I will see you in London. Libby, you make her come!"

"I will not let ye down, my lady. 'Twill be there, I will!" the ruddy-faced girl wailed, hugging her tight and blubbering into a wadded hankie.

Birdie gently wrapped her arms around the slumping shoulders of Sir Charles. Travers stood close to support the old man should he require it.

"You should not be out here without your chair. It is no good for you to be standing so long in the mists," she scolded him gently, biting back tears that threatened to overwhelm her. Temple came to stand behind her.

"You would scold me, my dear?" Sir Charles teased, cupping her cheek in the palm of his hand. "Temple, it will be a long trip with one such as this one." Gathering her into his trembling arms, he squeezed her tight. "Be happy, my love. Be happy." The familiar smell of musty wool, tobacco and hair wax filled her nostrils before he set her firmly from him. "Now, go!"

Gathering up the hem of her pelisse, Birdie mounted the iron steps and ducked into the chaise. A low rumbling came from the north. She turned her teary gaze to the young postilion, who looked up at the early morning skies. Sullen clouds rolled ominously behind the mist, threatening to turn into hard rain. Birdie sank back against the musty seat squabs facing the horses. The chaise swayed under Temple's weight as he followed her inside and latched the door behind him. Immediately the chaise rocked forward.

Leaning out one last time, Birdie waved to the gathering of people until the trees and wall bordering the yard obliterated them. Down the chaise flew to gain speed for the climb before them. She sank back and loosened the ribbons under her chin so that she could push the toque back. Temple watched her for a moment in silence, then he leaned forward and drew her to his side. Going willingly, Birdie raised wet eyes to him. He drew her mouth to his as his arm locked her to his side. Savoring the sweetness, he kissed her soulfully, lingeringly, setting her heart beating like that of a wild creature ensnared. For truly, she was ensnared by this man, her husband, her heart, body and soul.

"Ah, wife," he murmured against her mouth. "It will be a time before we have a warm bed beneath us. I have no idea how I shall manage to keep my hands from beneath your skirts the whole of this day."

Birdie sighed and snuggled against him. Turning her head, she could see Blanballyhaven, shadowy in the mist, as they topped the opposite rise. Condor drew in the horses momentarily as if knowing Birdie would desire this last look. Mystically it rose in the mists and the very sight brought fresh tears.

"Hey, little wren," Temple jested as he wiped them away. "No more tears, or I shall think you have no wish to be with me."

"Oh, no!" She rushed to reassure him. He chuckled and nestled her back to his chest, his arm around her pressing against her breasts. Birdie laid her head back on his shoulder and tried to explain her loss. "It is Sir Charles I weep for. He is not well and I fear I shall never see him again. I feel all sixes and sevens. I am sad, but I am happy, too."

A whip cracked and the chaise lurched forward with axles squealing in protest. The wheels slowly gathered speed and settled into a dull humming complaint, carrying her away from Blanballyhaven.

Chapter Fourteen

Temple was silent, for there was nothing to say in the face of her sorrow at leaving the only true home she had ever known. As the tears slipped down her cheeks, he gathered her even closer. Slipping the toque from her head, he tossed it to the other seat, burying his face in her hair. The fine mist gave way to rain thumping on the roof, which would turn to snow as they climbed higher. Birdie felt for Condor and the young postilion as she sleepily listened to the pattern of sound.

"Temple, tell me of our home in London," she whispered.

"Well, let's see. There's Daine Hall, a lavish little four-story town house, though large enough. It sits in Grosvenor Square with a park in the center where nannies walk with their charges on clement days."

The thought of her babies being taken to the park warmed Birdie. She longed for children. Lots of children. First would be a boy named Charles. And then a small daughter called Amaryllis. The third would be Henry, after his handsome father.... Temple continued.

"Stannisburn is a great rambling castle of a place. Once an abbey, then refurbished as the royal summer house, it was given to the Charlton family for services rendered the crown. Through marriage it came into the Daine family, with the stipulation that the unworthy bridegroom add Charlton behind his sire name of Daine. Hence a branch of the family called Daine-Charlton—as I will become once Uncle Charles has passed and I succeed. So, my lovely lady, do not become too used to the name of Lady Daine, for it will soon be Lady Daine-Charlton, Marquise of Stannisburn."

"To go from no name to so many," murmured Birdie, bewildered. "What of your father? And mother? Are there no brothers or sisters?"

"Stannisburn first. It is a wonderful, picturesque, typical English country house. Which, my dear, means there's a lake in the front, a great wooded park in the rear, and it looks great in the rain," he teased, kissing her temple as punctuation. "And for the other, my mother died when I was quite young. I barely remember her. I was firstborn and my only sibling perished with her at birth. My father took to drink and warm women, but never remarried. I spent every year in a boarding school from the age of six on. He was killed when I was in Oxford . . . riding accident. So no brothers or sisters. What of you, my dear?" Silence rang loud through the chaise. Birdie tensed and sat away from him as he spoke again. "I am sorry, Birdie. I did not think."

"'Tis quite all right. Indeed, I must get used to the questions, for I fear there will be a multitude of them from a race of people who value bloodlines so very much. And I fear you will suffer embarrassment, also, my lord husband, for your wife's pedigree is definitely a mystery. Besides that fact, I have managed to steal the most eligible man of their set from beneath their very stiff noses."

Temple watched her reach for her personals case and, releasing the catch, open the fine leather lid. "Really, Birdie, while I will admit they can be stuffy about such things, I doubt—"

Bringing forth a garnet velvet jewelry pouch tied with deep green, cross-grained ribbons, she drew out the treasured miniature. "This is my mother. Her name was Amaryllis and she died when I was five or so." She carefully handed it to Temple. "I never knew her last name or anything of her family. But I am positive she was a lady of quality. All I know of my father is her admonishment that he was a terrible man and I should never seek him out."

Temple studied the miniature, quickly coming to the same conclusion as Sir Charles. It was an expensive piece and obviously done by a master. The resemblance was great, especially about the mouth and chin. Something stirred inside his memory.

"I would swear I know her. She is familiar for some reason," he mused aloud. His brow furrowed in thought. "I have seen her somewhere."

Birdie's eyes grew huge. Breathlessly, she exclaimed, "Do you truly think you have see her? Quickly, tell me! I would wish for nothing else than to know who I am . . . and to know what terrible thing happened to her!"

"She could not have been much older than yourself when this was painted," he pondered, peering intently into the eyes of the miniature. "But I can't for the life of me remember or think what but—" Glancing up at Birdie's expectant face, he kissed her. "Give me time, little wren, and I am sure I shall put a name or place…or something to this face.''

Birdie tried to hide her disappointment as she wrapped the miniature back into its velvet-and-satin pouch. With a sigh, she thrust the pouch into her reticule.

Sorry for her disappointment, Temple took her by the hand. ''I will really try to remember, Birdie. Just a little more patience,'' he promised, then sought to distract her. Shifting her to the seat opposite, he flipped the quilted curtains over the windows and adjusted the little ember heater at their feet. ''Come. We'll play a game to pass the time,'' he said, pushing Birdie straight against the squabs. ''You just sit there quietly. Lean back and relax.''

''I am not very good at games,'' Birdie cautioned, her dark eyebrows drawing down with the furrowing of her brow.

''This is one I am sure you shall be very good at, indeed,'' he assured her with a wicked grin. ''Now, here are the rules. You must sit very still, put your hands on the seat at your sides…there, don't raise them and sit very still. If you move, you will lose the game.'' Leaning back against his seat, and crossing his buckskin-clad legs in a casual manner, he studied her.

Birdie sat very straight and stared at his face expectantly. Her brown eyes danced in merriment and her lovely mouth twitched with the effort of containing her smile. Temple's gray eyes roamed over her face, drinking in the smooth curves, the delicate brows, the sooty lashes framing sherry brown eyes. Leaning forward, he began to unbutton her fawn wool pelisse, clumsily taking his own sweet time with much brushing of her breasts.

''Temple!'' She giggled, quickly discerning the nature of his game.

''Don't move or you lose,'' he cautioned, wagging a finger beneath her nose. ''And you do not want to lose, as the forfeit will be expensive.''

Flipping the pelisse back on either side, he bared the soft fawn merino gown beneath, fitted tightly to her diaphragm, a prim tatted collar around her throat. Reclining again, he allowed his eyes the pleasure of the generous swells of her bosom. With his imagination, he could see the creamy flesh topped by pink nipples that hardened so nicely when he suckled them. He could see her breath quickening by the rise and fall of her breasts. Leaning forward again, he picked up one small booted foot in his hand and, flexing her knee, set it on the seat beside him. Relaxing back, he caressed the foot and ankle through the thin leather.

"Cor, man!" Birdie gasped and giggled, straining to remain motionless. "Don't be thinking you can take advantage of my person through the guise of a bloody game!"

"What have we here?" Temple's eyebrows climbed to his hairline as he pulled a thin blade from the leather strip tied to her ankle. Holding it aloft, he tested the edge with his thumb and found it very sharp. "My lady wife travels armed?"

"Aye, 'tis a habit to wear it. A lady never knows when a so-called gentleman will think to take unfair advantage."

"Can you use it? Or is it only for threatening?" he teased, slipping it back into its hiding place, caressing her calf as he did so.

"Condor taught me to use it, so you had best beware of what you're about beneath my skirts, my fine laddie. Have you not been threatened with bodily harm by a lady before, what with your lecherous ways?"

"Not once!" he declared with a wicked grin, placing her other foot outside his opposite thigh. With a devilish grin, he ran his hands up her silk-covered calves to her knees.

"Temple!" she gasped, making a move to close her knees in embarrassment.

"Don't move!" he ordered sharply. "Or you pay forfeit." Abruptly he tossed her skirts up to her waist. She squealed in surprise and clamped her knees together. Then, as he shook his finger at her in admonishment, she slowly relaxed them again with a giggle. He leaned back and looked at her.

"And now," he mused, "about your speech." Fingering the thin skin of her half boots, he eased his eyes up her legs. "While I do not mind in the least what you say when we are in private . . ." He could see the tops of her black silk stockings and the pink ribbons tying them above her knees. There was a delicious span of white thigh before his gaze reached the thin, linen pantalets stretched tightly between her legs, hinting at a darker shadow beneath. My God! She was delectable. A groan escaped him. "Er, I do think we should work on better control in public. Mustn't shock the Royals, now, must we?" Exerting a slight pressure on her ankles with his hands, he opened her knees a bit wider. "What would you say, just a cue, mind you, whenever you seem about to lose your proper English, I will, say, tweak your right nipple—" quickly leaning forward, he demonstrated "—just to remind you!"

"C-cad!" she stammered. "That would m-most definitely take their minds off my grammar." Birdie felt herself moisten and trembled under his heated gaze. Being wed to this man was going to be a glorious romp. She saw him squirm in his seat and adjust the tightness of his trousers, never taking his eyes from her.

"Oh, my dear! I give you my word of honor that they would find it amusing . . . very amusing, indeed."

"Would that be your word as a gentleman, my lord husband?"

"Oh, absolutely, my lady wife!" Again she gave in to the slight pressure on her ankles.

"Th-then I fear I shall require someone else's word, for you, my lord husband, are no . . . oh!"

So engrossed were they in their game, they did not readily respond to a shout from the top of the chaise and the quickening of pace and the pounding of hooves. Suddenly the chaise bounded into the air, roughly jolting Birdie from her seat and into Temple's arms. The chaise landed hard, with a sharp crack of the axle, and slewed sideways. Temple grabbed the hand strap set in the ceiling with one hand and held tightly to Birdie, even as the chaise turned over. Violently flung from their seats, they piled hard atop each other as the chaise settled on its side. Both lay still for a moment, stunned.

A shot rang out in the rain, followed by a groan of pain. The door above their heads jerked open and Birdie blinked as raindrops struck her face. A man's head and shoulders almost obliterated what little light the gray day provided. She was unable to discern his face, merely his blackened silhouette.

"Be ye all right, me lassie?" he called down.

Birdie put her hand on the seat beside her and tried to take some of her weight from the strangely quiet Temple. Under her flattened fingers, broken glass shifted, pricking her hand. Without heeding the stinging pain, she levered herself off him. He groaned and passed a shaking hand over his forehead.

"Temple?"

"If ye give me yer hand, me lassie, I will pull ye out," came the voice over her head again. "Just reach up to me now."

Shakily gaining her feet, Birdie reached up to the man's outstretched hands. With another grunt, Temple began to lever himself into an upright position, also. Standing on the side of the overturned chaise, the man lifted her out, rudely groping her breasts in the process. As soon as she was sitting on the side of the chaise, Birdie wrenched her body from his grasp with a scalding frown at his gall. Temple's head appeared over the door. Blood seeped down the side of his handsome face from a deep gash over one eye.

Leaping to the ground, Birdie quickly surveyed the scene, trying to understand what had happened. The chaise lay on its side and baggage was strewn across the mud. One of her portmanteaus had been thrown from the top and had opened on impact.

Her lacy shifts, gleaming white in the gray rain, had tumbled in the wet roadway to be trampled beneath the horses' hooves. The uneasy team danced softly on the soaked ground, dragging the overturned chaise a few feet. With her heart in her mouth, she put her hand out to the nearest horse. Dear, God, don't let them bolt. Not with Temple inside and hurt. One of the riders moved to the horses' heads and grasped the leathers. Dear Condor lay on the ground with blood spreading ever wider across his back. Pain tore through her chest at the loss of the man who had so patiently taught her to ride. Mattie's son. How she would grieve. Temple jumped unsteadily to the ground beside her and gathered her into his arms.

"Birdie, are you hurt?" he asked with a slight slur. Pulling a handkerchief from his waistcoat, he held it tightly to his forehead, the cloth startlingly white against the sun-browned skin of his face. Without waiting for an answer, he shoved her behind him and faced the men. "What is the meaning of this outrage?"

Besides the two men on foot, three others sat their horses on the far side of the chaise. All the men wore rough, deeply soiled clothing and expressions of varied greedy amusement. Birdie kept her attention on the tallest, most formidable-looking of them. He boldly sat a heavy-bodied bay stallion and sported an open sneer on his face. It seemed reasonable to assume he was the leader of this ragged group of malcontents.

"Yer money and yer jewels!" one rider, a thin monkey-faced man, demanded in a high-pitched voice. He erupted with a cackle of laughter at his own idea of a prank. Birdie shuddered and pulled the pelisse tighter about her.

Temple weaved on his feet, his face ashen against the startling claret of the blood flowing freely from the deep gash on his forehead. Nevertheless, he stood straight and his voice still carried authority as he attempted to barter. "I will give you what money we carry. But leave us the chaise horses so we might reach Buncrana."

"I think ye can barely maintain yer feet, English," the tall man said in a soft voice. "I think I must shoot ye here and save the trouble of hanging ye later."

"The devil, you say!" Temple's voice was weak and Birdie feared for him. He was badly shaken and perhaps grievously injured, as well. She steadied him with her arm. What were they talking about? Hanging?

The tall man rode around the chaise, crowding the stallion close to Birdie and Temple. Temple began to sag to the ground as he lost consciousness, carrying Birdie with him. She cried out, but there was no one to help her. Her gaze darted to Condor, then looked around for the young postilion. Pray God, he had gotten away. There was no one to help her. Somehow she must save Temple...and herself. Standing straight, guarding her husband, she squared her shoulders and refused to be cowed by these ruffians. Hadn't she faced worse before? Perhaps, but never had she felt so helpless.

She snapped her head up to stare into the eyes of the tall rebel. He was a handsome brute, if unkempt, and sat the horse with an ease that made him and the magnificent beast seem as one. Again he crowded the horse close. So close Birdie could smell the sweat from his lathered hide. She put out a hand to keep the horse from pushing her to the side of the chaise and trampling Temple.

"What say ye, Lady English?" he taunted slyly. "What would ye be bartering for yer man's life?"

"I say 'tis a bloody shame when an Irishman takes to the road." She threw the words out at him, her tone scalding and her brogue thick. "Do ye not know yer ancestors would hide their faces in shame at the sight of ye?"

Monkey-face rode closer to the leader. "Let's be done with this and away from here. Kill the woman and leave the man to fare as he will against the wolves. Paddy, cut the horses out of their traces."

The old man screeched at this. "Nay! Don't be wasting young flesh! I say we be taking the woman with us as a bed warmer!"

Birdie felt a terror she could not control for long. She thought of the knife in her boot. She would use the knife on herself before she became anyone's whore. Stepping astride Temple, Birdie shielded him with her skirt. She faced the tall man in hopes he was the leader and not the monkey-faced one. Her heaving breath knotted in her throat and she forced her tight voice out in a scream of defiance. "If ye be free Irishmen, then I spit on me name and me blood, too."

She found herself locked in a stare with the tall rebel. In his eyes there was a wildness that hinted at madness. Finally he spoke, breaking the silence. "And what be your name, lass?"

Searching quickly for something...anything...that would stop the men from doing murder, she spat at him. " 'Tis O'Donnell! Birdie O'Donnell!"

The man straightened in the saddle immediately. The name apparently meant something to him. "We take 'em both," he ordered.

Breathing a giant sigh of relief for the time bought with her lie, Birdie knelt beside the unconscious Temple to press her fingers against the faint pulse at the base of his throat. Thank God, she had guessed right. Not that she wanted to go with them, but it seemed the only way they would leave them here was to end their lives first.

Monkey-face wheeled his horse abruptly and screamed out in rage, "Damn it, Rory! Ye'll not be taking that woman anywhere!" Twisting suddenly, he raised his rifle and took aim at Birdie. Her heart stopped cold in her chest. He meant to shoot her. Without thinking of possible repercussions from her actions, she snatched the knife from her boot. With a quick underhanded flip, she threw it at Monkey-face. Her world stood still. All sound disappeared except the horrible gurgling he made, one hand clawing at the knife hilt protruding from his throat. Slowly he toppled from his horse and lay twisted in the mud. No one moved. Then, guns were raised and there was an ugly shout. The uneasy chaise horses shifted the carriage a few feet again, tossing their heads and snorting.

"No! Please, God, no," Birdie exclaimed softly. Suddenly she began to tremble, shaking to her very bones. She had gone too far. She could read murder in their furious faces. Desperately she searched the face of the tall man on the bay stallion. He seemed her only hope.

The rebel narrowed his eyes and stared at her. She held her breath. Slowly, he swung down from the dancing bay and stepped over the dead man. He calmly retrieved her knife. Wiping the bloody blade unceremoniously on the still chest, he slipped it into his pocket.

"The lass will ride John Ditty's horse. Seems she bought it. Throw the man over one of the carriage horses and let's leave this place."

The other men slowly moved to carry out his orders, casting sidelong glances at Birdie and muttering beneath their breath. She ignored them as best she could. Granting them the treatment a lady would any servant.

Chapter Fifteen

The rain that had pounded the track to mud lower down the mountain turned to white snowflakes the size of Birdie's hand as they rode higher. They rode in single file, the tall man on the bay in the lead, then Birdie. Somewhere behind her Temple had been slung head down over the back of one of the chaise horses. Still unconscious and, at least for now, alive, but Birdie could not say for how long. Though it was barely afternoon, the gray sky heavy with snow brought darkness early.

Not the first hour had passed before Birdie's thighs were rubbed tender and stinging from the stiff, ill-kept leather of the saddle. Her back ached from the rough gait of the animal. Boulders and rocks, fast disappearing beneath the heavy snowfall, were strewn on the path beneath the horse's hooves and gaunt fills loomed around them. They climbed higher and higher. A mood of foreboding was in the air and Birdie urged her old mount forward in an effort to reach a destination and end this misery.

"Easy lass," the tall man cautioned. " 'Tis not a goat ye ride. The footing be treacherous here."

"Aye," she mumbled through lips stiff with cold. She knew the man's words were wise for the drop was formidable. Never had she been so cold and miserable. Perhaps her memory was faulty, but even barefoot in Haymarket come January, she hadn't been this cold. She could not stop herself from asking, "How much farther?"

"Through the glen and yon forest," he called, pointing the way. "From the hills beyond there, we should be able to see Glencolumbkille."

Worried about Temple and heartened by the rebel's willingness to talk to her, she ventured to ask, "Please, 'tis not too much to ask, I would know of me man. 'Twould not hold ye back more than a moment.''

Pulling the bay around, he brought the party to a halt. Casting his narrowed eyes over Birdie's worried face, he called to the man leading the chaise horse. "Paddy! The man?''

" 'Tis awake and cussing, Rory.''

"Please, if his nob is cracked, hanging head down 'twill do him no good.'' She begged, putting pleading into her eyes, "Let him ride double with me.''

"Bring the man up, Paddy,'' he called again, without taking his eyes off Birdie's face. "He'll ride the lass's horse.'' With a sigh, Birdie breathed a silent, *Thank God!* "The lass will ride with me.''

Her head snapped around to stare at the tall man's sneering face. "Th-that will n-not do,'' she stammered. "I can go double with me man.''

"Ye'll ride with me if you want yer man to be riding head up,'' he said, a touch of steel in his voice. "Make up yer mind, lass, for we'll not stop again.''

She gave him a curt nod and slid down the horse's side. Dropping her eyes from the piercing blue ones, she shuddered at their look of avid interest. Pray, God, she was able to carry on this hoax long enough to gain freedom for both Temple and her.

Roughly shoving Temple forward with a laugh, the old man turned back to his own horse. Rushing to Temple, Birdie grabbed his arm to support him. His head was down and his walk shaky, but at least he was conscious. Dried and fresh blood matted his hair on his forehead and along one side of his face to stain his neckcloth a rusty brown. The wound looked terrible, and Birdie feared for him.

"Birdie,'' Temple whispered weakly. "Are you . . .''

"I'm fine, Temple. Here, take this horse. 'Twill probably die under you before he reaches fodder, but at least you'll be riding upright.'' Forcing a light tone into her voice, she thought to ease his worry. Dragging himself into the saddle, he looked down at Birdie. She could see fever and pain raging in his eyes. He braced himself upright with both hands, his eyes glazed, his breathing rapid, and sweat rolled down his face despite the cold.

"Hang on, darling. It can't be much farther,'' she whispered to him, but was unsure he heard. She knotted the leathers to the saddle horn and prayed the old horse would follow the other's lead without guidance, for Temple was not capable of directing him otherwise.

"Enough dawdling, lass. Come here!'' Rory shouted to her.

In the hopes she could deter trouble with a willingness to comply, she ran to the side of the bay. Reaching a hand to turn the stirrup, she squealed in surprise to suddenly find herself lifted by a hard arm around her waist. The excitable stallion sidled dangerously close to the drop. Rory lifted her in one swoop onto the saddle before him with a snort of laughter. Sliding his arm around her to hold the reins, he laid his other hand possessively upon her belly. Shoving at the rock-hard arm, she cursed him without thinking.

"Do not be thinking ye can manhandle me, Irish scum!" she taunted, forgetting for a moment that she needed his protection.

With a deep laugh, he whispered into her ear, "Patience, me pretty lassie. We can play yer games in the warmth of a cabin in just a few hours."

Instantly ceasing her struggles, she stared straight ahead. Inciting this man to anger would not get Temple to a warm haven any faster. And that must be her priority above all else. With a laugh, the rebel nudged the stallion forward. Looking straight ahead, she concentrated on the rhythm of the horse's hooves. The cadence drummed in her mind and she allowed it to numb her as a defense against her fears. Finally, exhausted, she sagged back against the strong chest and let her mind go blank. She slept.

Suddenly the drumming stopped, and Birdie came instantly awake. Twisting, she attempted to see behind them, to see if Temple was still upright, but was unable to see beyond the Irishman's wide shoulders. Leaving the narrow, rocky path, they moved into high grass that, mixed with snow, muffled the horses' hoofbeats. The bay was urged into a trot and then a canter. In less than an hour they burst through a line of trees and climbed a steep ridge. They reined up at the ridge's peak.

"There!" The word thundered in her ear. Birdie followed the spiraling smoke of a peat fire to its source. Leaning against the back of a mountain, forbidding and gloomy, was a small grouping of buildings. "Glencolumbkille," the man's voice rumbled in his chest, then he set the stallion down the other side of the ridge.

As they drew near, Birdie saw that it was a small, shabby town of hovels and poverty. The pounding of hooves brought people from the warmth of their fires to stare. Weak candlelight behind them turned them into pale silhouettes in their doorways and windows. Glencolumbkille may have once been a thriving town, but now the only activity came from a public house, which rattled music and noise into the otherwise quiet street.

Thankfully, they moved past this and toward a lane of bow houses, all alike even to the poles on their upper windowsills, hanging forgotten laundry, frozen stiff in the cold. Birdie shuddered. If these houses had ever had grace and beauty, age and weather had robbed them of it. They tottered like old men, bent under the weight of families, all gathered now in the doorways. Mattie had been a child here. These were the streets where she had played. These were the houses where she had lived. Birdie shuddered again.

The blowing stallion pulled up before a cabin, somewhat more substantial than the others, with a gated fence and a small-paned window. Throwing a leg over the stallion's back, the man vaulted to the ground, then turned to lift Birdie down. Holding her close, he slid her body the length of his, sneering at her discomfort. Ignoring him as best she could, she looked around but did not see Temple or the others.

"Where did ye take me husband?" she demanded.

"Do not be concerning yerself about that one no more," he snorted, spinning to march on the cabin.

Birdie's legs, stiff from the long ride in the cold, barely supported her. Stumbling, she followed the rebel to the door of the house. There was no light, no warmth from a cheery fireplace to invite her inside, so she wearily leaned against the doorjamb and listened to him fumbling in the dark.

"Damn woman let the fire go out!" he bellowed. The sound of wooden furniture being kicked across the room was followed by another snort of anger.

The place smelled of wood rot and overcrowding and poverty. Birdie remembered the smells well. All smells of her childhood. The weak light, when it came, did little to dispel the horror of the place. A table of sorts stood in the middle of the room with a stool drawn up to it. The mate lay against the far wall, where the vicious kick had sent it. A stone hearth, cold and black, took up one entire wall. Through a door in the back wall, she could make out the dim shape of a bed. No curtains softened the windows. No rug warmed the floor.

"Get in here! Sit," he ordered, kicking the stool from the table. "And do not be moving until I come back for ye."

Cautiously, Birdie slid onto the stool at the table. Rory left with a slam of the door and a roared oath. Instantly, she was off the stool and through the door leading to the sleeping chamber. Unable to see anything in the dark, she retreated to the main room for the candle. Halting for just a second, until she heard the horse move rapidly down the lane, she dashed into the little room at the back. Tiny and square, it held nothing more than a narrow bed and a row of pegs along the wall for clothing. Frantically she searched for a means of escape. But there was only a window, high and small. Too small for even her slight frame to squeeze through.

Swinging back to the main room, she was almost to the door when it opened. With a squeak of alarm, she found herself face-to-face with a woman so bound about with a man's coat that she had no form. As if guessing Birdie's intent, she took the candle from her hand with a look of open contempt. Crossing the room, she slammed it on the table. Digging in the pockets of the giant coat she wore, she drew forth candle stubs. Lighting one, she dribbled enough wax to stick the rest upright in a small circle. When lit, they filled the room with a weak glow.

"Who are you, lass?" Birdie asked. "Will you please help me?"

The woman turned to stare at her for a moment, her face closed. "I'll be having no questions from the likes of ye!" she snapped. Turning, she busied herself with the fire and slamming things about the shelves nearby. Birdie moved out of her way and leaned wearily against the table.

In a small amount of time, the fire was burning brightly and the teakettle rattled. As the room warmed, the woman removed her coat and then the shawl wound round her head. Surprised, Birdie realized she was quite young. Possibly close to her own age. And perhaps pretty if bathed and groomed. But now her face was gray with winter-chapped cheeks, her dark hair hung in strings from a haphazard bun on the nape of her neck, greasy for want of washing, and her gown was nothing but a rag of unrecognizable style.

Dipping a cloth into a pail of water, the girl took a swipe at the table, then laid tin plates and cups out. Slamming a loaf of bread and a pot of jam down next, she glared at Birdie. Taking the glare as a broad hint, Birdie picked up the knife and began to slice the stale bread. With a great blast of cold air, the Irishman stomped into the room, dragging a bundle of rags in one beefy hand. He threw the lot into the corner and Birdie gasped to realize it was a person . . . thin and indistinguishable as woman or child.

"Where did ye find her, Rory?" the girl asked.

Ignoring her question, the Irishman shrugged out of the great coat, shaking snow from its folds. Walking to the fire, he carefully spread it to dry. It was the act of a man who did not know how soon he might be forced out into the snow again. Dragging the second stool back to the table, he seated himself. With a frightened glance at the still figure in the corner, Birdie prayed that Temple was somewhere warm and being cared for.

"Where . . ." Birdie began.

"Nay!" he shouted, halting her question with an upheld hand.

The dark-haired girl threw her shawl back over her head with a speculative look at the man. When he did not speak to her, she bundled into her coat and slipped out the door into the cold. Birdie clasped her hands tightly in front of her to stop their shaking. She watched the Irishman. Unconcerned, he poured tea in both tin cups and tossed a slice of bread on the second plate.

"Sit!" Birdie slid onto the stool with a glance at the bundle in the corner. Answering as if she had asked the question aloud, he said, "She'll not be eating on this night. But ye...*eat*" he thundered at her.

Birdie jumped at his shout, then stared down at the stale bread. However was she to escape a man who would starve that poor, ragged bundle of humanity? His barely leashed cruelty frightened her. Cold, exhausted, terrified, she felt her bravado slip to the toes of her boots, but she dragged it back again.

"I cannot. Not until I'm sure me man is well cared for," she whispered. She felt tears gathering in her eyes but could do nothing to stop them. They slipped down her cheeks to fall upon her dirty hands clasped tightly in her lap.

The rebel studied her. Reaching across, he flipped her hair from her forehead. She jerked her head up to stare at him with huge eyes. The circle of candles on the table bounced red fires among the tangled ringlets. "How is it an O'Donnell is wed to an Englishman? Wasn't ye taught at yer mam's knee that 'twas them that stole our land?" he asked, his strong, white teeth biting into the bread.

Birdie ignored his question, buying time to think. "What be yer name, man?" she countered, glaring at him. She knew she must fabricate a story that he would believe. Something so convincing, so valuable that it could buy two lives and freedom.

"'Tis Rory...Rory O'Donnell," he declared, head lifted in pride.

So that was why her ploy had worked so far? He thought them clansmen. Drawing a deep breath, Birdie pushed the tiredness from her mind. If only she was warm and less weary, she would be more equal to this deadly game. The images of Maude and old Maybelle flitted through her mind. She had never given in to them, and neither would she give in to this man. Her spine straightened and her resolve became strong.

"And why does an O'Donnell skulk in the mountains, robbing travelers under the guise of hatred for the English?" she sneered, thinking he reacted best to her disgust.

"'Tis not a pretended hatred I feel for the bastards. They stole our land, destroyed our name and scattered the clan to the four winds."

He narrowed his eyes at her. Birdie saw mad hatred there and she felt fear creep up her spine. "'Twas two hundred years ago, man! Ye cannot carry the fight alive in yer breast for all time," she whispered, thinking to calm him. Instead, her words incited him to rage. He slammed his fist down on the table, spilling the cups across the surface.

"I cannot lay down the hatred, woman! I will rule me lands one day under the name of O'Donnell!" Rising to his awesome height, he leaned over the table. Bringing his face close to hers, he whispered in a terrible voice, "And I be thinking I will not be stopping me men from killing yon Englishman. 'Twould be one less of the bastards to hate, now wouldn't it? Just as I be thinking any lass, even be she O'Donnell, that would crawl on her belly into their beds to spread her legs is not fit to live the same life as me."

Using the only weapon she had, Birdie glared back at him. Without moving her face away from his terrible black anger, she whispered just as strongly, "And I be thinking yer mam must have lain with her brother, Rory O'Donnell. For ye be a fool, if there ever was one. Ye hide yerself in these mountains and make yer people live less than animals in this dead town when there be land at Blanballyhaven for the asking of any O'Donnell."

"I will not work me own land as a tenant!" he bellowed. He slammed his fist down again, rattling the dishes. The creature in the corner whimpered and tried to make itself smaller.

Inwardly Birdie quailed before his terrible anger. But she could not back down now. To do so would be to lose what ground she had gained. She raised her voice to overcome the fear she felt gnawing at her gut. She must make him listen before he stormed out to order Temple's death.

"'Tis going to take strong sons to reclaim Ireland. Can ye make strong sons on a supper of bread and jam? Nay! But ye can on meat and potatoes. At Blanballyhaven, where land is set aside for any O'Donnell and his sons, rents are low, there is no flogging, no half-hanging, and ye be free to hunt the land as yer own."

"I don't need to work under the English at Blanballyhaven! I build a stronghold *here*. I'll breed strong sons *here* to reclaim Ireland!" he roared.

"How strong would yer hold be at Blanballyhaven? Where ye have twenty acres to work as yer own, and ye have twelve strong sons beside ye, each with twenty acres of their own, and they have twelve strong sons, each with twenty acres? Use yer head, man! Ye waste yer life on thieving and ye waste yer seed on loose women, for all yer grand talk about savin' Ireland! I spit on ye for shaming meself for carrying the same name as the likes of ye!"

Rory stood erect and stared at her. His eyes narrowed and he shoved his hands deep into his pockets in indecision. Never had he had a woman stand up to him as this one did. Or speak words of such sense. "How do ye know so much about Blanballyhaven?"

he asked softly. His voice, soft and caressing, frightened her more than his thundering shout.

Rising to her feet, Birdie drew herself up proudly, her face and voice full of blessed Libby Fitzwaters's hauteur, and played her trump card. The card she prayed would save Temple's life and spare her. "'Twill be my sons that rule Ireland and O'Donnell land. While yers starve in this hellhole or dance at the end of hangmen's ropes as thieves!" She softened her voice. "While ye'd hide in the mountains, nursing yer hatred, I have wed the heir to the O'Donnell ancestral stronghold. Blanballyhaven!"

The man's eyes widened, then abruptly narrowed. A calculating look came over his face. "I must think this out. Do not talk to me again this night. Go to bed." As he turned his back on her and started to resume his poor supper, Birdie pressed her advantage.

"I will not sleep nor eat till I know he is well cared for," she stated. She raised her chin when he would turn on her in anger. Seeing her determined stance, he cursed under his breath for her strong will. Grabbing her arm roughly, he slammed open the door and dragged her in a running step down the snow covered lane. Gasping at the icy air filling her lungs, she ran to keep up with his long stride. But for his strong grip she would have fallen. Her trailing skirts wound wetly around her legs and her boots became heavy with snow and mud. Not ten hovels down the lane, he flung open the door and shoved her inside. Falling painfully against the wall, Birdie slipped to her knees. Grasping her arm again, he pulled her to her feet and turned her toward the fireplace.

Temple lay on a bed of straw before a hearth with a fire burning brightly. His wet clothes had been removed and a thin blanket was thrown over him, leaving his broad chest bare and beautiful in the firelight. The same girl was kneeling beside him, holding a bowl and spoon. She looked up, startled, at the noisy intrusion.

"What's this, Rory? Ye be thinking to keep them together?" she asked with an insolent look at Birdie's frightened white face.

"Shut up, Shanna," he spat at her. "There be yer Englishman." He gave Birdie a shake that rattled her teeth. "Nothing but a cracked head. Shanna will not let him suffer. In fact, she will see that he is pleasured in every possible way, won't ye, girl?"

"Temple..." Birdie whispered. She would have rushed to his side except for the restraining hand on her arm. He looked so pale and was not conscious, for he did not stir upon his pallet. Oh, God help her if he died, for her very soul would die with him.

"Come. Ye've seen enough." Rory dragged her back out the door and to the hovel next to it. "Ye can sleep in here tonight. 'Twill change yer mind about things tomorrow." Opening the door, he pushed her so violently into the room that she fell to her hands and knees. The door slammed behind her.

Wearily she raised her head and eased back on her heels. There was no light except for the dying firelight, but still she could make out twenty or so pairs of eyes staring at her. Pushing herself to her feet, she made her way to the only vacant place she saw. Carefully, she stepped over and around bodies, some so still she doubted only slumber claimed them. The fawn pelisse that had begun the day so beautiful was wet and muddy. Still, she was thankful for it, gathering it around her as she sat down with her back to the damp, stone wall. Breathing a deep, weary sigh, she surveyed the quarters. In these people, who lay as close to her as her own breath, she saw her past, but, God as her witness, she would never allow it to be her future.

Chapter Sixteen

Dawn could not come too early for Birdie. She eased her aching body erect and, stepping over the sleeping forms, slipped out the door. Quickly, she ran the short distance to the cabin where Temple was captive. Pressing her ear to the wood, she listened for movement. Hearing silence, she eased the door open and peered through the crack. Perceiving no danger except possibly the girl rolled tightly in her blanket, she slithered into the room, eyes seeking the still form of her husband. He seemed not to have moved the entire night. Tiptoeing lest she wake the girl and have an alarm sounded, Birdie knelt beside him.

Temple's bed was of straw, as hers had been, but he had a blanket spread beneath him to protect his bare back, as well as one tossed over him. The fire still burned brightly as if someone had fed it only recently. Birdie placed her hand on the flushed forehead. He was very hot to the touch, lips dry and cracked, as if a great fever consumed him. The cut on his forehead had been washed and left uncovered. The gash was deep, red and angry, and would probably leave a scar, but what worried Birdie was the purple-and-blue swelling, which told of a severe blow dealt him when the chaise had overturned. She leaned forward and touched her lips to his dry ones, silently begging him to open his eyes. But he did not stir.

"He hasn't moved since 'twas laid there." A voice behind her startled her. Whirling around she saw Shanna's black eyes watching her. There didn't seem to be as much anger and hatred in them this morning, for which Birdie was thankful. "His head be broken, but not so bad they can't ransom him."

Hope sprang into Birdie's eyes. Ransom! "Is that why they've kept him alive?" she asked. If they ransomed Temple, then rescuers would know where to find her. That is, if they refused to release her, too. Temple, with plenty of men from Blanballyhaven, would come back to rescue her. But Oliver was waiting in Buncrana. Surely he would raise the alarm when they did not arrive on schedule. Although she doubted anyone could find this place without a guide.

Sweeping a look over Birdie's dirty, disheveled figure, Shanna was pleased to see the high-and-mighty lass didn't look so pretty anymore. A satisfied look came into her eyes. The lass's nice clothes were ruined and her face was white with fatigue. If Shanna took real good care of the Englishman, some of those velvets and silks she'd seen in the lass's fancy cases would be hers. Then she would be far prettier. She had Rory's promise on it. It wasn't fair that one girl should have so much while she, Shanna, had nothing. Didn't she like pretty things as much as any? Her foul temper came back. "Unless they be drinking too much and decide to hang him for fun," she sneered, then abruptly rolled over to face the wall as if the conversation bored her.

Birdie sighed deeply. Turning back to Temple, she caressed his cheek. Shadowed rough with stubble, it burned her hand. Leaning forward, she laid a cheek on his chest. Oh, Temple! Was their happiness to be cut so short? How she longed for his strong arms to enfold her and tell her it would be all right. She needed him to wake up strong and well. To protect her and save them. She was so frightened. She wasn't strong enough or crafty enough to do it by herself. So deep was her grief, she failed to hear the door open.

"Thought to find ye here. Come—" Rory stood massive in the doorway "—and do not let me be catching ye here again." His tone was soft and he held his hand out to her in a gentle manner, but the threat was obvious. Birdie rose and, carefully avoiding his hand, swept out the door.

The lane was coming awake as people rose and faced another day. The smell of peat smoke filled the air, which meant there was a peat bog nearby. Birdie thought to remember that, just in case they made their escape on foot. Peat bogs were dangerous. Striding through the deep snow, Rory led Birdie back to his cabin. She half ran to keep up and stumbled as he threw open the door and shoved her inside. This time the room was warm and the smell of roasting game filled her nostrils, causing her empty stomach to rumble. The bundle of rags stood upright in front of the fire, slowly turning the spit. Not surprised to discover it was a woman, Birdie turned to sneer at Rory.

"Another of yer fortunate houseguests?"

"Aye, and ye'd best watch yer tongue or ye'll soon be taking her place," he threatened.

Birdie didn't question his meaning but turned her eyes to the woman. A pathetic sight, she looked quite elderly with her stooped posture. Birdie could not properly judge her age without seeing her face, and dirty gray hair, knotted beyond belief, hid that. The woman didn't acknowledge their presence. In fact, she seemed not to know anyone else was in the room.

"What's her name?" Birdie asked Rory.

With a cruel grin, he shrugged his shoulders. "Never asked her."

Appalled, Birdie turned startled eyes to him. "What kind of monster are ye, man?"

"A hungry one. Woman, put some food on the damn table!" he commanded, but still the woman didn't look up. She continued to slowly turn the spit as if in a trance. "Ye do it," he stormed at Birdie, then cursed something unintelligible under his breath before slamming out the door.

With only a moment's hesitation, Birdie moved to the fire, speaking to the woman. "You go sit down now. I'll see to the food," Birdie offered softly. When the woman showed no sign of hearing, she touched her hand on the spit.

Frantically, the woman crouched and fought to retain her hold. "No! No! No! He told me to do it!" she shrieked.

Startled, Birdie fell back. The woman's speech was refined! A shudder ran through her body. God help us! Was this to be her fate? Desiring nothing more than avoiding Rory's anger, she wanted to get breakfast on the table before his return.

She spoke firmly to the poor woman. "No! Go sit!" The woman cowered at the stern voice, then crept into the corner. "Not there!" Birdie said, shocked. "Sit at the table." The woman turned terrified eyes toward Birdie and mutely shook her head. "Is it Rory O'Donnell that you are afraid of?" Birdie whispered, and saw the woman try to make herself smaller at the very mention of the name. "I guess that answers that," she said, quickly searching bags of supplies stacked on the table.

As she busied herself, the tension and worry began to ease. Maybe a good meal would put Rory in a better humor and she could ascertain his intent for Temple. His use for her was plain enough, she thought, casting a glance at the pathetic creature huddled in the corner. Armed with the knowledge of the possible ransom, her mind eased somewhat. For Temple's sake, anyway.

The supplies in the cabin were not abundant, and after finding a woman's dress inside one of the bags, she realized they were stolen goods. She thought of her beautiful gowns, the satin nightdress . . . Her heart stood still. Her mother's miniature! Tucked inside her reticule. Last seen lying on the chaise seat while she and

Temple played their silly game. Tears gathered in her eyes. The miniature had been her security against the world. Had one of the men picked it up and stuffed it into one of the cases? Or was it buried under snow on the trail? Beside poor Condor's body.

"Oh, mam!" she cried, putting her face into her hands. Racking sobs tore from her throat. Her exhausted body trembled with their force.

The slattern inched forward in a crouched position, the tangles of greasy hair hanging in her face. With nervous glances at the door, she fluttered her hands about. "Hurry! Hurry before he comes back."

The door slammed open on its hinges, once again sending the woman crawling to her corner in a scurry of fear. Birdie quickly straightened and scrubbed at her face. She would not let him see her misery. Rory's large frame filled the room. He seated himself at the table, scraping the floor with muddy boots. Slamming food on the table without much ceremony, Birdie sat across from him. When she tried to get the woman to join them at the table, she cringed deeper into her corner with animallike whimpers.

"Do not fash yerself about her. Eat up!" he ordered. "There's no comfort in a skinny woman."

A little alarm went off in Birdie's head. "I will be doing no more than cooking for the likes of ye, O'Donnell. And ye should not be expecting more."

Swinging his head back with a lusty laugh, he grinned broadly at her. Grabbing her wrist, he ran his fingers up her arm. " 'Tis always a pleasure to tame a cat."

"Enjoy this then," she exclaimed as she kicked at his shins beneath the table. Whatever happened as a result of her action, she knew it would be forever worth the astonished look on his face. So much for her bravado, the next minute she was away from the table and backing toward the door. Moving around the side of the table, she sought to keep it between them. "And don't ye be thinking I'll stand for ye to be taking the back of yer hand to me, neither!"

Rory stood abruptly knocking his stool to the dirty floor. "Ye be much too bonny for me to be caring what ye be wanting, lass. Besides, I be making a plan for the two of us. Ye'll be my ticket out of here."

Rory slung the table across the room, scattering food and dishes. The woman began a high keening that set the hairs on the back of Birdie's neck on edge.

"Is that what ye did to her? Forced her to your bed?" she taunted, flicking her eyes to the door, gauging her chances of reaching it before he was on her. She waited too long. Rory caught her arm and wrenched it behind her back, forcing her close to him. She was sure he was going to break her arm as she struggled to escape his hot breath.

"Ye can't fight me, 'cause I always get what I want. *Look at her!*" He forced her head to the side. "I take what I want and I use it till it's all gone!"

Jerking around, Birdie spat full in his face, then turned her face away when he raised his hand to strike her. A shout and the sound of horses outside the door halted his hand in midair. Abruptly he released her, pushing her against the wall. Without looking back to see her crumple against the wall, he slammed out the door, pulling his coat on. The shrill keening went on and on. With shaking hands, Birdie shoved herself along the wall toward the woman. Speaking softly and rocking her in her arms, she calmed her until blessed silence fell.

Keeping a constant, one-sided conversation going with the woman, Birdie quickly set the cabin to rights, all the while in the back of her mind letting enough time go by to either see Rory returning or assure his departure for a long time. His attack had badly shaken Birdie. She knew she must plan and plan right away.

When it became apparent he would not return soon, she bathed quickly and changed her dress for the one in the bag. Baggy and an unbecoming shade of brown, it was at least clean. She wasted another hour pacing the cabin floor and finally gave in to her need to see Temple. When a quick survey of the lane showed no activity, she slipped out the door and ran with pounding heart to Shanna's cabin.

Temple was alone, and with a deep sigh of relief she saw he was sleeping peacefully. His face was still very pale beneath the healthy beginning of a beard, and the wound on his forehead, while red, raw and angry, had at last clotted over. Kneeling, she tenderly pressed a kiss on his hot forehead. He opened his eyes immediately.

"Birdie . . ." he whispered.

"I'm here, dearest. I brought you some food. Can you eat?"

"Where have you been?" he demanded, struggling to sit up. His attempt failed, and he was forced back with a grimace of pain.

"Please lie still, darling. You'll only hurt yourself," she whispered, pushing him back. He brushed her hands aside.

"I want an answer!"

There was a sharp command in his voice and suddenly it was too much for Birdie. She dropped her face into her hands but did not let tears overwhelm her. When he did not touch her, she looked up to see his fever-bright eyes on her. Tired or not, frightened or not, she must not let Temple know how desperate her situation was. Fretting about her would not make him mend any faster, and he must be well enough to travel should they decide to ransom him soon. No, the truth was not the best thing to hand him at this moment. Never a talented liar, Birdie twisted her hands in her lap.

"They...uh, they put me with an old woman...just down the s-street. She's very ill. I've nursed her all night and all day. I am tired and..." She tapered off, reading disbelief in his face.

Temple regarded her with narrowed eyes. He knew she was lying. He knew she wasn't with any old woman. Shanna had told him, in great detail, of the handsome Irishman, leader of the rebels. So why was Birdie lying? What was she hiding? Though there were dark circles under her tired eyes, she did not look to be mistreated. Was it as Shanna said, that she had a place of honor among these Irish rebels? Right now he was too weak to push her for the truth, but if Birdie would play false with her lies, he would place his trust in Shanna. He could appeal to that one's greed, bribe her with money or clothes—hell, even an offer to take her away from this miserable place—in exchange for the truth. She had too much to gain to lie to him.

"I—I must get back," Birdie whispered. She had not been comforted by his distance, but she was too worried by his frailness to throw herself on his chest and wail for him to save her. Tenderly she laid a hand on his forehead, sick to find it still burning with raging fever. "Does your head pain you much?"

"Not much," he lied. "But too much to fight my way out of here. Must bide my time. I must be stronger." His voice drifted off as his eyes closed.

Birdie leaned her forehead on his chest for a moment. Why had he said fight *my* way out? And bide *my* time? As if he were only concerned with himself? Why had he not held her and consoled her? Heaven help her, but she felt so alone. But she did not have time to spare. Placing a light kiss on his chest, she forced herself off the floor. With a last glance at the man she loved, and holding her breath that O'Donnell hadn't returned, she ran back to Rory's cabin.

Fighting the feelings of despair, she scrubbed at her fawn gown, not having much luck in removing the spots from the fine merino. Finally giving it up as hopeless, she threw the scrubbing rag on the table. The gown was ruined, no doubt about it. Even Franny could not repair the damage done to this one. Dear Franny! Did she think Birdie was safe with Temple, on her way to London? Her throat tightened with tears.

Chapter Seventeen

Hours later, Temple roused again from a feverish sleep. Soft hands stroked his bare chest. The room was dark and warm from the dying fire. A shapely body snuggled close to his side. A leg was thrown over his thigh. In his feverish state, his body reacted to the sensual touch and he smiled. Turning onto his side, he cradled the woman to him.

"Birdie," he whispered into the eager, seeking mouth. A low, lusty chuckle halted him. In a flood of memory, he recalled where he was, the accident . . . and Birdie somewhere else in this godforsaken place. Jerking away from the woman, he gripped her throat with his hand. "Who are you?" he demanded, holding her up to the dying fire in an attempt to see her face. Sharp claws savagely raked his bare chest, drawing blood. Abruptly loosening his grip, he flung her away from him. "Hell's teeth!"

"Would ye be thinking to throttle me, Englishman?" Shanna snarled. Swiftly lighting a stub of candle, she faced her attacker.

Temple slid cold eyes over her body, wantoningly displayed in a blush satin nightdress. "You should not sneak into a man's bed, girl. Especially a man who is being held against his will."

"Ye didn't seem to mind when you thought 'twas yer precious Birdie, now did ye?" she snapped at him, using both hands to fling her heavy, dark hair from her face. Seeing the absence of desire in the man, she smoothed the satin over her hips in a seductive gesture.

"She is my wife," Temple stated. He wanted nothing from this one except answers. He dabbed at the bloody scratches on his chest. They stung like fire.

"Here, Englishman," she said. Standing over him, she tilted a bottle of whiskey over his chest, turning the sting into real pain as the alcohol splashed over the scratches. "Can't be having ye get infected, now, can we?"

"Bloody hell!" he exclaimed again, jerking upright. The abrupt movement made his head throb and the room tilt this way and that. He forced himself to breathe deeply to forestall losing consciousness.

Tipping the bottle to her mouth, Shanna sucked greedily. "Best be putting that one out of yer head. O'Donnell will not give her up. She be O'Donnell, too, and ye know what that means."

"No, I do not know what that means. Make yourself clear?" demanded Temple. He fought to keep his voice noncommittal, when he truly wanted to choke the truth out of her. "Won't my wife be ransomed with me?"

Shanna straddled his body and handed the bottle down to him. "Drink or no answers!" she bargained. He took a long pull on the bottle to appease her, grimacing as the raw liquor hit his belly. "Nay, me fine English lord," she sneered, enjoying tormenting the man who would reject her, "she will not be ransomed. The man fancies his own babes to be the O'Donnell blood to inherit Blanballyhaven."

Swinging her body around the room in a slightly tipsy dance, she fell heavily over his legs with a breathless laugh. Holding his head with both hands, Temple tried to understand what this witch was telling him. If only his head didn't throb until all reasonable thought deserted him, maybe he could sort it out. "What? Speak plain, for God's sake!"

"Drink!" she ordered, and smirked when he did her bidding readily this time. "Yon lassie be of O'Donnell blood by her own admission. And surely ye be knowing that Blanballyhaven is where the heart and soul of all O'Donnells tarry. Wedding ye means her babes will be the masters of Blanballyhaven one fine day." Shanna doubled over with laughter. "Rory O'Donnell means for those babes to be his, not yers, Englishman. 'Twill be bedding yer bride, and with her willing consent, until her belly swells with his babe." She paused to see if he was following her tale. "Don't ye see? Once again the O'Donnell stronghold will be ruled by O'Donnells! And ye'll be a rotting corpse in the dung heap."

Temple's head spun in pain, confusion and whiskey. Could this be true? Birdie . . . Irish? An O'Donnell? What had she said about her mother? The O'Donnell cook at Blanballyhaven? No, the lady in the miniature! Was she part of some elaborate scheme by these foolish Irish rebels? Was this the truth behind the strangeness of her tale? He had to find out and soon. But he couldn't do that here. He must escape if he was to find out the truth. And this greedy girl could well be the means of that escape. Stroking his hand up the girl's leg, he lightly pinched her thigh.

"You know, if that's the truth and he means to keep her, then I will be without a wife."

The girl's eyes grew very round and she swilled from the bottle before extending it to him. Temple tightened his neck muscles against the blinding pain in his head and tilted the bottle to pour the fiery whiskey down his throat.

"'Tis the truth, I swear," Shanna coaxed. "'Twas all planned."

"What do you mean 'all planned'?" he asked, tipping the bottle to his lips. "How long ago?"

"Long, long ago," she admitted, trying to give him the answers she thought he wanted to hear. "Long before I was born."

Grinding his teeth together, Temple took another long pull from the bottle. The fire burned down into his gut. But not as hotly as the pain in his heart. So he'd been played a fool! Duped like a simpleton. That did not sit well with him. It was a mortal wound to his pride. And to think he had almost fallen in love with her. Well, he would have his revenge in some manner, someday.

"Ah, Shanna, we should leave here. This is no place for a sweet lass like yourself," he crooned. She stared at him with huge, disbelieving eyes.

"Will ye take me with ye? Will ye make me a lady?" she cajoled.

Temple gritted his teeth. So this one wanted to be a lady, too. Did all the Irish lassies wish to be ladies? "Yes, I'll make you a lady just like the other one. As long as we leave here, soon," he mocked.

Birdie jerked awake, confused for a moment, aware only of terror left over from a nightmare. Slowly moving her head, she took in the room and remembered . . . the nightmare was real. Listening to the silence in the house, she knew Rory had not returned. Quickly sitting up, she thought to take advantage of his absence to check on Temple once more. Wrapping her head and shoulders in the blanket against the falling snow, she slipped wrapped slices of game into her pocket. Good red meat to strengthen his blood, she thought. She prayed that he was stronger, so they could make a plan. Slipping through the door, she could hear tinny music, probably from the crowded public house. She shuddered to think of ending up there, servicing the needs of the men who gathered there. Running lightly toward Temple, she fought to dispel such thoughts from her head for they were too gruesome to contemplate.

Slipping into the warmth that was Temple's prison, Birdie shrugged off the blanket. "Temple?" Her voice died in her throat. Her husband lay propped against a mound of blankets, the firelight tinting his bare chest a golden hue and bouncing from one rounded muscle to another, leading her eyes to do the same. He looked up at her. His eyes seemed clearer and his color heightened but healthier. Her eyes traveled on to the body of Shanna lying across his lap. She caught her breath in a painful gasp. The feeling of having intruded upon an intimate moment surged through her.

"I see ye're getting all the tending ye be needin'," she grated, hating herself for feeling embarrassed and uncertain. As if she were the one in the wrong. She dropped her gaze to the tops of her boots as it hurt too much to see him with another in his arms. Why was she trembling so? Why wasn't she flinging accusations at his head for the faithless husband he was? "I shouldna have cum . . ."

Her heavy brogue seeped into Temple's fogged brain and stunned him. Spoken like a native and with such ease. It saddened him that he had been so gullible. He had fallen into his great-uncle's plan when all instincts had warned something foul was in the wind. The lonely old man must have been more senile than he had thought to mistake this one for a lady! He frowned. He would not feel sad when anger felt better!

"Go then!" he barked. His harshness came from the hurt deep inside him. It was difficult for his self-regard to allow they had bested him. And now he was forced to lie weakened at their mercy. But his day would come. He would seek his revenge against them all. Against her in particular, for, God help him, he had loved her. Loved her sweetness. Loved her warmth. She had filled an emptiness inside him that he hadn't even known was there. He'd been prepared to give her everything, but all she'd had for him was lies and deceit.

Birdie heard only the harshness of his voice and quickly stepped backward through the door into the cold and darkness. Numb with rejection, she turned to run, then stumbled to a halt to lean against a rough, stone wall as tears blinded her. Still holding the slices of meat in her hand, she flung them from her as far as she could. Obviously her husband did not need strengthening. Never had the thought occurred to her, while her every thought had been to keep them alive and to keep Rory from having his way with her, that Temple, her husband, would turn to carnal pleasures. With each thought, she cried harder.

She was never going to be a lady to him! Not all the pretty clothes or the proper manners were going to change his view of her. And for all his fancy promises, he didn't think twice to replace her with another. Finally exhausted, she collected herself enough to stumble down the lane. Temple might think of her as less, but she knew different. Inside, she knew different. It was then that she pictured Shanna, lying back against Temple's chest, her hand lingering in a caress over the dark hair of his chest, laughing at his humiliated wife—and wearing the blush satin nightdress that Libby had stitched for her wedding night.

The house was silent when she crept in. Shunning the bed again, Birdie took a place on the floor beside the woman, who shuddered and moaned in her sleep. She rolled into a blanket before the fire, but sleep did not release her from her anguish for a long time.

Chapter Eighteen

Birdie woke, just before first light, to the sound of whimpers. When she opened her eyes, she saw Rory kneeling over the woman, gripping her arm. Wide-eyed with terror, the woman attempted to inch away, her head sliding up the wall.

Birdie fought her way out of her tangled blanket. "Leave her alone! Why must ye be terrorizing her that way?"

"'Tis easy to terrorize this one. Doesn't have much mind left now. It wouldn't take much to be relieving her of the rest." He smirked, shaking the woman as if she were a rag doll. Her whimpers turned into the incoherent babbling of an insane person. "See what I mean?"

"Stop it! Stop it!" Birdie screamed, grabbing his forearm and trying to drag him away from the hysterical woman.

"She's not hurt," he countered, abruptly flinging the woman against the wall, where she curled into a knot and rocked herself.

"Why must ye be doing that?" Birdie demanded. She leaned back against the wall, face defiant. "Why must ye be making her mind to fly like that?"

"Because I want ye to understand me powers. There be something I would have from ye, lass, but I would be having it willingly."

This took Birdie by surprise. She had never doubted he would take her into his bed when he pleased, but to be holding off for her consent? "'Tisn't a thing I'd be giving ye willingly, O'Donnell!"

"Come, seat yerself," he coaxed, pulling the stool away from the table for her. He swung his leg over the other stool and yelled, "Woman, get up off the floor and make some coffee!"

The demented woman did not move but lay against the wall, rocking herself gently. Birdie swiftly moved to stir up the fire, hoping to spare the woman further abuse. He followed her with his eyes.

"Mayhap 'twas rougher on ye than I needed to be at first, but 'tis vital to me and the cause," he began in a wheedling tone, as if hoping to gain good graces. "Me name is all there is left to me, and to see an O'Donnell wed to the English was too much. I saw bloody rage, ye know?"

"And how can I be changing that?" Birdie asked, trying to bring him back to the point. She needed none of his sweet talk this morning. She sliced bread and set out cold meat to keep her hands busy and to stay away from the table, out of his reach.

"With yon Englishman dead, ye will be mistress of Blanbally-haven until another heir be found. And yer son, *our son*, with O'Donnell blood from both of us, must be that heir. Don't ye see? I must have the first male babe from yer belly to be carrying me own blood!" He leaned toward her in earnest. The fire in his eyes made him seem as demented as the moaning, rocking woman.

Birdie's mind reeled. Lord have mercy! In her attempt to save their lives, she had landed them in a far worse fix. This did nothing but sign a death warrant for Temple. She must think and she must think fast. Her brow knit as she scanned and discarded ways to escape this latest trap. Buying time, she retrieved coffee and with exaggerated slowness, filled two cups.

"I only be human, Birdie. I do get carried away with me hatred. But 'tis only what ye planned all along, to put O'Donnell blood back into Blanballyhaven with yer own son. What's better than to have him full-blooded Irish? And full-blooded O'Donnell?"

Darting a glance at his eyes begging her to believe him, Birdie shuddered. The man was totally insane. Totally out of touch with reality.

Taking her silence for weakening, Rory pushed on, his tone soft and wheedling. "I know I took to the road to feed me people, but mayhap the love of a good woman could help me with this anger. Just get to know me a little, Birdie—" he caught her hand in his "—and let me show ye I am no monster."

Birdie gently pulled her hand from his but held her silence. She did not want to push him to anger again, but she must appear to be thinking seriously about this plan. She needed to gain time to turn it all to her advantage.

"I swear I will not force ye, lass. I will not mistreat ye…as long as ye work with me to put a babe into yer belly. But it must be a lad, not a lass, ye know that? If 'tis a lass, we must try again."

"It wouldn't work, Rory, if you kill the Englishman. Surely you see that. The lad must be raised to take his rightful place in their society. Educated to live in their world. Don't you see that? 'Tis the only way he can help the Irish people. They would pay him no heed if he be a rabble-rouser," she reasoned. Regardless of what Temple had done to her, heedless of the way he had hurt her with his deception, she could not stand by and let this band of rebels end his life. She must appear to play into their hands, even if it meant she had to agree to this madman's plan. After they trusted her, she could escape somehow. But she must see Temple safe first. Once away from her, he could rescue her. Surely he would send some-one after her even if he no longer, or had never, wanted her for a wife.

Rory shook his head. "'Tis a young man he be, lassie. He could live as long as the old one, and that'd be too late. I must see Blan-ballyhaven in Irish hands before me own death. No, he must die. And then ye must grasp the power and raise our sons at Blanbal-lyhaven, with English teachers if ye must, as there is sense in what ye say, but they must be raised knowing what their blood means!"

"The Englishman's death does no good, Rory. Ye don't under-stand—"

Rory's head came up and his gentle demeanor slipped into a snarl before he caught himself. "No! 'Tis ye who will not under-stand! He will die! Ye must want that, too, seeing as how ye be one of us!"

"I am *not* one of ye, Rory! I'm no thief, nor murderer!" she shouted before she could help herself. Better he be angry with her than calmly plotting to murder Temple.

Rory's gentle demeanor slipped back into place. "You be a smart lass, Birdie. I know I can depend on you to help me plan this thing out, to get what we both want for our people." He rose from the table and gave her what he must have thought was a friendly grin. Tipping an imaginary hat to her, he left, supposedly leaving her to ponder and plan.

Birdie knew she must think. Somehow she must think of a rea-son that Temple be spared. She must get Temple ransomed. And away from Shanna! She shook her head at her absurdity. As if that truly mattered, when their very lives were at stake. Temple. Beau-tiful Temple, her husband. Was one night of blissful love all she was to have with the man she had pledged to love, honor and obey till death parted them? She shuddered to think of Temple dead. Better he live apart from her than be dead and moldering in a shallow grave in the high mountains of Ireland.

She was no fool, nor had she been taken in by Rory's sweet temper this morning. He was a ruthless killer and parted from reality in his reasoning. He was fired by one thing and one thing only: regaining control of Blanballyhaven. And as long as he thought her O'Donnell, he had use of her. She must be very careful. He must trust her and think her as fired by revenge as he. If he believed that, he would be less apt to mistreat her in any way. As long as she was not hurt, escape was possible. A sense of despair filled her. Pray God she was right about this.

Picking up the dirty dishpan, she walked to the door to fling its contents into the snow. Sitting astride his bay stallion in the roadway, Rory beckoned to her. Behind him rode two other men leading the sorry nag she had killed a man for, saddled and waiting for her.

"Wrap yerself up warm, lass. 'Tis off for a ride, we are."

With little choice in the matter, Birdie found herself mounted and galloping behind him through the heavy trees. She paid close attention to their route with the ever present thought of escape in her head. If only she could keep on riding, straight over the mountain to the warm hearth of Mattie's kitchen and the welcoming arms of Sir Charles.

Topping a rise after an hour's gallop from Glencolumbkille, they paused to let the horses blow. Then Rory abruptly wheeled his stallion and led the group down the rise and across a stream that dissected the trail. In unison, they pulled their horses to a halt again in the middle of a well-worn trail. Rory pointed toward a column of smoke drifting lazily up from a campfire. Out of his pocket, he pulled a black handkerchief and, while Birdie watched with dawning horror, tied it snugly over his face.

"Rory, no! *No!*" she screamed, dragging her old mount's head around. She must get out of here. She could not be a party to this!

"Not so fast, me lassie," Rory barked, snatching the reins of her old horse and halting her attempt to flee. "'Tis just tending a bit of business, we are."

The next moment they were thundering down the trail and into the camp. Birdie gripped the saddle for support. Once more she screamed, but was paid no heed by the three rebels bent on robbery and murder. They burst like thunderclouds into the clearing where three wagons sat. The people, a ragged group of men, women and children, caught unawares, could only stand with open mouths and gasps of surprise.

With an explosion of gunfire, Rory shot one man through the heart. Horrified, Birdie felt her mind go numb. In one motion, she was off her horse and onto the ground, running toward the dead man. A woman near her screamed a high-pitched wail and fell over the man, trying to stop the flow of blood with her hands. Birdie hovered helplessly over the man and wife. She could not believe this was happening. And there was nothing she could do to stop it.

"Get their goods, Birdie O'Donnell," Rory commanded, shoving the dancing bay between her and the distraught woman.

"No! No! No!" she screamed, beating his leg with her fists.

Rory leveled his pistols at the screaming woman, who wailed over her dead husband. "If ye do not obey me, and quickly, lass," he warned in that soft, dangerous tone, "I will not be thinking twice about ending the poor woman's suffering."

"No! Please no," she begged, clutching his leg. "Wh-what am I to do?"

Birdie knew that words would never save these people from this madman. She watched the people being crowded into the center of the clearing. They gathered about their rickety wagons, which carried the supplies and meager belongings that represented their entire miserable lives. Men shoved women behind them, who in turn shoved children behind their skirts.

"Get that man's hat and collect whatever they have." He swung his pistol barrel in a half circle over the people's heads and gave a shouted order. "Any of ye thinking to give me beautiful partner any trouble . . . and he'll earn a bullet."

"I'm not—" Birdie wanted to explain but stopped. No one listened. When she approached the first man, he looked at her with hatred and fear in his eyes.

"The Lord will see you burn in hell for this day, woman!" the man hissed at her as he placed a battered watch into the hat. It was a thing of little value except to its owner, who had so little.

His words brought tears to blind her. How could these people think she was other than a victim like themselves? Couldn't they take one look at Rory and tell that he was mad? Didn't the man lying dead on the ground tell them anything? She rushed along the line of people, keeping her head down in shame at her part, willing or not, in adding to the misery of their lives. The two riders loaded staples from the wagons onto the backs of the settlers' horses.

"Come along, Birdie," Rory coaxed gently, neighborly concern heavy in his voice. "We be needing to be getting home and leaving these good people to be burying their dead." At her horse, Birdie hesitated. Rory seemed to read her mind and leaned close. "If ye do not be getting on the damn horse, lass, I'll be killing the lot of them. I be having a liking for it, anyway."

Birdie mounted her old horse in resignation. She gripped the saddle as Rory again took the reins and led them out of the clearing in a thunder of hooves. Stopping again on the rise, he pulled his mask off and grinned at her, smug in his sick, demented humor.

"Now ye be one of us for sure, Birdie O'Donnell!"

"And ye be a fool, Rory O'Donnell!" she blazed out at him. "Don't ye realize ye would brand me son as the son of a murderer and thief! Ye do no good for yer people with yer stupidity!" No sooner had the heated words left her mouth than she knew she had made a mistake. She bit her lip in horror as his eyes narrowed and angry blood rushed to turn his face black. She should have known better than to confront him in front of his men.

"Ye may be right, lass. 'Twas not thinking clearly, now was I?" he all but whispered. God, how she hated that soft tone. Turning to the men, he nodded back in the direction of the camp. "Lads, best be shutting their mouths and eyes for good. Me woman here thinks it best if they live to carry no tales."

"No!" Birdie screamed as two of the men turned their horses and rode down the hill. The third, without looking up, strung the lead ropes together on the pack animals and set about balancing their loads. Rory tossed her leathers back to her with a smirk.

Birdie sat on the horse sobbing great, gulping sobs. Her heart was rent with the agony and realization that innocent people, some of them mere children, would die today because of her thoughtless words. How was she ever to live with that knowledge? Her mind moved away from the horror of the fact and tears streamed down her face. The old horse followed Rory's bay down the rise with no guidance from her. By the time they had reached Glencolumbkille, he was cursing her roundly for being a coward and a weakling. Jerking the stallion to a halt in front of the cabin, he roared at her in anger.

"Damn ye, Birdie O'Donnell, for being a weak woman!" He swung off the bay and stormed into the house.

Birdie sat astride her horse, numb to the very core of her damaged soul. She still had not moved when Rory stalked back out to sling a knapsack of food behind his saddle.

"Be getting down off the damn horse, woman!" he bellowed. When she didn't move, he roughly pulled her down, yelling into her face. "I'll not be coming back tonight. If I do, I'll be killing ye for sure! Now get yerself in the cabin and stay there!"

Birdie collapsed in a heap by the gate, drawing her knees to her chest as he mounted and spun the bay away to thunder down the path. She didn't cry or make a sound. She just lay there, dead inside. Hours later, the woman, cautiously peering out the door, found her. Creeping toward the girl, she tentatively stroked her face. Birdie did not move.

"Birdie?" she whispered, timidly glancing around to see if anyone else heard. "You're going to freeze, Birdie."

Shivering, the haggard woman summoned all the courage left in her demented mind and ran toward the cabin where Birdie had said Temple lived. She ran crouched over, ducking and dodging into the shadows whenever possible, even though the lane was deserted.

Temple was restlessly pacing the length of the small room. He flexed his powerful arms across his bare chest, seeking to renew strength in muscles gone soft with illness. His anger rode high, threatening to burst free into violence. The situation had gone far enough. Now that he was stronger, he would end it. He spun when he heard the door creak open, inch by inch. Startled, he witnessed a head with stringy gray hair peer around the door, then a claw-like hand beckoned for him to come to her.

"Good Lord, now what?" he muttered, approaching the hag. Though she had beckoned to him, the very act of his approach seemed to fill her with terror. She turned and scurried ahead of him. When he halted, she again signaled to him. Glancing about for a trap, he followed her into the lane.

"Birdie!" she whispered. "Birdie!" She pointed down the lane to the small figure lying in the snow and mud.

"My God!" cried Temple, breaking into a run. Kneeling beside her, he gathered her tenderly into his arms, staring hard at the white face. When nothing seemed broken except her spirit, he swung her into his arms. He must get her out of the cold. The hag stood in front of a house, motioning to him. One look around the clean room, with its smell of roasting meat and freshly baked bread, and he knew this was where she had been living with the Irishman. That was something he did not want to think of this minute. Striding forcefully through the main room into the bedroom, he gently laid her on the lumpy mattress.

"What happened to her?" he demanded of the hovering woman. At the sound of his loud, commanding voice she disappeared with a quiet click of the door. "Wait!" he called, striding quickly to the door. Wrenching it open, he looked both directions but the hag had disappeared as if into thin air. With a mighty heave, he crashed the door closed. Turning, he raked his hand through his hair, then grabbed Birdie's shoulders and lifted her into a sitting position. "Damn you, Birdie!" he yelled into her face. "Why did you do this to us?" He shook her, heedless of her russet curls whipping his face.

Tears seeped from beneath Birdie's lashes. She drew a shuddering breath. Never had Temple felt so helpless. He wanted to cradle her close to him and protect her, but whatever had happened this time, she had brought it upon herself. A wild sobbing overtook her. She clutched at him with all her strength, as if she could never get close enough, and sobbed against his bare chest. He held her, stroking her back until she was drained of tears.

"Now tell me!" he said when she quieted. "What happened?" Wanting desperately to believe she was not in league with these people, he shook her again. "Tell me, damn it!"

"No," she whispered, her eyes closing to shut out unwanted pictures. She could never tell anyone. Ever! For to speak the words would make it true. In her mind, she could see the bodies, grotesquely sprawled over the clearing, left for nature and wild animals to dispose of, and it was all her fault. "Just leave me be! Let me die!" she whispered, a sob breaking from her colorless lips. Birdie closed her eyes, for she feared he would see the horror of her life if he looked deep enough.

"Stop it, Birdie. It's always best to be alive. Just hush!" demanded Temple. When she lay back in his arms so limply, he feared she would slip back to that dark place where her mind left her body. He felt helpless in the face of her broken spirit. He caressed her cheek and neck with his large hand, wiping away the traces of her tears. She lay back in his arms with her eyes closed, pale as death, again looking like the child he had married. She shivered and gave a long sigh. Heartened by that, he claimed her lips, demanding and plundering, kissing her as if he were breathing the breath of life into her battered spirit. His desire became savage, fundamental in its purpose of bringing her back to the present, willing her to live, to fight. He touched the tiny buttons at the front of her gown, fumbling ineffectually, then suddenly ripping them loose with a simple, quick jerk. Pushing her chemise aside, he claimed her nipples greedily, his touch lusty and sure as he rubbed them to delicate, tender peaks.

It felt so good to be held by him, touched by him again. Birdie could almost forget where they were and all that had happened. Clasping him to her, she allowed love to pour from her body to his, silently begging him to forgive her for something he knew nothing of. Defenseless against his forceful mouth as it dragged over hers again and again, she offered it, and her body, freely. She wanted him. But not in this bed. Not in this place. Not where Rory could find them and end Temple's life as he had ended all life he touched.

"Temple, wait," she panted, pushing at his hands. But Temple, being both forceful in manner and formidable in body, would not take no for an answer.

"No, I'll not wait. You were mine first," he grated, slanting his demanding mouth over hers. He would wait for nothing. He would take what was, or had been at one time, his and his alone. The thought of another being with her tore at his guts.

Suddenly the only thing that mattered to Birdie was that Temple was here. And that she loved him above all else. Nuzzling her husband's lean cheek with her lips, she clumsily sought his mouth. He gave a deep groan as he kissed her, the sound low and responsive. Impatient, he ripped and tugged until she was freed of the skirt and petticoat tangle, and her pale skin gleamed in the weak light of the room.

Birdie responded with great urgency. Having never been taught that a lady rarely admits to enjoyment during lovemaking, she reacted to his ardor with the trust of a child. She began kissing him back with enthusiasm born of desire. The desire to be close to him, and the desire to forget. She slid her fingertips over the smooth bulk of his chest, sifting through the silken hairs. Arching her back and sucking in her belly as his fingertip explored the secret hollow of her body, she protested when he pulled his mouth from hers, then sighed with contentment as his lips encircled her nipple. She swallowed hard, her head rolling back, and arched her body upward in an instinctive reaction to the growing heat in her belly.

"Temple..." she gasped. He did not seem to hear her. She pushed at his chest. A part of Birdie's mind told her that they were being foolish and careless, but she was unable to think of it for long. Her hands dragged at him. She wanted to feel his weight, smell his smell, take him inside of her.

Temple levered himself above her. Her eagerness combined with her artlessness was almost more than he could bear. Before, on their one night together, he had been aware of the exquisite tenderness of her innocence, and there had been a degree of self-restraint in his loving, as he had been conscious of hurting her. Now all constraints were gone, all deliberation had vanished. He took her forcefully, her hands on his hips urging him to more...deeper...harder.

Temple gripped her waist and rolled to his back, bringing her on top of him. With his hands on her hips to steady her, he let her grind against him, ride him as she needed. He watched her face, glorying in the look of pure, undiluted pleasure, until she peaked on that pleasure. She gave a little cry and sagged limply across him, her breasts pillowing against the wiry black hair on his chest.

Temple could hold back no more. Rolling her to her back, he ground himself into the very depth of her and spent himself with a strangled cry.

Temple levered himself up to stare down at Birdie. Her eyes were glazed, her mouth soft, her hair in sweaty curls about her face. There was a wonder in her eyes that turned soft when she looked at his face. She raised a hand to stroke his rough cheek, and it was as if the touch brought her back to the harsh reality of the danger to Temple should Rory return.

"Sheesh man! You must be getting out of here! Before Rory comes back!" she cried, frantically pushing at him. "Get out!"

Temple narrowed his eyes. First, he must know the truth. And he must hear it from her own lips. "Birdie—" he forced her to lie still beneath him, to look at him "—I must know. And I will have the truth! Are you one with these murderers?"

Birdie, seared by the word *murderers,* thought of the innocent settlers, people she had murdered as surely as if she had pulled the trigger that sent the lead through their hearts. She averted her eyes in shame lest he see pictured there the man lying on the ground, his life's blood flowing over his wife's frantic hands. Nodding her head, she affirmed his suppositions and admitted in a dull voice that, yes, she was one with them, without fully realizing the consequence of her admission.

Temple gasped as if someone had struck him. Disbelief, then rage and finally pain filled his chest. Her obvious shame gave credence to her admission. There was nothing else he needed from her. Abruptly leaving her body, he quickly covered himself.

"That seems to be that, doesn't it? At least I thank you for your honesty, Birdie," he murmured. "If nothing else." Without waiting for her response, he quit the room quietly.

Birdie rolled to her side and buried her face in the lumpy mattress, weeping soundlessly. Had either of them looked into the other's eyes, they would have recognized the pain there. They would have seen that their pain was of misunderstanding and delusion, and so very unnecessary.

Chapter Nineteen

The sour, damp hackney coach, hired at the docks by George Hughett, rattled and lurched along the washed-out London streets. Not the best way to approach the ancestral home for the first time, but then Birdie had not expected the streets to be lined with well-wishers awaiting the arrival of a slum child turned marquise. How innocent she had been. Or perhaps naive and idealistic. Had it really been less than two years since she had married Temple and become a lady? Had Sir Charles ever gone to London that spring, expecting to see her triumph in society? Was he here now? At Daine Hall? Please God, let him be here, she fervently prayed.

Married at sixteen, widowed less than a month later. Such rotten luck! Could she only be eighteen now? Such a small amount of years to have lived so much. Just two years. Smoothing the russet hair back from her temple, she traced a finger over the scar on her forehead, nearly invisible, but not so the memory of the beating that had put it there. Two years of hell. An eternity with a madman.

It had been winter when she had married Temple. It had been winter when they had murdered him. It had been winter when she had run with Rory and his band of murderers the wild length of Ireland. Winter, and all around her men had died while the tiny seeds of spring had snuggled in Mother Earth's womb, merely waiting to launch new life to cover the battle scars and graves. The seeds planted in her womb had also taken root that winter. The little heartbeats had held tenaciously to life inside her body throughout the cold, the misery, the hardships.

Birdie's arms tightened around her sleeping daughter, even as her eyes sought her fretful son fussing on the surgeon's lap. The twins were identical. Chubby little creatures with angel faces framed by inky ringlets and big gray eyes. Images of Temple and truly a sign of God's goodness and the existence of miracles. Today her dreams would become reality. Her children would finally take their rightful places in the haut ton. Charles Templeton Daine would go to Eton as appropriate for the Marquis of Daine-Charlton. And Amaryllis Matilda Daine would have her season and make a brilliant marriage.

Birdie sighed and closed her eyes in weariness. Her immediate wish just now was to bathe and bed the babies, then crawl into a warm, unmoving bed for at least a fortnight. Undertaking a long and difficult sea voyage with two small children, without clothing or proper necessities, was something she never wanted to repeat. Though her fellow passengers had been most supportive, it had been an unbearable and exhausting ordeal. Her sober traveling dress had been a parting gift from the poor box at the Bantry rectory and a welcome one at that, although it would have been nice if the donor had weighed perhaps a stone or two less. If she had, the dress might not have looked quite so comical on her slight frame. If it had not been for the kindness and support of dear George, she feared she would not have survived the trip. And if it hadn't been for the miraculous rescue and expert care of dear George, she would not have survived to the end of the year.

Staring around the window curtain, heedless of the water that whipped in occasionally, Birdie peered out in worry. "Do you think there will be problems connected with the inheritance?" she asked George for the hundredth time.

"I know of no other relation to claim the title, do you? Though they do tend to come out of the woodwork over such as this. But we must not get ahead of ourselves. We can't even know for sure that Sir Charles has passed. It's only been two years, though I know he was ill. It's true that I have been at the end of the world, but surely I would have heard," stated George rationally. He shifted a fractious Charles in his arms.

"Oh, God, please let him be alive," Birdie prayed. She wrapped her arms around Amaryllis, rocking herself back and forth, more for her own comfort than the sleeping babe's.

"Birdie, there were too many people present at your wedding who can be brought forward. They cannot hinder you. Legal documents can be obtained from Ireland to confirm your marriage if need be, and the timing of the birth of your children is well within the limits contesting their legitimacy, even allowing for the early arrival of twins," George assured her once again, as he had done repeatedly over the long voyage, ever patient with her, and longing to help her in any way she should require.

Rain drummed like pebbles on the cab wall, and wetness seeped
around the ill-fitted curtains. Birdie shivered in the chill and damp
of the gathering dusk. Just when she thought to inquire how much
longer, they turned into a pretty little square. Tilting the window
shade would only result in a spray of water drops for her and waking Amaryllis, so she had no first impression of Daine Hall. A
sheet of rain slapped the curtain as they changed direction and
water dribbled down to wet the mud-stained hem of her gown,
further soaking her icy feet. A blue streak of lightning streaked
through the sky, closely followed by a clap of thunder. Heaven help
her. Would this miserable journey never be over? As the cab rumbled to a stop, George leaned over to settle Charles against her side.
The baby whined tiredly. Setting his beaver topper securely upon
his head, George made ready to descend into the storm.

"I will alert the servants and perhaps secure some blankets for
the babies," he said, twisting the latch on the door. Rain swirled
in briefly, then he was gone. Birdie waited, listening to the furious
rain pelting the hackney, battling the sound of her pounding heart.
Tension settled in her shoulders and she breathed deeply to calm
herself. A moment later, the door beside her was wrenched open.
Birdie stifled a scream, drawing her babies close to her. George's
grim face appeared, and behind him stood a footman holding aloft
an umbrella, useless against the wind and rain.

Flinging a blanket over Charles, he shouted above the noise.
"Birdie, wait here. I'll come back." He slammed the door and
disappeared, only to reappear momentarily to do the same with
Amaryllis.

Birdie gathered her skirts and ducked her head to climb down,
only to have her arm caught roughly by strong fingers. Gasping in
shocked outrage, she was lifted from her seat and set down hard
on her heels beside the cab. The rain soaked her hair instantly and
a vicious blast of wind billowed her oversize draperies and flung her
hard against a body. The man, rain coursing down his great coat
and a beaver jammed down tight over his eyes, swore sharply, the
wind snatching away his words but not his tone. Roughly he swung
her into his arms and started away from the cab. Blinded by the
driving rain, Birdie could only press her face against his broad
shoulder. She felt his arms tighten as he climbed upward. Abruptly
the rain ceased pelting them and she heard the slamming of a heavy
door.

"You may let go of my coat now," breathed a stern voice in her
ear.

Birdie snatched her fingers from the lapel as though scorched.
She was set down none too gently and steadied by an impersonal

hand under her elbow when she would sway. Shaking out her wet skirts, she knew she must look ridiculous. Pretty much like a drowned tabby cat. Water dripped from her nose and hastily she brushed it away. Speechless with anger at such rough treatment, she glared up into a pair of steel gray eyes so familiar that she thought to lose consciousness.

"Temple! Rory told me . . ." she whispered, then cried out in shock. "I thought you were *dead!*"

The scowl never left his face. "I live," he stated simply.

Birdie stared at the familiar face, the curly black locks and the eyes, the scar on his forehead, silvery now and well healed. He looked so good. Too good, in fact. Well rested, well dressed and well fed. A trembling so desperate that she was forced to clasp her arms about her midriff to physically hold herself together began at her feet and swept her body. She wanted to scream and throw herself at him. Claw those enchanting, mesmerizing eyes out of their sockets, rip his handsome face with her nails.

A stabbing pain filled her, like a knife thrust to the heart, at the realization that she had been sorely used and abandoned. Her love turned as a weapon against her, her most delicate sensibilities trampled upon like so many weeds underfoot. Remembering . . . to have given so freely of herself . . . having flung her heart at his feet . . . and then for him to escape, not more than an hour after bedding her; leaving her there to bear the brunt of Rory's sadistic cruelty for two long, miserable years . . . mourning him, revering his memory while trying to protect herself and his own babies . . . to have him merely say, *I live?* It was too much.

"You heartless snake!" she rasped.

"Birdie?" George, still holding Amaryllis swathed in her blanket, stepped forward. She had endured so much, and been so desperately ill that fateful day he had chanced upon her near the docks of Bantry, that he was greatly concerned for her mental and physical state. He could see both slipping, perhaps beyond repair, right before his eyes.

"You—" she snapped, unable to tear her eyes from Temple. "You contemptible—"

"I, my dear?" He mockingly tilted an eyebrow. "*I* did nothing."

That was the last straw. She was only too aware he had done nothing. Nothing for her and nothing for his children. She hurled herself at him. Her hand closed into a fist and flashed toward him, smashing sharply into his cheek. Though the blow was powered by all the hatred and frustration she could summon, he neither winced nor even blinked. Screaming out the pain and humiliation of two long years of hopelessness and torture, she began pummeling his chest. He took blow after blow, then finally gripped her wrists and stretched her arms outward to bring her under restraint. Beyond control, she jerked one hand free. She brought it down, her nails gouging his cheek, opening four troughs that quickly filled with blood.

"Bloody damn!" he yelped, flinging her away from him and holding his cheek. Birdie fell to her knees and could not rise as tears overwhelmed her. Great ripping sobs tore her chest, and she could not catch her breath.

"For God's sake, man! Have you taken leave of your senses?" George entreated, frowning at his lordship. He started toward Birdie.

"Leave her!" Temple roared. "She is my wife and your assistance will not be needed here."

His shout brought both tired babies to tears. Birdie raised her face and hatred shot through her eyes at this man she had loved with her whole being.

"Hell's teeth! What are those?" he demanded, waving his hand toward the two babies swaddled in blankets and shrieking at the tops of their powerful little lungs.

Leaping to her feet, Birdie jumped between Temple and her children. She looked fierce and prepared to do battle if he so much as moved toward them.

"They're mine!" she screamed. "Don't you touch them!"

"Madam, I would not even think of it." Temple's jaw stood out as he clenched his teeth. He turned to the footman holding a wailing Charles and raked a hand through raven hair. "For God's sake, take them to the nursery or something! I'll send Franny to you right away."

"Yes, Franny," she whimpered. "Oh, yes, Franny." Calming somewhat, Birdie bit back a sob of thankfulness.

"Thank God," he said. Motioning a second footman forward to relieve George of the screaming Amaryllis, he turned his back and withdrew into the library, to slam the door sharply behind him.

Birdie jumped at the slamming of the door. Taking both hands, she rubbed roughly at her face, much like an exhausted child.

"Birdie, I cannot leave you here like this," pleaded George. He stepped to her to gather her into his arms. "Come back to the ship with me. We'll think of something different. You can't stay here. Not like this!"

"Dear George, twice you have rescued me. But I am still his wife and I must stay here. Please do not worry about me. Just go, and know that I owe you my life and the lives of my children." Birdie swayed tiredly and grasped the polished banister to keep from falling. She turned unsteadily to mount the stairs. George jerked toward her but did not touch her.

"Birdie, the ship will be in port a fortnight at least. Do not hesitate to call on me. One word and I will be here to take you and the children away. Do you understand?" He stepped to the stairs and looked up at her with all his love in his eyes. She turned to throw herself into his arms with a sob.

"Oh, George, I shall never forget you and all we have shared. Stay well." With these parting words, fresh tears blinded her. She wept as if never to stop. George held her close for a moment, then spun and flung himself out the front door into the rain. Neither saw a stone-faced Temple standing in the open door of the library.

Blindly Birdie followed the footmen to the fourth-floor nursery. Wiping her eyes on the sleeve of the muddy traveling dress, she burst into the room to see both wailing children sitting on a single bed in an icy, cold room with the uneasy footmen edging out the door. Anger ripped through her heart that her children, who had suffered so much, should be subjected to such a cold welcome, just when she had promised them they would be safe here.

"Stop!" she ordered. Her tone froze the footmen in their tracks.

"Yes, m-miss," one of the young men stammered.

"From this moment on, you will address me and my children as befits our position in this house. Do I make myself clear?" At the footman's stricken nod, she demanded again, "*Do* I make myself clear?"

"Y-yes, my lady."

"Excellent. First of all, send a maid to clean and warm this nursery. My children and I will require hot...not cold...hot baths and some semblance of night clothing."

"Yes, my lady."

"Now, show me the mistress's bedchamber," she commanded. Scooping both children into her arms, she glared at the flustered footman when he hesitated to lead the way.

The long walk down one flight of stairs and along numerous corridors carrying a baby on each hip was exhausting for the drained Birdie. Only her anger helped her bear up under the strain. Once inside the large, airy bedchamber, she plopped both dirty, tired children in the middle of the large bed with a sigh and dismissed the man with a wave of her hand. Sinking to her knees beside the bed, she gathered her babies close to her and kissed their little tear-streaked faces.

"Everything will be all right, my dears. We're home now and this is where we'll stay," she whispered soothingly, fighting to keep her own tears in check. The door behind her opened with such force that it slammed back against the frame. Birdie started and turned quickly to protect her babies from this new threat.

"Lord have mercy, 'tis me lass!" The wail came from a plump woman flying at Birdie. Birdie's eyes widened at the sight of her and sobs broke from her own throat. Both babies, hungry and upset, began to wail afresh. The plump woman fell on all three, gathering them to her bosom, tears of her own streaming down her rosy cheeks.

"Oh, Franny!" Birdie gasped in sobs. "Oh, Franny! I've needed you so much!" She wasn't alone anymore. Finally there was an ally in the enemy camp. Franny would help her protect her children.

"Good heavens, what a racket! I'm ashamed of all of you!" Snapping around, Birdie flung herself at the voice without so much as a look, hugging the woman hard. Such hauteur could only belong to Libby Fitzwaters. Her arms were untangled and she was pushed back a step as the older woman demanded again, "Here, I believe I said to stop this infernal noise."

"I'm sorry, Libby." Birdie's tears turned to a watery giggle as she stepped back, wiping her eyes on the sleeve of her dress.

"A lady uses a handkerchief," Libby admonished, whipping a spotless linen from her sleeve and pressing it into her hand. "Franny, see to those suffering children immediately."

"Yes, Libby," Franny said with a wide grin. Picking up Amaryllis and cuddling her close, she soothed her with kisses and baby talk in her blessed Irish brogue. The crying diminished as both babies recognized a kind soul they could wrap around their chubby fingers.

"I will attend your needs, my lady. Franny, take the children to the nursery and see to them properly," Libby ordered, rolling up the sleeves of her gown above her elbows as if preparing for war. Franny stood holding a nodding baby on each ample hip, beaming with watery happiness at Birdie.

Birdie gave a deep sigh. At last she was home. "Oh, Libby, I shall never rest until I am easy about my babies first. If you will find food and nightclothes for the three of us, I will help Franny bath and feed them," she said. "Tomorrow will be soon enough to move them to the nursery. Tonight I n-need them close to me."

"As you wish, my lady. I'll have infant cots brought down from the nursery and set into the dressing room. I can clearly see that my lady needs her rest, also," said Libby. Birdie glanced back in surprise. Libby had never capitulated so easily before, and Birdie truly felt she was home at last.

Through the bathing and feeding of the babies, Birdie sketchily told her tale of the last two years. Franny clucked and moaned over the treatment she had endured, all the time thinking Temple dead. Now, with the babies tucked into their cots, and Libby brushing her drying hair in long, smooth strokes, the tension began to ease from her body. Perhaps, just perhaps the horror was finally over, she thought. Franny came into the bedchamber on tiptoe.

"They're sound asleep. Such little lambs they be, the both of them."

"Franny, seat yourself here, by the fire. I need to talk to the both of you."

"It is not proper, my lady," Libby scolded. "You should not encourage familiarity with the servants."

"Friends, Libby. Dear friends," she said, smiling at the formidable woman. "I need my friends around me to feel safe."

Seating herself on the edge of the chair, Franny patted Birdie's cold hand and clicked her tongue. "To think . . . an O'Donnell!"

"Let it go now, Franny. He's dead and so is his evil. George Hughett appearing on that dock at just the right moment can only be seen as yet another of God's merciful miracles. But Temple being alive . . . so many sleepless nights, and so many nightmares about how horribly Rory told me he died." She sighed, as if the burdens of the world rested on her shoulders. "The nights I've cried myself to sleep, praying for rescue. And all the while my beloved husband was alive and well. What a fool I was! He still had his inheritance, but without a slum wife," she said bitterly. "I could have killed him downstairs."

Franny's eyes narrowed. "There be a better way, slower . . ."

"Franny! You will not speak of the master that way!" Libby admonished her severely. She silenced the plump maid with such a terrible, threatening look that Birdie knew Franny was in for the scolding of her life when they were out of her sight. How she had missed these dear people. Weary tears slipped down her cheeks.

"I—I fear for my children . . . and I don't want Temple to see them. He might not allow me to stay here. If he realizes they are his, he might try to take them from me. I need time to sort all this out, but if I must leave, I cannot leave my babies behind."

Franny crossed her arms over her bosom with a defiant look at Libby. "Do not fash yerself about them little lambs. I will tend them and ye just sleep until ye are healed. The fairies as my witness, no one will touch a finger to them little lambs while I am alive!"

The statement was rash and exaggerated but exactly what Birdie needed to hear, and her mind eased for the first time since she had kissed the black ringlets on their heads and realized they were Temple's . . . and not Rory's.

"Now that your mind is eased on that score," Libby said, "it's off to bed with you, my lady. And you are not to rise at all tomorrow. We must strengthen your health. You've quite lost your looks, my lady."

Birdie smiled at the foolishness of the woman's insinuation that she'd had nothing more to worry about for the past two years than the state of her complexion. She slid into the bed and propped herself back against the pillows with a deep sigh.

"And you, Libby. Do you and Travers fair well?"

"As well as any, my lady," Libby answered tartly. She shooed Franny toward the dressing room and closed the door. "Now, to sleep with you."

No sooner had she shut her eyes than the hall door to the bedchamber opened and Temple boldly strolled into the room. Birdie sat up quickly, scraping her very soul for enough strength to withstand this dreaded confrontation. Temple's face was forbidding, indeed. Four crimson furrows angled down to his jaw, the flesh angry and raw around them. Birdie thought to call for Franny. As if reading her mind, he abruptly raised his hand to still her.

"Do not! I shall only require four minutes of your time. One for each of these," he said, indicating the marks.

"I am sorry about your cheek," she said icily. "I was going for your eye."

"Nevertheless," he said, standing stiffly just inside the door. "Despite what has transpired between us, you are still my wife, I regretfully say. I could divorce you if I chose, but I refuse to bring scandal—any more scandal—to my name, and therefore . . ."

"Divorce me!" she cried. "You think to punish *me?* When I am the one wronged? You—"

"No!" he shouted. "I will not discuss the right or the wrong with you!" His shout brought Franny through the dressing room door, concern written on her face. "Leave us!" Temple ordered, his face black with rage. The maid stood her ground, arms crossed over her bosom, until Birdie nodded to her, then she still hesitated before closing the door. Temple continued only when they had privacy again. "I will publicly acknowledge you as my wife and you will conduct yourself as my wife, bringing no further shame to the name of Daine-Charlton. Is that understood?"

For a moment, Birdie was stunned. Daine-Charlton? That meant Sir Charles was dead. Oh, no, please don't let it be true. "Sir Charles?" she whispered, her eyes pleading for him to say it wasn't so.

"Dead last year," he answered curtly. "I will have your word on this matter, Birdie. Tonight!"

Tears gathered again in her eyes. Sir Charles died never knowing she was safe, never seeing the children that would carry his blood and name on through the ages. Great silent sobs shook her body. Tears streamed down her face. Grief, as deep as what she had felt when she thought Temple had been killed in the mountains, tore at her heart. Wrapping her arms tightly across her chest, she rocked back and forth, trying to control herself, but her anguish was too great to be denied. Deep moans escaped her as she fought to keep body and soul together.

Temple waited uncomfortably for her to regain some composure. He must allow her this sadness, for it would seem she had been genuinely fond of the old man. When she did not seem to recover at all, he stepped to the side of the bed with a frown. Easing himself onto it, he touched her shoulder, then gathered her into his arms. Deeply immersed in her grief, she allowed him to draw her against the velvet lapel of the dressing gown but could not cease her silent sobbing, or her rocking, as if she were unaware he was there with her.

"Birdie, you mustn't. He would not want you to," he said, attempting to soothe her, one hand stroking her hair.

As she quieted and grew still, Temple became aware of the pillows of her soft breasts against his arm. His body stirred as his mind betrayed him and memories of making love with this responsive child flooded his mind. But then the thought that she had lain with another and bore the bastard's children quickly followed. Anger infused him again and he jerked her face up to glare at her. Her beauty was still considerable, despite the obvious exhaustion etched there. The tears had softened her eyes, which wanted to close with fatigue. Her lips were parted and tempting. He fleetingly thought to lay his there, to taste her again.

Who else had thought to do the same the past two years? The Irish rebel? And the man she had clung to so heatedly in the entry hall? Probably others, too. Who claimed paternity for her two children? His little virgin bride was soiled goods now, proper slum goods, even down to her two bastards. His mouth formed a grim line and he released her abruptly, standing to glare down at her in disgust. Or was it disgust with himself for wanting her still?

"Just so we understand each other. I will not denounce your children as not of my blood, although rumors will race throughout the ton, but you are not to flaunt them, either. I will have your word on this, Birdie, or I shall petition the queen for divorce on the morrow. I feel, under the circumstances, the petition would not be denied. Do you understand me?''

Emotionally exhausted and barely above consciousness, Birdie nodded her head. She would have agreed to anything if he would just go away and let blessed sleep numb her grief. She sank back to the pillows as her eyes drifted closed.

''Damn, Birdie!'' he breathed in irritation. ''Whatever happened to that guileless child I married at Blanballyhaven?''

She opened her eyes and smiled sadly. It was a smile full of secret amusement, deep heartbreak and infinite bitterness. She whispered softly, allowing her eyes to close, ''Perhaps I have finally become the nightmare you always thought I was, Temple.''

Chapter Twenty

When the disagreeable Viscount Sayers had obligingly departed the world in answer to his wife's twenty years of nightly prayers, Lady Emily Sayers had wasted no time in removing her two children to London with the idea of snaring a major share of the fortunes there. For weren't her two children, Sophia, with her extraordinary silver looks, and dear Oliver, her golden lion, by far the most marvelous creatures that had ever moved in the circles to which she aspired?

Although what had at one time seemed a promising fire now appeared to be damp ashes. Who would have thought, for all the attention he had paid Sophia, that the disagreeable Lord Daine-Charlton would have returned from Ireland with not only the expected title of Marquis of Stannisburn but the rumor, if not the physical presence, of a wife! To have all one's carefully laid groundwork go for naught had been exasperating. And now, the wife *would* mysteriously materialize in London. Most distressing, indeed!

Seated now in her grand salon, newly decorated in her own sense of high style, which consisted of a myriad of stripes and patterns to challenge the eye, the plump woman of middle years was fretting on that very subject. She had quite despaired of Oliver ever making a suitable marriage as nothing, simply nothing and no one, suited his finicky tastes. No, she'd best put her eggs in Sophia's basket, for Ollie was not to be trusted. It must lie upon her daughter's delicate shoulders to secure their place in society and replenish the failing coffers.

Basically a foolish woman, for all her lofty aspirations, Lady Sayers masked a greedy, self-indulgent manner behind a guise of inept, girlish fluttering. But what she lacked in intelligence to carry forth her plan, her daughter made up for. For here was one truly devious to her very core. A fact her mother either ignored or was unaware of.

"Sophia, I have only glimpsed the marquise from a distance, but you should not discount her. It was difficult to tell, she would flit in and out of the chaise in such a hurry, but I would swear there was great beauty there. Although it is rumored to be a disagreeable marriage and she may be sent to the country by the marquis, be prepared for her to take London by the ears if she does stay for the season."

"Nonsense! She is a child," said Sophia, delicately lifting the teacup from her saucer. "She hasn't a clue as how to go on in society. She'll make a fool of herself right off the cuff. Besides, Mama, Lord Daine-Charlton has told me practically point-blank that he intends to divorce her. So why should I worry?"

"Well, I have no idea how you have gained his lordship's confidence in such private matters ... I mean, he wouldn't be telling you this if he didn't harbor strong feelings for you. So—" Lady Sayers twittered, fluttering her hands over her ample bosom "—perhaps all is not lost?"

Sophia touched her teacup to rest lightly on her bottom lip and smiled a bit. Her mother had no idea, indeed, and she would never know, either, for she would be aghast if she did. "You worry much too much, Mama."

"I am just appalled to realize this opportunity..." Lady Sayers sighed deeply. "Well, you see, it'd be like starting over again. Setting our sights on another, you understand?"

"Mama, the girl is untutored. Barely out of the schoolroom, if she was ever in one in the first place. One hears the most awful rumors about her background. Why, if they ever spread, she'll be ruined before she even begins." A terrible smile crossed the tinted mouth for a moment. Luckily, Lady Sayers was not privy to it, although it is doubtful she would have understood, or cared, had she noticed. "I have told you, Mama, how the old marquis forced the marriage."

"I do hope it all comes off as planned tonight," Lady Sayers fretted. "I mean, she has just made her curtsy to the queen, and the princess's birthday ball is her first venture into society. Are you positive, Sophia, that it's the right move to start her here...I mean, dinner here first, then on to the ball? Won't it appear that...well, that we support her? Placing our stamp of approval on the chit?"

"What a worrier you are, Mama." Sophia's laugh tinkled. "Of course it is a major move on our part to begin the worst night of the girl's life here with us. We must be sure that the play is written in our favor from the beginning. You will see, all will work out as planned. I do mean to be the Marquise of Stannisburn. And now I am off to rest the afternoon away. 'Twill be a long, eventful night."

Birdie had seen little of her husband the last month. He dined at his club or with friends every night and quit the house before she came downstairs in the mornings. She tried not to be disappointed and busied herself with her children and dressmakers and such, readying herself to enter society. All in all, she should have been content. But it was hard to realize and accept that she was here at last. A lady in her own town house in Grosvenor Square. It was everything she had dreamed of as a child, and yet she was not happy. Instead, she felt she was living in a house with an advancing thunderstorm. She could feel the tension, smell the fear. She knew it was brewing, and it was wearing at her natural vitality.

At length came the day, three weeks after making her curtsy to the queen, that Temple came in search of her in the small back sitting room, called appropriately enough, for the color of its furnishings, the yellow room. Facing east and catching the sunrise, it was a place Birdie frequented in the mornings, sitting with the children, listening to Franny's detailed descriptions of their brilliance and accomplishments. At these times, she was truly and completely content.

Temple opened the door and stepped into the yellow room. Birdie looked up somewhat startled, and with no little feeling of having her privacy violated. She would have liked to say she had become quite used to not seeing him, but that would not be the truth. She sensed him in the hallways, smelled him in the library and heard him late at night through the connecting door in the dressing rooms. She yearned painfully for the closeness she mistakenly had thought they were developing at Blanballyhaven and abhorred the aloofness he extended toward her when escorting her to St. James Palace to be presented to Queen Adelaide.

"My lord," she greeted him formally, breathing a small sigh of relief that Franny had just now returned to the nursery with the babies.

"I will take no more than a moment of your time," he said, moving to stand with his back to the small fire. He stood erect, glancing neither right nor left but looking straight into Birdie's eyes.

She promptly laid aside the book she was holding and gave him her full attention. She raised her eyes with what she hoped was a calm expression to coolly return his stare. He was still gorgeous, she thought. The well-fitting jacket of black superfine was overshadowed by an intricately tied cravat that must have earned Travers a bonus. She smiled the slightest smile at the thought. An extravagant fall of lace spilled from his cuffs, half hiding his hands, causing Birdie to wonder to which of the many sets of the ton he belonged. Buff trousers, showing not the slightest wrinkle, were strapped tightly beneath gleaming Hessians, and he carried a caped coat over his arm, indicating that he was on his way out again.

The raven locks, so like his son's, were disarrayed already, as if he had raked his hand through them repeatedly before confronting her. Travers must despair of him, she thought. Though the ensemble was plain in the extreme, he looked outstanding and distinguished. She thought to query where he was running to so early in the day but refrained, as it was not to be her place to inquire into her husband's business. Clearing his throat, he addressed her. His voice, once so loved, brought her attention away from his person and back to his face.

"As I previously informed you, we will be attending Lady Sayers's dinner party before the princess's ball. Normally, it is not an invitation I would accept, the Lady Sayers being somewhat distracting, but the guest list is distinguished, and it is time we made our appearance as a couple. I shall call for you promptly at nine o'clock. Please do not keep me waiting."

"As you wish, my lord," Birdie answered, politely with a slight incline of her head.

The sunlight touched her hair, playfully suggesting he, too, should feel the silkiness of it. He saw that the extended rest had erased the exhaustion from her face, and she was, again, perfection. Her manner was correct, polite, everything it should be, yet it made him sad. Where was the child? Where was the innocence? The frankness he had fallen in love with such a short time ago? She blushed prettily beneath his gaze, satisfying some of his longings. As he looked at her soft skin so delicately tinted, his stern expression was eased suddenly by a wry smile.

For a moment, his feelings of having been ill-used by this infant left him. He wished to dispel the tension that existed between them. Her presence in the house was a tangible, warm thing. She had made Daine Hall a home. A home he wished to be included in but seemed forever racing away from with innumerable socials that were proving to be a bloody bore, for even there she dominated his thoughts.

"Birdie, I would suggest a truce between us. We cannot live like this for the rest of our lives," he began, clearing his throat with a nervousness he did not wish to admit. He attempted levity. "Besides, my health will not long stand the pace of my present activities."

A truce? Birdie toyed with the idea. A truce? A termination of hostility. Simply forgive and forget? Without answers? But would it be possible to swallow her anger, her pain at his desertion? How was she to forget the way he had raised his eyebrow in such a mocking manner and said, "I did nothing"? How she wanted to fly into his face and demand to know why he had done nothing . . . nothing while she had fought for their lives. The fact that he had promised her a chance, had encouraged her love with such dishonesty froze her heart. Lies! All lies! No, she feared she could not forget so easily. Rising from the sofa, she paced to the window overlooking the carefully manicured garden beyond.

"A truce," she began, then turned fully to study every minute detail of his beautiful face. How she wanted to question him. How she wanted some direct honesty from him. Had he been warm and well fed at Blanballyhaven while she had chewed jerky on the cold trail, dressed in thin rags against the freezing snow? Had he refused to join in the search for her the morning she had fought off rape in front of twenty jeering men? Had he been making love on satin-and-lace sheets the night that Rory had savaged her body over and over again in the rotten straw of a burned-out homestead?

Closing her eyes for a moment, she fought the desire to confront him. Where were you, dear husband, while I screamed and writhed, forcing your babies from my body with a madman as a midwife? Dancing at the palace? And where were you when Rory, realizing those babies were yours and not his, was driving his fists into my face? Her hand came up to touch the almost invisible scar at her hairline. No, she could never forgive because she could not forget. She refused to forget. To swallow this without answers would be to fester inside with rot. No, she wanted no truce.

"A truce, my lord?" she sneered. "As far as I am concerned, our differences are irreconcilable."

Temple nodded slightly, his face immobile as he watched the play of emotions cross her expressive face. Obviously the thought that he could set her and her bastards on the street never crossed her arrogant little mind. But when he thought to mention the fact, he was disgusted with himself. Threatening defenseless women and children gave him no pleasure. Temple stared at her for a moment with intensity. He sought to discomfort her, punish her for refusing an offer that he felt was generous on his part indeed, but she did not lower her gaze from his.

"As you wish," he said. Walking to the door, he left quietly, closing it firmly behind him as if that would stop him from wanting to go back to her. He stood there pondering. He wanted to open it again. He wanted to take her into his arms. To what? To shake her senseless? Or to kiss her breathless? The frank, outrageous child who would thump him in the head with her boots was who he wanted back. Where had she gone? Or had she ever been anything more than a flight of his imagination? The callous woman that child had turned out to be was a disappointment. He jerked his hand from the doorknob and quit the house in a dark mood.

Birdie, despite her outward calm, stood with bated breath, watching the door. Every sense in her expected him to reopen the door. She willed it to happen, but when it did not, she paced the floor in agitation. Why was her heart thumping as if it were a bird attempting to escape a cage? What did she want from him? She ran the tip of her tongue over dry lips. Scooping the book from the settee abruptly, she threw it across the room.

"Damn him to hell! He promised to give our marriage a chance. A promise that took him two days to break! But even then, all he had to do was take me with him when he flew Glencolumbkille. I shall never forgive him that! I hate him! I will not yearn for him! You hear me? I *will* not want him!"

Chapter Twenty-One

As promised, Birdie descended the staircase promptly at nine. Temple, waiting in the drawing room with a glass of spirits, looked up as she entered. Interest, and a reawakening of amazement at her beauty, flickered in his eyes before he shuttered them. She was regal, her coloring set off by the simple gown of bronze satin, topped by a cloak of luscious bronze velvet lined in the matching satin. The richness of her russet hair burned brightly in the candlelight. The whiteness of her skin had mellowed to ivory and her eyes shone warmly. She moved with such grace, her steps so measured, that the hem of her gown seemed to glide over the floor.

Suddenly Temple experienced the longing to put the past behind him and gather her into his arms. But no sooner had the thought entered his mind than it was replaced sternly with sanity. She had already denied him a truce. He would not humble himself to offer again. Taking her elbow rather roughly, he accompanied her to the waiting carriage for a silent, uncomfortable ride to the viscountess's dinner party.

Upon entering the Sayers's drawing room on the arm of her husband, Birdie was confronted with a sea of faces turning to stare at her and an abrupt halt of all conversations, leaving a silence that was deafening. With an effort, Birdie kept her eyes up and her spine straight. The lords and ladies of the ton studied her as if she had a dirty face or as if there were something distastefully wrong with her appearance. Temple stiffly performed the introductions, his expressive mouth tight. Several older ladies openly snubbed her by nodding curtly, then turning their backs. Birdie paled and cast a worried glance at Temple's set face. Surely he would not lay these snubs at her door? It was as she'd always declaimed. The ton was unforgiving of anyone or anything that did not meld into their mold of correctness.

"Lady Daine-Charlton?" Sophia mouthed with a mere dismissing flick of her pale eyes, before turning avid attention to Temple. "*My* Lord Daine-Charlton, how pleasant to see *you* here."

The possessive way she emphasized her words did not escape Birdie and she raised an eyebrow slightly. Since her presence had been apparently forgotten, it was possible to study the girl quite openly. Her pale face was arrestingly beautiful in an odd sort of way, she decided. Her mouth was etched and shaded a vibrant red, her cheeks glowing as white marble against it, and her almost colorless eyes were framed by astonishingly silver lashes. She was slight of build and preened openly for Temple. Polished and somewhat older than she herself was, Sophia Sayers possessed a confidence and self-assurance that made Birdie feel terribly young and gauche.

"Tem—Lord Daine-Charlton, London drawing rooms have been languishing without you," she now said to him, her tone indescribably intimate and her eyes limpid. She stood quite close to him, everything about her manner brazenly excluding his wife. Birdie remained silent and fingered her bronzed fan nervously as she watched them together. It was obvious to anyone observing the trio, anyone who cared to look beneath the bland conversation, that Temple and the silver Sophia had been lovers, and possibly were still.

It came as no surprise to Birdie that Temple was a man of experience. That had been obvious even to her innocence on their wedding night. But to stand face-to-face with someone he had known as intimately as he had known her brought a numbing dejection to her heart. Had he held this silver beauty as closely as he had her? The very thought of Temple kissing that red mouth, intimately entwining with her, was more than unpleasant. It was sickening. Was this the woman he had planned to wed? The one he had been in love with? The one he wished for every day of his life, every day he was bound to her?

With a secretive smile at Birdie's pale face, Sophia excused herself, pleading hostess duties, well pleased with herself for having firmly put the little upstart in her place. And for all the company to see.

Temple turned to Birdie, sensing her nervousness even though her proudly held head disguised it well from the rapidly swelling company in the drawing room. Touched by her vulnerability, he took her elbow and removed them from the center of the floor, away from open curiosity. Try as he might, he could not stop himself from wanting to shield her as one would a tender child. This disgusted him, as he did not want to feel that for her. In fact, he did not wish to feel anything for her. Watching her now, staring at the richness of the company in their silks and satin, he leaned forward to murmur into her ear.

"My dear, it is considered very poor manners to be so straightforward with one's words or with one's gaze. Such a direct look is usually reserved for the inexperience of little girls—" he paused to watch her face "—or the brassiness of harlots."

His words and tone implied her lack of breeding, and Birdie, flushing brilliantly in humiliation, dropped her eyes to her hands, tightly clutched her fan, looking very much like a chastised little girl and nothing like a harlot. Immediately, Temple regretted his words. But in truth, he was stung by her refusal to agree to a truce. She had no right to refuse any offer he made. He owed her nothing. Wasn't he the one wronged? Wronged by her participation in a scheme to defraud an old man. Although reason threw many an argument over that thought, for it was a farfetched idea that the Irish rebels could have instigated such a long-reaching plot. But she was guilty of conspiring with her Irish lover to hasten his demise, then returned with her two bastards to lay claim to his inheritance.

He had never looked at the children. Probably the younger was the boy and destined to be the heir, hence the time lapse before her return. With a snort of aversion, he turned from her. The fact of the matter was, he sternly told himself, she was cunning and conniving, though cleverly disguised by the most desirable body God had ever created. And if he must remain buckled to her, he would most definitely find a way to enjoy that body while spurning involvement with the rest of her. When dinner was announced, he took her elbow in a hard grasp and joined the company as they filed into the dining room.

An overelaborate affair, dinner was served in a great, hollow dining hall, lit by hundreds of candles wafting the heat and smell of beeswax repeatedly over Birdie, destroying any enjoyment of the food, which seemed heavy and slightly greasy in the first place. Directly across from her gaze was a vivid painting of ducks, geese and a few chickens hanging by their feet, dripping blood from their cut throats. She blanched and tried to stop her eyes from returning to it time and again throughout the prolonged meal.

Seated to Lord Oliver Sayers's right, and next to an elderly Lord Arlington, Birdie could not keep her eyes from straying the length of the table to where Temple was seated, with obvious forethought, beside the sophisticated Lady Sophia. With an astute street sense, Birdie surmised that, while the lady might portray a silver mink, there lurked a ferret just beneath the surface that bore watching.

Lord Arlington was bending her ear with a detailed report of the marvelous regimen his new physician had prescribed. In view of the fact that his lordship wolfed down every one of Lady Sayers's rich, greasy courses, from the thick, gamy mutton to the undercooked lemon tart, Birdie felt his dedication a trifle suspect, but as no one else deemed to notice, she thought it senseless to remark upon it. As he rambled on, her eyes wandered to Sophia's sparse bosom, shoved so high by padding in an attempt to display it to advantage that it was barely covered by the daring décolletage of her gown.

Despite this provocative display, Sophia apparently feared that Birdie's faithless husband might miss the magnificence of the exposed flesh, for she managed to lean well over the table every thirty seconds or so, and Birdie soon began to wager with herself as to whether she would eventually plunge her rose bodice into her plate. Unfortunately, to her great disappointment, she did not.

"You seem amused, Lady Daine-Charlton. Do you wish to share your thoughts with me?" a cool voice murmured into her ear.

Startled, Birdie leaned away from Oliver. "I do beg your pardon, Lord Sayers."

"I was merely trying to rescue you from the dribble on your right by diverting your attention to your left . . . and me," Oliver said. His smile was open and seemed genuine. Hungry for acceptance from at least one member of a gathering, Birdie relaxed and returned the smile with one of her own.

"I must say I welcome the diversion, my lord, although I would not want it said that I am a poor dinner partner," teased Birdie.

"I assure you no one would say that about such a beautiful lady," he countered, though his thoughts were quite different behind his mask of civility. He then continued with an expression that hinted at something less than respect for women in general. "Could it be possible that there lives *one* beautiful woman who does not know the power she wields with that very beauty?"

"I, my lord, have never found it to be particularly powerful. Speaking from the absurd assumption that beauty applies to myself," she flung back with a radiant smile that left no doubt of her beauty.

"You mean to say that not once in your life have you had occasion to notice that men would live and die for a beautiful woman? Honesty now!" chastised Oliver with delicate brows tilted upward.

Birdie laughed at his question. "I have, indeed, found that men will go to whatever lengths required to obtain, for however short a time, something they cannot carry away with them for any lasting purpose."

Covering his eyes with a slender hand in pretend pain, he replied, "Not so. To hold beauty in one's hand—" he swept that hand outward and his eyes slipped down significantly to her deep neckline "—even for a moment, is to commit that beauty to memory forever."

"*That*, my Lord Sayers, has nothing whatsoever to do with beauty," she replied with a set face. "*That* has to do with power, control . . . winning and losing."

"Exactly as I said," he agreed with a slight bow of his head, as if she had merely proven his point.

Birdie thought for a moment, then laughed. She liked this man. He may speak in riddles but he did speak truth. She laughed again.

Temple looked the length of the table to see his wife's merriment and was unsure if he was pleased she was enjoying herself or jealous that it was with someone else. God help her if she was trying to snare another man to use for her own selfish purposes. He would not be a willing cuckold for her.

When at last Lady Sayers signaled the ladies to leave the gentlemen to their port, Birdie excused herself to attend her needs in the bedchamber set aside for the ladies' use. Returning as slowly as possible to the drawing room, she dreaded spending another hour in the company of these unfriendly women and wished they were leaving immediately for the ball. Never had she thought in her youthful dreams that society could be such a crushing, tedious bore. Pausing to draw a deep, strengthening breath at the doorway, she suddenly wished she had entered with the others, for now she must suffer their stares as if appearing center stage. Bits of conversation floated toward her through the curtained doorway.

"I tell you, she *is* the bastard daughter of the old Lord Daine-Charlton," one shrill voice piped rudely. "Marrying her off to his great-nephew was the only way he could give her a name . . . and an immense fortune, I might add."

"*No!*" came more than one shocked gasp.

"Levina, that cannot be true! I have heard he was to marry her himself—the old marquis, I mean—if the great-nephew refused! Rumor has it she was the old man's mistress for years, and when he thought to die, well, he would pass her on with the title, so to speak." A high titter sounded throughout the room.

"But why ever didn't she come back to London when Lord Daine returned? Why now?"

Sophia's unmistakable cool voice wafted through the room, stilling all the rest. "I have an answer for that. She ran off with her

Irish lover on her wedding night. Poor Temple—I mean Lord Daine-Charlton—was actually relieved, but now she turns up here, on his doorstep, literally in the arms of another man . . . a common seaman, no less! *And* . . ." she paused dramatically, though she didn't need to build the suspense as the ladies, to the last one, were sitting on the edge of their seats, fairly drooling over this juicy bone. *"With a child!"*

In unison, the ladies drew in their breath in outraged sensibilities. Birdie waited for no more. She turned and fled blindly down the hall. Hearing the men rising from the dining room, she dodged into a dark sitting room off the main hall. A fire had been lit and the dim room closed cozily around her, protecting her from the pain. Leaning over the back of a chair to steady herself, she pressed fingers into her eyes to stop the tears. Tears of rage as well as pain, and no small amount of shame. There was only one way that Sophia could know of certain parts of that tale. Temple had to have told her, probably while curled around her in some bedchamber. The wicked cat!

She was probably his mistress even now. The gossip! The rumors! How was she to hold her head up in society? Temple had demanded no scandal. But she had not caused the stories. He had! This scandal was of his making, but would that make any difference to him? Would he still put her into the street with her babies, believing them to be O'Donnell's bastards? If she proved to him the blood of the children was his blood, to protect them and assure them a home and their rightful place, what then? He might still put her aside, but without her babies. No! She would not live without them! They were all she had!

Drifting around to the front of the chair, she sank into its concealing shadows. Her head ached abominably from the candle scent and heat. Her thoughts reeled wildly in despondency. If she begged, perhaps he would allow her to retire to the country and live quietly there. Anywhere but here, where his mistress was thrown in her face. Surely he would not force her to stand up in a society that did not want—or choose to acknowledge—her. Sophia's criticism and open lies would circulate through every drawing room in London. Lies perpetrated by Temple's uncharitable confidences. Oh, why hadn't she begged George to return with her to Blanballyhaven instead of London? Even with Sir Charles passed, Mattie would have taken her in. In despair, she raised her eyes to the ornate ceiling and to heaven beyond.

"Oh, Sir Charles, why didn't you let me stay at Blanballyhaven with you? I am so—" she dabbed at tears gathering in her eyes "—very alone here. Mam, I need you! Help me know what to do!"

She listened but no answer was lovingly whispered in her ear, as her mother's spirit had deserted her when she had lost the miniature. Dropping her head against the back of the chair, she let her eyes rest on a large portrait of two lovely young women that hung over the mantel, dimly lit by the firelight and a lonely, solitary candle on the mantel. The elder was seated on a gilt chair with her hands folded demurely in her lap, while the younger one, fresh and lovely, sat at her feet, resting her hands lightly on the woman's knee. The girl's smile was so sweet and her beautiful face, reflected in the flickering light, seemed to move and speak directly to her.

"Have strength, dear little bird. Always remember, you are a lady. You are of nobility."

"Yes, Mam, but I am so alone now," Birdie whispered back. Rising from the chair, she approached the portrait as if dazed.

"Beautiful, wasn't she?" a mocking voice came from behind her, and the room brightened somewhat with the addition of a candelabra that lit the gold hair and white, effeminate face of Oliver.

Spinning to confront the young man, she paled that he might have heard her words. "I could not bear to join the ladies. I hope you do not mind my slipping in here?" she pleaded.

"I could not blame you for anything, beautiful lady. Least of all wanting to avoid the gossipy cats in the drawing room," he insisted. "Think nothing of it."

Approaching her, he set the candles on the mantel in such a way that the portrait was bathed in warm light. Birdie's eyes were drawn back to the painting as if she were mesmerized. Oliver studied her with a calculating gaze. Her emotions played delightfully vividly over her face. Just how much did she know? Obviously not much, as she was greatly affected by the portrait, and stunned to find it in this house.

Birdie stared deeply into her mother's face. The realization that she was seeing a second picture of her mother, here in the house she must have called home, and that beside her stood a person who could answer all the questions she'd ever wanted to ask, was overwhelming. But she was afraid to ask those questions. She must move carefully before making claims, as she had no miniature to confirm her story.

"Yes, very beautiful," she whispered, then cleared her throat and asked in a stronger voice. "Who is . . . are they?"

"The woman seated on the chair is Sophia's and my mother—the girl at her feet was her younger sister...Amaryllis Lindley," Oliver stated offhandedly, as if unaware of the significance to Birdie. He watched her face closely. The resemblance really was remarkable when one knew to look for it.

"Amaryllis Lindley," she whispered aloud. But her thoughts ran wild. Lindley! I am Birdie Lindley! I have a name at last. Turning to the young man, she studied him. No taller than her, he seemed nicer, friendlier than when she had met him at Blanballyhaven. Her cousin. He was her cousin. Family! Biting the inside of her cheek, she tried to calm herself. "What happened to her? You said 'was.'"

"Well, now, I am not at all sure I should reveal that—family secrets, black sheep and all that," he drawled, enjoying the torment that played so openly over the young, fresh face. Never had he seen such yearning, such hunger. He could well imagine the will it took for her to answer as she did.

"I do not mean to pry. She is, as you say, very beautiful. One is always curious when someone has died so young."

"Whatever makes you say she died?" he asked, just to see her color in confusion and discomfort.

Birdie felt herself flush and quickly covered her slip. She must play this man carefully if she was to learn anything without giving away her secret. "I am sorry. I jumped to a wrong conclusion. Forgive me." Turning as if to take her leave of him, she bravely said, "Excuse me, Lord Sayers, I must return to the ladies before I am missed."

Correctly guessing his dear little cousin was holding her breath with each step she took toward the door, he allowed her to almost reach the doorway before granting reprieve and calling her back.

"Pray, forgive me, Lady Daine-Charlton. I am being inhospitable. To send you back to the ladies, which we have already established as a fate worse than having a flaming case of shingles, is despicable. Especially when I might entertain you with a story that really is not such a secret at all. In fact, probably was quite a scandal in its day. Come. Be seated," he entreated, waving a hand toward the chair. "Say you forgive me and I shall enthrall you with the story of my Auntie Amaryllis."

Birdie turned in a nonchalant way and put a teasing, slightly flirtatious smile on her lips. "I shall forgive you only because I would rather do anything than return to the drawing room," she quipped.

"I suppose I deserve to have my company placed second to a fate worse than death," he countered, giving her a deep bow. Taking her hand, he led her back to the chair where she could not help but look up at her mother again. He turned the opposing chair so that he might watch her expressive face at leisure.

"Quite a common tale, I believe, if the truth were known. It was when my mother was increasing, carrying one of my innumerable brothers and sisters she ultimately lost or whelped stillborn, that my Auntie Amaryllis came to stay. To assist my mother, you see. Sophia was young...say ten to my eight years of age. I believe Amaryllis must have been seventeen, and quite lovely. As one can see by the portrait. It was painted during that time, although the impending babe was apparently painted out by the overly sensitive artist." He laughed a cool, mocking laugh. Rising to splash whiskey into two glasses, he set one on the small table beside Birdie's chair.

"Please continue," she whispered as he seated himself. She fought to quail the urge to fidget in her chair.

"The foolish Amaryllis allowed herself to be seduced..." He paused to sip his libation, watching the rise and fall of Birdie's bosom stop as she held her breath. So, the little chit knew nothing! "By a young footman, I believe the tale goes. When it was discovered, she ran away, presumably with the young man. For the family never heard another word of her."

"But...d-did no one search? The family? Her parents? A young girl...alone."

"Her father, my grandpapa, was Lord Alfred Lindley. He passed long before I was old enough to remember him. And Grandmama, old and quite feeble in the head...well, there wasn't much anyone could do. Oh, Mother wanted to, being quite worried and heartbroken, you understand. After all, she was responsible for her, having her as a guest and all. But Father, ever practical Father, washed his hands of her. Said she had made her bed, now let her lie in it. If you will forgive my crassness."

As she turned to study the portrait again, her heart grieved for her mother. So young and so alone, with a baby coming, on the streets of London. Birdie prayed she had loved her footman, so at least she had had that to warm her cold nights. Stricken to her very core, she gazed at her mother with such longing and love that her lower lip began to tremble and her eyes misted with unshed tears.

Oliver leaned closer and slipped the glass into her limp hand. She did not raise it to her lips, but just the act of holding it might be enough to damn her should anyone walk in on them. "No one will believe you, of course," he murmured, his gaze never wavering from hers.

"Wh-what?" She looked at him quickly, so shocked at his statement she doubted that she had heard him correctly.

"I said no one will believe you," he repeated.

Anger began to replace shock. Had they all, the whole family, known about her? Willingly left her there, with Maude Abbott, after her mother had died? She leapt to her feet. "You knew! That she is . . . was my mother? You knew about me all along?"

Oliver smiled a tight little smile. Oh, she is delicious, he thought. So innocent, so easy to hurt. Fearing she would storm out, just when he was having such a delightful time, he decided to soothe her somewhat.

"We knew there was a child somewhere. Your reaction to the portrait was reason enough for me to guess the other. But what difference does it make?" He paused to sip leisurely from his glass before rising to his feet as manners dictated. Waving a hand to the chair again, he pleaded soulfully, "Please be seated so that I may, also. I am fearsome weary."

Without thinking, Birdie did as he begged, still holding the glass of whiskey. Oliver smiled at the picture they presented. Cozied into a dimly lit room, before a romantic fire, sharing a late-night libation. Foolish girl! Foolish wife! Foolish act for one warned to cause no scandal.

"What do you mean it doesn't matter?" demanded Birdie. "It matters a great deal to me!" She leaned toward him, rapt in her anger.

Oliver smiled again. Oh, yes, my little cousin, lean forward so that I might feast my eyes on those bountiful charms. He could feel his body tighten with excitement. "I mean, dear cousin, you have made a good marriage. You have a place in society, and your husband has not seen fit to denounce your child . . . yet. What do you think he will do if he learns you are the daughter of a common footman? What will society say? I daresay you will be shunned by the ton. Quite a stickler for blood, you know. No, I'd say it's a secret best allowed to remain a secret."

Birdie thought best to rise and strike the smug expression from his face, anything to erase the arrogance there, then abruptly depart his company. But as good as the idea was, she was not quick enough to save herself.

"Birdie!"

Leaping to her feet, she spun guiltily toward the door, spilling the whiskey on her skirt before she remembered she held it. There stood an obviously irate Temple, followed by Lady Sayers, Lord Arlington, Sophia and a gaggle of gossipy ladies glaring down their noses at the indiscretion they saw. Instantly, their mouths disappeared behind their hands and whispers erupted. Sophia gave a catty, self-satisfied smirk that only Birdie could see. What she didn't see, nor anyone else notice, was the slight raise of Oliver's glass in a salute to his sister. Quite pleased with himself, he was.

"Temple, I—I..." she stammered. Quickly she set the glass down on the table and rubbed her hand on her skirt, belatedly realizing how this must look to her husband and the others crowding the doorway.

"Come, Birdie, We are ready to depart for St. James," Temple muttered through clenched teeth. Taking her elbow, he led her from the sitting room with a purposeful stride. Birdie cast a glance over her shoulder for one last look at her mother's smiling, happy face.

"Do not look to him! He will not come to your aid, my dear," he rasped in her ear as he half dragged her down the hall to the delight of the company.

Chapter Twenty-Two

"The Marquis and Marquise of Stannisburn,"

All heads turned. Everyone stared. The pair descended the staircase of St. James Palace in stately silence. They were the most gossiped-about couple of this season. The couple whose most private lives, in the most intimate of detail, were discussed in drawing rooms across London with equal fervor. They presented an elegant pair, even if both faces were a trifle set. They reached the bottom of the stairs and joined the receiving line as if unaware of the attention their presence drew, though if one looked closely, the marquise's splendid bosom, so attractively displayed in bronze and gold, rose and fell a trifle fast.

"Magnificent pair, are they not?" murmured a droll voice in Sophia's ear. Oliver was standing behind her, his eye alight with mischief. "She looks every inch a marquise."

"Damn you, Ollie," she pouted. "I don't need your nonsense at this moment! It should be me entering on his arm, not that little nobody!"

"Little nobody? Are you forgetting she's family?"

"What are you babbling about? I refuse to recognize her as anyone important to me!" Sophia spoke over her shoulder as she was unable to take her eyes off the disgusting sight of Temple standing next to the chit, prepared to present himself and his wife to the Royals. Then she forced herself to relax. Temple loved *her*. Hadn't he told her so? Why, he had even spoken of divorce, hadn't he? He had no stomach for scandal, but for love of his Sophia Sayers, he would petition the queen to dissolve the marriage. And with both Ollie and her working against her, the chit could not hope to avoid shaming herself, now could she?

"Well, dear sister, refuse to recognize her if you will, but the fact is that she is Auntie Amaryllis's long-lost child!" Ollie hissed into her ear.

Sophia slowly turned to him with bitter eyes. "That makes no difference to me! And the situation would have never reached this state except for your ineptness, now would it, little brother?"

"Spilt milk . . . now we must merely turn it to our advantage. Retire with me away from this crush and I will tell you how the plot sets at this moment," he said, taking her arm to turn her away from the dance floor. "Come. He will be busy with his wife for a time. We have time before you can claim him again."

Stepping forward a step at a time to curtsy before the diminutive Princess Victoria and express her birthday wishes, Birdie drew in a quivering breath. Glitter, glamour, the rainbow flash of jewels, scent of flowers mingled with expensive perfumes, all swept around her in a heady wave. She was suddenly overwhelmed by it all. She was small and insignificant, the intruder they all believed her to be.

Temple watched her face with a mixture of feelings. Tenderness as he again saw the child bride, and weariness for a feigned innocence that had once before proven itself false. Those huge, beautiful eyes of hers were opened so wide that she had the look of a child on Christmas morn. Confusion brushed him again. Could one who looked so innocent, so vulnerable, be so calculating? A tremor swept through him.

Birdie, her hand resting on his arm, felt the tremor and leaned toward him to inquire in a hushed voice, "Temple! What is it? You're trembling! My lord, if you are terrified of facing this mass, then I shall surrender immediately!"

Temple looked down at her with dazed eyes, then recovering quickly, he said in his customary mocking voice, "I am quite well. Come, step forward. Bend your knee prettily for the princess."

Almost immediately afterward, Temple disappeared into the ballrooms, leaving Birdie trapped on the fringes with that old fool, Arlington, as chaperon. When she saw Temple standing up with Sophia for a set of country dances, her impatience burst. She would not sit in the matrons' line as a wallflower while her husband groped his mistress before the entire ton. Turning away from the sight with disgust, she moved toward the sound of music at the other end of the ballroom. It was a shocking squeeze, and before she realized it or intended it, she had separated from the fumbling Lord Arlington.

Determined to enjoy herself, she accepted an invitation from an amiable young gallant. This enchanted evening was a golden bubble, she told herself, something that might not happen for her again, and she did intend to enjoy herself. Once the ice was broken by the first young lord daring enough to brave gossip by leading the notorious marquise onto the floor, she found herself surrounded by a steady stream of admiring young Tulips of the ton. Unaware of the frowning countenance of more than one matron, she flitted from one amusing companion to another. As she grew flushed, excited by all the flattering attention she was receiving, her sherry brown eyes glowed and her shining russet ringlets began to fall in charming disarray, drawing many eyes, including the disapproving ones of her husband.

Leaning nonchalantly against a marble pillar within easy view of the dance floor, sipping ice champagne, Temple watched his wife. He was aware he was imbibing too much, but he did not particularly care. Even the knowledge that champagne did tend to leave behind a rather nasty head, and a foul mood to accompany it, did not deter him. Unlike whiskey, it did not affect his rationality, or his ability to think. For instance, at the present time, he thought it an admirable idea to thunder his fist into the faces of several young swains, then forcibly drag his wife from the dance floor, away from all the cursed male eyes greedily drinking of her beauty, and carry her home to bed. His bed! His body hungered for the responsive child bride that had been taken from him in Ireland. Draining his glass, Temple glanced around impatiently for a servant to replenish it.

"Darling Temple," Sophia's purring voice broke into his reverie. "I have been waiting for you to come to me, but since you will not, I came to you."

"Sophia." Temple acknowledged her with barely a nod. Catching the gay sound of Birdie's laughter wafting across the floor, he frowned and hardened his mouth. Certainly there was no lack of encouragement from her. How dare she smile like that. How dare she! He clenched the stem of his glass tightly and his frown deepened to a thundercloud.

Sophia's eyes narrowed speculatively, then widened. Oh dear, she thought. Cousin Birdie is calling attention to herself and her husband isn't happy about that! Perhaps I should circulate a bit and see if any of the dowagers have noticed. A word here . . . a word there. Sophia slipped away but Temple's attention was not caught by her departure.

"Confound it!" he muttered, searching for a servant to take note of his empty glass. "Does the Duchess of Kent retain so few servants?" When his eyes returned to the dance floor, Birdie was gone.

Refusing several invitations, Birdie eased from the circle of admirers with relief. The crush from the dance floor only intensified when she left it. Slowly she was able to make her way toward the columns at the door, which would protect her somewhat if she put her back against one. Truly it seemed a waste to dress with such care and then be in a crowd so dense that your gown could not be seen! But at least she would be grateful if the fragile stuff suffered no damage. Bending as best she could, she sought to examine it.

"I am gratified to see that you are in one piece."

"Temple!" she breathed, mortified beyond measure to be caught in such an undignified posture as examining one's costume.

"I had not thought to find you unescorted," he stated with a frown. "But as you are, perhaps you will favor me with your hand for the next dance?" He had meant for his statement to be a setdown, to send her eyes to the floor as a reprimand well received, but again he was confounded to find her readily standing up to him.

"I shall be pleased to take the dance floor with you, my lord, but only if you are quite finished mauling the other ladies," she countered sweetly as she gave him her hand to be led through the throng to the dance floor.

Being swept into the waltz, Birdie found herself held tightly in Temple's strong arms and swung onto the floor without her having much to say about it. This was a moment of revelation for her. She was appalled to find his warm hand upon her waist flaming through the fabric of her gown as if to scorch her. Surely, he was holding her too closely, for on some of the turns, her breasts grazed his shirt ruffles. The very touch of him set her face to blushing and she could not raise her eyes.

The waltz was wonderfully drifting, their feet moving at a leisurely pace, and Temple was an excellent partner, leading her firmly but smoothly across the floor with no misstep. Birdie relaxed in his hold, giving herself to the music, the steps, and to the firmness of his arms. His steps became more intricate, the half turns becoming full circles, the dips lower, and as she rose from them, her thighs brushed against his hard, muscled ones, and her breasts crushed the ruffles on his shirtfront. She dared not speak a word, for their mouths were almost touching, and his breath stirred the curls on her cheek.

"Birdie?" His soft voice so near made her tremble. Confused, she glanced into his eyes. He looked down into hers with a sensual smile. "Is this the mauling you spoke of?"

Mutely she shook her head. Dancing in his arms was the most seductive thing she had ever experienced. The movement, the closeness, the feel of his quickened breath paralleled his lovemaking. The momentum and the turns brought their bodies closer, and as they moved together, Birdie felt herself become pliant and responsive to him, the tightness in her belly pulsing with what he had taught her was desire. A desire she had thought deadened by Rory's abuse. Deny it if she wished, swear hatred for this man all she wanted, the truth remained that she had loved him then, she loved him now, and she would love him always.

Acknowledging her feelings, giving herself up to it, somehow lessened the pain. If this was to be the only way she could be in his arms, if this was the only time she was to experience his embrace, she prayed the music would last forever. Memories flooded her senses...Temple, his eyes hot with desire, his body tense with need of her, his tenderness in teaching her. I want him to hold me again, she thought, her cheeks flaming. I want him to need me desperately, moan my name, press me tightly against his body. She trembled uncontrollably. When her legs would have let her crumble, Temple gripped her tightly to him and danced on, carrying her as easily as a doll.

The waltz ended with Birdie visibly shaken. Now that the spell on her body was released with the removal of his hand, sanity returned. Hopelessness and anger ran through her. Acknowledging her love only increased the distance between them, for now she must protect herself on another level. Too many secrets to be kept. He must never learn of her feelings for him. The babies, her love and now the secret of her father's low birth and her mother's shame. Too many secrets! Too many walls to scale!

Escorting her from the floor, Temple avoided looking at her, ashamed of himself for making her a spectacle on the dance floor. A gale threatened from the flapping of so many fans held in so many matrons' hands. Eyes and whispers followed them, making him realize how unfair he had been. He could not lay scandals at her door when he was the one creating them, he thought sourly.

Birdie's brow furrowed with pain. The heat, the candles, the bright lights all conspired to tear her head apart. She desired nothing more than to quit the ball and to quit Temple's presence. The squeeze at the door gave her the opportunity she had been longing for. She eased away from Temple's hand on her elbow and allowed a couple to intrude between her and her escort. And in that moment, she made her escape into the crowd. The crush prevented her escape with any satisfying speed, and in a thrice she found herself trapped against the terrace doors with no room to advance. With no thought of safety or propriety, she slipped the latch and stepped through.

Darkness surrounded her along with the smell of grass and trees. The cool air refreshed her flushed cheeks and the sweet music drifted through the door, muted and undisturbed by voices, heat and candle wax. If she could have imagined paradise, it would be a lifetime of moments such as this. Tensing at a soft gasp from the far end of the terrace, she stepped away from the light of the tall doors. The rustle of silk and a murmur of lovemaking drifted to her. She had no wish to disturb lovers far more fortunate than her, yet the thought of reentering the ballroom was intolerable. As the terrace seemed to wrap the building, she felt her way in the opposite direction and slipped around the corner unseen. There she strolled the length of it. Here, others enjoyed the cool night air, and flares were set at intervals throughout the maze of pathways for strolls. She moved to lean on the stone baluster and gazed down at the gardens. Below the terrace, looking up at her with admiring laughter on his pale face, stood Oliver Sayers.

"Pray, stand there," he called to her, "while I drink my fill of the sight. A beautiful marble maiden, an angel from another world."

A small part of her mind suggested that Oliver should be thoroughly snubbed for his role in compromising her earlier, but another part of her was desperately lonely for a friendly face. And she must accept a large share of responsibility for what had transpired, for had she had her wits about her she would not have sat there alone with him, nor would she have accepted the glass even to hold in her hand. Also, she could have called Temple's attention to the portrait, and might have, if he had been alone when confronting her, for it was not something she wished to share with society at large. But then, he would have learned of her father, and it was as Oliver warned, common, common, common. So why should she shun Oliver? After all, he was family. Her family. She leaned over the baluster and answered back.

"If you would be calling Ireland another world, then you may be right. But not otherwise, you know."

He appeared to consider. "I think this bears discussion. Shall I come up or would you come down, my lady cousin?"

Birdie glanced over her shoulder. She had no illusions about Temple. He would not take kindly that she had escaped him. She realized, also, the first place he was bound to look for her was the terrace. With a wave of her hand, she moved rapidly toward the steps and bounded down them eagerly, as if escaping the hounds.

Oliver held up his hand to help her down the last broad step that led between rock gardens to the graveled walk beyond. Once on the walk, she withdrew her hand from his, and she noted with gratitude that he did not attempt to retain it. In fact, as they strolled away from the building, down the walk leading farther into the gardens, he put himself out to be amusing. The paths were not crowded, but there were other couples and small groups coming and going. Surely, Birdie thought, there could be no criticism of her strolling in the company of this small member of the ton.

He was, she decided, a bounder in his own quiet way, but he was family, even if that knowledge was privy only to the two of them. Clearly she was out of range for consideration as a dalliance for him. And as a married lady she was allowed some freedoms. So she would allow herself to enjoy his company. It was frankly admiring, which was a sharp contrast to the brooding of the forbidding man she was buckled with.

"Did you ever see anything so vulgar," Oliver mimicked, "as to invite so many people that movement is offensive? I swear I shall be libeled for taking advantage of several ladies on the morrow."

"Without good cause, I am certain, Lord Sayers," she teased with a serious shake of her head. They both burst into laughter as they reached a turn in the path. She hesitated. But beyond, the flares flickered reassuringly, and she allowed Oliver to urge her gently forward.

"Should you like something cooling to drink?" he inquired. "I should have thought of it before we left the palace."

"Oh, I would!" she exclaimed, for truly her throat was parched. "But..."

"No buts! Here is a bench. If you will wait for me, I shall bring you..." He paused in a quandary. "What shall I bring you? A lemon squash?"

"That would be wonderful. But had I not better come with you?" She looked around her at the stone bench, the shrubs.

"And have Lord Arlington whisk you away? The only straightforward conversation I've had this night?" Oliver exclaimed in mocking despair.

"I'll wait here," she agreed with a comical shudder, waving Oliver off down the path. In truth, it was not Arlington she wished to avoid, but Temple. If he had given up the search for her by now, as she devoutly hoped, he would be boiling mad at her, and that was a confrontation she would not enjoy.

But now, sitting alone on the remote bench, she began to reconsider her position. Surely she had been wrong to allow herself to be lured so far from the dancing, and while there were voices beyond, and now and then footsteps on the gravel, she felt very secluded. Not that she was afraid, for on the scale of her life, this was tame indeed, but the ever present concern of what people would say disturbed her. But then, when had they given her a fair chance to form an opinion based on her acquaintance? To hell with them!

"I am sorry to have been so long." Oliver rounded the turn with two tall, frosty glasses in his hands. "Had a devil of a time locating anyone. The place is an abominable crush!" His tone was normal. Surely if he was attempting to seduce her, he would be acting differently—more secretively or something? The drink was cold and welcoming on her throat. She began to drink thirstily.

"Were you frightened, here alone?" he asked, sitting beside her on the bench. "Did anyone come?"

"No," she said with a shake of her head and a rueful smile. "And I assure you, I have been in more frightening situations than this. I appreciate the drink. It's very delicious." It tickled her nose. "It's by far the best lemon squash I've tasted. So tingly."

Oliver laughed. "The Duchess of Kent does not stint on the bubble water."

She had half finished her drink before she spoke again. She wanted to speak of her mother and the Lindley family but was unsure how to venture into the conversation. The drink was upsetting her stomach. The cold liquid must have been too much for her after being so overheated, for she feared she was going to be ill. At least she was feeling very strange, indeed.

"I—I think..." she began, passing a hand weakly over her flushed brow. Suddenly it was hard to breathe and she was very, very warm. She fanned her hand before her face.

"I say, Cousin, are you quite all right?" Oliver asked, solicitous of her. His arm, which stole around behind her, now encircled her shoulders and turned her toward him. "Rest your head on my shoulder until you have recovered."

Fascinated, she watched the glass slide from her fingers and fall to the gravel. As if in slow motion, the delicate bowl separated from the stem. Birdie suppressed a giggle, for it certainly was not funny to have broken the Duchess of Kent's stemware. She glanced up at Oliver's face. His smile was still admiring but there was a quality in it now that turned her blood to ice. She had seen that look over and over again. The blighter was going for the queen's jewels!

The ridiculous thought made her giggle. Whatever was wrong with her? Although he truly was not doing anything except looking at her as if he intended to devour her, the situation was not a laughing matter. She giggled again. The rotter had spiked her lemonade! The fool! Did he think she would allow such privileges? Obviously so, for he seemed to think he could take them. His hand was caressing her cheek, her ear and then her throat, and she appeared unable to command her body enough to stop him.

"Don't do that!" she managed to say, but the sting of her words was lost in the delightful giggle that followed. "Or...or..."

"Or what, my kitten?" He chuckled deep in his throat at her helplessness. He loved compromising a woman, especially one as innocent as this one. For all her being married, she was very virginal.

Again the giggle erupted. "Or I'll be having to lop off yer bloody balls with me knife and stuff them down yer th-throat to...till ye strangle!" She sputtered, before bursting into full-throated laughter.

"Good God!" exclaimed Oliver.

He was so surprised he momentarily released her from his hold. His sudden release, combined with his arm being jerked from around her shoulders by her irate husband, toppled Birdie backward off the bench. She tumbled head over heels into the shrubbery in a great flurry of bronze-striped skirts and frothy petticoats. Laughing outrageously, she was unable to extract herself.

Temple was seething with rage. Having hurled Sayers away from Birdie, he stood with his back to her, confronting the smirking bastard. Resisting the urge to slam a fist into his face, he asked coolly, "I must admit to a certain curiosity, Sayers. How did you think you would come out of this with credit?"

"I quite imagine," drawled Oliver, flipping the lace at his cuffs fastidiously, "that you will give me all the credit I shall need on this."

"I don't understand your meaning," Temple stated. His jaw worked as he fought to control himself. Both men were unaware of Birdie's struggle in the bushes, as she floundered in her skirts and petticoats behind them, giggling outrageously.

"It's simply that I doubt very much you will find much credit to yourself if you go about with this tale. Discovering another, shall we say, entangled with your young wife in the dark?" cautioned Oliver.

A little silence greeted this crass remark. Birdie writhed to a halt, panting with giggles and overcome with dizziness. Lying helplessly entangled, with twigs in her hair, she had laughed until she was too weak to struggle further.

"I should call you out for that," said Temple with a studied air of carelessness. "Too bad that dueling has lost its ton." Then, with a savage intensity, he added, "But I warn you, Sayers, one more word from you and I will deal with you...swords, pistols, whatever your choice. Although my own preference runs along the lines of horsewhipping."

Oliver was shaken. He had no wish to confront Templeton Daine-Charlton at the opposite end of Hyde Park, no matter what the weapon. His style was more sneaking around and plotting destruction than open bloodletting. Besides, he had accomplished his task, which was to cause his dear little cousin to shame herself once more. So with a courtly bow, he backed the four or five paces from Temple and disappeared down the path.

Turning to Birdie, Temple gave an exasperated snort at her dilemma. She sat on the ground behind the bench, tangled among the bushes and trapped by petticoats gone awry. Leaning over to grasp her hand, he was almost pulled into the bushes headfirst. Birdie giggled again and plopped back on her fanny with a jarring bump.

"'Tis hopeless, man. I will not be leaving this place tonight," she lamented. Giggles overcame her.

In the dire face of this dilemma, disastrous should someone venture around the corner, an expedient resolution was called for. Temple took what he felt was the best line of action. Approaching through the bushes, snagging his silk hose in the process, he picked her up bodily and sat her on the bench with a thud. Steadying her with his hand, he rounded to the front of the bench and pulled her to her feet. Her giggles came again, and he smelled whiskey on her breath.

"Saved my life, you did," she sighed with relief, throwing her arms around his neck. "I should just kiss you for being my hero."

"And I should paddle you until you could never sit again. I am absolutely outraged with you at this moment. Do not even speak another word to me until I get us out of this fix and safely home," he raged in a whisper, twitching her gown into some sort of decent order.

"'Twasn't as it seemed," she commenced to explain with a sad shake of her dizzy head.

Temple halted her words with a finger pointed sternly beneath her nose. "Not one word, do you hear me?" When she grinned impishly at him, he shook her roughly. This action brought more giggles erupting from her lips, and her legs wobbled, threatening to give out. Gritting his teeth, he swung her into his arms and strolled off in the direction he prayed would lead to the carriage yard. He didn't dare take her through the palace. Nor could he hope the intoxicated Birdie could control herself, for she was fairly foxed. His lips tightened to think of her sitting in the garden imbibing with Sayers. Much the same as at the dinner party. He hefted her higher in his strong arms, and she wrapped her arms around his neck and snuggled her face sweetly against his cheek.

"Ah, Temple. Don't be mad at me," she whispered, her breath tickling his ear. "I didn't do it on purpose. 'Twas the devil! I owe you my life for saving me from the devil." Slipping her little pink tongue out, she stuck it into his ear with a giggle.

"Birdie, stop it!" he whispered violently, shaking her in his arms. "Behave yourself now."

Suddenly he stopped. There were voices on the path ahead of them, speaking so quietly that he could not tell if they were coming or going. Best he take no chances. Stepping from the path, he stood behind a line of shrubbery. The voices did not come nearer but neither did they recede.

"Damn, they must be standing on the path," he whispered to Birdie. Hoisting her more securely in his arms to even her weight, he muttered in irritation, "Sh. Be quiet or we'll be found out for sure." She giggled again and rubbed her cheek against his shoulder. Stepping backward farther into the bushes he hoped would conceal their presence, and not knowing how long the people on the path would stand there, he eased onto a stone bench placed there, holding her on his lap. "Hush now, or I swear I'll throttle you here and now!"

With a contented sigh, she did not remove her hands from behind his neck but caressed the crisp curls there. Raising her face, she pulled his mouth down to hers with half-closed eyes.

"Birdie..." he began, attempting to turn his face away.

"Sh! Don't let them hear you," she cautioned, following his face with hers until she could gently place her lips upon his again. She moved them sweetly, as a child would, teasing his mouth open with her tongue. Temple made a move to turn his head away from her, but she took his head between her hands and again placed her mouth against his.

Giving in to the sensations and her sweetness, Temple shifted his arms around her. Drawing her body tightly to him, he found her bodice and, with a quick twist, released her warm breast to his hand, teasing the nipple erect with his fingers. Birdie sucked her breath in sharply and arched her back, her heart pounding wildly. Her mind befuddled by the alcohol, her body became responsive and open to his wishes, she let her head loll back and surrendered completely. With a groan of unleashed desire, he lifted her and, flipping her bronze satin draperies and petticoats up as a cushion, laid her on her back on the bench.

To Birdie, the cold of the stone was a minor thing compared to the hot, probing hands beneath her skirts, then the weight of Temple, her beloved Temple, pressing down on her breasts with the studs of his ruffled dress shirt as he freed himself and entered her in one hard thrust.

"Ah . . ." she gasped, only to have the sound cut off by his urgent mouth capturing hers. The torrid thrusting was delicious, filling her to extreme. Gripping him tightly with her legs, she raised her hips to meet him with each thrust, urging him on with her hands and her mouth.

Suddenly Temple became very still. Birdie squirmed beneath him. The voices were louder. The speakers had finally decided to move on down the path, coming toward them rather than going the other way. As they leisurely strolled past the thinly veiled screen of bushes, once again they stopped to discuss a point of religion. Hearing snatches of their conversation, Temple could only guess them to be men of the cloth.

Lying pillowed on Birdie's soft body, he looked down at the girl he had married in such haste. The flare's light, coming through the foliage of the shrubbery, patterned shadow and light across her face. Her hair had come undone and curled like crushed silk over the bench and the ground. A pulse beat rapidly at the base of her throat and her brown eyes were riveted to his. She looked so young, so vulnerable lying there, with her lovely face, indeed, her whole lush body, his for the taking. He sank slowly back upon her yielding softness, pressing a gentle kiss upon her slightly parted, expectant mouth to swallow her gasp as he flexed his hips, driving deep inside her.

Barely resisting the urge to giggle, Birdie lifted her head to recapture his lips. As his mouth took possession of hers once more, she could no longer control or hope to prevent the love that coursed through her veins like molten lava. Her arms clung tightly around his neck in hungry need, pulling his head closer to hers, her kiss becoming more demanding. Soon neither would care if they were heard or seen, only that their passion be fulfilled. As if taking pity on the lovers, the pair on the gravel path moved on at the same leisurely pace, and finally they were alone in their shadowed love nest.

"Oh, Temple, love me! Please love me!" she begged, her eager hands pulling at his hips. Her meaning was double-edged, for her heart needed his caring and devotion as much as her body needed his thrusting.

Her pleading only served to make Temple want to hold back, despite their precarious position. Hooking his hands behind her knees to raise her silk-clad legs high, he opened her fully to him.

Slowly he thrust into her, varying his stroke until her molten insides pulsed and grasped around him and her cries filled the night. Devouring her mouth, he took her cries on his tongue. Only then did he allow his own passion full rein to flow inside her slick heat.

Chapter Twenty-Three

The marquis and marquise arrived at Daine Hall in such disarray that Hudson, opening the door for them, feared a terrible accident and fluttered about them wringing his hands in unaccustomed agitation. Temple carried the limp Birdie straight up to her room and laid her on the bed.

"And what have you done to her *now?*" Libby demanded, hands on hips and with a glower that quite sent him back to the schoolroom.

Quickly he relinquished care of his tipsy wife to her and escaped to the sanctum of his own bedchamber. Obviously the housekeeper thought whatever had befallen her mistress his fault. And in truth, he admitted as he poured himself a healthy dollop of whiskey, much of her disarray was. Pausing with the glass halfway to his mouth, he thought of the very feel of her, the satin of her skin and her lush curves. Tossing the spirits to the back of his throat, he closed his eyes as the burn filled his throat and traveled to the pit of his stomach. Deriding himself for a fool, he stripped his shirt from his back and threw it into the corner with a vengeance.

When had she taken over his life? Jerking the thin dancing slippers from his feet, he threw them in the same direction as the shirt, then unrolled the ruined silk stockings. He gave a little chuckle remembering her trapped behind the bench, her petticoats frothing around her head, her eyes glowing in delight and that delicious mouth merry. When had been the last time he had seen her that happy? In the chaise just before the attack? The thought disconcerted him greatly. Had she been happy during the past two years?

Before the wedding, what little time he had spent with her had merely branded her a child, and a precocious child at that. She'd been shy in front of strangers in the library. Then outraged on the hillside, bopping him a good one on the side of the head with her boots, but so deliciously innocent in her first kiss. When had he started to desire her? That morning in the library? When she offered her absurd plot to disappear? Or laughing with that teasingly tempting mouth over poor Travers's plight? Whatever the moment, what mattered now was that he realized he had missed her. He had missed her greatly, regardless of what or whom he had used to distract himself. She was inside him body and soul. And she was his, by damn! She belonged to him and no one else!

Temple strolled to refill the glass. Slamming the spirits to the back of his throat, he gritted his teeth against the burn. Was that what galled him to dire actions? Jealously that perhaps she wasn't his and his alone? She'd refused a truce and a new beginning, and been caught twice in blatant flirtations in one day. Perhaps she could never be his in the way he wanted.

Wandering to the window, he stared past his reflection into the darkness below. He was no longer master of his emotions, and they threatened to run away with him. His desire was the easiest to understand, for she was perfection of form. But it was more than that. He wanted to protect her, care for her, spend time before the home fires with her. These were things he had never felt with any woman. Even upon returning to London, he had been filled with a hunger for her that his hate could not burn away.

With a snort of disgust at his weak will, he tossed the stockings he found in his hand toward a chair and walked through his dressing room to the connecting door to Birdie's dressing room. Hesitating before the door, he contemplated his actions. If he entered her room, it must be with total commitment in his mind. Could he set aside his anger? Take her into his arms, knowing others had been there, as well? Could he forget and build a life from this day forward, putting aside all of the past? Yes, he could. With a few honest answers from her, he would make every effort to reclaim her as his and his alone. With her promises of continued honesty, he could.

"If the door is unlocked, I will take it as a sign that this is the right thing to do," he muttered, bargaining with himself. "If it's locked? Then I shall consider it over. I will send her to the country and be done with it." The door was unlocked. Which was just as well, for he had no doubt he would have detoured through the hall in his bare feet to reach her.

Moving lightly to the bed, he gazed down at the lovely young girl. Touching a lucifer to the candle on the night table, he bathed the bed in yellow light. She slept on her back with her slender arms flung over her head. It would seem the outraged Libby had forgone the labor of preparing her limp form for bed, as her hair was unbound and she still wore the lacy, thin cambric chemise instead of a nightdress. The low neckline had slipped off one luscious white shoulder, revealing a snowy expanse of breast and one peeking pink nipple. Her hair spread over the pillow in a riot of color and would be a painful tangle by morning. His body responded to the wanton sight of her. God, she did stir him!

Not wanting to wake her just yet, he carefully stroked the winking nipple with a forefinger. It puckered shyly. Flipping the coverlet from her, he caught his breath at her sensuality. Lying with one knee drawn up and flung out to the side, she was as abandoned in sleep as she was in lovemaking. Hooking the chemise hem with his finger, he drew it slowly the length of her thigh, baring white skin and shadowed curves to his hot gaze. Feasting his eyes over her strong calves and lightly muscled thighs, he groaned softly.

Flipping the thin fabric onto her belly, he traced his fingertips along the petal-soft alabaster of her inner thigh, then across those sparse curls barely hiding the valley beneath. She did not stir in her sleep. Drawing the line again, he marveled at the satin feel of her. The floral scent she used wafted upward to fill his nostrils. The fingers stroked the line again. Up the thigh, across the curls, lingering a bit this time to slip down lightly over the valley, then up over her belly, moving the cambric higher. Small silver lines, shimmering in the candlelight, striped her flat, taut belly. Signs of having carried a child . . . another man's child.

Temple caught his breath as pain knifed through his belly. He withdrew his hand, then, extending it slowly, he traced his fingertips over each one in acceptance, sealing the pact with himself to accept everything about her. Soon he would plant his own babe in her womb, and it would be his child that swelled her belly. The thought pleased him enough to bring a smile to his face. She turned restlessly. The soft protest she made in her throat was so childish that it caught at his heart. With a tender smile, he gently pushed the ringlets from her face, gazing at the soft, flushed cheeks, the tempting lips, baring another silver scar high on her forehead. Small as it was, Temple knew it spoke of a deep, vicious wound. There was so much he didn't know about this woman-child.

Temple's brow furrowed in thought. In the barouche coming home, snuggled into the curve of his arm, she had offered confidences. Brushing his fingers over her forehead, over this scar, he now realized, she had mentioned being marked by Satan, calling the devil O'Donnell. It had been something about the devil in the bottle turning O'Donnell mean. That damned brogue of hers had been so thick he had not fully understood. Something about her children and O'Donnell, but she had withdrawn into silence when he had quizzed her. As he smoothed his finger across the scar, his lips tightened. Just one more mark put on her by the hand of another man, he thought. How he wished for a window into the soul of this woman-child . . . to know what had occupied her the two years they were apart. Birdie turned to her side and snuggled into the mattress, drawing her knees up and slipping a hand beneath her cheek.

"All right, have it your way, little wren," he whispered, planting a feather kiss on her brow near the scar. Sighing, he pulled the warming goose-down coverlet over her, gently tucking it around her. Raking a hand through his hair, he restlessly paced back to his room. Then, with an exasperated sigh, he began to dress to go out, cursing himself for giving Travers the office to retire early.

"Although there might as well be one of us snuggled next to his wife this night!" he muttered. The picture of slight, flighty Travers snuggled against the formidable frame of Libby Fitzwaters brought a wry grin to his face. "I do believe I'd pay money to see that," he muttered again, quickly tying a respectable cravat in spite of his Travers's absence.

The morning did not have a chance to arrive leisurely for Birdie. Awakened before first light with a head set on revenge and a stomach full of revolt, she threw one long, lovely leg over the side of the bed and got up in a tangle of cambric and Venetian lace. With a groan, she held her hand to her head until she could straighten upright, weakly tossing the matted tangle of ringlets back when they sat too heavy on her shoulders. Not having her hair braided for the night would make it a nightmare to brush out this morning, and, she reasoned, the way her head felt it might just remain snarled for the rest of the day. Dragging the coverlet from the bed, she climbed into the window seat and sat with her chin on her knees, her arms clasped about them, letting the tail end of the blue coverlet pile like a cloud on the floor. She looked thoughtfully out at the dark, deserted street and contemplated a life gone awry once more.

What had she done last night? With a moan, she laid her forehead on her knees. Damn that Oliver! He gloried in putting her in compromising positions. But at least she knew of her mother from him, though the information had done her little good. The knowledge she had so yearned for, what had she thought it would do for her? Prove to her that, indeed, she was a lady? Well, all it had proven was her commonness. She was the daughter of a footman, and her mother a young girl running away from her family in disgrace. So disgraced that they had not even bothered to search for her. Her uncle had forbid it. Maybe her Aunt Emily was of a kinder heart, but surely if she was, she would have flown to her newly discovered niece after Oliver exposed her existence.

Birdie's head came up from her knees. *If* Oliver had told! It was just possible he had said nothing. Hadn't he said secrets should remain secrets? What would she herself gain if she approached her aunt? A warm, tearful welcome? Perhaps. But more probable, a reawakening of the gossip and scandal of the lady and the footman that surely had flamed the tongues of the ton at the time. Temple finding out, then divorcing her as being common, especially since he had made it very clear at Glencolumbkille that he would take any opportunity to divest himself of her unwanted presence.

No, she would not approach her aunt. Nothing in her craved a closer union with that fractious woman at present. Perhaps later she would ask for details of her mother's life. But for the present, it was enough to know her name and why her dear mother had ended her life in the slums. And she had no interest in furthering relations with Sophia! Easing her head down to her knees again, she groaned with the ache in her temple! Temple! Her face flushed and she allowed that memory to come. In the gardens of St. James Palace, no less! The very thought of it brought a delicious sinking feeling in her belly, a warm liquid well of desire. No, she must not think of that. Rising quickly, she grabbed her head to keep it attached to her neck, then proceeded to the bellpull at a more leisurely pace.

"Last night meant nothing, you fool!" she admonished herself. "Can you think of any man who would turn down a female throwing herself at his head the way you did last night? Last night proved only that you can't hold your liquor, and that while you may look the part of the Marquise of Stannisburn, your actions come straight from the streets of Haymarket!"

Sinking into the chair before the dead fire, she pondered. What to do? She was thoroughly disgusted with herself and surely Temple was, as well. Would that she had accepted his truce when it was offered. Perhaps then she would have not been tipsy in the garden with Oliver. And thus never alone with Temple. If she had accepted the truce, just perhaps she could have begun the long journey toward feeling safe at last. If! If! If! No, society was not for her! How she longed for Blanballyhaven. To be away from all this, to raise her babies in peace and safety. But Blanballyhaven was too far, and with Sir Charles gone, would it even feel like home again?

She needed somewhere closer to make her own. Stannisburn, of course! She would pack and retire to the country. There she would have sanctuary. Rising, she rang again and rushed into the dressing room to begin tossing dresses over a chair for Franny to pack.

Discovering the marquis had not returned to Daine Hall the previous night only reinforced her need to get away. He hadn't wasted any time before taking to the streets again. She did not want a tomcat of a husband any more than he wanted a wife. Marshaling the servants with the efficiency of an army general, she had the traveling coach packed with essentials in a thrice, and instructions left for the rest to follow in two days' time.

Libby stood outside the coach, her hands and mouth clasped, fairly trembling with disapproval. "A wife's place is with her husband. If you will forgive my impertinence, my lady, you have a responsibility to stay beside your husband! I do not know what he did last night, as is right, for heaven knows the stink of spirits was all about you, but it is your moral duty to save his soul. Lecherous libertine that he is!"

"Libby! He *is* the master!" Franny gasped, startled to hear her speak that way of his lordship. Herself maybe... but Libby? And in front of the nursery maid and the children?

"Libby, I haven't time for your lectures. Just let me assure you that Lord Daine-Charlton did nothing last night that I did not ask for, libertine that *I* am," she responded, waving Franny into the coach. "And I seriously doubt the man even has a soul to save!"

"All this haste, it's all so unseemly. I really should be accompanying you, my lady," Libby admonished.

Hugging her tightly, Birdie could not resist teasing her. "I believe a woman's place is with her husband. Especially when he apparently has the blackened soul of the very devil. Besides, Libby, one would hear the wail of agony from Travers the width of London if I took you away from him."

Climbing in to seat herself across from Franny, Birdie lifted Charles to her lap. Snuggling him close, she dropped kisses on his raven ringlets. The horses were whipped up and they rolled out of Grosvenor Square. She paid scant attention to the crowded streets, or the passing miles, but reclined with her tired eyes closed, comforted by the weight of her sleeping baby against her breasts. Then a frown furrowed her brow and she raised her head suddenly.

"Franny, how far is it to Stannisburn?" she asked, giving the maid a searching look. What if it was days and days? And her without much over pin money in her reticule? She felt panic wash over her.

"I be having no idea, my lady. Never fashed meself to ask," Franny answered with a raised eyebrow at the young nursery maid, which only brought a negative shake of the wide-eyed girl's head.

Just as quickly as it came, the panic passed and Birdie's reason returned. "Well, it's no matter," she said. Leaning her head back against the leather squabs, she closed her eyes again. It was no insurmountable barrier for the Marquise of Stannisburn! If her name wasn't enough, she had her rings to barter for rooms. There must be a steward at Stannisburn to dispatch with funds to redeem them. She had survived a winter march across Ireland with a madman and an ancient steed. What terror could the civilized countryside of England and a well-sprung, oversize traveling coach hold?

She would never be afraid for her future again, she resolved. She would assess each situation as it advanced upon her, do her best and be satisfied with it. She tried to relax her neck and shake off the pain behind her eyes. Why ever did men find drink so pleasurable when it left such nasty aftereffects. It was no small wonder Rory was always so mean, for she felt slightly out of sorts herself just now.

Birdie breathed easier with each passing mile. To be away from Temple was to allow sanity to reign. The man's very presence caused her brain to cease to function. She could never be trusted not to want more of what they had shared in the garden. And wanting something that was never to be only brought suffering and grief. No, he took what she offered only because she was female and willing...nothing more.

It was just before dusk on the third day that a weary Birdie and two very tired maids tending two fussy children peered from the window of the coach to stare in awe at Stannisburn. The old abbey stood arrogantly against the green, resembling a small, sprawling castle with its spirals and peaks in a soft cream-colored stone that gleamed a mellow yellow in the dying sunlight. The large traveling coach negotiated the awkward turn into the long curved drive with practiced expertise. The five eager faces quickly switched windows, not wanting to lose sight of their new home.

Waking at his club with a raging headache from a night spent in self-destruction at Blue Ruin with the full idea of putting the temptress from his mind forever, Temple found the light of day reversing his decision completely. So the beginning of their marriage had been somewhat difficult. That did not mean they could not change their direction and make a decent go of it from this day forward, did it? Her playful mood of the previous evening had reflected back on the delightful child he had fallen in love with on their wedding night. It was that which colored his decision. He must admit it once and for all time, he enjoyed her company. He lusted after her body with a vengeance. So why not? Was her devious side any more devious than most females of his acquaintance?

He was honest enough to admit to no small discomfort that other men had stolen two years of her innocence from him and left their marks upon her body and soul. It also rubbed his heart sore that she had carried another man's babe in her womb. Twice, for there were two children, quite possibly with different fathers. And if one of them was a boy, the title would fall to him, even if Temple settled the fortune and personal holdings to his own offspring. That was a fact, unless Temple publicly renounced the boy. That was a hurdle that must be overcome with Birdie, but with loving help from her, he could conquer anything and, with children of his own, possibly come to love her children, as well, for they were a part of her. He was definitely willing to make a concerted effort if she was. He looked forward to an open, honest marriage full of mutual respect. He was willing to listen to her tale and forgive every ill, if she would only promise to deal honestly and fairly with him in the future. Returning to Daine Hall with these thoughts in his mind, he was reduced to staring openmouthed at Hudson at his answer to his inquiry of Birdie's whereabouts.

"Her ladyship left the house within an hour of first light, my lord, taking her maid, and, uh, the children with her." A decidedly uncomfortable expression crossed the butler's face, which then returned to passivity before the marquis's astonished stare. He folded the marquis's coat over his arm and extended his hand for the beaver topper and gloves.

"Left!" Temple yelled, further feeding the butler's discomfort. "Left for where? And how?"

Hudson shifted with divided loyalties, then cleared his throat again. "Her ladyship took the traveling coach, my lord. And, as she did not confide in me, I may only presume she was retiring to Stannisburn."

Rising to his full height, Temple threw his gloves on the entry floor with a force to crack the marble if they had been of any weight. Striding through to the library, he went directly to pour a rather stiff drink, considering the earliness of the hour. Blind rage clouded his reason.

Before God, he would beat her! He would lock her in her room on bread and water! He would...he would...Blast! Must she always be fleeing from him? Was he so formidable that she feared for her safety? Could she never stay put long enough to straighten out some of this blasted mess? Well, to bloody hell with her! He'd not be one of those husbands who gave chase from one end of the country to the other, forever retrieving their aberrant wives.

Thus Lord Daine-Charlton resumed his life as an attached and yet somewhat available Tulip of the ton. Although it was duly noted by the gossipmongers that his temperament was as foul as a dark and stormy day, and that he spent much more time at the Royal Fencing Academy and Gentleman Jim's Boxing Establishment than in the fashionable drawing rooms of fawning matrons, to the visible despair of one silver beauty.

Chapter Twenty-Four

The rout at Lady Westerland's was proving to be a dead bore. As it would seem more and more of the entertainments were becoming as the weeks passed. The marquis stood casually leaning against the doorframe, watching the elite of the ton mill and mingle. Maybe it was just the season growing thin, but he yearned for the crisp fresh air and good hunting of Stannisburn. Just because his wife had decided to take up residence there was no reason for him to spurn the place. The house was certainly large enough to accommodate the both of them admirably. Perhaps he would put together a group of twenty or so and sojourn down for a country party. It might be worth it just to see her astonishment....

A tug on his arm interrupted his muse. Turning slightly he met the pale eyes of Sophia, slanting up at him seductively. She tilted forward in a seemingly unconscious posture, a move that bared her small breasts almost to the nipple. A manipulative gesture that Temple recognized immediately. Strange that it no longer affected him. In fact, it only brought to mind fuller, more succulent mounds with pink responsive nipples.

"Were you thinking of me just now, Temple?" she quizzed, blinking her eyes coyly. "I felt so strongly drawn to join you."

"Would you like me to be thinking of you, dear Sophia?" he drawled. Without conscious thought, he dropped into the acceptable flattering, flirting banter one adopted with a former mistress. He brought his glass to his lips, effectively removing his arm from beneath her possessive hand.

Tapping her fan on his forearm, she scolded him. "You are bad, my lord. I will not allow you to trap me into confessions, not after ignoring me these long weeks past. Eight long weeks to be exact! Tell me, how do you fare now that your errant wife has run away again?"

Temple's eyes narrowed dangerously but Sophia either did not notice or, if she did, refused to back down with her open invitation. "I know what you are angling for, Sophia, and the answer is no," he said somewhat coldly. He had no intention of resuming an affair that had been over for a long time. She had mistaken the friendship he had offered her and Oliver upon his return from Ireland and obviously still entertained expectations. And now he regretted the confidences they had shared, confidences spoken from his need to release anger and hurt. Confidences that would undoubtedly come back to haunt him at some time or other, as she was persistent in her pursuit.

"I hear the word—" she paused to glance seductively through her lashes "—but I never, as you well know, take *no* for an answer. Not when it's something I truly want."

She laughed softly as she spoke, and despite himself, his mouth tilted sideways in a smile of sorts. "You are quite incorrigible," he said. Looking at her now, he wondered what their life would have been like if he had married her. As boring as this rout, he supposed. While she had been an entertaining mistress, amazingly versatile, in fact, and surprisingly experienced for an untried debutante, he had no desire to rekindle a flame that was nothing more than cold ashes and carried too few good memories, at that.

"And what could be more intriguing?" she inquired. "Mama has gone with Oliver to some country week. I pleaded fatigue just on the chance you might stop by the town house. They left this afternoon."

"No, Sophia," he repeated with a twinkle in his eye. He didn't mind sparring with her, for she was a quick wit, but he desired nothing else from her. Although, God knows, he could use the attentions of an experienced woman, for his body awoke in rebellion each morning, but something stopped him from accepting her blatant invitation. Whoever would have imagined it of Lord Daine-Charlton . . . celibate, by God!

A footman brought Sophia a glass of champagne and she sipped it delicately, allowing the tip of her tongue to play in the bubbles as suggestive temptation. She looked over the rim with her sensuous eyes. Framed as they were with the unusual silver lashes, the question in them was easily read.

"The answer is still no!"

"Could I have arranged anything better than I should be quite alone for two whole days . . . and nights?" she questioned.

"That was your arrangement, not mine."

She sipped a bit more champagne before she replied, "We will continue this conversation later, when you have come to me."

"No, Sophia," Temple answered more forcefully, becoming bored with the confrontation.

"If you do not come to me, I will come to you!" she threatened. "We have much to talk of, you and I!"

Temple's eyes became hard and so did his voice. "You would make threats to me, Sophia?"

Sophia just smiled at him as if he were a willing partner in the assignation and added, "I will give you until midnight. The french doors off the sitting room will be left unlatched. You *do* remember the sitting room?"

She turned away from him with a little flounce of her skirts and a sensuous sway of her hips. The action conveyed an unspoken invitation that was as dangerous as the swinging head of a cobra. Temple was furious, but there was nothing he could do that would prove satisfactory at that moment, or in polite society. Although he could not say his marriage was anything resembling a success, at least it had saved him from making the biggest mistake of his life, he reasoned. He was more than a little confounded with his total lack of judgment in thinking Sophia Sayers would make an admirable wife for anyone.

Quitting the rout immediately, he spent the intervening hours at his club. The problem of Sophia weighing upon his mind did nothing to improve his disposition on this night, and a quarter to midnight found him stepping through the french doors into the sitting room of the Sayers's town house. As he had expected, there were more than a few candles placed seductively about the room. Standing still, he listened intensely, pondering for a moment if this could be a trap of some sorts. He was a fool to come here to her. But it would be more foolish still to let her appear at Daine Hall, and he had no doubt that she would do exactly as she threatened. His lips hardened into a tight line as he moved into the room, watching the door to the hallway.

What advantage would a trap do her? An outraged mother or brother could not force a marriage, as he was most definitely unavailable. And an outright scandal would do her more damage than him. No, her only recourse to his repeated rejections was to attempt a seduction. Only by reengaging his affections could she hope to coerce him into setting Birdie aside through a petition for divorce.

With an irritated snort, he raked his hands across his face and through his hair, dreading the coming scene. Sophia was capable of staging one flaming snit when she wanted. The urge to quit the place was strong. That same urge followed him most places these days. He no sooner arrived at some amusement than he greatly desired to be anywhere else. With an explicit oath, he glanced about the room. He had spent many a stolen hour here with Sophia. She seemed to relish the excitement of discovery, always demanding more and more candles to brightly illuminate the room.

It was the same sitting room where Birdie had shared a cordial with Sayers on the night of the princess's birthday ball. His jaw tightened. He did not want to think of her here. Hell, he didn't want to think of *himself* here! To hell with Sophia! Let her make her scene on the front steps of Daine Hall. He was going to his club to douse all conscious thought in Blue Ruin. The decision made, he glanced about at the candles over the tabletops and along the mantel. To hell with them, too! Let Sophia worry about burning the place down about her ears!

He stepped quickly through the french doors, settling his topper firmly on his head. Thankful to have escaped before Sophia arrived, he passed into the darkness with a sigh of relief for the cool air. Not five steps across the terrace, he came to an abrupt halt. His face registered shock and then disbelief. Spinning, he reached the doors in two giant leaps, slamming into the room. Snatching a candlestick from the table, he approached the mantel, gray eyes widening. Holding the light high, he inspected the faces of the women in the portrait. Obviously the older one was Emily Sayers, the heaviness about the jawline already visible and captured by the artist. Then he had eyes only for the younger girl seated at her feet. The soft eyes, the ginger hair, the chin . . .

"Mother of God! It's the woman in Birdie's miniature!" he exclaimed. No wonder the face had seemed so familiar. Considering the hours spent closeted in this room with Sophia, he must have looked at that portrait a thousand times. Had they ever spoken of the portrait? His brow furrowed with thought, but nothing came to him. He thought to wait for Sophia to arrive, to shake the truth from her if necessary. But there would be no truth in Sophia for him this night.

The mental picture of Birdie came to him. She had been seated before this fireplace. Of course she would have looked at the portrait. Had Oliver brought her into this room? What had he told her? He remembered the way Birdie had strained to look back over her shoulder that night as he had fairly dragged her down the hall. It burned through his brain. She hadn't been looking back at Sayers but at the portrait! Back at her mother! The viscountess's younger sister? Probably. Birdie must be a . . . cousin? Did Oliver know that?

Flinging himself around, he slammed his hand on the mantel. He wanted to hit something. He wanted to hear a cry of pain and feel the breaking of something! Why hadn't she said something to him? Not one word the entire night! But then, if memory served, he had mentioned wringing her neck if she had spoken that one word. Clenching both fists, he shuddered. Emotions raged through him. How unfair he had been to Birdie! How alone she was! God only knew what Sayers had told her that night, especially as he had backed Sophia in hoping for a reunion between the two of them. Was that why Birdie had been with Sayers in the garden later? To learn more of her mother?

"Oh God! If this is truth..." he muttered, staring at the portrait. "What if there were other truths I have been blinded to by anger?" His face became pale and stricken. Ireland! Shanna declared... Even with her dying breath, Shanna had cried her tale was true, but what if— "God help me! I left her there." His hand passed over his face, trembling with shame. There was only one who could answer the questions that raged in his head. He must be away to Stannisburn posthaste! Heedless of notice, he slammed through the french doors again.

Not one second later Sophia, floating in a cloud of musk scent and wearing a long strand of black pearls and nothing else, stepped into the room to await the anticipated arrival of Temple. To wait...and wait...and wait a long time before she began throwing things.

Chapter Twenty-Five

The warm sun burned its way through the thin morning fog by lunchtime, and it had turned into a bright, crisp afternoon, with the sky tinted a deep blue. It was the kind of sun and sky rarely seen in Ireland, warm, bright, cloudless and wonderful. And yet Birdie missed the restlessness of the Irish mists and the vivid greens that came from abundant rain. But above all, she missed Sir Charles. She missed his gentle teasing and their ofttimes heated conversations. She missed being loved. How she longed for him to see her children. He would have been proud of them, growing so tall and sturdy. Proper Daines, they were! She smoothed a hand over her stomach and smiled contentedly. As would be this new babe being nurtured in her womb, well worth the mornings spent retching over the chamber bowl with Franny holding her head.

To feel so bad each morning, then to end in such sweetness. She sighed, and her brow furrowed a bit. How to tell Temple? If only she could guess his reaction. Would he be angry? Or, please God, would he be as pleased as she? Didn't all men want an heir? If so, how would he react to the knowledge that he'd had one for almost two years? Could he possibly understand why she had kept his children from him? Or would he simply refuse to acknowledge them? God help her, her heart would surely leave her if he denied this one, too. She really had no way of knowing how he would react about anything. She certainly hadn't expected him to allow her flight to the country to pass without one word of censure from him.

The gray mare moved smoothly beneath her, blowing mightily, full of herself. After the initial gallop, she had been content to fall into a sedate pace. Birdie idly reached down to stroke the silken mane. Having tried most of the horses in Stannisburn's dreadfully lacking stable, she had despaired of finding a suitable mount for herself, when this little beauty had turned up from some obscure origin. Birdie had promptly christened her Pigeon, in honor of her two babies' pigeon gray eyes. Since that day, she had spent nearly every afternoon astride the mare, roaming freely through the winding dales and valleys, only now carefully skirting fences and fallen trees that normally she would have sailed over.

She glanced over the rolling English countryside to Stannisburn in the distance and sighed with contentment. This was her home. She had effectively established herself as mistress, and her small but growing family was quite comfortably situated. Here was home, and here she meant to stay.

After three days' hard riding and the changing of horses at every available inn along the way, Temple was not in the mood to sit idly in the great hall to await Birdie's return. Securing yet another fresh mount, he sought her in the hills, having been given her direction by the stablemaster. He located her near the mouth of a small stream that eventually found its way down onto the flats and fed the lake in front of Stannisburn, where she sat perched on a rock with her skirts raked up high to bare long legs to the sun. Head tilted back, arms clasped about her drawn-up knees, she sat facing the sun's warming rays. The line of her thigh was exquisite and milk white, but would be pink and tender from the sun if she sat too long. Her long, tight ringlets shimmered like a fox's bush down the arch of her back.

His thought had been to rush up here and confront her immediately. But now, drinking in the picture of tranquillity, he merely wanted to join her in quietness and serenity. He sat his horse in silence, watching her with more longing on his face than he realized. How right she looked in this setting of green hills, blue water and yellow sun. She was a true child of nature. Perhaps he was seeing, at last, the Birdie his great-uncle had tried so hard to describe. Her horse raised its head from grazing to nicker to his gelding in the shadow of the trees. Birdie rolled her head to one side and looked directly at him. He pushed his mount forward, disappointed to see her flip her skirt down and sweep her hair up to bind it with a tie. Dismounting and leaving the gelding beside the gray mare, he came toward her slowly. She stood up, shaking her skirts down. All was silent between them except for the gentle ripple of the meandering stream.

As Temple reached up to steady her descent from the rock, he accidentally brushed against her full breasts. They both froze instantly. The immediacy of his desire washed over him without mercy. He inhaled sharply, wanting her uncontrollably. Visions of taking her there in the grass, of her hands grasping him, her head thrown back in ecstasy, flashed through his mind. The rush of his inwardly drawn breath dried his mouth. Taking that last step closer toward her, he gripped her waist and lifted her from the rock and against his body. As she came toward him, soft and pliant, he brought her down to capture her lips. The fire of uninhibited desire engulfed them both. Temple kissed her as a starving man gulps food.

"My God, Birdie! I swear I could take you here and now," he groaned in a hoarse whisper, when his body would shudder with longing.

Unsure of what to make of this unexpected greeting, Birdie moved away with a shaky laugh. She was afraid to be near him. She was terrified to trust this Temple, who would act so much like the Temple she had married, the Temple she loved with her very soul.

"I think you should not go so fast that I do something else stupid," she admonished, moving toward the gray mare.

He came to stand close to her side again, wanting to touch her, to hold her against him. "Birdie? Aren't you even going to ask me why I've followed you to Stannisburn?"

"No," she admitted simply. She straightened the leathers on Pigeon's saddle. Temple gripped her ankle and lifted her easily onto the mare's back. Fitting her foot into the stirrup, he slid his hand up the warmth of her calf. The rays of the sun touched on her glossy curls as she shook her head and looked down at him. He looked up at her, at the sweet curve of her lips as if she guarded some cherished secret, at the warmth of her sherry brown eyes and at that spot beneath her ear where he wished to press his lips. Suddenly he knew the truth of it all. And that truth was that she would haunt his dreams forever if he could not straighten this mess out and keep her within the circle of his arms for the rest of his life.

"And why not, little wren? I thought women and curiosity went hand in hand," he teased. His heart rode high in his throat. If he were not a man grown and above such things, he would have thought himself close to tears.

"While I will admit to a degree of curiosity as to the origin of this open show of goodwill from you—" she leaned down to brush his hand from beneath her skirts "—I naturally assume whatever it is will bring about a raging argument and I merely wish to forestall the spoiling of such a glorious afternoon."

"Can you not just believe that I missed you, and realizing your responsive nature feared being replaced in your affections? As your husband, I confess to having been extremely negligent. Can't have you taking up with a footman, now, can I?" he said.

Jerking her eyes to his, Birdie sought to read his face. Was there malice here, or had it been an innocent remark? If he knew of her father, then why was he so amicable? "Shall we discuss this over a tea tray?" she proposed.

"I think that would be very agreeable. Your chambers or mine, dear wife?" he teased with a sardonic tilt to his eyebrow.

Birdie, wanting so much to believe what he was seemingly promising, spun the mare and with a touch of her heel careened down the hill, spooking the gelding beyond Temple's reach.

Swinging aboard his excited mount, he quickly followed and entered the stableyard just as she disappeared into the house.

Leaving word that she would meet him in the library in one hour, Birdie rushed to bathe and change from her outdoor things. She hugged her hopes to herself. It would be wonderful indeed if this present mood of his would prevail, say, for the rest of their lives together?

"Move carefully, lass. Do not trust too easily. Make him prove himself worthy of your love, or you'll have it trampled over again," she scolded herself. Stepping behind the screen, she found a tub already prepared before the fire. The thick dressing gown and the towel warming before the fire had the efficient touch of dear Libby and . . . speak of the devil.

"It's about time you returned from the hills, my lady."

"Dear, Libby!" she cried, spinning to throw her arms about the woman.

Libby immediately disengaged herself, admonishing her charge. "My lady, a marquise does not hug her servants." Swiftly disrobing Birdie, she continued to deliver a scalding setdown. "Never have I witnessed such outrageous behavior! First, your ladyship dashing off at the crack of dawn. Then here's his lordship all in a stew. Telling us to pack up! We leave immediately, he demands. And to travel at such a pace is indecent! At least he has the presence of mind to travel with his man—" she raised her eyebrows with significant meaning at her wayward mistress "—not like some we know!"

Birdie dropped her chemise and soiled gown to the carpet and stepped naked into the bath. She slid down into the warm, sweetly scented water until it lapped under her chin. A sigh escaped her as she dawdled, knowing she should hurry as she was to meet Temple, but it felt too good to be here, scolded lovingly by Libby.

"Ah, Libby, 'tis a true gem ye be, even with all yer scolding."

Scooping up the soiled clothes, Libby frowned at them, then at Birdie, before tossing them in a heap. "Your speech is appalling! It is quite evident, my lady, that you cannot do without me. You were gallivanting about the countryside in a riding costume not fit for a servant! Not that you should be aboard a horse at all!" Taking a washing cloth and the delicately scented soap, she sudsed Birdie thoroughly, lecturing the entire time. "A lady should remain at home the moment she suspects she is increasing. Gentle walks in the garden, and only that after the first few months have passed with no sign of trouble. Plenty of bed rest and nourishing food. After all, you are eating for two, you know."

"How did you guess?" Birdie exclaimed, already knowing the answer. "I don't want his lordship to know just yet!"

"You cannot be unaware of Franny's propensity for gossip! And it is for you to inform your husband . . . not myself nor Mr. Travers."

"I'm glad you're here, Libby. We all need you."

"If his lordship requires Mr. Travers to accompany him, as is only proper, then I must accompany Mr. Travers. Foolish man would backslide if I relaxed my vigil." Wrapping the warmed towel about Birdie, she pointed a stern finger to a stool before the fire. "Sit! And do not move until your hair is completely dry. We cannot chance a chill. I shall return momentarily."

Patting herself dry, Birdie slipped into her dressing gown. Shaking the wet hair from her face, she walked over to the pier glass to stare at her reflection. Opening the dressing gown just enough to run her palm over the flat plane of her belly, she wondered if Temple would hate the sight of her swelling body. Then chided herself for assuming he would even be with her for the birth of his second son, for she had no doubt that this one would be a boy.

" 'Tis no matter, little Lord Henry. Your mam will be here for you always," she murmured, stroking her belly. With a warm maternal smile, she drew the dressing gown close and belted it loosely, wandering out onto the terrace. She knew she should hurry, and hell would pay if Libby caught her out here with a wet head, but unable to help herself, she leaned dreamily on the wall, allowing her eyes to roam over the manicured lawns, washed gold with afternoon sun. Franny was there, with Charles and Amaryllis. She laughed to see them racing over the grass, chasing one another on chubby legs. Busy and energetic as always.

"Gentle walks in the garden, indeed!" she mused. "Fourteen hours a day in a freezing saddle, dried beef strips to gnaw for nourishment and a beating a day could not stop those two from demanding a share in life! The Daines and the Lindleys make strong babies. Pray you have an easier start, little Lord Henry, than your brother and sister."

"I thought we were meeting downstairs, and here you are daw-dling on the terrace," rebuked Temple. He came up behind her and slipped his fingers into her damp hair, ruffling it to the slight breeze. Pulling her head against his chest, he dropped a kiss on her forehead near the small scar. "Whatever has made you so dreamy today, little wren?" he asked. Slipping his arm around her and in-side the dressing gown, he laid his hand over her warm belly.

Birdie merely smiled. She would hold her secret a little longer. Hug the joy to her heart for a while longer, in case he became an-gry and stormed about. This warm peace between them was so precious, and yet so fragile, she would strive to maintain it a bit more. Catching her breath in her throat, Birdie shivered in de-lightful anticipation as his hand moved over the satin flesh of her stomach. Tightening his hand in her wet hair, he arched her back to kiss her forehead again. His lips were hot and moist against her skin. She shivered in delight.

"Cold?" he murmured in her ear. The hand stroked lower and shifted through the sparse nether curls. He sank his teeth into her earlobe and tugged gently, sending shivers racing down her spine.

"You wished to tell me something earlier, Temple? We are alone at last," she murmured, turning into his arms with a languorous grace. Her dressing gown opened as she rubbed herself against his body. But instead of the hot look she expected, Temple was star-ing over her head with a scowl on his face.

"The hell we are!" he expounded.

Birdie followed the line of his stare down the drive to a fast-approaching coach. It was a large traveling coach, but not the sort local gentry would use to pay social calls. The four-horse team was dusty and steaming as if they had come a far piece at a fast pace.

"Damn! Bloody damn!" Temple swore and quit the terrace abruptly.

Birdie heard the paneled door to her chambers slam and felt a moment of confusion. Well, whoever it was, she reasoned, could do without her until dinner. She and little Lord Henry were going to rest for a few hours. Perhaps Papa would come back to join them. If not? Then she would dress to seduce him at dinner, de-spite unwelcome company. A smile caressed her face. Whatever he had come to tell her could not be bad or surely his behavior to-ward her would have been greatly different. What had been his main objection to marrying her? Her lack of background? Or the ultimatum from Sir Charles? Maybe it was time she asked him. And actually, she did not know why he had deserted her so harshly at Glencolumbkille, but perhaps a direct question was in order there, also. She intended to discover the truth about those things and, however possible, set it right. She loved him too much not to fight for him.

Remembering the feel of his palm against her skin sent a shiver through her again. No, she was not dead inside. Rory hadn't killed her after all. Not when her beloved Temple touched her! She certainly hoped he loved the sight of her swelled with his child, for his very touch seemed to plant a living seed into her womb. Charles and Amaryllis began on their wedding night. And Lord Henry? She stroked her belly lightly. In the garden at St. James Palace, for there was no other time. The memory of her abandon on that night brought a pink flush to her cheeks. She giggled, patting her belly again.

Perhaps if she could induce him into her bed this night, she would tell him of the babe, and maybe, if all went well, even introduce him to his son and daughter. The picture of the two of them standing over the cribs of their children, watching them sleep, warmed her even further.

Chapter Twenty-Six

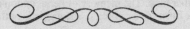

An hour before dinner, Birdie descended the staircase to join her husband in the main drawing room to receive her unwelcome guests. Magnificently attired in a gown of golden sparkles, with her hair allowed to riot into ringlets about her shoulders, she was breathtakingly lovely. Turning at her entrance, Temple visibly caught his breath. He was forced to place his hand on the back of a chair to steady himself for a moment at the mere sight of her. Every line of her figure was displayed with fluid grace, and her face was serene perfection.

"Birdie, there is something I must say to you before..." he began, thinking to warn her of the portrait and her mother's identity before their guests took the opportunity to make a sham of it, for he had no doubt the purpose of their uninvited presence was to cause trouble, but Oliver's arrival forestalled him.

"Ah, Cousin Birdie! It is a pleasure to see you again," Oliver drawled, drifting into the room. His blond good looks were as polished as if this were a ballroom instead of a country estate where he had not been invited. Birdie had just opened her mouth to answer when Sophia swept into the room behind him. She dramatically sailed across to envelop Birdie in the palest blue gauzy muslin, her cloying scent so strong Birdie's weak stomach turned alarmingly.

"Dear Birdie! I can't believe it! Our long-lost cousin!"

Birdie turned her face aside and tilted her eyebrows at Temple. Such a show! He dropped his head to hide his smile, greatly relieved at her pranking when he feared she would be upset. Sophia, prettily begging permission to kiss her newly discovered relation, wrapped her white-gloved arms sensuously around Temple's neck as she did so. Instantly, for all her finery, Birdie felt like an awkward schoolgirl. Oliver moved to the sideboard to assist himself to a before-dinner libation, quite as if he were the master of the place. Her upset had no time to settle before Lady Emily Sayers arrived. Flying full tilt to her, weeping copiously, she dragged the over-whelmed Birdie into her arms.

"Amaryllis's baby! Oh . . ."

"Lady Sayers! Really!" exclaimed Birdie. She shoved mightily at the bulk of the woman in an attempt to extract herself.

"No! No!" the lady wailed, mopping nonexistent tears from dry eyes. "You must call me Aunt Emily!"

Temple disengaged his arm from Sophia's clutching hands and, stepping forward, cleared his throat. "I believe there is a great deal of explaining to be done here."

Birdie waved him aside. "Please, Temple, it's quite all right. Oliver has told me everything."

Temple's brow creased in an uneasy frown. He wanted very much to demand that someone tell *him* everything! But, later, he vowed, he would have the whole story from Birdie or else. He'd had enough secrecy to last him a lifetime.

Lady Sayers was not to relinquish the center of attention to anyone. Dropping into a chair and fanning herself as if overcome by all the stirred emotions, she continued to lament, "Oh, how my heart is relieved. You can't imagine how horrible it's been. Now, after all these years, it's Amaryllis's baby. Dear, dear Beatrice—" she again dabbed at tears that weren't there "—you're named for Mama, you know. My mama . . . and Amaryllis's, of course. Papa called her Birdie, too."

Birdie placed a hand over her heart and dropped her eyes for a moment of privacy from the company. Beatrice! She was Beatrice Lindley! When she had recovered herself, she raised shining, tear-filled eyes to Temple. She had a name! He smiled at her, sharing the intimate moment as if he could read her mind and feel her emotions.

Lady Sayers would not be denied her moment in the sun. Her coy simpering—her quite obviously pretended onslaughts of weeping—sat at odds with her plump, tight-laced figure and heavy jaw, which hinted at her calculating nature. The marquis's ex-tremely unfortunate jilting of her beautiful Sophia could just pos-sibly be righted by this unexpected windfall of having her niece married to the man. The Sayerses could live on the bounty of Birdie's hospitality for a long time . . . a long time indeed. In fact, her very dress had already been charged to the chit's dressmaker's account. She smoothed the ruby satin skirt, proud of Sophia for having thought of it. Her daughter was right. The little upstart might as well be made to pay for interfering in their plans.

"I just cannot express how shocked, and of course, pleased, I was to learn of your identity, Beatrice, dear. And as soon as my darling Oliver told me what he suspected, I realized my duty and—" she paused dramatically to look appreciatively around the room "—here we are! Very elegant! A perfect setting. A most perfect setting, indeed!" Her small eyes rested pointedly and adoringly upon Sophia, leaving absolutely no doubt for the others as for whom the perfect setting was perfect for. "Beatrice... Mama's name, you know. You must tell me everything you remember of your mother. Oh, poor Amaryllis. I would know everything!" Then, without allowing time for Birdie to say one word, she let out a loud shriek of laughter and rapped the marquis a painful blow across the knuckles with the ivory sticks of her fan. "Rude man! Sneaking off and turning up here with such a prize!"

Temple opened his mouth to protest but Lady Sayers, fortifying herself with champagne served ironically enough by Oliver, was in full flight. Birdie smothered a laugh behind a delicate cough into her lace handkerchief. Casting an amused glance sideways, she met the catty, slanted eyes of Sophia. The brazen hussy had the gall to raise her glass the tiniest bit in a secret toast to her little cousin. Birdie was unsure why this tribe had descended upon Stannisburn, but it was not for the reason so far put forth.

Perhaps, she thought, just perhaps having a family was not to be the most coveted thing in life. She closed her eyes and prayed for strength, or that her newly found aunt would disappear, but when she opened them, Lady Sayers was still beaming with smug satisfaction and Temple had moved away. He stood before the fireplace now, engrossed in conversation with Sophia, while she was left to the mercies of the other two. She could not hear what they were saying but she saw Sophia laugh, and as Temple's back was partially to her, she could not see his face. Probably the rotter was grins from ear to ear, she thought distastefully.

There was no chance to converse with Temple alone before dinner was announced, as was Birdie's wish. She so desperately wanted to tell him she had not invited these people and under no circumstances was he to allow them license to move in, relations or not. Besides being quite positive they would not rouse easily once settled, she had no intention at all of spending any amount of time under the same roof as his calculating mistress! If he wanted Sophia, he could just remove to London and take her with him!

The announcement of dinner prompted Sophia to slip her arm through the marquis's, making it very plain in an exceedingly possessive way that she would go in on his arm. Oliver stepped forward and offered an arm to Birdie and his mother, turning her to follow the others into the dining room.

"Beatrice, you must give me a tour of Stannisburn," he stated. "It is most extraordinary, I believe. Quite a bit of history?"

"Oh, I would love that, too." Sophia tilted her face up adoringly to Temple. "To see all the changes the new bride has made in the different rooms."

Birdie fumed. She is informing me quite neatly that she is familiar with every room in this house, she thought hotly. She intends to set me in my place from the onset, but she has no idea that I've staked claim to Stannisburn as my own!

"I am surprised you could tear yourself away from London, Sophia. 'Tis still the season, after all." Temple's rich deep voice reached her as he seated Sophia to his right.

"Well, Temple, those abandoned..." implied Sophia, tilting her head so that she was mooning directly into Temple's eyes. Lady Emily and Oliver exchanged looks too full of meaning for Birdie's comfort. Laughter bubbled from Sophia's white throat as she threw back her head in such an attractive way. Birdie could only fume as she accepted her chair from Oliver.

"Such a long walk," Lady Sayers huffed in mock exertion, plopping heavily into the chair held by the footman. "I do not know how anyone could live in such a large house. I mean just two people—" She paused for emphasis, her meaning clearly a broad hint.

"Fortunately I am young and strong, Lady Sayers," responded Birdie. She absolutely refused to rise to *that* bait. "You must tell me about my family since your stay will be so short. Named for my grandmother..."

"Temple, this rug!" Sophia shrieked, refusing to allow the change of subject. Her voice easily carried the length of the table. "It was always my favorite! But wasn't it in your bedchamber—" She made a little face at Temple as if in apology for creating such a social blunder, and in front of his wife, of all people. "Oh, perhaps not."

On her lap, concealed by the heavy damask tablecloth, Birdie felt her nails bite into her palms. She hated that beautiful, taunting face smiling at her husband. She hated the innuendos and insinuations. It was only too obvious that Sophia's sophistication, her breeding, her background, everything about her, had prepared her from birth to be a marquise. She was everything Birdie could never be. She could feel Temple's eyes on her but refused to look at him.

"I could envy you, Beatrice," Sophia called shrilly down the length of the table.

"Envy me? Why?" Birdie raised her eyes and waited for a baited remark.

"Because you are the mistress of all this! And surely that is everything!"

Birdie gave her a wooden stare and answered reluctantly, "Yes, I suppose it is something, although not everything."

Sophia shrugged and looked away in boredom, as if her question had been mere politeness. Birdie studied the perfect picture Sophia made, her silver beauty glowing in the flattering candlelight. How she must hate me! She had always intended to have all this. But for Sir Charles's wild notion, it would have been a silver hostess tonight. Wealth and position meant so much to her. Her gaze wandered to Temple, looking so urbane, so sure of himself, putting himself out to draw Oliver into conversation. She had married him because she needed protection. It was pure chance that she loved him with her very soul.

The knife's edge that she walked was sharp. She could fall in either direction. Would he set her aside when he learned of her common blood? Would he take her children...her life...away from her? Could she do other than fight for his love? Fight to hold on to what she wanted? A little chill went through her and she quickly turned away lest Sophia see the pained expression that passed over her face. The wealth and position had not brought the protection Sir Charles had hoped. Would Sophia still envy her if she knew the true situation? Perhaps not envy, Birdie thought, but definitely exploit to her own advantage.

Sophia might not have been aware of Birdie's thoughts but Oliver was ever watchful. Stroking the delicate crystal glass in his fine hands, he watched every delicious expression that crossed his little cousin's face with enjoyment. Lady Sayers prattled on and on with no one listening. Stupid woman, Oliver reflected, thinking herself smart enough to live off the fringes of Birdie's life. A snort of disgust escaped his lips. He wanted to slap her hard enough to stop her senseless yammer. He did not intend to live off anyone's scraps.

Birdie excused herself soon after dinner, leaving Temple to entertain a company used to much later hours than she. Besides, even at the point of being rude, she had no intention of watching the play in the drawing room unfold. She was tired. And unable to conjure an effective manner in which to lure Temple away from that beautiful, worldly face and all those shared experiences that must inevitably be drawing them back together.

Toward dawn, lying sleepless in her bed, she heard the noisy party come up the stairs. And though she waited with barely drawn breath, long after the house quieted, there was no soft opening of the connecting door between her and Temple's rooms. She did not try to stop the tears from slipping down her face and soaking into her pillow. There had been such hope. Could it have only been hours earlier? Perhaps she could share a private morning with him, as the others would surely sleep till luncheon, and a private moment was definitely needed.

But it was not to be. Her face dropped miserably as she entered the breakfast room before seven to discover the whole despicable clan gathered there and making plans for the day. Obviously they were not returning to London immediately, as was her wish. It was with no little relief that she heard Temple explain that he would have to leave them to their own devices as he had estate business to attend. He gave Birdie a lengthy look of speculation, then added that he would attempt to be at their disposal for part of the afternoon. Without even a smile to warm her morning, he took his leave of them. Whatever had that questioning look meant? Surely he didn't think she wanted them to stay? He could not be that obtuse!

"If you can spare the time, Cousin Beatrice, I would love to see the grounds. Looks to be a fine morning," Oliver said with a friendly tilt of his head.

"Yes, we could all stroll. The roses are beginning to bloom in earnest," she said. Turning a quizzing look toward the two ladies, she breathed easier when they both declined. Birdie took note of their drooping eyelids and correctly assumed it was back to bed for both of them now that Temple had excused himself. She doubted she would see them again before he returned.

Oliver proved to be a cheerful and amusing companion, exclaiming with wonder and appreciation at the wide vistas and smooth lawns. Birdie listened to his calculated chatter, and although she realized some of it was carefully planned to drip poison into her heart, she could not help wondering how much truth there was inside the insinuations.

"You know, dear cousin, that your husband is labeled a rakehell and a heartbreaker," he said with such a happy laugh that Birdie could only look at him and assume she was meant to take no offense. After all, the two men were friends of some history. She kept her face controlled, for undoubtedly any remark she made would be relayed to Sophia, who in turn would taunt her with it at the dinner table tonight.

"Is that right?" she murmured noncommittally.

"You must not be annoyed by all the malicious gossip that the marquis was forced into this marriage," he added soothingly in his silken voice. "Merely jealousy on the part of passed-over ladies."

Does that include your own sister, dear cousin? Birdie wanted to ask spitefully. She might not have been in society long enough to gauge whether a gentleman commonly spoke in this candid manner to ladies of the ton, but she did know *she* did not like it. Even with his smile and sincerity, she sensed there was malice in every utterance. She just did not know what motive he might have. But to gain insight into his little game, she would smile and listen, instead of bursting into tears and rushing upstairs to fling herself on her bed. The desire for such an emotional display she laid at the door of her advancing pregnancy, nothing more. Pregnancy did tamper with one's emotions in the worst way.

"Oliver, I do believe it's you who are the rake," she cooed. "You scheme to turn me from my husband's side."

"No!" he exclaimed, placing a delicate hand over his heart as if she had wounded him deeply. "I merely do not wish you to live your life with your eyes closed. If only I had met you first."

Immediately, Birdie felt relief. Was that what all this blarney was about? Was he merely attempting to seduce her? She fought down the urge to laugh outright into his face. Biting her lip, she met his lovesick stare. The eyes that gazed into hers were hypnotic.

"Oh, stop this instantly! I resent you treating me as if I were a loose woman," she snapped, but then could not help laughing in his face, which tempered her reprimand. "Come, let us return to the house. Perhaps the ladies are downstairs by now."

"Your indignation does you credit," he said with a slight bow. Taking her elbow in a firm grip, he turned her from the path and planted her back against a tree, his arms holding her captive. "Beatrice!" he murmured raptly. "Could you not find it in your heart to love me . . . even a little?"

"Oliver . . ."

"I could make you unbelievably happy," he said, carrying her hand to the front of his pantaloons and pressing it there. "Me . . . and my best friend."

Birdie sighed. She was more than a little tired of men and their best friends. She jerked her hand away and wiped her palm on her skirt. "Let me go! I happen to be in love with my husband!"

"That will pass," he cautioned. Stepping back, he flicked the lace at his wrists. "You will tire of being second, possibly third, in his heart. Hear me, Beatrice, and pay heed. I only want to see you unhurt."

"What do you mean, third?" she demanded. So intent was his expression, so intense his voice that Birdie felt him to be speaking the truth. Or was this what Sir Charles had meant when he had said she would be defenseless against the honeyed words of gentlemen, gentlemen who lie so beautifully?

Every word he uttered left a raw wound in her heart. "First with Temple come Daine Hall and Stannisburn. Although Stannisburn belongs rightly to you now, by Lord Charles Daine-Charlton's bequest."

Birdie's eyebrows went up. Sir Charles had given her Stannisburn? This was news to her. She swept the mighty abbey in a glance. Most welcome news. She would never be without a home again.

"But second? Second will always be Sophia. The one he intended to wed all along."

Birdie riveted the slight man with intolerant eyes. "Are you accusing my husband of something? If so, speak plainly and we'll take it to him to verify."

"Lord Daine-Charlton has a mistress of the heart. One he will never divorce," the silken voice continued. "And her name is Sophia. And no matter her faults, he always takes her back. Would you—can you—truthfully say he has in the past and will in the future stand beside you against all others?"

Birdie wrenched away from him and started toward the lake with a determined step. No, she could not say he would stand beside her. Did he not leave her at Glencolumbkille? Did he not escape to save his own hide with no thought for her?

"If you want proof, Birdie," he called after her, "watch the summerhouse for lights tonight."

She spun in her tracks and confronted him. "What did you say?"

"You heard me. You are just such a little puppy, Cousin. I only want to protect you from hurt," he taunted. Without waiting for an answer, he strolled toward the house, exceedingly pleased with the afternoon's work.

Left alone in the garden, Birdie drew deep, even breaths to calm herself. Plucking a rose, she held it to her nose, concentrating on the sweetness. Though she would try to be calm, her eyes narrowed and she chewed on her bottom lip. Damn them all! If she must fight for what she wanted, then they would see her fight.

She'd made a home here and here she meant to stay...with her husband if at all possible.

"Just a little puppy, am I?" she muttered, shredding the rose to litter scarlet petals on the path. "I do believe it's not the size of the dog in the fight, *Cousin,* but the size of the fight in the dog!"

Chapter Twenty-Seven

The sitting room on the east side of the house was Birdie's favorite sanctuary at Stannisburn. The small room was papered and upholstered in a delicate floral of all the hues of a summer flower garden, and it was there that she routinely retired each morning to write in her journal, as the early morning light was so delicious. It irked her now to have the Sayerses invade this room, but it seemingly could not be helped. Given another chance, she would have barred the door and swallowed the key rather than entertain them here. Although the freshness of the floral setting did glare at odds with Sophia's overblown sophisticated style. It was much more suited to her own character, and that did set her at ease.

At present, the spirited conversation centered around horseflesh, much to Sophia's disappointment, as horses were a smelly bore and never one of her strong points. She was piqued that Birdie had become the center of attention and especially piqued that Temple's gray eyes should rest so warmly on his wife. Tapping her oval fingernail sharply against the stemmed glass in her hand, she pouted her lips. Something must be done. She was not going to sit in this dull little sitting room and watch both men slobber over another woman, cousin or no. Flipping her elaborately jeweled cuff back as if it bothered her, she leaned forward. The deep neckline of the ice blue silk gown gapped, baring her small breasts, winking pale nipples to anyone bothering to glance.

"I did not realize you were such an animal enthusiast, Cousin Beatrice," she drawled in her bored voice. "Did the woman who raised you in Haymarket slums have a rag wagon or something?"

Temple scowled and leaned forward to speak, but Birdie replied as if he had not moved. She was calm and well armed against Sophia's darts after the encounter with Oliver in the garden. For all their titles and fancy bloodlines, these were not nice people, and she was not going to expend a great deal of patience with their ill manners.

"No, Sophia. Maude Abbott ran a home, and I use that word loosely, of sorts for the abandoned children of street whores. She trained them to be pickpockets and thieves. I'm afraid my education in horses didn't begin until Blanballyhaven." Here she tinkled a little society laugh. "And I believe one could say I thoroughly completed it after I was kidnapped by the Irish rebels. You see, I was forced to accompany them through the mountains the entire length of Ireland. We were in the saddle most days, oh, perhaps sixteen hours, for well over ten months before it was over."

"Indeed. You must tell me of it sometime," Sophia said, stifling a yawn behind her hand. "I imagine you have quite a lot to say about the difference between English and Irish horses. I believe that, if not everything else relating to the subject, has not been discussed as of yet."

Determined the blond slut would not have the last word, Birdie merely smiled. "Actually, I did not have the opportunity to observe the purebred animals of Ireland. The rebels' lot were a sorry sight for the most part. Although I did have a rather interesting old gent for most of the trek. I cut his owner's throat with my ankle knife to keep him from shooting Temple—" Turning as if pondering seriously, she looked at Temple, pouting her luscious mouth in a fair imitation of Sophia. "Although I believe you were unconscious by then, darling, from your head wound?" Temple could only stare at his wife, who was magnificent in her anger. Flipping back as if she had not made such an astonishing statement, she continued. "Anyway, they said I had earned him. Actually, a pitiful mount—hardly worth a man's life. He was just the oldest thing but never faltered once. Ever willing despite deplorable conditions, but—" there was a touch of genuine sadness in her voice "—he swerved at just the worst possible moment during an English ambush. He took a deep saber cut across his neck that was meant for mine, you see...."

Her soft voice tapered off, leaving silence in the room. Even Sophia was staring at her in wonder. Could she be speaking the truth or making up a spiteful taradiddle? The pale blue eyes narrowed sharply and she started to open her mouth. Oliver saw the brawl coming and interrupted hurriedly to divert the anticipated clash.

"Well, I for one am a lover of excellent horseflesh and would enjoy a tour of the Stannisburn stables. If my charming cousin would be so good as to accompany me."

Birdie would have liked to tell him which river to jump into, but a guest was a guest after all. And as Temple seemed determined that they should stay, far be it for her to cry uncle.

"Of course, if that would please you, Oliver," she demurred sweetly. "Though I'm afraid Sir Charles neglected them terribly and Temple has yet to refurbish. Shall we make it an outing? Call Aunt Emily?"

"I shall accompany you, also, my dear," Temple interjected, rising smoothly with a flex of his strong thighs. "Though I doubt Lady Sayers is a dedicated horsewoman and will decline to leave her settee."

Sophia sniffed and rose from her chair to gracefully shake out her skirts. "Oh, I guess I might as well go along, too. Maybe these horses will be special. You will tell me all about them, won't you, Temple?" she cooed.

With a blatant snub, Temple took Birdie's elbow firmly in his hand. Looking up questioningly, she raised her eyebrows sarcastically. He merely grinned down at her. The small party was quickly let out the side door into the drive. At an ambling pace, they strolled leisurely to the stables. Temple tucked Birdie's hand under his arm, leaving Oliver to follow with a fuming Sophia bordering on a temper tantrum.

"What happened to the old horse that carried you across Ireland?" Temple asked her in a slightly teasing tone. "Did he fall during the, er, ambush?"

"No, the crush of horses and men was so tight, he couldn't go down. I put spurs to him as soon as there was an opening and he gave me the last that was in his heart. I'm afraid he died in midstride, carrying me away to safety. If that kind of courage could be bred..." Birdie said in a light voice, but her eyes had a sad, far-off stare.

Looking down at her, Temple tensed. Could what he thought to be a tall tale simply to put Sophia in her place truly be the way it was? Could a young girl have survived hardships of such magnitude? He shuddered inwardly. He remembered the knife strapped to her ankle. He had teased her about it in the coach not half an hour before they were attacked. His brow furrowed in thought and his hand unconsciously tightened in a protective manner over hers.

If such courage could be bred, indeed, then her children would be kings!

Having been Stannisburn's stablemaster for thirty of his fifty years, Jake Burke was taken aback by the number of invaders to his domain, but watched calmly enough while her ladyship made a fuss over a pair of newborn foals. He wondered a bit at the silvery lady that clung to his lordship's arm in such a possessive manner, but how did one figure the nobility anyhow! He nodded his grizzly head, not surprised as she stepped back hastily when one of the foals came too close to her skirts. She was obviously one of those females who had no business invading a man's stable, while he readily welcomed the mistress, for she was a true horsewoman. She rode for the enjoyment of it and was considerate of blooded cattle. High praise from a man who disliked women in general. Though he had to watch her, for if he didn't look sharp, she was apt to tack her own horse if she thought him too busy.

Sophia would not have argued with the stablemaster's assessment of her. She was bored within five minutes of entering the stable and wondered that Temple appeared to enjoy himself so thoroughly. She herself saw nothing entertaining in the spectacle of Birdie squatting in the straw to pet filthy animals, and therefore she was relieved when their visit was no longer than half an hour. But then Temple would release himself from her hand and turn back just as they reached the double door. She gave an exasperated, exaggerated sigh and stamped her foot in the straw.

"Birdie," began Temple, drawing her away from Oliver's side and walking her back to the gray mare's box. "You've yet to thank me for this little beauty. Do you not like her?"

Birdie jerked her round eyes up to his face. "*You* sent me Pigeon?"

"Of course. I received a note from Burke—" he nodded in the direction of the stablemaster "—informing me that you were quite accomplished in the saddle and there wasn't a horse in the whole of the stable worthy of you. Rather told me to mind my manners and send you a proper blooded mount!"

Turning to the stablemaster with eyes shining, Birdie impulsively held out her hand to him. "Oh, thank you, Burke. I can never tell you how I appreciate what you did. She's truly lovely and a real goer!"

Taking her offered hand gingerly, Burke bowed over it slightly and cleared his throat with embarrassment. Strangely, her sincere gratitude brought a tear to his old eyes, as much to his surprise as

Temple's. "Ye be welcome, my lady. There's just some that deserve a good horse." Dropping her hand, he shuffled backward instantly, gruffly clearing his throat.

"Birdie! I sent the damn horse! He just told me to," Temple exclaimed in a stage whisper, looking every bit like little Charles when he didn't get his way. Birdie laughed at his pretended pain. "And I thank you very, very much, my lord. Now come along. Our company awaits." She moved toward the door and the waiting Sayerses with an enthusiasm that was all playacting.

Using the same small door into the house once more and entering the narrow hallway, Birdie and Oliver led the way. Sophia held Temple to the rear, deliberately keeping their pace slow as she talked intimately of London. When she saw the others turn the corner and out of sight, she pretended to stumble. And as expected, Temple automatically put his arm about her.

Sophia leaned against him, limping a bit on one foot. "It's just my ankle. It will be better in a moment." She looked up at him with a brave smile.

Temple felt her soft curves under his hand and suspected her turned ankle was purely pretense. Knowing Birdie was alone with Oliver, he was not willing to be duped. He smiled a tight smile.

"Sophia, I understand you too well for your own good."

"Do you, Temple?" asked Sophia with a pout. She straightened and slipped her arms around his neck, pressing intimately against him.

"Sophia, this is not . . ." commenced Temple. He gripped her waist to set her away from him when she reached up to urgently press her lips to his.

Temple turned his head away from her and met Birdie's outraged stare down the hallway. At once, he loosened Sophia's arms and stepped away from her in what he imagined must look like a guilty move. Spinning, Birdie ran down the hallway to catch up to Oliver. Slipping her arm through his, she brightly smiled up at his quizzical look.

"They'll be along momentarily," she said, pulling him toward the drawing room.

A few moments later Temple and Sophia joined them. Sophia's expression was complacent. She had not meant to have a witness to the interlude with Temple, but nothing could have been more fortuitous than to have Birdie chance upon them. She rather thought she might have scored more points in that one moment than Ollie had in all his encounters.

When Sophia said she wished to change her gown for the hem was quite soiled, Oliver seized the opportunity to escape to the library for a smoke. Birdie rose, also, commenting that she was quite fatigued and would rest until dinner. She swept from the room, fully aware of Temple's eyes on her back.

With a disgruntled sigh, she allowed Libby to slip off the dress and order her to the chaise. Lying back with the light throw across her legs, she stared moodily out the window at the sunny day. What she really wanted to do was take Pigeon out for a rioting gallop through the fields, but was rather trapped in her room unless she wished Oliver to accompany her. Hearing the door open softly, she stiffened to see Temple.

"I hope you do not mind my company, Birdie," he said with a faintly worried look, strolling toward her.

Birdie looked up at him coolly. "Indeed, my lord, I would much prefer to be alone just now." She returned her gaze to the window as if greatly interested in the view.

He ignored her snub and seated himself opposite the chaise in a fragile chair of oriental lacquer, looking extremely uncomfortable. "Birdie, I feel compelled to offer you an explanation. I realize you were disgusted by the display you witnessed. I can only say it was not as it seemed."

"Pray do not go any further, my lord. I do not ask for any confession," she snapped, angry with herself for caring so much. "Indeed, your private affairs are no concern of mine. I would just ask you to confine your, uh, liaisons to London, and perhaps out of my immediate family?"

Temple raised an eyebrow at the hard note in her voice. "Birdie, I am not making an admission. However—"

"Then pray leave off the topic! I have no desire to discuss your alliance with my cousin," exclaimed Birdie, rudely interrupting him. Though she wanted to appear blasé and worldly, she felt compelled to add, "Though to flaunt your, what shall we call it, relationship . . ."

"Exactly what do you accuse me of, Birdie?"

Fine color rose in her cheeks. She did not stop to analyze her hurt and anger. "You are a rakehell, Temple! Entirely without shame or conscience!"

Temple laughed at this, though the humor did not ease the tense lines around his mouth. Mockery lit his eyes. "Am I to believe you are jealous?"

Birdie jumped to her feet. The throw tumbled to the carpet. "You are..." Stepping close and raising her hand, she had thought to slap his smug face. Snatching her wrist in midair, he pushed her off-balance and she plopped roughly back on the chaise.

"Never mind what I am. What of you?" demanded Temple.

"What do you mean?"

"When did you discover the identity of your mother?"

"That has no bearing on this discussion," she countered. Caution took over and she tensed. She had been waiting for this discussion since the unwelcome arrival of her dubious relations and the opening scene in the drawing room. Temple raised an eyebrow in question but did not speak. Clearly he was waiting for an answer and was not to be put off with evasions.

"The night of the ball. When I overheard them, the old biddies in the drawing room, ripping my character to shreds with their lies, I ran away...to that small parlor? The portrait was there...of Mama and Lady Sayers...Aunt Emily," she said, clasping her hands in her lap, not raising her eyes to meet his. Please do not let him ask the story, she silently prayed.

"And? What happened?" he prompted gently. "I assume Sayers told you of her. How did she come to end her life in the slums, er, Haymarket?"

Rising in discomfort, Birdie paced to the window. How much to tell him? "She came to stay with her sister, Aunt Emily, to help while she was increasing. Something happened and she ran away."

"But did no one look for her?" he asked, leaning back in the chair.

"No, Edmund Sayers refused to allow that. He said she had made her bed and...and..." Birdie stammered. Sinking into the chaise again, she looked at Temple. Tears welled in her eyes at the thought of her mother, so young, so alone, turned into the streets without a care from her family. "No, no one looked for her—" her voice filled with raw pain "—either."

"Why did she run away, Birdie?" he urged gently.

"Th-they don't know," she whispered, looking down to cover her lie. "And I can't get Aunt Emily to talk to me about her. You've seen how she is."

"Well, there is still time." He patted her hand. Reaching into his pocket, he drew forth a small package wrapped in pale pink fabric. "I have something for you." Opening her hand, he placed the cool object in it and closed her fingers tightly about it before she could make out what it was. Without releasing her hand, he pulled

her to her feet. "Come, slip into a pretty gown. I promised Oliver
we would show them the family portrait gallery. You haven't been
there, have you?"

"No, my explorations have not taken me quite that far," she
admitted, conscious of the warmth of his hand clasping hers. "I
suppose if I must. I shall be no more than a moment."

Raising her hand, he planted a light kiss on her wrist and left.
Drifting across to her dressing room, Birdie leaned against the door
and sighed. Why must he always take away her reason? Not thirty
minutes before, he was kissing Sophia. Then, just now, he was
merely kind to her and she melted. Damn him! Looking down at
her closed fingers, she sighed. As she slowly unwrapped the pink
fabric, a gasp escaped her. In her palm lay the miniature of her
mother. Somehow he had retrieved it from her lost reticule. Had
he gone back to look for her after all? A tear slid down her cheek,
but she dashed it away resolutely.

"Do not be losing yer mind, me lassie," she chided herself. "The
man's a charmer, for sure, and probably sweet-talked it away from
Shanna with his winning ways." Gripping it tightly, she closed her
eyes and willed her mother's presence to come to her. "Mam, talk
to me. Did you love your footman, Mam? More than your own
life? For that's what he cost you." Thinking hard, the words
popped into her head as if she had heard them yesterday.

"Always remember, Birdie. Your father is a gentleman, and that
makes you a lady. But he is a terrible man and you must never go
to him."

Birdie blinked her eyes. Her mother had said that! Not a footman but a gentleman! One of Lord Sayers's friends perhaps,
someone invited to their town house enough times to seduce the
younger sister of Lady Sayers? A bad person certainly, but a gentleman. Oliver lied to her! Her eyes narrowed sharply. Moving toward the mirror, she stared into her own face. Why would he lie to
her? Or had he lied? He hadn't been very old then. He might have
just repeated rumors. Best she give him the benefit of the doubt,
although Birdie felt her mother would have said Oliver Sayers was
a bad person, also.

Slipping into a gown of moss green silk, she proudly pinned the
miniature to her bodice. Fluffing her russet curls, she swept from
the room to join the others in the portrait gallery, greatly
strengthened by her mother's presence and the knowledge that her
father had not, after all, been a footman.

"I can remember as a boy when the gallery was used for formal balls," lectured Temple. "The musicians played at the far end and the dancers filled the room end to end. The press would be so great that all of the windows would be thrown open to let in cool air."

The long gallery was a drafty wing with tall, slanting windows on one side. Rows of portraits hung opposite the windows. The visitors' footsteps and voices echoed in the vastness.

"How magnificent to give a ball here!" squealed Sophia, looking with laughing eyes up into Temple's face. He returned her smile in an absentminded way. She leaned against him, demanding more attention.

"And how would you have knowledge of the windows, my lord?" Oliver asked with a knowing smile and wink for Birdie, extending himself to be entertaining.

Temple laughed, but Sophia frowned at her brother for distracting the marquis from her. "I was in the garden...about halfway up that tree there. Imagine my dismay when Lord Daine-Charlton came out for air and chose to stop beneath that very tree. I was petrified and prayed earnestly for the opportunity to regain the safety of my room without discovery. Promising the heavens above never to stray from the path of the good little boy again."

Birdie and Oliver laughed heartily. Sophia gave an obligatory smile to hide the irritation of Temple's warm smile for Birdie. She slid both hands around his forearm again and turned him away.

"How provoking to be sure. Pray, show me that large portrait, Temple." He obligingly escorted her toward the portrait indicated, leaving Birdie and Oliver to follow at their own pace.

Oliver grimaced and said softly, "Sophia is truly a marvel to observe. It's no wonder the marquis has always found it impossible to stay from her side." Birdie merely set her teeth in silence and urged him to move quicker to join the others. She would not be drawn into that discussion again!

"Cousin Beatrice? This next portrait should be of particular interest to you. It's Temple as a very young boy," Sophia called, smiling like a cat stealing cream when Birdie moved to stand before the tall canvas. "We haven't met your children yet! I'm sure they look just like this...*oh!* Oh, I am sorry! Temple, please forgive me?"

Birdie glanced, then stared openly at the portrait's merry young face with sober gray eyes and tousled black curls. She felt shock like a physical blow. The group was astonished when her face turned chalk white. Temple saw her sway and, pushing Sophia aside, swiftly caught her arm.

"Birdie! Are you all right?" He folded her into his arms and held her upright. "I think we'd best sit for a moment." Dazed, Birdie shivered. Temple stared keenly at her. He had felt the shiver and knew that she was operating under some sort of strong emotion. He led her to a settee.

Oliver and Sophia trailed behind. Sophia fumed and clenched her teeth. Once again, Birdie had snatched the attention with this unexpected performance. Just when she had made such a telling shot. Damn the chit!

"I quite admire your sensibility, dear Beatrice. It speaks volumes, I must say?" she sneered. Temple's head shot up and he glared hard at the smirking girl, as if the thought of delivering her a harsh setdown rather pleased him. Oliver glanced from one face to the other, eyebrows tilting in dawning interest.

"Come along, Sophia," prodded Oliver, taking his sister's arm and forcefully escorting her the length of the room.

"Ollie! What are you doing? Don't you see? We could have pushed the fact that her bastards aren't even Daines," she whispered harshly. She attempted to jerk her arm from his hand.

"Open your eyes!" he grated at her blindness. "You do nothing but drive him to protect her. He is done with you! We must try another tack. You will never bring him to the mark now for he loves his wife!"

"You lie!" Sophia raged. "He doesn't love her! He loves me!"

"Shut up! We have better things to discuss. Now listen to me, for we might not have much time." Oliver gripped her arm tightly, causing her to wince.

"Ollie, careful . . . you're bruising me," she whined, and followed him farther away from the stricken Birdie only through necessity.

"Thank God," sighed Birdie in relief. She leaned her head back against the settee, closing her eyes against the dizziness and nausea. Calm down, little Lord Henry, she thought, longing to place her hand over her belly to comfort him. Sensing Temple's closeness, she didn't dare. He drew her hand into his and she allowed it to rest there, enjoying the warmth against her suddenly icy flesh. After a moment or two Birdie straightened and started to pull her hand away. His fingers tightened and she looked up into his piercing eyes. "Let me go, Temple," she said breathlessly. She was not at all sure of the meaning of her words, for he held her captive in many ways.

He did not appear to hear her request. "Why did the portrait affect you so, Birdie?" he asked.

Her eyes seemed to look beyond him. "Don't be silly! The portrait had nothing to do with it. I merely felt faint for a moment. I didn't sleep well last night."

"Are you certain?" he quizzed with suspicion. She dropped her head and did not answer. He rose and gently drew her to her feet. "I think we have toured enough of the gallery for one afternoon."

"Oh, no! I should very much like to continue. I am fully recovered, I assure you. I shall not embarrass you again, my lord."

"I am not so easily embarrassed," he assured her with a smile to melt her heart, and drew her hand over his elbow, tucking her tightly against his side. "Very well, little wren. I shall treat you to a commentary on each and every ancestor who has the misfortune to fall upon my stern gaze. And I shall not allow you away from my arm, so pray do not beg."

Birdie laughed. Sophia heard her from her distance away from them. She frowned at the sight of Temple escorting his wife slowly down the gallery in the opposite direction. The result of having underestimated her rival irritated her. "Come, Ollie. The chit seems to have recovered. Let us rejoin them."

But Oliver held a firm hold on her slim arm. "I think not, Sophia. You've botched enough chances these past two days. From now on, we will do this my way. Understand?"

Sophia's eyes sparkled like fiery diamonds as she glared at her brother. "Who are you to order me about, Ollie?"

A dangerous glint lit his eyes and he tightened his grip on her arm until she gasped in pain and would have sunk to her knees had he not supported her. He wanted nothing more than to drive her to her knees in his frustration, but now was not the time. He glanced down the gallery, noting that they were unobserved and unwanted. He released Sophia's arm and stepped away from her to collect himself.

"Go join your mother. *Go!*" he ordered when she would hesitate. Then he slowly followed his fleeing sister from the gallery.

Birdie let Temple lead her through the rows of portraits. She was silent and deeply lost in thought as he kept up an amusing commentary on each ancestor. Sophia's words haunted her terribly. When would one of them demand to see the children? Surely

Temple would veto the idea, as he had never shown the least interest in meeting them. But however would she keep their parentage
from Temple if they were brought down?

One look at either Charles or Amaryllis, and even a perfect
stranger would see the remarkable resemblance. The portrait of
Temple could just as easily have been a portrait of either baby. The
ebony curls grew the exact same way on their foreheads and the
gray eyes had the same direct look. The chin, the stance... No, she
needed more security before she allowed that to happen. Her brow
furrowed in thought, then smoothed into a small smile with more
than a bit of devil in it. Ah, the pleasure of watching Sophia's face
if she turned those albino eyes on not one, but two perfect images
of Temple. Not his babies indeed?

Temple smiled down at her, pleased to see her enjoyment of his
company.

Chapter Twenty-Eight

"No! I refuse to be drawn into spying on a roaming tomcat of a husband!" Birdie sternly told her reflection. "If a man cannot be trusted to stay in his own—" Tossing the brush down on her dressing table, she frowned disagreeably. "Sheesh!"

Racing down the staircase on bare feet, trailing the froth of cambric and lace she had foolishly worn to bed with the hope that her husband might come to her, she passed the pier mirror in the hallway. Her white cambric nightdress flaring widely caused her to pause. She would stand out like an apparition, she thought, looking down at herself. Turning, she stared back up the gently curved staircase, fully aware that if she climbed those stairs to dress, the courage to descend again would be gone. No, she must go now or never know for certain. And for her own peace of mind she must know now and for all time. The certainty would enable her to set her face firmly in another direction if her worst fears were realized.

Slipping to the cloakroom, she swept a dark cloak around the gown and raised the hood over her head to shield her white face. Easing out the side door of the dining room, she drew the chilly air into her lungs and shivered as her feet hit the flagstones. Allowing time for her eyes to adjust, though it took little with the moon so bright, she ran swiftly the fifty yards to the summerhouse, keeping to the shadows as much as possible.

Studying the white board and lattice building, she shivered. A silly thing actually, having only a main room below and a few bedchambers above, it was never used. Built by some ancestor on a whim, probably a woman with more blunt than sense, she could not even imagine what its original use had been.

"Please God," she whispered. "Let this be nothing more than another of Oliver's games."

Watching the upper windows for a light that would indicate someone was making illicit use of it this night, she held her breath, but her prayers were not to be answered, for there was the flicker of a candle through the shutters in one of the bedchambers. Her heart plummeted to the bottom of her stomach. The urge to retrace her steps to her own bed was almost overwhelming. Did she really want to know for sure? For if it was Temple with Sophia, then it meant the death of all her hopes.

"In for a penny, in for a pound, lass. Don't back down now!" she admonished herself. Wrapping the cloak tightly about the nightdress, she worked her way around the building to the exterior set of stairs. It seemed an eternity before she was able to scramble over the rail and along the sun porch toward the lighted room. Pausing for a moment to catch her breath, she caressed a hand over the imagined mound of her babe beneath the cloak. She so desperately did not want to move to the window. But she had to know the truth.

Dropping to a crouch beside the window, she cursed the shutters. She could hear low murmuring voices inside but could not see the speakers. And she must see with her own eyes, must confirm the heartache and turn her love to hate. Sliding her finger into the shutter, she carefully eased the wooden blade up until her eyes had access to the whole room, and though it was only lit by the wavering light of a flickering candle, which cast eerie shadows, what she saw made her bite her lip to still a gasp of anguish. A woman's cape, dress, chemise, boots and stockings lay in a trail from the door to the narrow bed. There, Sophia writhed, seemingly in agony, astride a man's nude body. Birdie peered closely, but she was unable to make out the man's face or enough of his body to identify Temple. Gnawing her lip, she waited until Sophia's groans grew to a crescendo, her body convulsing one last time, and she fell forward onto her partner. She watched as the wanton girl left the bed and moved to retrieve her chemise. Careless of her nudity, she flung her silver mane over her shoulder and swung to address the man on the bed.

"Temple darling, you were a beast tonight! I swear I shall have to wear a high-necked gown to hide the marks from dear little cousin Beatrice. Or do you even care, my love?"

Birdie gasped, pain knifing through her heart. Well, she knew now, didn't she? Wasn't that what she wanted? To know for sure?

Blinded by tears, she fled across the sun porch and down the stairs, heedless of the noise she made.

Sophia stepped into the chemise and began to draw it up her body. Hearing the noise, she moved to the window. Swinging the shutters wide, she watched Birdie run across the lawn with her dark cloak waving behind her, no longer caring if the white cambric flapped brightly in the moonlight.

"Our little bird has flown, darling. You may come out of the shadows now." She smirked with glee at the other's torment. "Did you hear me, Ollie?"

Oliver lay still and watched his sister's fingers lazily lacing the ribbon up the front of her chemise. "Yes, I hear you. But I do not think you should dress yourself as yet. Just because the play is over..." he said. Snagging the lacy hemline on a languid finger, he forced her closer to the bed.

"Ollie, be careful! You'll tear it." Sophia pouted her lips in a seductive way. "What do you think she'll do now? Run away to Ireland so Temple will divorce her and marry me?" Slipping the chemise off her shoulder, he planted small kisses along the whiteness there. "Oliver, stop," Sophia chided, slapping at him. "Enough!"

"Sorry, little sister, I am merely carried away," he said, lying back on the bed. "Actually, I don't think Daine is enamored of you, or your body, any longer. You could never bring him to heel while Beatrice lives, and maybe not even with her dead. It now makes more sense to dispose of him and bring the little bird, as rightful heir to the fortune, into my bed."

"No, Ollie," she whined. "I want to be a marquise."

Oliver's eyes moved down her body. "You seem to have lost your touch, little sister, and now you must pay a forfeit."

"No, Ollie!" Sophia moved away from the bed, her body shrinking from him. "No more!"

"Come here, sister," Oliver coaxed in a wheedling voice. He watched her back away. Sophia was afraid of him when he was in this state, but more afraid to run away, for he would only find her. And once he did, it was always worse.

Birdie's bare feet flew up the stairs. The cloak, catching at her feet, threatened to send her tumbling backward. Tears blinded her as she tore into her bedchamber and crashed the door shut behind her.

"Damn him! Damn him!" she sobbed. Pacing back and forth the width of her room, she hugged herself tightly with her own arms. The only arms that had ever held her with any lasting comfort. "Damn him to hell!"

"Birdie, whatever is wrong?" Temple stood in the open doorway to the connecting dressing room, contemplating her distress with a frown of worry on his face. "Where the hell have you been?"

Spinning around, she stared at him in shock. He was fully dressed and his hair was messed as it always was when he had been running his hand through it. Was it possible that he could have dressed and followed her so fast? Had he seen her from the window and followed her here?

"Birdie? Answer me!" he demanded angrily, taking in the wet hem of her nightdress, her bare feet and the cloak thrown on the floor in one sweeping glance, as well as her unbound hair rippling around her shoulders. "Have you been meeting someone?"

"Meeting someone!" she snarled at him in disbelief. "You *dare* to try turning the tables and accusing *me* of meeting someone? You pig!"

"I mean it, Birdie!" he grated, advancing toward her. When he came within striking distance, Birdie swung her arm with open palm toward his set face. But responding quickly, he caught it midstroke in a paralyzing grip. "No! I will never allow you to strike me again. Now tell me where you have been!"

"I saw you, Temple!"

"You saw me? Where? I have been here, in the library all night. I just came upstairs, heard your sobbing and thought you were having a nightmare. A nightmare! Not an argument with a lover!"

"How dare you stand there and accuse me! You can't put me off with your lies any longer. For once, listen to me? *I saw you with Sophia!* In the summerhouse, not five minutes ago," she sobbed in anger and pain. "I have had enough lies from you to last me a lifetime. Get your hands off me and stay away from me forever!"

"Birdie, if I had been in the summerhouse just five minutes ago, how could I be here so fast?" he demanded. Shaking her to stop her tirade, which seemed to border on hysteria, he vowed his innocence. "Birdie, it wasn't me! And I'll prove it to you!"

Turning to sweep the cloak from the floor, he threw it around her shoulders and pulled her struggling body out the door into the corridor.

"No! No! I will not go back there," she cried, flinging the cloak to the floor again. Anger overcame hurt and she grabbed for the doorjamb, battling his greater strength. "Do you hear me? I will not go anywhere with you!"

"Yes, you will! I have had enough of this nonsense," Temple insisted. "While I will freely admit Sophia is probably in the summerhouse, it isn't, nor was it, with me. And I will prove it to you."

Swinging her slight body easily into his arms, he ignored her protests as he clattered noisily down the stairs and strode toward the front door. The night footman jumped to open it for him. The young man's entire face seemed eyes as he ogled this strange sight! The master carrying the mistress out the front door in the middle of the night—and in her night rail! No one would believe him!

Libby, gray hair tidily braided and large body shrouded in a voluminous night rail of flannelette, stormed from the hall. "What is the meaning of this!" she demanded. "Unhand her immediately...er, my lord!"

With barely a pause in his stride, Temple ordered over his shoulder, "Go back to your husband's bed, madam! Else I shall order him to beat you within an inch of your life or lose his employment!"

Quickly, over his shoulder, Birdie waved Libby away. She would not see her friends punished for standing up to her husband. Temple bore her across the lawn in powerful strides, coming to a halt at the door of the summerhouse.

"Temple..." she began as he eased her to her feet.

"Sh. Let's not give them time to, er, regain their composure, my dear," he whispered. Tapping a forefinger teasingly against her open lips, he winked at her, as if catching Sophia were a great joke.

"Temple, I will *not* go up there," Birdie whispered, pulling back. Why she was whispering if she did not intend to follow him up those stairs, she did not stop to reason. Perhaps if she was honest with herself, she would admit that nothing short of wild horses could have kept her away.

"Sh..." he warned. Putting a finger to his lips again and raising an eyebrow, he mimicked the comedy of walking in on sly-puss Sophia frolicking with the boot boy. He gripped her hand tightly in his to quietly pull her up the stairs behind him. After a good laugh, by God, he would order Sophia from Stannisburn, sending her irritating brother and whining mother with her. He had tried to tolerate them, to give Birdie a chance to have her family, but enough was enough. He wanted nothing more than to be alone with his wife and begin to build their own family.

"Which?" he whispered close to her ear, indicating the two bedroom doors. Pointing toward the closest door, Birdie could not speak for her heart was wedged high in her throat. Walking boldly to the door, Temple swung it open. Almost immediately, his eyes hardened and he clenched his jaw. Birdie stepped to his side, and though he moved to block her view, he was not quick enough. Her breath escaped in a gasp of disbelief.

Even dimly lit with the one candle, the scene was clearly defined. Sophia, her pale body now devoid of the chemise, was snuggled in the crook of Oliver's arm, just tilting a champagne flute to her lips. The silver hair was fanned wildly over the pillow, and over Oliver's bare chest. Birdie gasped and clutched Temple's arm. With a strangled cry she tore from Temple's side and ran down the stairs, out the front door and into the cool night air, barely reaching the shrubbery before sobs overcame her.

Temple allowed his disgust to become plainly etched on his face. "I want both of you, and your mother, out of my house within the hour. Your carriage will be at the front door. Be in it or I will personally assist you. I believe I have made myself clear," he ordered, then spun to follow Birdie's retreat into the night.

Gripping her arms, he gently pulled her against his chest. Behind them, Sophia could be heard screaming accusations at Oliver. A sharp word cut the yells short, then came wild sobbing. Birdie placed both hands over her ears to shut out the sounds. Sweeping her into his arms, Temple cradled her to his chest. Giant strides carried her away from the ugliness, back to the house, up the staircase and into her bedchamber. Laying her on the bed, he wiped her eyes with the skirt of her nightdress.

"There are some people, Birdie, who are . . . sick. I'm sorry you had to see that ugliness, but they will be gone within the hour and we never have to see them again." He gently smoothed her hair from her forehead. "I know you are shocked. I know . . ."

"You know nothing!"

"You must try to calm down, Birdie," cautioned Temple. Gathering her into his arms, he rocked her tightly against him. "Birdie, I'd never . . . never let anyone hurt you! You must believe that!"

"Then why did you leave me there? Why?" she demanded, pushing herself away from him. She evaded him when he would draw her close again, her eyes searching his face. Temple could only stand guilty before her. Shrugging his shoulders helplessly, he tried to explain his actions, when in truth he felt guilty as hell...just as if he had knowingly caused all her horror.

"I thought it was a plot to dupe my uncle. I thought you were one of them. Hell, Birdie, I don't know what I thought!"

"A plot? I was a child, Temple! I could have been killed when that carriage ran over me. If it hadn't been for George Hughett, the ship's surgeon, I would have died!" she insisted. Leaping from the bed, she paced to the window. "Then later, if George hadn't found me... I escaped Rory with nothing, not even clothing... and my babies. My babies..." She shivered. Temple came to stand by her, then gently wrapped his arms around her again.

"Hush now, little wren." Holding her tightly against him, he whispered into her hair. "You are frozen through and through. You're going to be ill. Hush now. It's over and we'll work together to overcome the nightmares until all the bad memories are replaced with good ones. Cling to me, and I'll take care of you... and your babies." Soothing her with his voice and hands, he felt the tenseness slowly ebb away. Raising her face to stare into her eyes with worry, he could see she was emotionally exhausted. "I don't want to leave you, Birdie, but I must see that our...guests are hurried on their way as I have instructed. Climb into bed and I shall return as soon as I am done."

Libby's fully dressed, tightly corseted figure loomed to fill the doorway. Her hands were braced upon broad hips, and she was outraged to the very point of violent trembling. "I think, Lord Daine-Charlton, that you have done just about as much harm as I will allow for one night," she announced inflexibly. "If you will leave us now, my lord, I shall see if I can keep your wife from los—"

"Libby!" Birdie wailed, barely stopping her before she blurted out her precious secret.

Temple turned with an angry gasp to confront this high-minded servant who would admonish him in his own household. Birdie, relieved of his supporting arms, swayed precariously with bees buzzing in her ears. Dragging her hand over her forehead and rapidly blinking her eyes, she fought for control over her narrowing vision. Oh, drat this business of having babies, she thought. It would seem as if your body turned against you just when you needed it the most. With a resigned sigh—limply, gracefully—she drifted to the floor in a swoon, pooling prettily in a great froth of tatted cambric and lace, never hearing the cry of distress from Temple, or the terrible tongue-lashing he received from Libby.

Chapter Twenty-Nine

The moon drifted behind clouds, cloaking the road with dense shadows. A small, lightweight curricle stood in the center of the track with one lantern attached to its side. As if unconcerned with drawing attention, it burned brightly. There were two men standing near, passing a bottle of cheap swill across the span between them. The horses moved restlessly, jingling their harness, as if they had been waiting a long time.

In the distance sounded the regular cadence of a horse's approaching stride. Instantly alert, the men straightened and moved closer to the curricle. Stowing the bottle, they pulled back coats to check pistols jammed into belts. Anxious to have the work done, and return to their own business with well-oiled pockets, they shifted their weight from foot to foot as the man drew rein and swung from his horse. Casually he approached them, drawing off his gloves and studying them with a pair of cold eyes. He stopped in the circle of the lantern so that the light fell on his face. The lantern flame shot gold fire through his hair and flickered over a boyish face with incredibly pretty features.

"Come closer," he said in a soft voice. The men shifted uncomfortably again and edged closer. For a moment no one spoke, and then the larger of the two, urged by a sharp elbow in the ribs, raised his eyes fleetingly to the cold pale ones, but could not sustain the contact long enough for his purpose. He moved back again.

From behind his bulk, a smallish man with a squashed face screwed up his courage to ask, "So, Gov, what have ye for us to do?"

Softly, in a little singsong voice, Oliver began to speak. "There is a lady, a soft, white-skinned lady, that I am going to take tonight, quiet like. I'll bring her to you. I will pay good coin for your part, and then after I am finished, er, enjoying the lady, I want the two of you to have a piece of her. A sort of reward, you understand."

The small man licked his lips greedily. "And then what are we to do with her? After, I mean?"

"I plan to burn her," Oliver whispered in a satanic voice, gently flicking the lace back from his hands to take a pinch of snuff with a slightly feminine gesture.

"See here, Gov," said the larger thug, moving wearily away from the lantern light until his face was hidden in the shadows. "What say we just pop her off, quick like."

"It will be as I say, or else I can see that the two of you join her in the flames of hell," Oliver threatened in a voice that sent chills to run across the man's scalp. Unceremoniously handing the leathers of his mount to the man, he motioned the smaller one to swing atop the curricle before him. "We shall be back within the hour."

"Gov!" the large man called urgently, placing a staying hand out. "If ye be doing the snatching and the burning, why do ye have need of us?"

"Just be here when I return."

"What if ye don't come back?" he asked tentatively.

"Sell the horse!"

As the curricle bowled away, the large man grabbed at the bottle in his pocket. Shoving it into his mouth, he drank greedily. Then, moving closer to the horse, he nervously looked around as if expecting the very devil to leap at him from the trees.

"I can tell ye, hoss, that be one bad toff. He means for Chiv, and me, too, to burn with that lady. Ye can mark me words on it!"

Less than an hour later, Oliver leaned comfortably against the dusty seat of the hired conveyance and smirked with satisfaction. He lit a slender cigar and flipped the lucifer away, watching the tiny light arch through the darkness of the passing countryside. Fitting the tapered end into his sensuous mouth, he smiled to think how incredibly clever he was. So far the plan was working as perfectly as if his little cousin were cooperating of her own free will.

"Foolish, foolish girl," he muttered. "Prancing about on the terrace with no care of evil lurking in the darkness." Blowing a thin line of smoke upward, he chuckled low in his throat. Extending his elegantly clad foot, he nudged Birdie roughly. "Come on, my pretty," he sneered. "Wake up!" When she did not readily respond, he reached across the seat to jerk her upright. Birdie cried out as the sudden movement ripped her throbbing head. The curricle swung into a turn without slowing, careening crazily. Frantically, she grasped the ceiling strap. "Incompetent bastards!" Oliver muttered. "Shameful, isn't it? The caliber of criminals available for hire these days? You tell them and tell them, but they don't listen."

Carefully, she held her head and tried to think of how she had come to be here in the middle of the night. She remembered the summerhouse, the crying jag, Temple...Libby putting her to bed, waking and restless a day and a half later. Throwing on a dressing gown—she glanced down to see it was what she wore still—walking on the terrace. Something sweet-smelling thrust over her face, and, of course, enter Oliver. She raised her head to glare in his direction, just in case he could see better in the dark than she could.

"You'll never get away with this, Oliver!" she challenged. "Temple will be right behind you! He'll come for me!"

"Like he did last time?" Oliver said, watching the pained expression cross her face. "Honestly, I hope he does, for I have planned the party with his presence in mind."

Birdie took a deep breath to calm the panic racing through her. Remember, Beatrice Lindley Daine-Charlton, wit can overcome strength. She forced herself to confront him in a calm manner. "Perhaps you would like to tell me, *Cousin,* just what you hope to gain by all this?"

"It's all quite simple, Beatrice," he drawled. Like most madmen, Oliver was thrilled to speak of his plan, his genius, to a captive audience, so to speak. "As your husband simply refuses to succumb to Sophia's greedy clutches by putting you aside, it has fallen to me to secure the Daine-Charlton fortune."

"And you think I will turn to you in my time of grief once you have disposed of the nuisance of my husband? Enthralling, Cousin. Stupid, but enthralling," Birdie retorted. The moon broke its cloud cover as bright as day. Oliver looked so smug that she wanted to scream and lash out. But her experience with Rory had taught her, above all else, to appear calm. Violence only begot violence. She gave an exaggerated sigh. "Although I suppose I should be flattered. It is not every day one has proposals before one's first husband is even dead."

Oliver stared at her, a smile curling his lips. "My dear, you are truly magnificent! But I fear I would make you a poor husband, for I have only loved one woman in my entire life. The lovely Sophia. She captured my heart long, long ago, although she is never jealous if I sample another's charms—as long as the attraction is fleeting. Oh yes, I did promise my accomplices a treat, also. I didn't think you would mind, as it will be the last thing you ever do.''

"I'm sure I should be honored, my lord, but indeed, I cannot find it within me to thank you," she managed to answer in a quip. Shivering uncontrollably, she clenched her hands in her lap.

Oliver pretended hurt. "Really, Beatrice! I think you might try to exhibit more enthusiasm. I mean, after all my careful planning."

"I swear, Cousin Oliver, I do believe you are quite out of your mind," she openly sneered at him.

"Ah, yes—" he smiled at her, dipping the arrow of truth in the poison and preparing to release it into her heart "—about that cousin thing. We are related, it's quite true, but much closer than that. You see, dear Daddy unfortunately had a taste for young female flesh. He was constantly being put out of my mother's bedchamber by her attending physician—all those babies." Pausing to draw on his cigar, he watched her rapt expression in the moonlight. "But then a man does have his needs, and I imagine dear Amaryllis was such a juicy little piece. How clumsy of him to put a brat in her belly before the end of that first year, don't you think...*sister*, dear.''

"No!" Birdie jerked forward in outrage. She wanted to reach for him, to rip the filthy lie from his lips. "He couldn't! Not his own wife's little sister! My mother would have told...gone to her sister to stop it!"

"What? Tell a beloved sister such a tawdry tale? A bedridden woman in fear of losing her baby? Come now, sister. You aren't using your head! Besides, they never tell!" He referred to all abused women. "They bury their shame and never tell." The curricle drew to a shuddering halt. "Ah, here we are. Watch your step now. One wouldn't want you to hurt yourself."

Birdie could not stop the buzzing in her ears. Her mind reeled with shock. So she had been right. Her father had not been a footman but a sick, depraved viscount. Not so hard to fathom when one knew his son and daughter—her half brother and half sister!

Chapter Thirty

Temple was an expert shot. Had he been asked to place a wager on it, he would have readily bet he could load a pistol with his eyes shut, but now that his trial came, he found it no easy task. The frail light went from moonlight to darkness with the blinking of an eye each time the clouds shifted. Crouching in the trees off to the left of the road, he listened to the shifting of his horse tied behind him. If the restless animal did not settle soon, he would be forced to waste valuable time moving him farther back to escape notice. He watched the curricle standing clearly on the grassy edge of the road, quite obviously meant to be seen. They expected him to blunder forward into a trap probably. The curricle horses stamped impatiently and were soothed by a man leaning against the damned thing in plain sight of Temple's narrowed gaze. One man seemed to be all there was at this point, but he had no doubt there were others.

Rechecking his newly loaded pistols, he knew he should wait for his men, as they could not be more than a quarter of an hour behind him, but a quarter of an hour could mean Birdie's death at the hands of Sayers. Another glance satisfied him there was only one guard, and though a large man, he appeared so cocky that he was not as alert as he should be. He was lolling at his ease against the side of the rig, and as Temple watched, he drew a cigar from an inner pocket and lit it, striking the lucifer against the wooden side with an absurdly loud rasp. The light flared briefly, showing the contours of the man's mangled face, then died as it arched through the air. Prodded into reluctant motion by the nervous shifting of the curricle team, the tough moved round to their heads, cursing them in broken English. Temple knew they sensed his own restless horse.

With barely thirty feet between him and the curricle, he cautiously started across the road as soon as the cloud cover shifted, moving as slowly as nerve allowed, waiting always for the crunch of rock to betray him. Rounding behind the curricle, he eased up beside the horse, calming him with a gentle hand on the sweaty withers.

"Hey," he whispered, striking the man a sharp blow on the side of his head as he spun toward him. He fell like a stone. Temple smiled a hard smile. That should keep this one out of the way for the time it took to settle with Sayers.

A hill stretched up into the darkness on his left. A line of trees flanked the road a few feet away, but beyond that, as far as he could see, was open land. He could see no barn but knew there must be one, as he'd been sent a personalized invitation to a sick party. The note, hastily penned in a man's script and weighted with a pearl-handled knife, had been tossed through the window into the library. Rather a sissy weapon for a man, but knowing Sayers's tastes as he now did, he easily labeled the man a coward and a woman killer. The very thought of Birdie in that monster's clutches turned his belly. Touching the pistols in his belt and the knife in his boot, he struck off in the direction he thought the barn would be. He could tarry no longer. He must surprise Sayers before he knew Burke and the men of Stannisburn reinforced his back.

The going was difficult. The light from the moon was intermittent and the darkness heavy when it came. The urge to rush forward was almost overwhelming. Would Birdie die this night without his having the chance to tell her how deeply he loved her? And had, in all truth, loved her since their wedding night? With an effort, he attempted to clear his head of all such thoughts. He must concentrate on the matters at hand.

The top of the hill afforded a view of a deep valley, wooded on one side. He hesitated for a moment, wondering how many men awaited him. He could do Birdie no good dead. He must move with caution, though every nerve screamed for him to dash down there and demand her release. Toward his left, the roof outline just visible against the deep blue, stood the barn. As he stared, he thought he caught the flicker of a light somewhere inside. He plotted a course by moonlight, then waited for the clouds to make all dark. As soon as the clouds moved, he darted off on his mental route in a crouching run. Racing down the hill under cover of darkness eased the knotted tension in his thighs, though he was navigating almost blindly. Arriving just as the moon broke from the cloud cover, he leaned his back against the wall and forced his breathing to slow.

Cautiously circling the building, he found there to be two doors, a large double door in one end and a smaller door on the side. Above, high up on the wall, was a square opening over which a large metal hook was sunk deep into the wall. As he stared up, the wind caught at a rope hanging there and swung it gently to and fro. The rope, used for hauling bundles of straw to the loft, had been left on the hook and afforded him a method of entry. It would be easy to grasp the rope and walk up the side of the wall, except for the fact that he would not have a free hand to wield a weapon. Another perfect trap.

Cautiously he made his way to the small door. Testing the latch, he found it stiff but operational. Waiting again for darkness to come, he took a deep breath to calm his pounding heart. Silence came from inside the barn. When the cloud moved across the face of the moon, he drew his pistol and eased the door open an inch, hesitating at the sound the rusty latch made. No alarm sounded, and through the crack he could see a lantern sitting in the middle of the floor, casting a flickering light over Birdie, sitting bound hand and foot in the straw. Checking the moon, Temple eased the door open just enough to slip his body through. Instantly, he crouched to protect his head from any blow that might come. Nothing moved. He could see no one but Birdie. Cautiously, he stepped forward, his eyes fixed on her. Her head came up, turning toward him with eyes flashing warning above the white handkerchief stuffed into her mouth, but it came too late. A voice, smooth and mocking, sounded above him, causing him to freeze.

"So, Lord Daine-Charlton, at last you are here! I confess I expected you a while ago, but I suppose it is of little consequence. Although Beatrice must have been wondering if you were going to be negligent in your duties as her protector... again."

Slowly Temple turned. Crouching above him, a pistol carelessly aimed at Temple's head, was Oliver, a mocking smile on his lips that seemed strangely out of context with his boyish looks. Oliver tilted his head and clicked his tongue.

"Don't women just cause the most trouble? I wonder sometimes at our persistence in dealing with them. Kindly move over next to your wife—" he laughed a lazy laugh "—and if you would be so good to remove her gag. I would not miss her comments for the world. So much wit for one woman."

Complying with the order, Temple bent to Birdie and gently removed the handkerchief. Her eyes brimmed with tears as he cupped her face with his hand in silent reassurance. Turning her face, she pressed her mouth into his palm.

"I suppose," Oliver drawled, descending the ladder from the loft, "that I should leave the two of you alone. Such a private moment, but alas . . . Your pistols and your sword, Daine."

"I have no sword," Temple snapped. He tossed one pistol into the straw at Oliver's feet.

"What! A gentleman without a gentleman's weapon? Tsk! Tsk! Surely you do not intend for me to believe you would come unarmed except for one small pistol? Do not play me for a fool." Temple merely shrugged and said nothing. Growing impatient, Oliver called sharply over his shoulder, "Chiv, come here."

Instantly the small weasel of a man appeared from the opposite wall. Temple tensed in surprise. He had begun to hope that Sayers was alone in the barn. Grinning wickedly, the man ran his hands over Temple's pockets, pulling out the second pistol from his waistband and a gold watch, which he dropped into his own pocket. "He be clean now, Gov."

"Excellent!" Oliver relaxed. Waving his pistol toward Birdie, he instructed, "Now, my lord, if you will please be seated next to your wife, our friend here will bind you somewhat. Just enough to discourage your participation during our little games."

Temple, highly reluctant to allow his hands bound, glanced briefly at Birdie, whose brown eyes were huge and apprehensive. He knew he must never sit bound while Sayers terrorized her, and since his men were slow in their rescue he must do something, but could he move fast enough to prevent it?

Sensing his thoughts, Oliver stepped abruptly to him and dealt him a brutal blow on the head with his pistol butt. Stunned, Temple slumped to one knee in the straw. Chiv quickly leapt to bind his wrists behind his back. Then, without cutting the rope, he stretched it to Temple's ankles, giving him a kick so that he rolled over onto his stomach. His ankles tightly tied, his legs bent at the knees, he was completely helpless.

"Temple!" Birdie gasped. Turning to Oliver in helpless rage, she railed at him. "You filthy bastard! You'll hang for this! I swear—"

"Tsk, tsk, my dear, such language to use to your own kin." Oliver clicked his tongue and shook his head in a disapproving manner. "I fear your upbringing has been somewhat lacking. Chiv, go fetch Harry... that is if you want to watch the pleasure my little half sister gives me."

Licking his lips and casting glittering eyes toward Birdie, Chiv bobbed his head and darted out the door.

"What do you hope to gain by this, Sayers?" Temple demanded, struggling to roll to his side so that he could see the demented man's face.

"Why...a fortune! Your fortune actually," Oliver explained as if the answer were obvious. "I thought you understood that. It would have been so easy if you had just wed Sophia. Afterward, a small arranged accident, and my love and I could have lived happily. But you would insist on that journey to Ireland before declaring yourself. Then to be so obstinate as to wed some little nobody upon a whim of your great-uncle's... Really, that was so tedious." He shook his head in disgust and leaned casually against the ladder. "But, still, all would have been fine except for my little sister's charms overcoming O'Donnell's sense of loyalty. If he had merely followed my instructions and made you a widower that day on the trek to Buncrana, you would have come back to London and Sophia—"

"You! It was you and Rory? Together?" screamed Birdie, fighting to loosen her bounds.

"Not together, Beatrice. I merely hired him to do a task he wasn't equal to," Oliver corrected. He turned back to Temple. "But, for all my carefully laid plans, like a bad penny, she would turn up again. The hope of a divorce gave us pause for a while. Though, even with her bastards and her shameful behavior in society, you refused to set her aside. You are ever a contrary, my lord. Just as your entry here. I sincerely thought you would climb the rope Chiv left so invitingly convenient."

"I still do not see what you hope to gain. It would seem all your plans have come to naught," Temple persisted, hoping to gain time by prompting the boasting the man seemed to relish.

"Well, when you seemed to lose your desire for my silver Sophia, Birdie's demise seemed ineffective. But with your demise, I had thought to wed your widow, for as you might have noticed, she is a desirable child." With this last remark, he stepped to Birdie to cup her chin in his hand. With a strangled cry, she twisted away.

"You bloody pig!" she screamed. "Take your hands from me body or I'll take them off at the wrists!"

With a laugh, he stepped back. "She is such a fighter, and doesn't the slut come out in her when she's angry!" Then with a deep sigh of apparent regret, he shook his head. "Alas, I have come to notice she would make a somewhat reluctant bride, though I had thought at one time, with the proper training...but my lovely Sophia does not desire her presence around as a reminder of the fact that she can never be a marquise. She's most upset over that, my lord."

"You are an animal . . . a madman!" Birdie proclaimed.

"Yes, a madman. They called my father that, too. And I suppose it must have appeared so to someone who did not understand. But Sophia understands, and so shall you before this night is over. Pain can bring great pleasure, also. Especially from one who knows how to make it linger, as I do." Leisurely he pulled a slender cigar from a case, fingering it but not lighting the end. "I'm surprised, dear sister, that you have no questions about our father. Very unforgiving man, you know. Actually I hated him."

The pale eyes narrowed. "Though with the act that earned my immediate ejection from his household—sent to boarding school is their polite way of phrasing it, I believe—I did manage to best him at last." He paused with an expectant, almost eagerly anticipating look on his face, which turned to open disappointment when neither encouraged his confession. Leaning forward with an insane glint in his eyes and a slick sheen of perspiration on his brow, he whispered into Birdie's cringing face. "You see, I became Sophia's lover. As I will with you. He'll be furious with me for marking you first, but I don't care. I'll laugh in his face, I will. You just wait and see! I'm not afraid. I'll laugh right in his face!"

Birdie shuddered to see the demented glaze of his eyes. His sick hatred for his father had rotted his soul.

"Sayers! You waste your time," Temple shouted to divert his attention from Birdie. "If you kill both of us, you will have no claim on the title or the fortune. This does not serve you."

"Oh, but it does!" he said softly. Bending to Birdie again, he caressed her cheek with the cold barrel of the pistol. "What would be more natural than that the grieving family take over the rearing of the poor little orphans, Lord Charles and Lady Amaryllis? Such a tragedy it will be"

"No! Not my babies!" Birdie screamed. "I've already saved them from one madman. You may harm this babe I carry when you end my life, but you will not touch the other two. There are those who will stop you!"

"Breeding again, little sister?"

Temple opened his mouth in surprise, but before he could utter a word, the small door was thrown violently open as Chiv burst through it. Sayers spun and crouched with pistol ready.

"Harry's out cold, Gov. And there's riders coming. A regular mob from the sound of it!" he panted, winded from his wild run up the hill.

"My little bird," Oliver said, doffing an imaginary hat. "I regret that I will not be able to linger and instruct you in true pleasure, but as you see, I must be off before company comes. So, so sorry."

"Nay, Gov. Ye promised me the wench. And I mean to take her with me," Chiv protested, squatting beside Birdie to work at the knots at her ankles. "Ye have me word, I'll dispose of her right proper like when I'm done."

"Well, I must leave you. There is just time to prepare my defense . . . and clean up loose ends. One must be so careful, you know, when dealing with hardened criminals." Oliver sighed and shook his head. Turning, he placed a pistol shot neatly between Chiv's eyes. The man fell away backward with a piercing scream from Birdie. Oliver's laugh echoed through the barn. Picking up the lantern, he turned to face the bound pair.

"Oliver, what are you going to do?" Birdie asked in a small voice, her eyes looming huge in her pale face.

"A funeral pyre, my dear. A fitting end, do you not think? The loving husband dying at the side of his faithless wife! A sad accident with a lantern. I shall be ostracized by society for a while, but when they see how truly heartbroken I am at the loss of my love, dear Cousin Beatrice, they will forgive me. I shall never marry, and I shall be utterly devoted to Lord Charles and sweet little Amaryllis for the rest of my life. Yes, I truly believe society will forgive me."

"No! Not my Amaryllis!" Birdie shrieked. Thrashing wildly, she kicked at the ropes Chiv had loosened. Her skirt rode up her white thighs.

"No, sister! Do not attempt to seduce me, I haven't time." Again he laughed eerily. "I must prepare my defense."

Catching up the oil lamp and removing the glass cover, he exposed the feeble flame. Then, to Birdie's horror, he held his left arm over the flame until the fine cloth of his coat caught and smoldered. Then he flung the lamp into the dry, dusty straw, where it smashed, spilling the hot oil and igniting the straw instantly. The flame licked up his arm, and Oliver drew in his breath sharply as the burning cloth fell away and exposed the skin. Slowly stripping off the coat, he beat out the flames until just a thin column of smoke rose from the charred fabric. Despite the grayish tinge to his lips and the pain he must be experiencing, he laughed gaily and returned his rapidly blistering arm to the coat.

"I salute you, Sayers," Temple said dryly. "A sad accident, as you say. No doubt you tried to save us, even at your own peril, but were driven back by the strength of the flames."

Oliver laughed softly. "As you say, a sad, sad accident. Now I must be off. Someone should be at Stannisburn to console the children. Sophia will be there by now, but she severely lacks when it come to infants." His laugh followed him out the door and disappeared into the night.

"Temple, what do we do?" screamed Birdie, kicking frantically at the ever loosening ropes at her ankles. The fire rose in columns as the flames greedily devoured the dry straw at an alarming rate. The barn grew hotter as the blaze quickly covered one side and crept toward the straw at their backs.

Temple squirmed around until his feet were closer to her hands. "Knife! In my boot. Can you reach it?"

"Which leg, for God's sake?" she gasped. The smoke billowed in the barn and would soon overcome them. With an effort she turned her attention to fingering the tight fabric of his trousers up his leg. A slow process, as her hands were so tightly bound against her back.

"That one. You've almost got it. Careful now, don't drop it in this straw or we're lost for sure," he cautioned, unnecessarily.

"Got it! Give me your hands . . . Turn here quickly, Temple!"

Grasping the knife tightly, she managed to sever the rope in a matter of moments. Precious moments, as the fire and smoke were creeping closer. Temple struggled mightily as he felt the fibers slacken, until a final wrench completed the freedom of his hands. There was little time to spare. As he fumbled with the knots that bound his ankles, the flames reached their feet. Free at last, he leapt up, dragging Birdie back from the flames.

"Damn!" he choked, bending to tug on the ropes at her feet. Already loosened, they came away and she gained her feet, also. They took rapid steps backward away from the greedy fire. Taking no time to loosen the knots from her wrists, Temple hoisted her into his arms and moved quickly to the small door. Ramming a foot against it, he intended to kick it open, but it did no more than shudder with the force. He kicked it again and again.

"Damn! It's blocked!" Temple swore. Coughing, he dropped Birdie to her feet. Frantically, she worked the sharp blade against the ropes behind her back, coughing and blinking streaming, smarting eyes.

The flames had reached the roof of the barn. All the straw piled against the far wall was ablaze. The double doors charred black and smoked mightily. One of the main beams began to smolder, then glow. Before their eyes it burst into red flames. There was no way out. The ladder, ablaze now, blocked their access to the loft and escape through the small window there.

"The double doors . . . only chance . . ." Temple choked, waving toward the doors, which were smoking vigorously, weakened by heat. He only hoped weakened enough to crash through with a show of force. A glance at Birdie's billowing nightdress made his heat sink. He made a quick decision. Grasping her skirts, he threw them over her head to protect her hair and face.

"Get on my back. Quickly! For God's sake, hang on tight."

Suddenly, the ropes gave and her hands were free. There wasn't time for arguments, and ladylike appearances were not to bother with. She just jammed the knife into her pocket and wrapped the fabric tighter about her head. Climbing onto his back, she wound one arm round his neck and the other she slid beneath his right arm to clasp her own wrist.

"Whatever you do, don't let go! We'll only have one shot at this!"

He gave her no chance to protest. The flames between them and the double doors were a foot high and the enormous wooden door was beginning to glow. He took a deep breath, flung his arms over his face, then plunged shoulder first through the flames and toward the door. The momentum carried him into it, and with a hard jolt he burst through the burnt wood just as it burst outward in flames. They fell out onto the grass and rolled head over heels, a tight bundle of arms and legs. Behind them, the beam fell from the roof and the barn became an oven of death. Birdie's flimsy chambray had caught, and Temple dragged off his smoldering coat to smother the flames as she lay gasping and choking on the cool ground.

"Birdie! Are you hurt? Sweetheart?"

Coughing deeply, she waved her hand at him. Finally giving a deep sigh, she allowed herself to be dragged to her feet. "Just a little singed around the edges," she croaked, her voice hoarse from smoke. "I suppose Libby will give me hell when she finds out I'm out of bed . . . *and* taking strenuous exercise."

"Pray, love, don't gammon me at a time like this!" he said, pulling her tightly against him for a moment. "Oh, God, Birdie . . . if I had lost you!"

A crashing of the barn folding in on itself in a blaze of fire brought them apart. Birdie clenched her eyes shut with a muttered prayer. Temple held up his coat, still smoldering with a large hole through the front panel, then tossed it aside. He spread Birdie's skirts, looking for hot spots, then placed a scorched hand against her cheek.

"Ready? Let's get away from here. I have a score to settle with Sayers."

With his arm around her, they started up the hill. Progress this time was far easier, for several hundred yards beyond the fire was lit as daytime. As they approached the road, however, Temple became more cautious, laying a hand on Birdie's arm in warning. Peering from the cover of trees, they surveyed the scene. A group of men and horses milled restlessly about the curricle.

"Really now! I demand these accusations cease! I tell you the marquis and my cousin have perished in the fire. As you can see, I tried to save them. Indeed, I am badly burned," Oliver's voice rang out confidently.

" 'Twould seem to me if they had an accident in yonder barn, I would know where to look for the one responsible," the stable-master said, leaning over the small man menacingly.

"Really, man, I have told you," Oliver shouted, sorely tried. "He found my cousin and myself . . . uh, entangled. We struggled and the lamp was knocked over. I tried to save them, but it was useless." There was a short silence. "Now I am in pain and I refuse to be questioned by servants any longer."

Jake Burke was not to be put off. Raising his voice about the mutters of the footmen and stable hands, he angrily defended Birdie. "She wouldn't! Not her ladyship! Not with the sorry likes of you, she wouldn't!"

"Come on, love," whispered Temple. "This is where we rise from the dead." Grasping her waist, he stepped over a fallen tree and lifted her after him.

Their appearance caused heads to turn, and for a moment there was total silence. Then Jake Burke, relief blatant on his stern face, rushed toward them, both arms outstretched. His long stride carried him straight past Temple's extended hand to grasp a stunned Birdie to his chest. He patted her gently on the back.

"Praise God, my lady. I feared for ye, I did. Now, come on over here and just listen to the lies this fellow be telling."

Oliver blanched at the sight of them and began to stammer. "So—so you escaped. Sorry I was not of more help."

"Stow it, Sayers," Temple grated, advancing on the smaller man with fire in his eyes. "You would murder us for your own greed! It will give me great pleasure to see you hang!"

A peculiar choking sound came from Oliver. Then, taking a step backward, he produced Temple's own pistols from his belt to brandish in their direction. "Keep back! I shall not scruple to use them, I assure you! I have no desire to hang!" His voice was confident again.

A gasp came from Birdie and she stepped closer to Temple to mutter, "Please, God, don't take Temple from me now. Let this nightmare end!"

"Do not try to follow! I warn you, I shall not hesitate," Oliver shouted as he inched backward. Coming up against his horse, he slowly eased the reins from the back of the curricle. Thrusting one pistol into his belt, but keeping the other leveled, he swung himself into the saddle and gathered the reins. Then, with a maniacal laugh, he pulled the horse's head around.

Birdie's eyes widened and her mouth opened to scream. The pistol barrel swung slowly toward Temple, and a puff of smoke came from the mouth as Oliver's hand jerked. Burke lunged toward the horse with a warning shout.

"No!" Birdie screamed. There was a loud report. Temple spun to pull Birdie out of the line of fire as Burke slammed into the side of the horse, causing the startled animal to rear high and the shot to go awry.

Oliver Sayers gave a strangled oath. His face grimaced into a mask of hatred as Burke dragged him from the horse and slammed him facedown to the ground. The men, recovering from the shock, quickly stepped forward to bind the struggling malcontent tightly.

Burke gained his feet and swept his hat from his head to mop his face. "Bloody hell! That was a close one! He meant to do ye in for sure, my lord," he exclaimed.

Birdie grasped Temple's coat fiercely and burrowed her face into the wool. She shuddered mightily, then glanced up to whisper, "It's like living parts of one's life a second time, isn't it? We've been here before." She pulled away when he frowned in confusion. "He'll hang, I suppose." She spoke resolutely, for it seemed death followed her as closely as her own shadow.

"That will be for a judge to decide," Temple said, reaching to draw her back into his arms.

Eluding his hands, she stepped quickly to the horse Oliver had just released. Bundling her skirts to her knees, she swung easily into the saddle. "Then, I am going home. I have an overpowering urge to hold my babies."

Grabbing the bridle, Temple halted her. "Birdie, I think it best you ride inside the curricle."

"It's too slow and my urge is for speed. Remember, Sophia is at Stannisburn!" she warned, attempting to pull the horse's head around.

Again, Temple stopped her. The bright moonlight illuminated her soot-stained face. The night rail was ripped across the bodice, displaying the white tops of her breasts. The hiked skirt left her thighs bare and she had a wild look, with her singed hair tumbling down her back.

"Birdie, have you forgotten your, er, condition?"

"Hell's teeth, man! 'Tis no time to argue!" she shouted. She jerked the reins in her fury and fear, and the horse reared on its hind legs. Deliberately, she yanked the reins to draw in the beast, and at her doing so, the horse nearly pawed Temple before he released his hold. No sooner had the forefeet touched the ground than she had spun the animal toward home. Stretched into a full gallop within three strides, she raced toward Stannisburn and her children. Sliding one hand down to hold her belly, she whispered to the babe there.

"Hold tight, little Lord Henry. You must survive...as my Charles and Amaryllis must! No one must take you from me!"

Furious, Temple raked his hand through his hair. Was there no stopping her? Did she fear nothing? Kidnapped...nearly perishing in a fire...then racing off on a horse! She did not quite fit his mental picture of a lady who was increasing! Would she deliberately endanger the life of his child with this foolish behavior? Damn her to hell and back again!

"Wipe that smirk off your face, Burke, or I will wipe it off with my fist!" he growled at the grinning stablemaster as he commandeered a horse from a gaping footman.

"Aye, my lord," consented the old man. Ducking his head to hide the smile that would not leave his face, and in fact threatened to burst into a hearty laugh any moment, he dragged himself upon his horse. Yes, the young master had married a hell-raiser for sure. 'Twas as good a match as ever made. The old marquis would have been proud. Spurring his animal, he followed the lead of Lord Daine-Charlton as they flew after her ladyship.

Chapter Thirty-One

With her head start, Birdie reached the house before the mounted men, and very much ahead of the curricle bearing the bound Oliver Sayers. Giving only a thought to reining in, she swung from the horse's back and hit the ground running. The footman, hurrying to open the door for her, was knocked from his feet by the force of her entry. Landing with a thud, he slid across the smooth marble on his backside.

"Where's Lady Sayers?" she demanded, striding across the black-and-white marble entry hall. "Where's Franny? Is she with the children?"

"Uh, I—I—" he stammered. The young man could only gawk at her. Soot-blackened from head to toe, she was a staggering sight.

"Get up, man! Get up!" she ordered in frustration. Wasting no more time, she ran lightly up the stairs and into the family drawing room.

Sophia sat on the satin striped sofa, daintily rubbing a lotion into her soft hands. Her startled gaze raked Birdie from head to toe. To give her credit, she did not much more than flinch at the sight of her. Her composure was amazing. Clearly she meant to play the scene to the hilt, and to her advantage, regardless of the outcome of the kidnapping incident.

"New fashion trend, Cousin Beatrice?"

"Don't you mean Sister Beatrice?"

"Oh. I see Ollie has told you the whole story. Well, it's of no consequence really," she observed with a minute shrug.

The girl did not stop applying the lotion but rubbed and soothed until Birdie wished to scream. Her own two hands and face felt blistered beyond relief. She moved to gently tug at the bellpull.

"Sophia, have you always known about my mother?" she asked.

"Oh, yes. I was a big girl by then. Our rooms were connected through a common dressing room . . . mine and Amaryllis's," she admitted. "I heard most everything that happened in her room." She raised pale blue eyes to meet Birdie's, wanting to gauge her reactions, assess any chance of an advantage.

A footman came into the room with eyes agog. Word of her ladyship's appearance had spread rapidly below stairs. The whole household was astir with the excitement in the middle of the night. "You called, my lady?"

"Yes. Would you please ask the majordomo to attend me here. And ask that three or four footmen accompany him. Quickly now!" she instructed without taking her eyes from her enemy.

Sophia gained her feet and aimlessly approached Birdie. Her eyes widened, for the first time betraying a little doubt. "Where is Temple?"

"My *husband* is following with the curricle . . . and Oliver's in ropes."

"In ropes? Whatever happened to him?" Sophia calmly asked.

"The plot is exposed, Sophia. He attempted to burn me and Temple alive," Birdie explained. She narrowed her eyes at the girl's nonchalance. Her lack of emotion was unnerving. "But his worse offense was to threaten my children. Temple's son and daughter." She paused but saw no reaction from the silver beauty in front of her. "Don't you even care that Oliver will most probably hang?" she cried.

"I give this—" Sophia snapped her fingers and snorted "—for Ollie! He is nothing to me! However, Temple, as the Marquis of Stannisburn, is a different matter entirely. You'll need more than two bastard brats to hold him for long."

Birdie, suddenly very tired, wished for nothing more than her bed. She started to turn from the woman. "I perceive that we are about to have a discussion that does not affect my life in any way or another, and therefore I shan't listen to it," she stated.

"You and your airs!" Sophia hissed, finally losing her composure. "I'll not be outdone by a common Haymarket whore. You *will* make a fatal mistake, my fine lady, and Temple will set you aside. And I, for one, shall enjoy watching your speedy departure."

Birdie looked at her coolly. "How extremely vulgar you are."

Sophia gasped. "How dare you!" She slapped Birdie hard across the cheek. "Leave this house at once!"

Birdie immediately slapped her back, hard enough to rock her back on her heels. Sophia stared at her with shocked eyes, one hand shielding her stinging cheek as stormy tears gathered. Birdie's eyes blazed, yet she spoke softly.

"Do not presume to ever again deal me such treatment. I will not tolerate it! Furthermore, I will remind you that I am the mistress of Stannisburn while you are merely an uninvited interloper."

"Well . . ." Sophia sniffled, rubbing her reddened cheek.

"Ahem! My lady requested my presence?"

Turning to see the requested footmen crowding the doorway, preceded by the majordomo, Birdie marched over to them. "Mr. Wyatt, pray, listen and listen closely. I will expect my instructions carried out exactly in the manner I express them. Is that understood?"

With a deep bow of extreme correctness, the man answered gravely, "Of course, my lady."

"First, send a man to find Franny. Instruct her to go to the nursery immediately. She is to remain there until I join her. The footman is then to post himself outside the nursery door. No one is to be allowed to enter save myself. No one! Is that clear, Mr. Wyatt?"

"Yes, my lady." Again he bowed deeply. With an abrupt flip of his hand, one young, burly footman dashed off.

"Secondly, send one man to whichever rooms Sophia Sayers has claimed possession of. I'm presuming the elder Lady Sayers is not here?" She paused long enough to acknowledge the startled majordomo's negative head shake. "Excellent. Then have Sophia Sayers's belongings gathered and immediately carried to the entry hall. Immediately! Is that clear?"

"Yes, my lady." The bow was shallower this time and his bulging eyes darted to the outraged woman with the red cheek behind his mistress. He flapped his hands to shoo a footman away to do as bid.

"And lastly, have men lay hands on this . . . *lady*. I want her thrown bodily out the front door. On her bum, if necessary. Neither she nor her mother shall be allowed entry into this house again! Have I made myself perfectly clear?"

This time she received no bow at all. The majordomo could only stare with his mouth open as he dumbly nodded at Birdie. A scream of rage tore from Sophia's throat. She lunged for Birdie with hands curled into claws. The two remaining footmen needed no direction from Mr. Wyatt to carry out their duty. Grabbing the woman beneath the arms, they lifted her feet from the floor and departed the room with her kicking and screaming curses that Birdie had not heard since leaving Haymarket.

"Thank you, Mr. Wyatt. That will be all." She smiled sweetly at him and swept past. He bowed deeply, then dashed as fast as his pudgy body would carry him down the stairs to watch the eviction of Lady Sophia Sayers into the drive...on her bum.

Birdie entered her bedchamber in haste. "Libby!" she shouted. Pouring water into the washbasin, she gently laved her blistered face and arms. Flinging the smoke-infested night rail from her body, she wrapped herself into a thick robe. "Libby! Where are you, Libby?"

"I'm here, my lady!" Breathlessly, Libby rushed into the bedchamber. "I was just downstairs with the others watching the lady depart, er, so to speak. It was quite a show. My word! Whatever has he done to you this time?" Never had so many words, and in such a rush of emotions, passed over Libby's lips. Excitement and the hurried dash up the stairs had even flushed her face.

"I'll tell you later. Right now, a bath is what I need. I shall be in the nursery when it's prepared," Birdie said, patting the housekeeper on the hand as she rushed from the room.

"But you aren't even dressed! *Birdie!*" Libby squawked. Clamping both hands over her mouth, she blanched. Heaven help her! Libby Fitzwaters, for the first time in her life, had quite forgotten her place.

Holding her robe closed with her hand, for her stride wanted to throw it open with every step, Birdie ran the flight of stairs to the third floor and the length of the hall to the nursery. Nodding at the young footman standing outside the door with his arms folded over his chest, she slipped into the room.

Franny had been sitting in a rocker beside the fireplace, holding a fussing Amaryllis. Leaping to her feet, she appraised Birdie's sorry state with a sad shake of her head and a clicking of her tongue. "Whatever 'tis, lass, I know we will not rest till it be the end, huh, Birdie?" she soothed. Her hand gently cupped the reddened chin, then she hugged the smaller girl to her side with her free arm for a brief moment.

Tears sprang to Birdie's eyes and traced down her reddened cheeks. Scooping Amaryllis into her arms, she gathered the warm little body against her. Sinking down into the rocker, she rocked and crooned to the baby, needing the comfort of the holding and rocking more than the child. Charles, asleep in his infant cot, stirred and whimpered.

"He tried to burn us, Franny. He . . . Oliver had us tied up and he set fire to the straw. He tried once before, too. He hired Rory to kill me . . . in Ireland. He was as evil and as insane as Rory. Then he meant to shoot Temple. If it wasn't for Burke . . ." She moaned without raising her head from the baby's black curls.

"Saints preserve us!"

"Temple came for me this time. He saved me! 'Twas Oliver and Sophia! I just had Wyatt throw Sophia into the driveway...forcefully." She giggled. Her giggle changed to a laugh. The laugh grew louder until Amaryllis looked up at her mother, her tiny face puckering with uncertainty.

"Birdie, stop it!" Franny laid a hand on her shoulder and gave her a little shake. "Ye be in shock, lass . . . and ye be frightening Amaryllis."

The laughter changed again, to silent sobbing. Gathering Amaryllis tightly to her, Birdie rocked and wept. Franny smoothed her hand over her hair again and again, crooning to her softly.

In a flurry of gravel, Temple and the men rode into the driveway. Reining in the animal quickly, Temple vaulted from the saddle just in time to see two footmen exit the door with a struggling, screaming Sophia. There was no hesitation in their stride as they carried her, kicking and cursing, down the broad, granite steps to unceremoniously dump her in the gravel on her bottom. Dusting their hands as if they had just discarded rubbish, they ascended the steps again.

"What on earth?" Temple demanded with raised eyebrows.

"Her ladyship's expressed orders, my lord," they informed him. They folded their arms over their chests and positioned themselves before the doors, ready to repel the lady should she attempt to reenter the house. The door opened again and a third footman exited carrying half-packed traveling cases. This man did not even bother to descend the steps but threw the cases into the dirt from the top step. He also dusted his hands and returned to stand with the other two, arms folded determinedly.

Temple stared at them, then noted every window was crowded with faces, all watching the strange events of this usually stuffy, dignified household. Throwing back his head, he burst into joyous laughter. Sir Charles had warned him that Birdie would change his life, but he had never conceived of this. He had given Stannisburn a marquise to beat all others.

"Temple . . ." Sophia sobbed from the dirt.

He turned to the girl, the laughter dying in his throat. His hard eyes penetrated her silver beauty, seeing, instead, her black heart. "Burke!"

"Aye, my lord?" The stablemaster kneed his mount closer to the steps where Temple stood.

"As soon as the curricle arrives, load the lady into it with her brother and see them off the property posthaste."

"Aye, my lord."

"Temple, help me!" Rising beseechingly on her knees, Sophia begged, stretching out hands in a pretty, pleading manner that at one time he would have moved heaven and earth to change.

"God can only help you now, Sophia. And if I were you, I would consider leaving the country. There will be an inquest into the fire, and your brother's deadly plans will be exposed," he warned, then mounted the steps in a run and entered the house, ignoring her pitiful wailing.

Taking the stairs two at a time, he rushed into his wife's bed-chamber. Libby, busy laying out bath articles, turned with a small shriek at the sudden sight of the soot-blackened man standing there. He looked every bit as poorly used as her ladyship.

"Where is my wife?"

"In the nursery, my lord," Libby called after his retreating back. She sank to a chair beside the fireplace and placed a hand over her thumping heart. "This family will be the death of me yet!"

Broad strides carried Temple in the direction of the nursery. When he would reach for the door, the young footman posted there stepped in front of him and sketched a small bow. "Begging pardon, my lord, but . . . her ladyship's orders."

Temple pulled himself to his full height and glared at the footman. "Stand aside, man, or damned if I won't put you aside!" he thundered.

The footman did not change his polite expression, nor did he remove his bulk from in front of the nursery door. With a mighty scowl, Temple took the man's measure, considered his bulk and thought he could overturn him, though it would be a tussle and he had extended himself greatly already tonight.

"This goes too far. First Burke, now this! Even Mr. Wyatt! Would she turn the entire household against me?" he muttered for the enjoyment of the footman, who would repeat it in the kitchen later in exchange for minute details of the eviction of the silver lady.

"Birdie! Open this damn door!" he shouted, raking a hand through singed, smoke-reeking hair.

The door opened abruptly and Franny's plump face peered around the footman. Tapping him on the shoulder, the lady's maid gave the marquis permission to enter his own nursery.

Scowling strongly at the young man, Temple stepped around him into the room. He halted at the sight of Birdie rocking the baby and weeping quietly. "Is she all right?" he whispered to Franny. Concern furrowed his brow and clenched his hands into fists, but there was no one left to pummel for hurting Birdie.

"Aye, she be fine. Just leave her be till she has sobbed out the horror of it all. Whew! Ye be needing a bath, my lord, as bad as she does. I will just take meself off to tell Travers, though I imagine Libby has done it already," Franny said. Quickly slipping into the hall, she paused from her errand only long enough to post the footman on the opposite side of the hallway, well out of the range of words that might penetrate the nursery door.

Temple leaned quietly against the door, waiting for Birdie to quieten. Maybe Franny was right. Maybe a good cry was what was needed to release the horror. Perhaps he should try it himself, he thought, raking a weary hand over his tender blistered face and through his hair. This was the first time he had been in the nursery, or even on this floor, since he was a small boy. His eyes roamed the room, taking in the silly caricatures of animals doing human things that someone had painted on the walls. Child-size wicker chairs sat around a miniature table in one corner, and there were two white iron infant cots with slatted sides placed against one wall. A large, well-screened fireplace dominated the other wall, and two rockers were pulled comfortably toward the cheery blaze.

A small sound from one of the cots caught Temple's attention. The other child was just waking from sleep. A small hand grasped the rail at the end of the crib to pull himself to his feet. Temple watched as a small head covered in a mop of ebony curls appeared over the white ironwork. The chubby fist that scrubbed sleep from his eyes dropped and Temple looked into a pair of solemn gray eyes that duplicated his own. A stunned gasp escaped his lips, as if he had received a sharp jab in the belly. The face was his face from the portrait in the gallery. He stared into that little face. The baby stared back at him, in awe of this black-faced stranger who would invade his nursery in the middle of the night.

Tears gathered in Temple's eyes. He swallowed hard and moved to hold out his hands to the baby. After a moment's hesitation, the two little arms rose and Temple lifted his son to his shoulder. Cradling the boy, he carefully carried him to the fireplace. He sank to the rocker, facing Birdie. Burying his face in the soft hair, he inhaled the warm, powdery baby smell. Emotion raged inside him. Could this child truly be his? He leaned over to study the little face illuminated in the firelight. There was no denying the resemblance! There was nothing of Birdie there, except the curliness of the hair. His child! But Charles or Amaryllis? He could not tell. But the names... One for her dear mother and the other for his beloved great-uncle. Rage entered his heart. She would withhold his child from him? Why would she seek to wound him so?

"Birdie!" The stern word, released into the quiet room, cracked as a pistol shot. Birdie jumped and gasped, her head snapping up. The baby sitting on her lap stuffed fingers into her rosebud mouth and peeped around at him with wide gray eyes. Again, Temple was astounded. The face was the same cherub face framed with ebony ringlets and large, solemn gray eyes. A duplicate of the baby he held in his arms. "My God! Th-they are identical!"

They were both his children! And she carried another one in her womb this very minute. What had she said? His mind reeled with memories. That he need only touch her and a babe started in her womb. The night of the princess's birthday! It must have been that night, for there was no other time. And the twins? Their wedding night? Or the night of despair in the rebels' camp?

Birdie watched the emotions play over his face with a deep sorrow in her heart. She had planned so many different ways to spark this moment. She had wanted time, a quiet time, to explain to him. To share her deep love for him before telling him of his children. This was only one more thing Oliver and his hatred had stolen from her. Now she must face accusations and recriminations. She watched Temple cup his son's head with his hand and met his eyes openly when he would raise them accusingly to her.

"Why didn't you tell me?" Temple whispered, true anguish in his voice. His hand pressed the precious head of his child against his chest... protecting, claiming. "Do you hate me so much that you would deny me my own children?"

"No, Temple, I..." she began, then hesitated to sigh deeply before admitting, "Believe me when I say that I have tried very hard, but I can't seem to make myself hate you."

"When were you going to tell me of the child you carry in your womb? Or would you deny me that one, also? Why, Birdie?" he demanded in a stronger voice. Charles struggled to sit up and stared up at Temple.

Her head fell and she buried her face in the baby curls. "You left me there, to survive by my own efforts. And I meant to survive." Her head came up defiantly. "I would not die and leave a child alone in the world as I had been abandoned."

"But why keep them from me?" he asked again.

"Don't you remember? When I saw you at Daine Hall, you threatened me. Threatened to set me aside. Would you have allowed me to take your children with me into the streets? I think not. Can you imagine how I felt...standing there in the entry of Daine Hall? Knowing it had all been lies? Your promise to try and love me . . . to make our marriage one of trust? To realize that you had survived and never searched for me? I just could not trust you with my babies! Surely you must see that!"

"That is not the way of it, Birdie. Shanna told me of your O'Donnell blood. And of the plot. I tried not to believe her, but then you confirmed it. I asked you if you were one of them, and by your own mouth you said yes."

"O'Donnell blood! I said what I had to say to save your life and myself from their whorehouse. The Irish! Blood is thick, clan is everything! You know who I am! Who my mother and father were!" she cried out to him. "Shanna lied! Just as Rory lied when he said he had hunted you down to put a bullet between your eyes. I believed him...and mourned you every day. I thought you hadn't come for me because you were dead."

"Why did you say you were one of them? Birdie, I would never have left you there otherwise!" he demanded, his stern voice causing Charles to look up at him and pucker his face into tears. Tenderly Temple traced a dirty finger down the softness of the baby's cheek to soothe his fear. His voice softened. "I never would have left you. Except by your own admission—"

"I was . . . am one of them, Temple. A murderer! I have enough blood on my hands and soul—oh, not the first one—but the blood of innocent people. Men, women and children who died because I taunted Rory. He slaughtered them," she ended in a whisper. "Don't you see? It was my fault—"

"Birdie, I—"

The door swung wide and Franny bustled into the room. She smiled to see Birdie and Temple seated before the fire with the babies, as was right and proper, and about time, too.

"Go along now, my lady. Libby has a cool bath waiting for ye. Go on with ye and I'll be right behind ye as soon as Molly shows up to tend these babies," Franny ordered in a gruff, familiar manner. Taking Amaryllis from Birdie's lap, she plopped her into a crib. Busily, and with no nonsense, she hustled Birdie out of the room, sending her down the hall. Turning to Temple, she started to lift Charles from his arms, but they tightened about the baby.

"I'll just stay a moment more. Franny, which baby is this?"

"'Tis Master Charles...yer son," she stated in a matter-of-fact way, as if it were perfectly natural for him to be asking. "Little Missy Big Eyes staring at ye there be Missy Amaryllis...yer daughter."

Amaryllis, at the familiar teasing tone of Franny, grinned a wide grin and wrinkled her nose delightfully. Appreciating the audience, she jumped up and down on the feather mattress, squealing a high-pitched squeal. Temple was immediately captivated. He instantly recognized the exuberant joy of just being in the world that was reminiscent of her undauntable mother.

"And ye, my lord," Franny remarked, lifting Charles and hefting him to her hip, "stink like the inside of a chimney pot. There be a hot bath waiting for ye, also. Now, out with ye, or poor Molly will not be getting these babies back to sleep tonight!"

"All right, I'll go," he conceded. Rising, he planted a kiss on the top of the bouncing Amaryllis's head and started for the door. Turning, he looked at Franny holding his son. He smiled a tired smile that crinkled the tender skin at the corners of his eyes. "You are a good friend, Franny. I'm glad she's had you in her life."

Chapter Thirty-Two

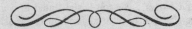

The bathwater was thankfully tepid, and yet it stung Birdie's scorched skin. Sinking her exhausted body lower, she ran her hands over the flat belly, whispering to her babe.

"Hold tight, little one. The horror is over. We'll lie in the bed all of tomorrow and rest. Just you hold tight now."

"Ye can bet ye will, for I will not be letting ye out!" warned Franny adamantly. "But ye be strong, and that babe will not let go easily."

"No, he'll not let go. My little Lord Henry is strong. The Daines and Lindleys make strong sons who will not let go easily."

"It's a miracle if you ask me. Considering the events of the last twenty-four hours! A miracle, you hear!" Libby huffed, shaking out a thick, flannelette night rail with a snap. Birdie smiled sleepily. She quite imagined Libby would rather be shaking her instead.

"What did his lordship say after I left the nursery, Franny?"

"He said I be a wonder and a jewel, and ye be lucky to have me by yer side," Franny said, easing her hands through the lather to massage Birdie's scalp with searching, soothing fingers.

The housekeeper turned to plant hands on broad hips. "Humph! Stuff and nonsense! My lady, I am going to the kitchen to make you a strong cup of restorative tea. Franny, lather that hair at least three times, although I seriously doubt the smoke will ever leave it."

Birdie giggled as Libby marched solidly from the room. She eased deeper into the water and closed her eyes. The lilac-scented lather turned her thick tresses a foamy white. The tenseness eased in her shoulders and she sighed deeply as Franny worked down the back of her neck.

"Whoever would have thought a stroll on the terrace could have such consequences. A man captured, and the whole household turned topsy-turvy in the middle of the night. Finally I know who my father was. Funny, but it seems of such little importance now," Birdie murmured as she gave in to Franny's hands. "I just want to raise my babies at Stannisburn, ride Pigeon through the fields on sunny days and be safe, with my husband at my side. It doesn't seem too much to ask, does it?" The hands left for a moment, only to return to work slowly through the lather in a sensuous movement. "It just appears everyone has a plan for my life, and they will go to any measure to see that it's lived their way. Maude, Flo, Sir Charles, Rory, Oliver... How can they presume to take over my life? Must I fight every day of my life to live my life as I choose?"

"Sh..." A hiss of admonishment sounded in her ear as she became agitated. The strong hands worked down to her shoulders, where they kneaded and stroked. Birdie allowed her head to roll and flop forward with a sigh. The room was quiet. The fire popped, flared and resettled itself.

"That feels so good, Franny. You'll have me asleep before I am rinsed. Remember my wedding night? You had me so relaxed and sleepy." She gave a little snort of laughter. "And then he almost didn't show up!" Her voice softened. "But when he did, he gave me Charles and Amaryllis."

The soapy hands smoothed across her chest and lifted her heavy breasts, tweaking the nipples.

"Franny!" she squealed, sitting up with a splash. The soap on her head slid down into her eyes. "Oh! Quick! It's burning my eyes."

A slow, steady stream of warmed water poured over her head. Birdie tilted her face back and held her breath. The water splashed in her face, running across her forehead, nose, reddened cheeks, to wash her heavy hair from her shoulders and down her back. Gripping the sides of the tub, she pulled herself to her feet. Squeezing her eyes shut, she rotated slowly, sputtering as another stream of warmed water cascaded over her to rinse the concealing soap from her body. It emerged pink and shiny from the water, delicately rounded and tautly muscled. Gentle hands beneath a warm towel patted her dry, lingering across her pert buttocks.

"Give me a towel! I can't see!" she demanded, holding out her hand, swiping at her face with the other. The hands with the towel moved to the front of her body, swiping around her nipple and stroking across the feminine curls in a leisurely manner, successfully avoiding her hands. Turning an indignant stare to the owner of the hands, Birdie squeaked, "You! I should have known!"

Temple, with a wide grin on his red face, stood holding the towel for her. "I had no idea, absolutely no idea at all, that being a lady's maid could involve such inviting opportunities."

Crimson with embarrassment, she snatched the towel from his hands, scrubbing vigorously at her face. "Ah..." she gasped as the tortured skin stung. When she opened her eyes again, Temple was across the room, leaning negligently against the mantel. Casually he lifted the crystal goblet of brandy he had carried in with him. His eyes drifted lazily over her body.

She fumbled with the towel, attempting to cover herself. "Wh-what are you doing in my—"

"Washing you," he interrupted calmly, giving her no chance to finish her question. His eyes crinkled with his amusement.

Birdie swore under her breath. Her vexation increased considerably when she discovered the towel too small to cover her completely. If it hid her breasts, the reddish triangle between her thighs peeped out. When she lowered it, her nipples popped over the edge of the top. Deciding to forgo the battle, she looked up at him flustered. "My robe, if you please?" she demanded, pointing.

With catlike grace, he moved toward her, his stride easy and controlled. His own hair was wet from his bath, and considerably shorter where Travers had trimmed the singed edges. He was wrapped in an enveloping ruby robe over black lounging trousers and ruby velvet slippers.

"That is the choice I think I would have made, also, though the decision would have been equally difficult for me. I must say your breasts are beautiful. I do so admire looking at them... stroking them, tasting them." He moved closer, teasing her choice of display.

Quickly, she tugged the towel higher to cover her breasts from his lusty gaze. "My robe, you cad!" she demanded.

"Ah, well, perhaps I was wrong. Perhaps my choice would have been..." Instantly casting his eyes lower, he grinned. His gaze drifted idly to the robe and then back to her. The smile on his face was pure enjoyment. "Here, let me assist you out of your tub. I would wager your toes are becoming quite pink and wrinkled."

"You are a rascal!" Birdie stated, accepting his hand. Once her feet touched the floor, she immediately moved to the fireplace and picked up the robe. Turning her back to him, affording him a delightful view of a tapering back and well-turned bottom, she slipped into her robe. She heard him move and sensed his nearness. Waves of desire flowed through her when he lightly touched her hair, stroking down it to lay his hand on her shoulder.

"One question . . . and an honest answer, please," he said. His voice was soft, but ready to turn hard if the answer was not to his liking. "Do you believe we can make our way back? To build a marriage on honesty and . . . love?"

"I . . ." She dropped her head and clutched the robe around her. Then turning to lift pleading eyes to his face, she cried, "I want to trust you, Temple. Truly I do, but . . ."

Taking her stricken face in his hand, he ran a thumb over her trembling mouth. Drawing away, she turned her back on him again in confusion. Temple's hand dropped to his side. "Birdie, it's not an excuse, but I thought myself in love with Sophia . . . heaven help me! I was angry when Uncle Charles forced our marriage. But I truly did resolve to make the best of it. He told me how special you were and begged me to give me time. I found your honesty so refreshing, but I was just so unreasonably angry. Then the way you responded to me . . . our wedding night . . . so innocent, so trusting. God, how I wanted to protect you. I never wanted you to change. I had fallen quite hopelessly in love with you."

Birdie's eyes sparkled at his admission of love. She so desperately wanted to be loved. "That's all I've ever . . ."

Putting his fingertips over her trembling lips, he halted her words. "When I thought I'd been duped, when I thought you had confessed to me, I was crushed. Desire for revenge infused every particle of my being. I refused to pursue you, no matter how Uncle Charles tried to convince me. That haunts me . . . how he railed and pleaded." His face saddened and he ran a hand over his eyes. "I shall never forgive myself for that. Hell, for more than just that. Such stupid male pride. I was a fool, Birdie. A blind and utter fool!"

"Oh, Temple . . ."

"I came back to London with you inside my heart and nothing could dislodge you. When you returned, I tried not to love you. But I ached for you, raged with it when I thought you preferred Sayers over me. You showed me that night at St. James Palace that I was a fool to even try not loving you. When I saw the portrait of your mother and came to you, there by the stream, I was determined to forget everything that had happened between us and make you love me. Then Sayers followed. I wanted to throw them off the place—would that I had now! But . . . well, you wanted family so desperately.''

''I think we could have solved a lot of problems if we had just sat down and talked sensibly, don't you?'' Birdie leaned her head onto his broad chest to sigh deeply. ''Oh, Temple, I have missed you so much.''

Swooping her into his arms, he held her close, breathing deeply of her scent. Seating her before the fire, he planted a lingering kiss on her sweet lips. ''It's all over now. And I know one or both of your watchdogs are outside the door at this very moment, fuming because I have you standing about with wet hair, so I must leave you to them.''

Clutching his sleeve, Birdie looked startled, then pleading. ''No! Stay!''

He chuckled, a low and dangerous sound. ''Ah, little wren. There is no way I can crawl into that bed with you at this moment. That would not be the rest you need. But I'll be close and you only need call out if you want me,'' he promised, planting a kiss on her forehead as he rose. The door had no chance to close behind him but swung wider to admit Franny and Libby hustling in to scold her lovingly into bed.

Hours and hours later, for day had come and gone and the sky was again dark, Birdie woke trembling from a dream, hands clutching the coverlet. The room was lit only by a fire burning brightly in the hearth. A dream hung heavy upon her, but it was no nightmare this time. With a deep intake of breath, she ran both palms across her belly and over her hips and thighs. Heat rose inside her. Aroused from sleep by a hot, throbbing dream in which Temple had lain over her body and touched her, she ached for him. Needed him, here, beside her . . . inside her, now.

''Temple?'' she whispered into the darkness.

''Yes, my love?'' His answer came from the direction of the fireplace.

Warmed by his nearness, she smiled drowsily. He had been with her, watching over her as she slept. Protecting her as she had always wanted someone to protect her. She watched as he moved to the foot of the bed, and she held out her arms to him, gratified when he readily slipped the robe from his body, fascinated by the way the muscles of his shoulders and chest, dimly lit by the firelight, rippled when he moved to her. The red glow from the fire mingled with the silver of the moon to lend a coppery sheen to his smooth skin.

"The mere sight of you heats my blood, Temple," she whispered.

"Ah, Birdie..." he murmured, his voice hoarse with unmistakable desire. He slid the nightdress up over her body in a slow movement, then over her head to toss it beside the bed. His gaze roamed over the blush of her body, sweeping downward to the smooth indentation of her waist and over the rounded curve of her hips. He leaned over to follow his eyes with a hot hand. "You are so beautiful."

Birdie gasped softly at his touch. She raised her arms to take his head in her hands, running fingers through the crisp, unruly curls to pull him into her embrace and into her bed. Tenderly guiding his lips to hers, she teased him with the tip of her tongue. "No, it's you who are beautiful," she countered.

He caressed the gentle plane of her belly, moving his hand upward to cup the fullness of her breast. She thrilled as her body responded to the sweetness of his touch. She guided his lips to her breasts and groaned as she felt him suckle them. Her body came alive beneath his touch, drawing him into a whirlpool of sensuousness. Wrapping his powerful arms around her, he crushed her almost ruthlessly, his excitement evident against her thigh. She could feel the pounding of his heart against her own. Rolling to her side, she allowed him to pull the length of her tight against him. She hid her face in the hollow of his neck and moved against him with all the yearning in her young body. Again his muscular thighs pressed against her and his breathing quickened. Her own breath grew heavy in his ear, accompanied with teasing flicks of her tongue.

"I have missed you, Birdie," he rumbled.

Her body was stretched taut with desire, every pore of her flesh aching for him. Throwing her leg over his hip, she pressed herself against him and moaned. She ached for fulfillment. Running her hands over the broad back and shoulders, she kissed the chest so near her face, nuzzling the wiry hair there.

"I have missed you, Temple," she whispered. "Promise me we'll never be apart again. I don't think I could stand it ever again."

"I promise you, Birdie, that I will do everything in my power to never be away from you," he promised. Dipping his head, he slanted his mouth over hers in a demanding kiss that snatched her breath away. He kissed her until she trembled uncontrollably and whimpered into his mouth. She drew her leg high over his thigh and pressed herself to him. He drew his breath sharply in through gritted teeth.

Birdie, lost in throbbing need, arched her back and cried out, "Oh, Temple! Hold me tight . . . never let me go."

He held her closer, running his hand over her back, lengthening the stroke each time until it caressed her firm buttock, then slipping his fingers into the cleft there with each stroke. She shivered with the flowering of desire his touch promised with each stroke, then giggled at her own wanton responses.

Temple pushed her to her back and leaned over her, holding her still when she would squirm against him. "I love you, Beatrice Daine-Charlton," he declared. "You are my life! You and our children."

"I know," she sighed softly, nuzzling his cheek.

He drew back farther to look into her face. "And just how did you know that when I have taken so long to discover it?" he demanded.

"I just knew you had to love me," she explained. "Because I loved you too much for you not to love me in return."

"Ah, smart woman," he teased, thrusting a tongue into her ear, chuckling as she flinched away from the wet tickle.

"Superior intellect," she whispered with a giggle. Splaying her hand over his back, she urged him to her, reveling in his hot breath on her neck. Burrowing against his chest, she put her tongue out to taste his flesh and shivered. Love filled her for this man who would share her life from this day forward. Wanting to touch him as deeply as he touched her, she slid her hand down the hard plane of his belly to tease with feather strokes. He drew in his breath sharply and grasped her hand to still the seeking fingertips.

"Temple?" Birdie pushed at his chest to look up at him in worry, for he did seem in agony.

"Ah, little wren, we will get to that later," he whispered, pressing her back. As his meaning dawned, she giggled again, delighting him. "Witch! I see I shall have to teach you manners. It's impolite to giggle at a man when he's without his trousers," he challenged. Drawing her hands over her head, he rendered her helpless beneath him by capturing them with one of his. Snaring her soft, teasing mouth, he probed her mouth with his tongue. His free fingers traced and tugged at her nipples, which peaked eagerly into points of sensitivity, shooting flashes of excitement down her belly.

"Oh, unfair," Birdie gasped and giggled. Trembling uncontrollably, she squirmed and fought the sensations. Throwing a leg over her thighs, he slowly explored her trapped body until she was panting in mindless yearning.

Finally taking pity on her arousal, he rose over her body to part her thighs with his knee and sank between them. Staring down at her, he could only marvel in wonder at this child-woman he had taken for a wife. Her face was flushed. A line of perspiration dotted the upper lip of her mouth, swollen and pouty from his kisses. The sherry brown eyes were half-closed and unfocused with desire. His heart felt it would burst with love for her.

"Enough lessons, little wren? Do you wish to laugh at me now?" he teased. He flexed his hips forward to rub sensitive parts together. "Or are you ready to admit that you are mine to do with as I will?"

Birdie jerked as his heat touched her, crying out in a hoarse voice. Lifting her legs to circle him, she drew him tighter to her body. Reaching to tangle her fingers in the raven's wing hair, she sighed in perfect happiness. "You're a terrible, teasing man, Temple, but I give you the queen's jewels of my own free will!"

* * * * *

Weddings by DeWilde

Since the turn of the century the elegant and fashionable DeWilde stores have helped brides around the world turn the fantasy of their "Special Day" into reality. But now the store and three generations of family are torn apart by the divorce of Grace and Jeffrey DeWilde. As family members face new challenges and loves—and a long-secret mystery—the lives of Grace and Jeffrey intermingle with store employees, friends and relatives in this fast-paced, glamorous, internationally set series. For weddings and romance, glamour and fun-filled entertainment, enter the world of DeWilde...

Twelve remarkable books, coming to you once a month, beginning in April 1996

Weddings by DeWilde begins with
Shattered Vows
by Jasmine Cresswell

Here's a preview!

"SPEND THE NIGHT with me, Lianne."

No softening lies, no beguiling promises, just the curt offer of a night of sex. She closed her eyes, shutting out temptation. She had never expected to feel this sort of relentless drive for sexual fulfillment, so she had no mechanisms in place for coping with it. "No." The one-word denial was all she could manage to articulate.

His grip on her arms tightened as if he might refuse to accept her answer. Shockingly, she wished for a split second that he would ignore her rejection and simply bundle her into the car and drive her straight to his flat, refusing to take no for an answer. All the pleasures of mindless sex, with none of the responsibility. For a couple of seconds he neither moved nor spoke. Then he released her, turning abruptly to open the door on the passenger side of his Jaguar. "I'll drive you home," he said, his voice hard and flat. "Get in."

The traffic was heavy, and the rain started again as an annoying drizzle that distorted depth perception made driving difficult, but Lianne didn't fool herself that the silence inside the car was caused by the driving conditions. The air around them crackled and sparked with their thwarted desire. Her body was still on fire. Why didn't Gabe say something? she thought, feeling aggrieved.

Perhaps because he was finding it as difficult as she was to think of something appropriate to say. He was thirty years old, long past the stage of needing to bed a woman just so he could record another sexual conquest in his little black book. He'd spent five months dating Julia, which suggested he was a man who valued friendship as an element in his relationships with women. Since he didn't seem to like her very much, he was probably as embarrassed as she was by the stupid, inexplicable intensity of their physical response to each other.

"Maybe we should just set aside a weekend to have wild, uninterrupted sex," she said, thinking aloud. "Maybe that way we'd get whatever it is we feel for each other out of our systems and be able to move on with the rest of our lives."

His mouth quirked into a rueful smile. "Isn't that supposed to be my line?"

"Why? Because you're the man? Are you sexist enough to believe that women don't have sexual urges? I'm just as aware of what's going on between us as you are, Gabe. Am I supposed to pretend I haven't noticed that we practically ignite whenever we touch? And that we have nothing much in common except mutual lust—and a good friend we betrayed?"

Coming in May from

The exciting third book in award-winning
author Theresa Michaels' Kincaid trilogy

ONCE A LAWMAN
The story of Conner Kincaid

"...another Theresa Michaels masterpiece. 5★s."
—*Affaire de Coeur*

"ONCE A LAWMAN is the breath-taking conclusion to
Ms. Michaels' outstanding trilogy."
—*Romantic Times*

Don't miss it!

If you would like to order your copy of *Once an Outlaw*
(HS #296) or the first book in the series, *Once a Maverick*
(HS #276), please send your name, address, zip or postal code
along with a check or money order (please do not send cash) for
$4.50 for each book ordered ($4.99 in Canada) plus 75¢ postage
and handling ($1.00 in Canada) payable to Harlequin Books, to:

In the U.S.:

3010 Walden Avenue
P. O. Box 1369
Buffalo, NY 14269-1369

In Canada:

P.O. Box 609
Fort Erie, Ontario
L2A 5X3

Please specify book title(s) with your order. Canadian residents
add applicable federal and provincial taxes.

HARLEQUIN®

Don't miss these Harlequin favorites by some of our most
distinguished authors!
And now, you can receive a discount by ordering two or more titles!

HT #25645	THREE GROOMS AND A WIFE by JoAnn Ross	$3.25 U.S./$3.75 CAN. ☐
HT #25648	JESSIE'S LAWMAN by Kristine Rolofson	$3.25 U.S./$3.75 CAN. ☐
HP #11725	THE WRONG KIND OF WIFE by Roberta Leigh	$3.25 U.S./$3.75 CAN. ☐
HP #11755	TIGER EYES by Robyn Donald	$3.25 U.S./$3.75 CAN. ☐
HR #03362	THE BABY BUSINESS by Rebecca Winters	$2.99 U.S./$3.50 CAN. ☐
HR #03375	THE BABY CAPER by Emma Goldrick	$2.99 U.S./$3.50 CAN. ☐
HS #70638	THE SECRET YEARS by Margot Dalton	$3.75 U.S./$4.25 CAN. ☐
HS #70655	PEACEKEEPER by Marisa Carroll	$3.75 U.S./$4.25 CAN. ☐
HI #22280	MIDNIGHT RIDER by Laura Pender	$2.99 U.S./$3.50 CAN. ☐
HI #22235	BEAUTY VS THE BEAST by M.J. Rogers	$3.50 U.S./$3.99 CAN. ☐
HAR #16531	TEDDY BEAR HEIR by Elda Minger	$3.50 U.S./$3.99 CAN. ☐
HAR #16596	COUNTERFEIT HUSBAND by Linda Randall Wisdom	$3.50 U.S./$3.99 CAN. ☐
HH #28795	PIECES OF SKY by Marianne Willman	$3.99 U.S./$4.50 CAN. ☐
HH #28855	SWEET SURRENDER by Julie Tetel	$4.50 U.S./$4.99 CAN. ☐

(limited quantities available on certain titles)

	AMOUNT	$
DEDUCT:	10% DISCOUNT FOR 2+ BOOKS	$
ADD:	POSTAGE & HANDLING	$
	($1.00 for one book, 50¢ for each additional)	
	APPLICABLE TAXES**	$_____
	TOTAL PAYABLE	$_____
	(check or money order—please do not send cash)	

To order, complete this form and send it, along with a check or money order for the
total above, payable to Harlequin Books, to: **In the U.S.:** 3010 Walden Avenue,
P.O. Box 9047, Buffalo, NY 14269-9047; **In Canada:** P.O. Box 613, Fort Erie, Ontario,
L2A 5X3.

Name: _____

Address: _____ City: _____

State/Prov.: _____ Zip/Postal Code: _____

**New York residents remit applicable sales taxes.
 Canadian residents remit applicable GST and provincial taxes.   HBACK-AJ3

This May, keep an eye out for
something heavenly from

SPARHAWK'S Angel

by *Miranda Jarrett*

"Delightful...5★s"
—*Affaire de Coeur*

Available wherever Harlequin books are sold.

BRIDE'S BAY RESORT

UNLOCK THE DOOR TO GREAT ROMANCE AT BRIDE'S BAY RESORT

Join Harlequin's new across-the-lines series, set in an exclusive hotel on an island off the coast of South Carolina.

Seven of your favorite authors will bring you exciting stories about fascinating heroes and heroines discovering love at Bride's Bay Resort.

Look for these fabulous stories coming to a store near you beginning in January 1996.

Harlequin American Romance #613 in January
Matchmaking Baby by Cathy Gillen Thacker

Harlequin Presents #1794 in February
Indiscretions by Robyn Donald

Harlequin Intrigue #362 in March
Love and Lies by Dawn Stewardson

Harlequin Romance #3404 in April
Make Believe Engagement by Day Leclaire

Harlequin Temptation #588 in May
Stranger in the Night by Roseanne Williams

Harlequin Superromance #695 in June
Married to a Stranger by Connie Bennett

Harlequin Historicals #324 in July
Dulcie's Gift by Ruth Langan

Visit Bride's Bay Resort each month wherever Harlequin books are sold.

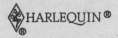

HARLEQUIN ®

BBAYG